PENGUIN BOOKS

RAGE

'Kellerman's psychological mysteries are first-class and this is one of the best' *Independent on Sunday*

'Tautly written with a truly chilling denouement' *Elle*

'A psychological thriller with real oomph' *Esquire*

'This is Kellerman on good form, strong on both characterisation and dialogue' *Sunday Telegraph*

'Kellerman picks up pace and the momentum does not let up' *Sunday Express*

'He writes stories of such multi-layered complexity they are among the most rewarding works in any genre of popular fiction . . . Kellerman grows stronger with every book' *Ireland on Sunday*

'Jonathan Kellerman has justly earned his reputation as a master of the psychological thriller' *People*

D1023419

Jonathan Kellerman is one of the world's most popular authors. He has brought his expertise as a clinical pyschologist to numerous bestselling tales of suspense (which have been translated into two dozen languages), including the Alex Delaware novels; *The Butcher's Theatre*, a story of serial killing in Jerusalem; *Billy Straight*, featuring Hollywood homicide detective Petra Connor; and *The Conspiracy Club*, a chilling hunt for a twenty-first-century Jack the Ripper. And with his wife Faye he is the co-author of the bestseller *Double Homicide*. He is also the author of numerous essays, short stories and scientific articles, two children's books and three volumes of pyschology, including *Savage Spawn: Reflections on Violent Children*. Kellerman won the Samuel Goldwyn, Edgar Allan Poe and Anthony Boucher awards and has been nominated for a Shamus award. He and Faye have four children and live in Los Angeles.

Books by Jonathan Kellerman

FICTION

Rage (2005)

Twisted (2004)

Therapy (2004)

The Conspiracy Club (2003)

A Cold Heart (2003)

The Murder Book (2002)

Flesh and Blood (2001)

Dr Death (2000)

Monster (1999)

Billy Straight (1998)

Survival of the Fittest (1997)

The Clinic (1997)

The Web (1996)

Self-Defense (1995)

Bad Love (1994)

Devil's Waltz (1993)

Private Eyes (1992)

Time Bomb (1990)

Silent Partner (1989)

The Butcher's Theatre (1988)

Over the Edge (1987)

Blood Test (1986)

When the Bough Breaks (1985)

NON-FICTION

Savage Spawn: Reflections on Violent Children (1999)

Helping the Fearful Child (1981)

Pyschological Aspects of Childhood Cancer (1980)

FOR CHILDREN, WRITTEN AND ILLUSTRATED

*Jonathan Kellerman's ABC of
Weird Creatures* (1995)

*Daddy, Daddy, Can You Touch
the Sky?* (1994)

WITH FAYE KELLERMAN

Double Homicide (2004)

RAGE

AN ALEX DELAWARE NOVEL

JONATHAN
KELLERMAN

PENGUIN BOOKS

PENGUIN BOOKS

Published by the Penguin Group
Penguin Books Ltd, 80 Strand, London WC2R ORL, England
Penguin Group (USA) Inc., 375 Hudson Street, New York, New York 10014, USA
Penguin Group (Canada), 90 Eglinton Avenue East, Suite 700, Toronto, Ontario, Canada M4P 2Y3
(a division of Pearson Penguin Canada Inc.)
Penguin Ireland, 25 St Stephen's Green, Dublin 2, Ireland (a division of Penguin Books Ltd)
Penguin Books Australia Ltd, 250 Camberwell Road,
Camberwell, Victoria 3124, Australia (a division of Pearson Australia Group Pty Ltd)
Penguin Books India Pvt Ltd, 11 Community Centre,
Panchsheel Park, New Delhi – 110 017, India
Penguin Group (NZ), cnr Airborne and Rosedale Roads, Albany,
Auckland 1310, New Zealand (a division of Pearson New Zealand Ltd)
Penguin Books (South Africa) (Pty) Ltd, 24 Sturdee Avenue,
Rosebank, Johannesburg 2196, South Africa

Penguin Books Ltd, Registered Offices: 80 Strand, London WC2R ORL, England

www.penguin.com

First published in the USA by Ballantine Books 2005
First published in Great Britain by Michael Joseph 2005
Published in Penguin Books 2006

1

Copyright © Jonathan Kellerman, 2005
All rights reserved

Typeset by Rowland Phototypesetting Ltd, Bury St Edmunds, Suffolk
Printed in England by Clays Ltd, St Ives plc

ISBN-13: 978–0–141–02194–2
ISBN-10: 0–141–02194–2

To my mother, Sylvia Kellerman

Special thanks to Larry Malmberg, P.I.,
and Detective Miguel Porras

I

On a slow, chilly Saturday in December, shortly after the Lakers overcame a sixteen-point halftime deficit and beat New Jersey, I got a call from a murderer.

I hadn't watched basketball since college, had returned to it because I was working at developing my leisure skills. The woman in my life was visiting her grandmother in Connecticut, the woman who used to be in my life was living in Seattle with her new guy – temporarily, she claimed, as if I had a right to care – and my caseload had just abated.

Three court cases in two months: two child-custody disputes, one relatively benign, the other nightmarish; and an injury consult on a fifteen-year-old girl who'd lost a hand in a car crash. Now all the papers were filed and I was ready for a week or two of nothing.

I'd downed a couple of beers during the game and was nearly dozing on my living room sofa. The distinctive squawk of the business phone roused me. Generally, I let my service pick up. Why I answered, I still can't say.

'Dr Delaware?'

I didn't recognize his voice. Eight years had passed.

'Speaking. Who's this?'

'Rand.'

Now I remembered. The same slurred voice deepened to a man's baritone. By now he'd be a man. Some kind of man.

'Where are you calling from, Rand?'

'I'm out.'

'Out of the C.Y.A.'

'I, uh ... yeah, I finished.'

As if it had been a course of study. Maybe it had been. 'When?'

'Coupla weeks.'

What could I say? *Congratulations? God help us?*

'What's on your mind, Rand?'

'Could I, uh, talk to you?'

'Go ahead.'

'Uh, not this ... like talk ... for real.'

'In person.'

'Yeah.'

The living room windows were dark. Six forty-five p.m. 'What do you want to talk about, Rand?'

'Uh, it would be ... I'm kinda ...'

'What's on your mind, Rand?'

No answer.

'Is it something about Kristal?'

'Ye-ah.' His voice broke and bisected the word.

'Where are you calling from?' I said.

'Not far from you.'

My home office address was unlisted. *How do you know where I live?*

I said, 'I'll come to you, Rand. Where are you?'

'Uh, I think . . . Westwood.'

'Westwood Village?'

'I think . . . lemme see . . .' I heard a clang as the phone dropped. Phone on a cord, traffic in the background. A pay booth. He was off the line for over a minute.

'It says Westwood. There's this big uh, a mall. With this bridge across.'

A mall. 'Westside Pavilion?'

'I guess.'

Two miles south of the village. Comfortable distance from my house in the Glen. 'Where in the mall are you?'

'Uh, I'm not in there. I kin see it across the street. There's a . . . I think it says Pizza. Two z's . . . yeah, pizza.'

Eight years and he could barely read. So much for rehab.

It took awhile but I got the approximate location: Westwood Boulevard, just north of Pico, east side of the street, a green and white and red sign shaped like a boot.

'I'll be there in fifteen, twenty minutes, Rand. Anything you want to tell me now?'

'Uh, I . . . can we meet at the pizza place?'

'You hungry?'

'I ate breakfast.'

'It's dinnertime.'

'I guess.'

3

'See you in twenty.'

'Okay . . . thanks.'

'You sure there's nothing you want to tell me before you see me?'

'Like what?'

'Anything at all.'

More traffic noise. Time stretched.

'Rand?'

'I'm not a bad person.'

2

What happened to Kristal Malley was no whodunit.

The day after Christmas, the two-year-old accompanied her mother to the Buy-Rite Plaza in Panorama City. The promise of MEGA-SALE!!! DEEP DISCOUNTS!!! had stuffed the shabby, fading mall with bargain-hunters. Teenagers on winter break loitered near the Happy Taste food court and congregated among the CD racks of Flip Disc Music. The black-lit box of din that was the Galaxy Video Emporium pulsed with hormones and hostility. The air reeked of caramel corn and mustard and body odor. Frigid air blew through the poorly fitting doors of the recently closed indoor ice-skating rink.

Kristal Malley, an active, moody toddler of twenty-five months, managed to elude her mother's attention and pull free of her grasp. Lara Malley claimed the lapse had been a matter of seconds; she'd turned her head to finger a blouse in the sale bin, felt her daughter's hand slip from hers, turned to grab her, found her gone. Elbowing her way through the throng of other shoppers, she'd searched for Kristal, calling out her name. Screaming it.

Mall security arrived; two sixty-year-old men with no professional police experience. Their requests for

Lara Malley to calm down so they could get the facts straight made her scream louder and she hit one of them on the shoulder. The guards restrained her and phoned the police.

Valley uniforms responded fourteen minutes later and a store-by-store search of the mall commenced. Every store was scrutinized. All bathrooms and storage areas were inspected. A troop of Eagle Scouts was summoned to help. K-9 units unleashed their dogs. The canines picked up the little girl's scent in the store where her mother had lost her. Then, overwhelmed by thousands of other smells, the dogs nosed their way toward the mall's eastern exit and floundered.

The search lasted six hours. Uniforms talked to each departing shopper. No one had seen Kristal. Night fell. Buy-Rite closed. Two Valley detectives stayed behind and reviewed the mall's security videotapes.

All four machines utilized by the security company were antiquated and poorly maintained, and the black-and-white films were hazy and dark, blank for minutes at a time.

The detectives concentrated on the time period immediately following Kristal Malley's reported disappearance. Even that wasn't simple; the machines' digital readouts were off by three to five hours. Finally, the right frames were located.

And there it was.

Long shot of a tiny figure dangling between two males. Kristal Malley had been wearing sweatpants and so did the figure. Tiny legs kicked.

Three figures exiting the mall at the east end. Nothing more; no cameras scanned the parking lot.

The tape was replayed as the D's scanned for details. The larger abductor wore a light-colored T-shirt, jeans, and light shoes, probably sneakers. Short, dark hair. From what the detectives could tell, he seemed heavily built.

No facial features. The camera, posted high in a corner, picked up frontal views of incoming shoppers but only the backs of those departing.

The second male was shorter and thinner than his companion, with longer hair that appeared blond. He wore a dark-colored tee, jeans, sneakers.

The lead detective, a DII named Sue Kramer said, 'They look like kids to me.'

'I agree,' said her partner, Fernando Reyes.

They continued viewing the tape. For an instant, Kristal Malley had twisted in her captor's grasp and the camera caught 2.3 seconds of her face.

Too distant and poorly focused to register anything but a tiny, pale disk. Sue Kramer said, 'Look at that body language. She's struggling.'

'And no one's noticing,' said Reyes, pointing to the stream of shoppers pouring in and out of the mall. People flowed around the little girl as if she were a piece of flotsam in a marina.

'Everyone probably figured they were horsing around,' said Kramer. 'Dear God.'

Lara Malley had already viewed the tape through tears and hyperventilated breathing, and she didn't recognize the two abductors.

'How can I?' she whimpered. 'Even if I knew them, they're so far away.'

Kramer and Reyes played it for her again. And again. Six more times. With each viewing, she shook her head more slowly. By the time a uniform entered the security room and announced 'The father's here,' the poor woman was nearly catatonic.

Figuring the video arcade attracted kids to the mall, the detectives brought in Galaxy's owner and the two clerks who'd been on duty, brothers named Lance and Preston Kukach, acned, high-school dropout geeks barely out of their teens.

It took only a second for the owner to say, 'The tape stinks but that's Troy.' He was a fifty-year-old Caltech-trained engineer named Al Nussbaum, who'd made more money during three years of renting out video machines than a decade at the Jet Propulsion Labs. That day, he'd taken his own kids horseback riding, had come in to check the receipts.

'Which one's Troy?' said Sue Kramer.

Nussbaum pointed to the smaller kid in the dark T-shirt. 'He comes in all the time, always wears that shirt. It's a Harley shirt, see the logo, here?'

His finger tapped the back of the tee. To Kramer and Reyes, the alleged winged logo was a faint gray smudge.

'What's Troy's last name?' said Kramer.

'Don't know, but he's a regular.' Nussbaum turned to Lance and Preston. The brothers nodded.

Fernie Reyes said, 'What kind of kid is he, guys?'

'Asshole,' said Lance.

'Caught him trying to steal scrip once,' said Preston. 'He leaned over the counter right when I was there and grabbed a roll. When I took it away he tried to whale on me, but I kicked his butt.'

'And you let him come *back*?' said Nussbaum.

The clerk flushed.

'We've got a policy,' Nussbaum told the detectives. 'You steal, you're out. Top of that, he *hit* you!'

Preston Kukach stared at the floor.

'Who's the other one?' said Sue Kramer, pointing to the larger boy.

Preston kept his head down.

'If you know, spit it out,' Al Nussbaum demanded.

'Don't know his name. He's here once in a while, never plays.'

'What does he do?' said Sue Kramer.

'Hangs out.'

'With who?'

'Troy.'

'Always Troy?'

'Yeah.'

'Troy plays and this one hangs.'

9

'Yeah.'

Al Nussbaum said, 'Now that you know who they are, why aren't you going after them pronto, finding that kid?'

Reyes turned to the clerks. 'What does hanging consist of?'

'He stands around while Troy plays,' said Lance.

'He ever try to steal?'

Head shakes from the Kukach brothers.

'Ever see either of them with little kids?'

'Nope,' said Lance.

'Never,' said Preston.

'What else can you tell us about them?' said Reyes.

Shrugs.

'Anything, guys. This is serious.'

'Spit it out,' said Al Nussbaum.

Lance said, 'I dunno, but maybe they live close by.'

'Why do you say that?' said Sue Kramer.

'Because I seen 'em leaving and walking out to the parking lot and keep going onto the street. No one picked 'em up in a car, y'know?'

'Leaving at which exit?'

'The one that goes out to the parking lot.'

Al Nussbaum said, 'Three exits go out to the parking lot, Lance.'

'The one near the garbage,' said Lance.

Fernie Reyes glanced at his partner and left.

No body in the Dumpsters out back near the eastern exit.

Five more hours of neighborhood canvass finally ID'd the two boys. Both of them lived in a low-income housing project set like a scar across the scrubby park that paralleled the rear of the mall. Two hundred shoddily built, federally financed one-bedroom units distributed among a quartet of three-story buildings, ringed by chain-link fencing in which dozens of holes had been cut. A scruffy, prisonlike place well known by uniforms who patrolled the area – 415 City, they called it, after the penal code for disturbing the peace.

The manager of Building 4 watched the video for a second and pointed to the smaller boy. 'Troy Turner. You guys been out here before on him. Last week, matter of fact.'

'Really,' said Sue Kramer.

'Yeah. He smacked his mother with a dinner plate, busted up the side of her face.' The manager massaged his own unshaved cheek. 'Before that, he was scaring some of the little kids.'

'Scaring them how?'

'Grabbing and shoving, waving a knife. You guys shoulda locked him up. So what'd he do?'

'Who's the bigger one?' said Reyes.

'Randolph Duchay. Kind of a retard but he doesn't cause problems. He done something, it's probably 'cause a Troy.'

'How old are they?' said Fernie Reyes.

'Lemme see,' said the manager. 'Troy's twelve I think, maybe the other one's thirteen.'

3

The detectives found the boys in the park.

There they were, sitting in the dark on some swings, smoking, the lighted ends of their cigarettes orange fireflies. Sue Kramer could smell the beer from yards away. As she and Reyes approached, Rand Duchay tossed his can of Bud onto the grass, but the smaller one, Troy Turner, didn't even try to hide it.

Taking a deep swig as she came face-to-face with him. Staring right back at her with the coldest fuck-you eyes she'd seen in a long time.

Ignore the eyes and he was a surprisingly small, frail-looking kid with pipe-stem arms and a pale triangular face under a mop of untrimmed dirty-blond hair. He'd shaved his head clean at the sides, which made the top-growth look even bigger. The manager had said he was twelve; he could've passed for younger.

Randolph Duchay was good-sized and broad-shouldered, with wavy, short brown hair and a puffy, thick-lipped face plagued by wet-looking zits. His arms had already started to pop veins and show some definition. Him, Sue would've placed at fifteen or sixteen.

Big and *scared*. Sue's flashlight picked up his fear

right away, the sweat on his brow and nose. A bead of moisture rolled off his pimply chin. Repeated eyeblinks.

She moved right in on him, pointed a finger in his face. 'Where's Kristal Malley?'

Randolph Duchay shook his head. Started to cry.

'Where is she?' she demanded.

The kid's shoulders rose and fell. He slammed his eyes shut and began rocking.

She hauled him to his feet. Fernie was doing the same to Troy Turner, asking the same question.

Turner tolerated being frisked with passivity. His face was as blank as a sidewalk.

Sue put pressure on Duchay's arm. The kid's biceps were rock hard; if he resisted he'd be a challenge. Her gun was on her hip, holstered, out of reach. 'Where the hell *is* she, Randy.'

'Rand,' said Troy Turner. 'He ain't no Randy.'

'Where's Kristal, Rand?'

No response. She squeezed harder, dug her nails in. Duchay squawked and pointed to the left. Past the swings and across the play area to a pair of cinder-block public lavatories.

'She's in the bathroom?' said Fernie Reyes.

Rand Duchay shook his head.

'Where *is* she?' Sue growled. 'Tell me *now.*'

Duchay pointed in the same direction.

But he was looking somewhere else. To the right of the lavs. South side of the cinder block, where a corner of dark metal stuck out.

Park Dumpsters. Oh, Lord.

She cuffed Duchay and put him in the back of the Crown Victoria. Ran over to look. By the time she got back, Troy was cuffed, too. Sitting next to his bud, still unruffled.

Fernie waited outside the car. When he saw her he raised an inquisitive eyebrow.

Sue shook her head.

He called the coroner.

The boys had made no attempt to conceal. Kristal's body lay atop five days' worth of park refuse, fully clothed but with one shoe off. The white sock underneath was grimy at the toe. The child's neck was broken like that of a cast-off doll. Delicate neck like that, Sue figured – hoped – she had died instantaneously. Several days later the coroner verified her guess: several broken cervical vertebrae, a ruptured windpipe, concomitant cranial bleeding. The body also bore two dozen bruises and internal injuries that could have proved fatal. No evidence of sexual assault.

'Does it really matter?' said the pathologist who'd done the post. A usually tough guy named Banerjee. When he reported to Sue and Fernie he looked defeated and old.

Placed in a holding cell at the station, Rand-not-Randy Duchay hunched, immobile and silent. He had stopped crying and his eyes were glassy and trancelike. His cell stank. Sue had smelled that feral reek plenty of times. Fear, guilt, hormones, whatever.

Troy Turner's cell smelled faintly of beer. The cans the detectives had found indicated each boy had downed three Buds. With Troy's body weight, not an insignificant amount, but there was nothing spacey about him. Dry-eyed, calm. He spent the ride to the station glancing out the window of the unmarked as it passed through dark Valley streets. As if this were a field trip.

When Sue asked him if there was anything he wanted to say, he gave a strange little grunting noise.

A grumpy old man's sound – annoyed. Like they'd messed up his plans.

'What's that, Troy?'

His eyes became slits. Sue had two kids, including a twelve-year-old son. Turner freaked her out. She forced herself to outstare him and he finally looked away and gave another grunt.

'Something on your mind, Troy?'

'Yeah.'

'What?'

'Can I have a smoke?'

Both boys, as it turned out, were thirteen, and Troy was the older one, a month from fourteen. Neither had known Kristal Malley. As the papers reported it, the pair had run out of change; as they left the video arcade they spied the little girl wandering around the mall looking lost. Deciding it would be 'cool' to 'fool around,' they gave Kristal some stale candy from Rand's gritty jeans pocket and she accompanied them willingly.

Despite evidence to the contrary, implications of sexual assault laced the local coverage. The story was picked up by the national press and the wire services, tilting toward the lurid, feeding sensation to their international clients.

That brought the usual swarm of talking heads, public intellectuals, and other misery pimps sounding off. Op-ed editors found themselves in a buyer's market.

The *obvious* root cause of such an outrage was: poverty; rampant societal breakdown; media violence; junk food and poor nutrition; the erosion of family values; godlessness; the failure of organized religion to meet the needs of the underclass; the absence of moral training in school; truancy; insufficient government funding for social programs; too much government control over the lives of the citizenry.

One genius, a pundit funded by the Ford Foundation, attempted to connect the crime to the post-Christmas sale season – pernicious materialism had led to frustration had led to murder. 'Acquisitional rage,' he called it. The same thing happens all the time in the favelas of Brazil.

'Shop till you drop it on someone,' Milo had remarked at the time. 'What an asshole.' We hadn't discussed the case much and I'd done most of the talking. He has solved hundreds of homicides but this one bothered him.

The media noise lasted awhile. Over at the Hall of Justice, the legal process kicked in, stealthy and gray. The boys were placed in the High Power ward at the county jail. With both of them too young to qualify for a 707 hearing to determine if they could be tried as adults, most experts felt the disposition would end up in Juvenile Court.

Citing the brutality of the crime, the District Attorney's Office made a special request to kick the case up to Superior Court. Troy Turner and Randolph Duchay's court-appointed P.D.s filed papers in strong opposition. A couple more days of editorial columns were devoted to that matter. Then another lull, as briefs were written and a hearing judge was appointed.

Juvey judge Thomas A. Laskin III – a former D.A. with experience prosecuting gang members – had a rep as a hard case. Courtroom whispers said it was going to get interesting.

I got the call three weeks after the murder.

'Dr Alex Delaware? Tom Laskin. We've never met but Judge Bonnaccio said you're the man for the job.'

Peter Bonnaccio had been presiding judge of Superior Court, Family Division for a couple of years, and I'd testified before him. I hadn't liked him much at first, thinking him hasty and superficial when making custody decisions. I'd been wrong. He talked fast, cracked jokes, was sometimes inappropriate. But plenty of thought went into his decisions and he was right more often than not.

I said, 'What job is that, Judge?'

'Tom. I'm the lucky guy who got handed the Kristal Malley murder and I need the defendants evaluated psychologically. The main issue, obviously, is, was there enough mature forethought and mental capacity prior to and during the commission of the crime to qualify the defendants for full, adult psychological capacity. The D.A.'s broken new ground, but from what I've seen the sixteen-year minimum for a 707 isn't inviolate. Issue Two – and this is as much personal as official – I'd like to know what makes them tick. I have three kids of my own and this one makes no sense to me.'

'It's a tough one,' I agreed. 'Unfortunately, I can't help you.'

'Pardon?'

'I'm not the man for the job.'

'Why not?'

'Psychological tests can reveal how someone's functioning intellectually and emotionally in the present, but they say nothing about past state of mind. On top of that, they were developed to measure things like learning disabilities and giftedness, not homicidal behavior. In terms of what made these boys tick, my training's even less helpful. We're good at creating rules about human behavior but lousy at understanding exceptions.'

'We're talking bizarre behavior, here,' said Laskin. 'Isn't that your bailiwick?'

'I've got opinions, but they're just that – my personal point of view.'

'All I want to know is were they thinking like kids or like grown-ups.'

'There's nothing scientifically definitive I could say about that. If other shrinks tell you different, they're lying.'

He laughed. 'Pete Bonnaccio said you could get like this. Which is exactly why I called you. Everything I do on this one is going to be put under the microscope. The last thing I need is one of the usual expert whores turning it into a circus. I didn't take Pete's word that you were unbiased, I talked to some other judges and a few cops. Even people who think you're a compulsive pain-in-the-ass admit you're not doctrinaire. What I need here is an open mind. But not so open your brain falls out.'

'Are you open-minded?' I said.

'What do you mean?'

'You really haven't made up your mind?'

I heard him breathing. Rapidly, then slower, as if forcing himself calm. 'No, I haven't made up my mind, Doctor. I just had a look at the autopsy photos. Went by the jail and looked at the defendants, too. In jail duds, with their hair cut, they look like they got kidnapped themselves. It just doesn't make sense.'

'I know, but –'

'Cut the crap, Doctor. I've got solid citizens clamoring for vengeance and the ACLU and their buddies wanting to make political hay. Bottom line: I'll evaluate the data and make up my own mind. But I need to be sure I've got the best information. If it's not you evaluating those boys, it'll be someone else – probably one of the whores. You want to opt out of your civic duty, fine. Next time something bad happens, tell yourself you did *your* best.'

'Impressive guilt trip.'

'Hey,' he said, laughing. 'Whatever works. So how about it? Talk to them, test them, do whatever the hell you want and report directly to me.'

'Let me think about it.'

'Don't think too long. Okay, decided yet?'

'I need to be clear,' I said. 'I could end up with no recommendation on adult versus juvey.'

'I'll deal with that if and when it happens.'

'I'd need unlimited access,' I said. 'And no time pressure.'

'Yes to the first, no to the second. I'm due to rule within thirty days. I can extend it to forty-five, maybe sixty, but if I don't act in a timely manner it leaves me open to all sorts of appeal static. You in?'

'Okay,' I said.

'What's your fee?'

I told him.

'Stiff,' he said, 'but not out of line. Send your bill directly to me. You might even get paid within a reasonable amount of time.'

20

'Comforting.'

'That's all the comfort you're going to get on this one.'

4

Social Services had evaluated the boys' families before settling them in the housing project. It took a subpoena but I got the records.

Troy Turner Jr. lived with his mother, a twenty-eight-year-old alcoholic and cocaine addict named Jane Hannabee. She'd been in and out of rehab for most of her adult life and had spent two years, as a teenager, at the state mental hospital in Camarillo. Her diagnoses ranged from mood disorder, depressed type, to personality disorder, narcissistic-borderline type, to schizoaffective disorder. Meaning no one really understood her. During her attempts at treatment, Troy had been sent to her parents in San Diego. Troy's grandfather, a retired army sergeant, found the boy's wild ways intolerable. He'd been dead for seven years, his wife for six.

A habitual felon and addict named Troy Wayne Turner was the boy's alleged father. Jane Hannabee claimed that at age fifteen, she'd shared a rock and a one-night stand with the thirty-nine-year-old in a San Fernando motel. Turner had recently turned to bank robbery to support his habit, and after his tryst with Hannabee was caught fleeing from a Bank of America in Covina. Sentenced to ten years at

San Quentin, he succumbed three years later to liver disease, never meeting, or acknowledging, his son.

Shortly after her boy's arrest, Jane Hannabee had left 415 City for parts unknown.

Rand Duchay's parents were long-distance truckers who'd perished on the Grapevine in a thirty-vehicle winter pile-up. Six months old at the time of the crash, Rand had been riding in the truck, swaddled in a storage compartment behind the front seat. He had survived without obvious injury, lived all his life with his grandparents, Elmer and Margaret Sieff, uneducated people who'd failed at farming and a number of small businesses. Elmer died when Rand was four and Margaret, afflicted with diabetes and circulatory problems, moved to the project when her money ran out. The way the social workers saw it, she'd done her best.

As far as I could tell, neither boy had spent much time in school and no one had noticed.

I put in my request to visit the prisoners and the A.D.A.s assigned to the case requested a prior meeting. So did the boy's deputy public defenders. I didn't need priming by either side and refused. When all the lawyers protested I had Judge Laskin run interference. A day later, I was authorized to enter the jail.

I'd been to the county jail before, was used to the grayness, the wait, the gates, the forms. The squinty scrutiny by reflexively suspicious deputy sheriffs as I stood in the sally port. I knew the High Power ward, too, had visited a patient there, years ago. Another kid who'd teetered over the edge. As I walked down the corridor with a deputy escort, moans and giggles sprayed from distant cells and the air filled with the battling stenches of excreta and disinfectant. The world might change but this place didn't.

Psych evaluations had been ordered alphabetically: Randolph Duchay, first. He was curled up on a cot in his cell, facing front but sleeping. I motioned to the deputy to hold back and took a few seconds to observe.

Big for his age, but in the cold, unadorned, custard yellow space, he looked insignificant.

The furnishings were a sink, a chair, a lidless toilet, a shelf for personal items that was bare. Weeks behind bars had left him sallow, with sooty half-moons under his eyes and chapped lips and a slack face ravaged by furious acne. His hair had been clipped short. Even from a distance I could see the scourge of pimples stretching up into his scalp.

I motioned that I was ready and the deputy unlocked the cell. As the door clicked behind me, the boy looked up. Dull brown eyes barely took the time to focus before closing.

The deputy said, 'I pass through every quarter hour. You need me sooner, holler.'

I thanked him, put my briefcase down, sat in the chair. When he left, I said, 'Hello, Rand. I'm Dr Delaware.'

'H'lo.' Hoarse, phlegmy voice, barely above a whisper. He coughed. Blinked several times. Remained prone.

'Got a cold?' I said.

Head shake.

'How are they treating you?'

No response, then he half sat, remaining slumped so low that his trunk nearly paralleled the cot. Big torso, disproportionately short legs. His ears were low-set, flaring on top, folded over in an odd way. Stubby fingers. Webbed neck. A mouth that never fully closed. His front teeth were small and ragged. The overall picture: 'soft signs' – suggestions of abnormality that didn't qualify for any formal syndrome.

'I'm a psychologist, Rand. Know what that is?'

'Kinda doctor.'

'Right. Know what kind?'

'Hnnh.'

'Psychologists don't give shots or examine your body.'

He flinched. Like any other inmate he'd been subjected to the full course of physical scrutiny.

I said, 'I deal with how you're feeling emotionally.'

His eyes floated upward. I touched my forehead. 'What's in your mind.'

'Like a shrink.'

'You know about shrinks.'

'Crazy nuts.'

'Shrinks are for crazy nuts.'

'Hnnh.'

'Who told you that, Rand?'

'Gram.'

'Your grandmother.'

'Hnnh.'

'What else did she say about shrinks?'

'If I didn't do right she'd send me.'

'To a shrink.'

'Hnnh.'

'What does "do right" mean?'

'Bein' good.'

'How long ago did your grandmother tell you that?'

He thought about that, seemed to be really working at figuring it out. Gave up and stared at his knees.

'Was it after you were in jail or before?'

'Before.'

'Was your grandmother angry at you when she said it?'

'Kinda.'

'What made her angry?'

His grainy skin reddened. 'Stuff.'

'Stuff,' I said.

No answer.

'Has Gram been to see you, here?'

'I guess.'

'You guess?'

'Yeah.'

'How often does she come?'

'Sometimes.'

'She have anything else to say?'

Silence.

'Nothing?' I said.

'She brang me to eat.'

'What's she bring you?'

'Oreos,' he said. 'She's mad.'

'Why's that?'

'Because I ruined it.'

'Ruined what?'

'Everything.'

'How'd you do that?'

His eyes fluttered. The lids dropped. 'My sin.'

'Your sin.'

'Killing that baby.' He lay back down, flung an arm over his eyes.

'You feel bad about that,' I said.

No answer.

'Killing the baby,' I prompted.

He rolled away from me, faced the wall.

'How do you feel about what happened to the baby, Rand?'

Several seconds passed.

'Rand?'

'He laughed.'

'Who laughed?'

'Troy.'

'Troy laughed.'

'Hnnh.'

'When?'

'When he hit her.'

'Troy laughed when he hit Kristal.'

Silence.

'Did Troy do anything else to Kristal?'

He was inert for nearly a minute, then rolled back toward me. His eyelids lifted halfway. Licked his lips.

'This is tough to talk about,' I said.

Small nod.

'What else did Troy do to the baby?'

Sitting up with the stiff, labored movements of an old man, he encircled his own neck with his hands and pantomimed choking. More than mime; his eyes widened, his face turned scarlet, his tongue thrust forward.

I said, 'Troy choked the baby.'

His knuckles whitened as he squeezed harder.

'That's enough, Rand.'

He began to rock as his fingers dug into his flesh. I got up, pried his hands loose. Strong kid; it took some doing. He gasped, made a retching sound, flopped back down. I stood by his side until his breathing slowed. He drew his knees up toward his chest. Pressure marks splotched his neck.

I made a note to request suicide watch. 'Don't do that again, Rand.'

'Sorry.'

'You feel bad about what happened to the baby.'

No response.

'You watched Troy choke and hit the baby and thinking about it makes you feel really bad.'

Someone's radio spat a hip-hop number. Footsteps from afar sounded but no one approached.

I said, 'You feel bad about watching Troy.'

He mumbled.

'What's that, Rand?'

His lips moved soundlessly.

'What, Rand?'

The deputy who'd escorted me strolled by, scanned the cell, and moved on. Fifteen minutes hadn't passed. The staff was taking special care.

'Rand?'

He said, 'I hit her, too.'

For the next week, I saw him every day for two hourly sessions, once in the morning, once in the afternoon. Instead of opening up, he regressed, refusing to divulge anything more about the murder. Much of my time was devoted to formal testing. The clinical interview was a challenge. Some days he remained resolutely mute; the most I could hope for were passive, monosyllabic answers to yes-no questions.

When I brought up the abduction, he seemed confused about why he'd participated, more stunned than horrified. Part of that was denial, but I suspected his low intellect was also a factor. When you comb through the histories of seriously violent kids, you often find head injuries. I wondered about the crash that had killed his parents but had spared him obvious damage.

His Wechsler Intelligence scores were no shock:

Full Score I.Q. of 79, with severe deficits in verbal reasoning, language formation, factual knowledge, and mathematical logic.

Tom Laskin wanted to know if he'd been functioning as an adult when he killed Kristal Malley. Even if Rand was thirty-five years old, that might've been a relevant question.

The T.A.T. and the Rorschach were pretty much useless: He was too depressed and intellectually impoverished to produce meaningful responses to the cards. His Peabody I.Q. score was no higher than the more verbally influenced Wechsler. His Draw-a-Person was a tiny, limbless, stick figure with two strands of hair and no mouth. My request to free-draw elicited a blank stare. When I suggested he draw himself and Troy he resisted by feigning sleep.

'Just draw anything, then.'

He lay there, breathing through his mouth. His acne had grown even worse. Suggesting a dermatologic consult would have elicited smirks from the jail staff.

'Rand?'

'Hnnh.'

'Draw something.'

'Can't.'

'Why not?'

His mouth twisted as if his teeth hurt. 'Can't.'

'Sit up and do it, anyway.' My hard tone made him blink. He stared at me but couldn't hold it past a few seconds. Pitiful attention span. Maybe part of that was sensory deprivation due to being locked up, but my guess was he'd always had trouble concentrating.

I handed him the pencil and the paper and the drawing board. He sat there for a while, finally put the board in his lap, gripped the pencil. The point froze on the paper.

'Draw,' I said.

His hand began circling lazily, floating above the paper. Finally making contact, as he created flabby, barely visible, concentric ellipses. The page began to fill. Darker ellipses. His eyes shut as he scrawled. For two weeks he'd done that a lot – blinding himself to his hellish reality.

Today, his pencil hand moved faster. The ellipses grew more angular. Flatter, darker. Sharpening to jagged, spearlike shapes.

He kept going, tongue tip snaking between his lips. The paper became a storm of black. His free hand fisted and gathered the hem of his jail shirt as his drawing hand moved faster. The pencil dug in and the page puckered. Ripped. He slashed downward. Circled faster. Digging in harder, as the paper shredded. The pencil went through to the drawing board, hit the glossy, fiberboard surface and slid out from his hand.

Landing on the floor of the cell.

He moved quickly, retrieved it. Exhaled. Held the yellow nub in a grubby, moist palm. 'Sorry.'

The paper was confetti. The pencil's graphite tip

had broken off, leaving behind splintered wood. Sharp little spikes.

I took the pencil. Put it in my pocket.

After my final visit, walking to the subterranean parking lot, I heard someone call my name and turned to see a heavy woman in a flowered dress leaning on an aluminum cane. The dirty-milk sky matched her complexion. I'd awakened to sunny blue Beverly Glen firmament, but cheer had eluded the grimy corner of East L.A. dominated by the jail.

She took a few steps toward me and the cane clunked on pavement. 'You're the psychologist, right? I'm Rand's gram.'

I walked to her, held out my hand.

'Margaret Sieff,' she said, in a smoker's voice. Her free arm remained at her side. The dress was a scratchy-looking cotton print, relenting at the seams. Camellias and lilies and delphiniums and greenery sprawled across an aqua background. Her hair was white, short, curly, thinning so severely that patches of pink scalp shone through. Blue eyes took me in. Small, sharp, searching eyes. Nothing like her grandson's.

'You been here all week but I never heard from you. You don' figger to talk to me?'

'I plan to when I'm finished evaluating Rand.'

'Evaluatin'.' The word seemed to distress her. 'What you figger you can do for him?'

'I've been asked by Judge Laskin to –'

'I know all that,' she said. 'You're supposed to say was he a kid or an aldult. Ain't that cristo clear? What *I'm* askin' is what can you *do* for him?'

'What's crystal clear, Mrs Sieff?'

'The boy's dumb. Screwy.' She pinged her waxy forehead with an index finger. 'Din't talk till he was four, still don't talk so good.'

'You're saying Rand's —'

'I'm saying Randolph ain't never gonna be no *aldult*.'

Which was as good a diagnosis as the jargon in my notes.

Behind her, rising above both of us, the concrete grid of the jail was the world's largest window shade. 'You coming or going, ma'am?'

'My appointment's not for a coupla hours. With the buses from the Valley it's hard to figger, so I get here early. 'Cause if I'm late, those bastards don' lemme in at all.'

'How about a cup of coffee?'

'You payin'?'

'I am.'

'Then, fine.'

5

Jails spread a very specific commercial rash, a trickle-down of cheap lawyers, bail-bond outfits, translation services, fast-food joints. I knew of a hamburger stand nearby but the walk through the parking lot was too much for Margaret Sieff's stiff legs. She waited by the entrance as I pulled up in my car. When I got out to open her door, she said, 'Fancy-dancy caddy. Must be nice being rich.'

My Seville's a '79, with a rebuilt engine. At that time it was well into its third vinyl roof, and a second paint job was already losing the battle with corrosive air. I took her cane and braced her elbow as she struggled to get in. When she finally settled, she said, 'How much they payin' you to evaluate?'

I said, 'That's not your concern, ma'am.'

That made her smile.

I drove to the burger joint, set her up at an out-door table, went inside, and waited in line behind a motorcycle cop who'd outgrown his tailored shirt, an A.D.A. who looked fifteen, and a pair of scruffy, mustachioed guys with faded gang tattoos. Those two paid with coins and it took awhile for the kid behind the counter to do the math. When I finally reached the front, I ordered two cardboard-flavored coffees.

When I returned to Margaret Sieff, she said, 'I'm hungry.' I went back in and got her a cheeseburger.

She snatched the food from me, ate ravenously, made token attempts at daintiness – quick dabs of paper napkin on mottled chin – before returning to her spirited attack. 'That hit the spot,' she said, scraping ketchup onto a finger and licking it off. 'I tell you, sometimes I could eat five a those.'

'What do you want to tell me about Rand?'

'Other than him being a dummy?'

'Must've been hard raising him.'

'Everything's hard,' she said. 'Raising his mama was hard.'

'Your daughter had problems.'

'Tricia was a dummy, just like him. So was that fool she went and married. It was *his* fault they got killed. All those speeding tickets *and* his drinking. So they give him a truck.' She laughed. 'Idjits. *That's* who they give a truck to.'

I said, 'Tricia had trouble in school.'

Her glare said she was starting to doubt my intelligence. 'That's what I said, ain't it?'

'What kind of trouble?'

She sighed. 'When she even bothered to go to school, she hated reading, hated 'rithmetic, hated everything. We were in Arizona back then and mostly she snuck away and ran around the desert with bad influences.'

'Where in Arizona?'

Instead of answering, she said, 'It was hot as hell. My husband's big idea, he was gonna grow cactuses because he heard you could make big money growing cactuses and selling 'em to tourists. "Be easy, Margie, no water, just keep 'em in pots till they're big enough." Yeah, and make sure the dog don't eat 'em and die from spikes in the guts, then you have to set up a stand on the highway and breathe all that heat and dust and hope some tourist'll bother to stop.'

She gave her empty cup another glance. 'I sat at that stand day after day, watching people speed right by me. People going somewhere.'

She pouted. 'Guess what? Even cactus need water.'

She held out her cup. I got her a refill.

'So Tricia grew up in Arizona,' I said.

'And Nevada and Oklahoma and before that we lived in Waco, Texas, and before that southern Indiana. So what? This ain't about where we lived. It's about Randolph and the bad thing he did.' She pressed forward against the table, bosom settling on grease-spotted blue plastic.

'Okay,' I said, 'let's talk about that.'

Her lips folded inward, tugging her nose downward. Her blue eyes had darkened to granite pebbles. 'I told him don't be hanging with that little monster. Now, all our lives is turned to shit.'

'Troy Turner.'

'Mister, I don't even want to hear that name.

Sinful monster, I knew he'd get Randolph in trouble.' She finished the refill, squeezed the cup and folded it over, placed her hand over the misshapen wad. Her mouth trembled. 'Didn't think it would be trouble like this.'

'What scared you about Troy?'

'Me? I weren't scareda that little shit. I was *worried*. For Randolph. 'Cause he's stupid, does whatever you tell him.'

'Is Troy stupid?'

'He's evil. You wanna do somethin' useful, sir? Tell the judge that without bad influence Randolph never woulda – never *coulda* done anything like this. And that's all I'm gonna say about it 'cause Randolph's lawyer said you weren't necessarily on our side.'

'I'm on no one's side, Mrs Sieff. The judge appointed me so that I could –'

'The judge is *against* us, we were some rich nigger it would be different,' she snapped. 'And from where I'm sittin', what you're doin's a waste of time and money. 'Cause Randolph don't have a chance, he's gonna get sent somewhere. Could be an aldult jail or could be someplace with little monsters.'

She shrugged. Her eyes were wet and she swiped them angrily. 'Same difference. He ain't gettin' out for a long, long time and my life's turned to shit.'

'Do you think he should be released?'

'Why not?'

'He murdered a two-year-old girl.'

'The *monster* did it,' she said. 'Randolph was just too stupid not to get outta there.'

Her grandson had told me otherwise.

'You want blame,' she said, 'there's plenty to go around. What kinda mother is that, leaving a baby all alone? They should be puttin' *her* on trial, too.'

I fought to remain expressionless. Must've failed, because she held out a palm. 'Hey, I ain't sayin' it was *all* her fault. I'm sayin' everything should be ... considered. 'Cause everything had to be movin' together for it to happen, know what I mean? Like all the astrology signs being in place. Like all the pieces in the puzzle fittin' together.'

'Lots of things played a role,' I said.

''Zactly. First off, she leaves her baby alone. Second, the baby goes and wanders off. Third, Randolph goes with that monster to the mall even though I told him not to. Fourth, my legs were hurtin', so I lay down to sleep it off and Randolph sneaked off. See what I mean? It's like a ... like a movie. Starring the devil, with us being the people the devil's workin' against. Like no matter what we do, everything goes to hell.'

She struggled upright, stood bracing herself with her cane. 'Take me back, okay? I get over there too late, those bastards gonna love lockin' me out.'

6

I drove Margaret Sieff back to the jail, went home, and picked up messages. Rand Duchay's P.D., a man named Lauritz Montez, had left two.

He didn't bother with small talk. 'You're finished with my client, so can we finally talk?'

'Feel free to state any relevant facts, Mr Montez.'

'Only one fact, Doctor, but it's the crucial one. Randy's obviously impaired. No way you couldn't have found that. What's the extent of it?'

No one called the kid Randy.

I said, 'It'll all be in my report.'

'Spare me,' said Montez. 'This isn't the stuff of forensic debate.'

I said, 'You know how it goes. Judge Laskin sees everything first.'

'Yeah, yeah ... so, what'd you think of that grand-mother? You bought her lunch. See that as conflict of interest?'

'I'm pretty busy, Mr Montez –'

'Easy, just kidding. So what do you think of her? Seriously.'

'At the risk of repeating myself –'

'Come on, Doctor. You can't be harboring any serious doubt about competence. You might want to know that I'm having my own expert conduct a full psychometric battery. Herbert Davidson, endowed professor from Stanford, acknowledged authority in the field.'

'Read his textbook in grad school,' I said.

'Be a shame if your results run far afield from his.'

'Be a damn shame,' I said.

'So when do I get your report?'

'When Judge Laskin sends it to you.'

'Sure,' he said. 'Following orders. God forbid anyone should think independently.'

Troy Turner was housed as far from Rand as possible, in a corner cell past a dark twist of corridor. The deputy who walked me over said, 'You're gonna love this one.'

He was an iron-pumper named Sherrill with a shaved head and a massive, straw-colored mustache. Usually, he projected the confidence of a strong man. Today he looked distracted.

'Tough kid?' I said.

He slowed his pace. 'I got kids. Four of my own plus a stepkid. On top of that, I spent three years working juvey crime, so I understand kids. Unlike some of the other guys, I know punks can start off as victims. But this one . . .' he shook his head.

'He do something in here?' I said.

'Naw, it's just the way he *is*.' He stopped. Behind us were empty cells. 'Doc, if anything I'm telling you gets out, we're never going to have any trust between us.'

'This is off the record.'

'I mean it,' he said. 'I'm talking to you because word is you're straight and you're doing your best for Judge Laskin and we all respect Judge Laskin, 'cause he knows the way the real world is.'

I waited.

He looked over his shoulder, stopped again. Silence all around; only on High Power could a jail be this quiet. Up a few feet was an occupied cell and I could see the inmate checking us out. Well-groomed, gray-haired, middle-aged. Copy of *Time* magazine in one hand.

Sherrill drew me farther up the hall, muttering, 'That one's Russian Mafia, cut your throat as easy as smile at you.' When we were alone, he said, 'I don't talk much to prisoners, life's too short, why fill your life with garbage. But this one, being a kid, I tried to be friendly. Turner reacts by shining me on. Completely. Making like I'm invisible. One time, I'd been off-shift, and when I got back he looked like he'd lost some weight. I brought him some breakfast, threw in some extra toast because he seemed pitiful. He snatched up a piece, gobbled like a hyena. I asked him if he understood why he was in here. This time, he doesn't shine me on, he comes right out and says, "'Causa what I did." But not with any feeling. He could've been ordering fries and a Coke. Then he takes another piece of toast from the breakfast tray and looks me in the eye and starts chewing. Real slowly, real sloppy. Pieces are falling out of his mouth, and then he starts dribbling and drooling, rolling his eyes. Acting like an idiot, like it's a big joke. I stand there and he keeps it up and then he spits it all out on the floor and says, "What?" Like I'm annoying him. And I say you didn't answer my question, dude. Why're you in here? And he says, "I fucked that baby *up* is why." Then he grinds the toast into the floor with his foot and says, "This shit *sucks,* dude. Gimme some *real* food."'

'Remorseful,' I said.

'Doc, God help me for saying it – if you repeat this I'll totally deny it – but some sperm deserve to be drowned before they get a chance to swim.'

7

Small boy, stick arms, heart-shaped face. Expect-
ant brown eyes widened as I entered his cell. The
pinched, wounded features of a Dickensian orphan.

I introduced myself.

He said, 'Pleased to meet you.' It rolled out easy,
like a rehearsed line, but if there was sarcasm I wasn't
catching it.

I sat down and he said, 'That chair's not real
comfortable.'

'Not much choice around here,' I said.

'You kin sit on the bed and I kin sit there.'

'Thanks, Troy, but I'm fine.'

'Okay.' He straightened his posture, rested a hand
on each knee.

I took out my notepad. Looked at his hands.
Narrow, white, long-fingered hands, grimy around
the cuticles but the nails had been clipped neatly.
Delicate hands. It wouldn't take much strength to
strangle a baby, but still . . .

'Troy, I'm a psychologist.'

'To talk to me about my feelings.'

'Someone told you that.'

'Miz Weider.'

Sydney Weider was his primary P.D. She'd been

more persistent than Lauritz Montez about meeting me before I began my evaluation, had gotten aggressive when I refused. Laskin had termed her 'a pit bull. Mark my word, she's already making notes for the appellate attorneys.'

'What did Ms Weider tell you about me?'

'You're gonna ask questions and I should cooperate.' He smiled, as if demonstrating.

I said, 'Is there anything you want to talk about?'

'I guess,' he said.

'What's that?'

'I should talk about her.'

'Her?'

'The baby.'

'Everyone calls her a baby,' I said, 'but she was more like a toddler, right?'

The term was new to him. 'I guess.'

'Kristal was two years old, Troy. She walked and talked a little.'

'I didn't hear her talk.'

'Ever see her before?'

'No way.'

I said, 'Why'd you decide to take her?'

'She followed us.'

'Where?'

'Out.'

'Out of the mall.'

'Yeah.' The camera had caught Kristal dangling, kicking her legs. The police had assumed it was a

44

struggle, but both defense briefs suggested that all three kids had been horsing around.

As if that mattered.

I said, 'Why'd Kristal follow you?'

Shrug.

'Can you think of any reason at all, Troy?'

'Probably she thought we were cool.'

'Why would she think that?'

''Cause she was little and we're big.'

'Big is cool.'

'Yup.'

'Okay,' I said. 'Kristal followed you and then what happened?'

'We went to the park and smoked and had some beer.'

'All of you.'

'Yup.'

'Where'd you get the beer?'

His eyes half closed. Suddenly wary. 'We had it.'

'You had it with you at the mall?'

'From before.'

'Where'd you keep it?'

'At the park.'

'Where at the park?'

Hesitation. 'Behind a tree.'

'Hidden.'

'Yup.'

'So you drank and smoked. All three of you.'

'Yup.'

'Kristal drank and smoked.'

'She tried to. She wasn't no good at it.'

'Kristal had trouble drinking and smoking,' I said.

'It made her cough.'

'So what'd you do?'

'Kept trying.'

'To make Kristal smoke?'

'To help her.'

'How'd that go?'

'Not so good.'

'What happened?'

'She coughed some more.'

'Anything else?'

'She threw up.'

'Where?'

'On my shirt.' Now the eyes were slits.

'You didn't like that,' I said.

'It smelled shit – smelled bad.'

'Kind of gross.'

'Yup.'

'What'd you do about that?'

'About what?'

'Being barfed on.'

'Pushed her away.'

'Where'd you push Kristal?'

He placed his hands on his chest.

'Where did she land?' I said.

'On the floor.'

'The floor of the park.'

'The grass.'

'She land hard?'

'It was grass.'

'Soft.'

'Yup.'

'Did you push her pretty hard?'

No answer.

'Troy?'

'I didn't do nothing serious,' he said. 'She sat on her butt and started crying real loud. Rand gave her some beer.'

'Why?'

Shrug. 'I guess to keep her quiet.'

'Rand's idea.'

'Yup.'

The coroner's report had found traces of Budweiser in Kristal's tiny stomach. Her lungs, too – the child had aspirated beer.

I said, 'It was Rand's idea to give Kristal beer.'

'I said that.'

'Why do you think Rand had that idea?'

'He's stupid.'

'Rand is.'

'Yup.'

'You hang out with him a lot.'

'He hangs out with *me*.' Flint had come into his voice. He realized it. Smiled. 'Most of the time, he's okay.'

'What happens when he's not okay?'

'He does stupid things. Like that.'

'That?'

'Giving the baby beer.'

'How'd Kristal like the beer?'

'Not too good.'

'She throw up some more?'

'She made puffy noises.' His cheeks inflated and he exhaled noisily. 'Stuff started coming out of her nose. Then she started yelling.'

'Yelling loud?'

'Kind of.'

'Pretty annoying.'

His eyes were hyphens. 'It wasn't cool.'

'What'd you do about that?'

'Nothing.'

'Kristal threw up on you and yelled loud and annoyed you but you didn't do anything at all?'

'Didn't have to,' he said. A tiny smirk skipped across his lips. Lasted for less than a second before his features settled into childish innocence. If I'd been writing notes, I would've missed the whole thing.

'Why didn't you have to do anything, Troy?'

'Rand did.'

'Rand solved the problem.'

'Yup.'

'How?'

'Shook her and hit her and put his hand on her neck.'

'Rand put his hand on Kristal's neck.'

'He choked her.'

'Show me how Rand choked Kristal.'

48

He hesitated.

I said, 'You were there, Troy.'

'Like this,' he said, grazing his own neck with a limp hand. Pressing ineffectually with the back of the hand, then releasing.

'That's how,' he said.

'Then what happened?'

'The baby blooped over.' He tilted to one side, in demonstration, lowered himself in slow motion to the cot. Sat up again. 'Like that.'

'Kristal fell over after Rand choked her.'

'Yup.'

'How'd you feel when you saw that?'

'Bad,' he said, too quickly. 'Very bad. Sir.'

'Why'd you feel bad, Troy?'

'She wasn't moving.' Fluttering eyelashes. 'I shoulda stopped it.'

'You should've stopped Rand from choking Kristal.'

'Yup.'

His lips curled upward and I watched for the return of the smirk. But something happened to his eyes that softened the expression.

The resigned, world-weary smile of one who'd seen it all but had managed to maintain his dignity.

'I'm very sorry,' he said. 'It was up to me. I'm the smart one.'

He was.

Full-scale I.Q. score of 117, which put him in the

top twenty-five percent. Given an abstract reasoning subtest in the ninetieth percentile and spotty school attendance that weakened his knowledge base, I figured it for an underestimate.

Worlds apart, intellectually, from Rand Duchay.

I shoulda stopped it.

Maybe Sydney Weider's coaching had fallen short. Or she'd told him the facts and he'd blocked them out.

Or he'd simply chosen to lie, figuring me for a gullible jerk.

I'd read the coroner's report.

Traces of Kristal Malley's skin had been found under Troy's fingernails, not Rand's.

For the rest of our sessions he cooperated fully, blithely lying every step of the way.

When I asked about his mother he told me she was trying to be an actress and that she visited him all the time. The logbooks said she'd been there once. Deputy Sherrill told me Jane Hannabee had been obviously stoned, the visit had lasted ten minutes, and she'd left looking angry.

'Once you see her, Doc, maybe you understand something about the kid. But not all of it, right? Other punks have crackhead skanks for mothers and they do bad stuff, but not this bad.'

According to Troy, his father had died 'in the army. Shooting terrorists.'

When I asked him what a terrorist was, he said,

'It's like a criminal but usually they're niggers and they blow stuff up.'

I revisited the murder several times and his position remained the same: Kristal had gone with him and Rand voluntarily; Rand had committed all the violence. Troy felt bad about not intervening.

On the sixth session, he substituted 'guilty' for bad.

'You feel guilty.'

'Real guilty, sir.'

'About what?'

'Not stopping it, sir. It's gonna delay my life.'

'Delay it, how?'

'I was gonna be rich soon, now it's gonna be later.'

'Why?'

''Cause they're gonna lock me up somewhere.'

'In jail.'

Shrug.

'How long do you think they'll lock you up?'

'You could tell them the truth, sir, and maybe it wouldn't have to be so long.' He cocked his head, almost girlishly. His smile had a feminine cast to it, too. He had a dozen smiles; first time I'd seen this variant.

'You think that if I tell them the truth, your sentence could be shorter.'

'The judge likes you.'

'Someone tell you that?'

'Nope.'

When most people lie they give off a 'tell' – a shift in posture, subtle changes in eye movement, tone of voice. This kid could fabricate so coolly I was willing to bet he'd fool the polygraph.

'Troy, do you ever get scared?'

'Of what?'

'Anything?'

He thought. 'I get scared of doing bad things.'

'Why's that?'

'I don't want to be bad.'

'Are you ever bad?'

'Sometimes. Like everyone.'

'Everyone's bad sometimes.'

'No one's perfect,' he said. 'Except God.'

'Are you religious?'

'Drew and Cherish say I am, sir.'

'Who're Drew and Cherish?'

'Ministers.'

'They visit you?'

'Yup. Sir.'

'Do you find that helpful?'

'Yessir. Very helpful.'

'How do Drew and Cherish help you?'

'Tell me I'm gonna be okay. Tell me everyone makes mistakes.'

'So,' I said, 'you think sometimes you're bad. Like how?'

'Not going to school. Not reading books.' He stood, took a volume from the bottom shelf. Black cardboard covers. *Holy Bible* in green script.

'Drew and Cherish give you that?'

'Yessir. And I read it.'

'What are you reading about.'

A second's pause. 'Day Two.'

'Of creation?'

'Yessir. God made heaven.'

'What does heaven mean to you?'

'A good place.'

'What's good about it?'

'You're rich and you get cool stuff.'

'What kind of cool stuff?'

'Whatever you want.'

'Who goes to heaven?'

'Good people.'

'People who don't do really bad things.'

'No one's perfect,' he said and his voice tightened.

'That's for sure,' I said.

'I'm going to heaven,' he said.

'After you're delayed.'

'Yessir.'

'You talked before about getting rich. How're you planning to do that?' I said.

Rebirth of the smirk. This time it endured, and his eyes drilled into mine and his delicate little hands became bony little fists.

''Cause I'm smart,' he said. 'Can I go to sleep, now? 'Cause I'm tired. *Sir.*'

The rest of the sessions were unproductive, as he wavered between claims of fatigue and feeling 'sick.'

My attempts to elicit specific symptoms were fruitless. A physical by a jail doctor had produced nothing. The last time I saw him, he was reading the Bible and ignored me as I sat down.

'Interesting?' I said.

'Yup.'

'What are you up to?'

He put the book facedown on the cot and stared past me.

'Troy?'

'I'm feeling sick.'

'Where?'

'All over.'

'Dr Bronsky checked you out and said you're fine.'

'I'm sick.'

'This may be the last time I come to see you,' I said. 'Anything you want to tell me?'

'What are you gonna tell the judge?'

'I'll just report what we talked about.'

He smiled.

'You're happy about that.'

'You're a good person, sir. You like to help people.'

I got up and picked up the Bible. Small gray smudges marked his place. Genesis, chapter four. Cain and Abel.

'Quite a story,' I said.

'Yessir.'

'What do you think of it?'

'Of what?'

'Cain killing his brother, getting cursed.'

'He deserved it.'

'Cain did?'

'Yessir.'

'Why's that?'

'He did sin.'

'The sin of murder.'

'Exactly,' he said, taking the Bible from me and closing it softly. 'Like Rand. He's going to hell.'

8

I met with both public defenders in a conference room at the jail.

Lauritz Montez was there when I arrived, a slightly built man, thirty or so, with dark hair pulled back into a ponytail. An extravagant waxed mustache overpowered a fuzzy chin-beard. He wore a vintage gray tweed three-piece suit and a skinny blue bow tie that was more like a shoelace.

Sydney Weider breezed in a few seconds later. She was older – early forties – thin and tall, with efficient blond hair and wide pale eyes. Her tailored black suit and crocodile bag and big pearl earrings were beyond a P.D.'s salary. Maybe the rock on her finger explained that. Maybe that was a sexist assumption and she'd cleaned up in the stock market.

She sat down and twisted the ring so the diamond faced inward. Put on a pair of tiny little gold-plated reading glasses and said, 'Well, here we are.' Her words came out crowded together. Big hurry to express herself.

Both of them had wanted individual meetings. I told them we'd start out together and see how it went.

It didn't need to go further. They worked on me

individually but their goals were identical: emphasizing the youth and criminal inexperience of their clients, pointing out the wretchedness of each boy's upbringing, letting me know that anything other than a juvenile trial would be cruel and inhuman.

By the end of the hour, they were working as a team. From talking to Troy I sensed Weider would be laying everything on Rand, but it wasn't my place to bring that up.

As she warmed up, she talked even faster, seemed to dominate Montez. Ending up with a long dissertation on the evils of video games and public housing, she snapped her Filofax shut, removed her glasses, and cross-examined me with her eyes.

'What's your report going to say?' Machine-gun burst.

'I haven't written it yet.'

'You must have come to some conclusions.'

'I'll be reporting to Judge Laskin. He'll send you copies.'

'So it's going to be like that,' she said.

'Per Judge Laskin, that's the way it has to be.'

She collected her papers and fiddled with her ring. 'Think about this, Dr Delaware: Psychology's a mushy soft science and psychologists can be made to look pretty vulnerable on the stand.'

'I'm sure they can.'

'More than vulnerable,' she said. 'Downright ludicrous.'

'I'm sure some of them deserve it.'

She sat up straighter, tried to stare me down, looked disgusted when she failed. 'Doctor, you can't seriously be considering these kids for an adult trial.'

'It won't be up to me –'

'Judge Laskin is relying on your expertise, so for all practical purposes it *will* be up to you, Doctor.'

'From what I've seen, Judge Laskin is a pretty independent guy.'

Montez said, 'All we're aiming for is basic justice, Doctor. Let's give these kids a chance at rehabilitation.'

Weider said, 'Doctor, we'll be bringing in our own experts.'

I said, 'Mr Montez has already hired Professor Davidson from Stanford.'

Weider turned and eyed her colleague. He twirled a mustache and nodded. 'It took awhile to get his fees authorized, but he's on board.'

Weider shot him a cold smile. 'How funny, Lauritz. I called Davidson last week. His secretary told me he had a prior commitment.'

'If you want him for your kid, maybe we can work something out,' said Montez.

'No need,' said Weider, breezily. 'I've got LaMaria from Cal.'

I said, 'Do either of you have a theory as to why your clients murdered Kristal Malley?'

They swiveled toward me.

Weider said, 'Doctor, exactly what are you asking?'

'What you think your clients' motive was.'

'Isn't motivation *your* thing, Doctor?'

'I'd imagine it would be yours, too.'

She stood, shook her head, stared down at me. 'You really think I'm going to lay my strategy out right here?'

'I'm not interested in strategy,' I said. 'Just insight.'

'Doctor, I don't have any insight. Which is precisely my point vis-à-vis your report: A fresh perspective is required. I hope you're prepared to deliver that.'

Montez's eyes followed Weider as she walked to the door. 'See you in court, Doctor.'

Montez left a second later; he avoided looking at me.

I sat there for a while. Wondering what I was going to do.

As I entered the jail parking lot, Sydney Weider called out my name. She was standing next to an ice-blue BMW convertible, tapping the croc bag against a long, lean thigh. To her left stood two women and a man.

Weider waved as if we were old buddies. I walked over. When I reached her, she smiled as if we'd just shared a pleasant afternoon. She drew one of the women close. 'Doctor, this is Troy's mom, Jane.'

Jane Hannabee was several inches shorter than the attorney and she seemed to shrink further under Weider's grasp. My files put her at twenty-eight. Her sallow face was scored with paper-cut wrinkles. Her long-sleeved knit top was bisected by a wide red stripe and looked brand new. So did her baggy jeans and her white sneakers. A snake tattoo coiled up past the sweater's crewneck. Its triangular head terminated just behind her left ear. Fangs bared, some sort of adder.

She had a thin body, thin lips, thin nose, lank brown hair that hung past her shoulders. Three holes punched in each ear but no earrings. A tiny black dot on her right nostril said that region had once been pierced. A caved-in mouth foretold missing teeth. Her eyes were blue and red-rimmed.

Crusted makeup failed to mask a bruise on her left cheek.

The police report said Troy had hit her from time to time.

She looked older than Weider.

I said, 'Pleased to meet you.'

Jane Hannabee bit her lip and looked down at the oil-spotted floor of the parking garage and slipped me cold, dry fingers.

Sydney Weider said, 'Doctor, I'm sure you'd like to talk to Ms Hannabee.'

'Absolutely. Let's set it up.'

'How about now?'

Taking control.

I smiled at her and she smiled back.

'You *do* have time for Troy's mother, Doctor.'

'Of course,' I said.

Weider turned to the other two people. 'Thanks for bringing her.'

'Anytime,' said the man. He was in his late twenties, solidly built, with thick, wavy dark hair that reminded me of an overripe artichoke. Broad, pleasant face, meaty shoulders, a wrestler's flaring neck. He wore a corduroy suit the color of peanut butter, black boots, a navy blue shirt with long collar points, and a baby blue tie.

His white-gold wedding band was speckled with tiny blue stones and matched the one on the hand of the woman next to him.

She was around his age, slightly heavy, and extremely pretty with long, teased hair bleached nearly white and swept back at the sides. A white linen dress flared under a soft pink cardigan. A thin silver chain and crucifix circled her neck. Her skin was bronze and flawless.

The man stepped forward and blocked her face from view. 'Drew Daney, sir.' Thick fingers but a gentle grip.

Sydney Weider said, 'Doctor, these are some supporters of Troy.'

That made it sound as if the kid were running for office. Maybe the analogy wasn't that far off: This *was* going to be a campaign.

Drew Daney said, 'This is my wife, Cherish.'

The blond woman said, 'I can't see anything, honey.' Drew Daney retreated and Cherish Daney's smile came into view.

'Troy's supporters,' I said.

'Spiritual advisers,' said Cherish Daney.

'Ministers?'

'Not yet,' said Drew. 'We're theology students, at Fulton Seminary. Doctor, thanks so much for being there for Troy. He needs all the support he can get.'

I said, 'Are you ministering to Rand Duchay as well?'

'We will if we're asked. Wherever we're needed –'

Sydney Weider said 'Let's get going' and gripped Jane Hannabee harder. Hannabee winced and started to shake. Maternal anguish or some sort of dope jones? I told myself that was wrongheaded thinking. Give her a chance.

Cherish Daney said, 'We'd better get going to see Troy.'

Her husband looked at his sports watch. 'Oh, boy, we'd better.'

Cherish moved toward Jane Hannabee, as if to embrace the woman, but changed her mind and gave a small wave and said, 'God bless you, Jane. Be well.'

Hannabee hung her head.

Drew Daney said, 'Good to meet you, Doctor. Good luck.'

The two of them walked off toward the jail's electric gate, keeping up a brisk pace, arm in arm.

Sydney Weider watched them for a few seconds, expressionless, then she turned to me. 'Getting another interview room in the jail is going to be a hassle. How about I let you guys talk in my car?'

Jane Hannabee sat behind the wheel of Weider's BMW and looked as if she'd been abducted by aliens. I took the passenger seat. Sydney Weider was a few yards away, pacing and smoking and talking on her cell phone.

'Is there anything you want to tell me, Ms Hannabee?'

She didn't answer.

'Ma'am?'

Staring at the instrument panel, she said, 'Don't let them kill Troy.'

Flat voice, slight twang. A plea, but no passion.

'Them,' I said.

She scratched her arm through her sleeve, rolled up the fabric, and worked on bare, flaccid skin. More tattoos embroidered her forearm, crude and dark and gothic. Weider had probably bought her the fresh clothes, dressed her up with an eye toward camouflage.

'In prison,' she said. 'When they send him up, he's gonna have a bad name. It's gonna be cool to hurt him.'

'What kind of bad name?'

'Baby killer,' she said. 'Even though he didn't do it. The niggers and the Mexicans will say it's cool to get him.'

'Troy didn't kill Kristal,' I said, 'but his reputation will put him in danger in prison.'

She didn't answer.

I said, 'Who did kill Kristal?'

'Troy's *my* baby.' She held her mouth open, as if needing more breath. Behind the desiccated lips were three teeth, brown and attenuated. I realized she was smiling.

'I did the best I could,' she said. 'You kin believe that or not.'

I nodded.

'You don' believe me,' she said.

'I'm sure raising a son alone was hard.'

'I got rid of the others.'

'The others?'

'I got knocked up four times.'

'Abortions?'

'Three. The last one hurt me.'

'You kept Troy.'

'I felt like I deserved it.'

'Deserved having a child.'

'Yeah,' she said. 'That's a woman's right.'

'To have a child.'

'You don' believe that?'

'You wanted Troy,' I said. 'You did your best raising him.'

'You don' believe that. You're gonna send him off to prison.'

'I'm going to write a report about Troy's psychological status – what's going on in his head – and give it to the judge. So anything you can tell me about Troy could help.'

'You sayin' he's crazy?'

'No,' I said. 'I don't think he's one bit crazy.'

The directness of the answer startled her. 'He's not,' she insisted, as if we remained in dispute. 'He's *real* smart. He always was smart.'

'He's very bright,' I said.

'Yeah,' she said. 'I want him to go to college.' She turned and shot me another smile, closemouthed, subtle. Its arc matched the coil of snake on her neck and the effect was unnerving. 'I figured he kin be a doctor or something else to get rich.'

Troy had talked about getting rich. Unperturbed. As if the charges against him were an inconvenience along the road to affluence. His mother's delusions made my eyes hurt.

She placed her hands on the BMW's steering wheel. Pressed down on the inactive gas pedal. Muttered, 'This is somethin'.'

'The car?'

She eyed Weider through the windshield. 'You think she's gonna help Troy?'

'She seems to be a good lawyer.'

'You don' ever answer a question, do you?'

'Let's talk about Troy,' I said. 'You want him to go to college.'

'He ain't goin' there now. *You're* sending him to prison.'

'Ms Hannabee, I can't send him anywhere –'

'The judge hates him.'

'Why do you say that?'

She reached over and touched my arm. Stroked it. 'I know men. They're all hate and jumping.'

'Jumping?'

'On women,' she said, working her way up toward my shoulder. Touching my cheek. I removed her hand.

She gave me a knowing smile. 'If there's something a man needs, I know it.'

I shifted backward, touched the door panel. 'Is there anything you want to tell me about Troy?'

'I know men,' she repeated.

I caught her gaze and held it. She touched the bruise on her cheek. Her lips quivered.

'Where'd you get that?' I said.

'You think I'm ugly.'

'No, but I would like to know –'

'I used to be hot,' she said. 'My tits were like water balloons, I used to dance.' She pressed her palms to her chest.

'Ms Hannabee –'

'You don't have to call me that. Miz. I'm no Miz.'

'Jane –'

She wheeled, grabbed my arm again. Claw-fingers bit through the wool of my sleeve. No seductiveness this time. Desperation, as cold fear brightened her eyes and I caught a glimpse of the girl she'd once been.

66

'*Please*,' she said. 'Troy didn't kill no *baby*. The retard did it. Everyone knows it.'

'Everyone?'

'He's the big one, Troy's little. Troy's my little man. It weren't his fault he hooked up with the retard.'

'Rand's the guilty one,' I said.

Her grip on my arm tightened further. 'Zactly.'

'Did Troy tell you that Rand killed the baby?'

'Yeah.'

I glanced down at her fingers. She coughed and sniffed and removed them.

'He'll get better,' she said.

'Who will?'

'Troy. You give him a chance and he'll get better and go to college.'

'You think he's sick.'

She stared at me. 'Everyone's sick. Being alive's being sick. We got to be forgiving. Like Jesus.'

I said nothing.

She said, 'You understand? About forgiving?'

'It's a wonderful quality,' I said. 'Being able to forgive.'

'I forgive everyone.'

'Everyone who hurts you?'

'Yeah, why not? Who cares what happened before? Same with Troy, what he did is over. And he didn't even do it. The retard did.'

She turned in the seat, bumped her hip against the steering wheel and flinched. 'You gonna help him?'

'I'll do my best to be truthful.'

'You should,' she said. Leaning closer. Her scent was a strange mixture of old laundry and too-sweet perfume. 'You could look like him.'

'Like who?'

'Jesus.' She smiled, ran a tongue over her lips. 'Yeah, definitely. Put a beard on you, a little more hair and yeah, sure. You could be a real cute Jesus.'

9

Tom Laskin's clerk called me a couple of days later to check on my report. I told her I needed another week, picking the time arbitrarily, not sure why I was asking for an extension.

I spent ten more days on the case, interviewing the social workers and the eligibility officers who covered 415 City, visiting the project and chatting with neighbors, anyone who claimed to have something to offer. Each time, Margaret Sieff was out. Jane Hannabee had moved and no one knew where.

I visited the boys' school. No one – not the principal or the guidance counselor or the teachers – had more than a vague remembrance of Troy or Rand. The last time either boy had been graded was a year ago. C minuses and a couple of D's for Rand, which was social promotion; my testing had shown him to be illiterate with math skills at the second-grade level. B's and C's and D's for Troy. He'd been judged 'bright but disruptive.'

To the project workers, the young killers were names on forms. The residents all agreed that prior to his arrest, Rand Duchay had been viewed as a harmless oaf. Everyone I spoke to was certain he'd been turned bad by Troy Turner.

No divided opinions on Troy, either. He was seen as cunning, nasty, mean, 'evil.' Scary despite his small size. Several residents claimed he'd threatened their children but the details were vague. One woman, young and black and nervous, stepped forward as I was leaving the project and said, 'That boy done nasty things to my daughter.'

'How old's your daughter?'

'Gonna be six next month.'

'What happened?'

She shook her head and hurried away and I didn't go after her.

I asked to reinterview the boys but was blocked from doing so by Montez and Weider.

'They're adamant,' Tom Laskin informed me. 'Went so far as to file motions to keep you away.'

'What's the problem?' I said.

'My feeling is it's mostly Weider. She's a manic shark.'

'She does talk fast.'

'Everything's conflict with her, even when it doesn't need to be,' said Laskin. 'She says you've had more than enough time with her client, doesn't want his head messed up before she brings her own experts in. Montez is a loafer, takes the path of least resistance. I could probably push it, Alex, but if I'm reversed I'd prefer it not be for something picayune. Do you really need more time?'

'Why would I mess up their clients' heads?'

'Don't take it personally,' he said. 'It's lawyer crap. Their basic premise is that you're biased for the prosecution.'

'I haven't spoken a word to the D.A.'

'It's gamesmanship. They're setting the stage so if you do say something they don't like, they've precharacterized it as impeachable.'

'Okay,' I said.

'Don't worry, I'll protect you when you get up on the stand. So when can I expect your compiled psychological wisdom on my desk?'

'Soon.'

'Soon is better than the alternative.'

I sat down to write my report, starting with the easy part – the crime scene, the background information, the test results. But even that was a struggle, and I hadn't gotten far when Lauritz Montez called me.

'How's it going, Doctor?'

I said, 'Have you changed your mind about my talking to Rand?'

'Maybe,' he said. 'My client cooperated fully the first time, didn't he? You'll make a point of stressing that, right?'

'I'll do my best to be unbiased.'

'Look,' said Montez, 'the motion was Weider's idea. You know what she's like.'

'Actually, I don't.'

'Whatever,' he said. 'You do remember Rand cooperating fully.'

'I do.'

'Good.' His voice was tight. 'He's pretty depressed.'

'That doesn't surprise me.'

'Poor kid,' he said.

I didn't answer.

'The reason I'm calling, Dr Delaware, is that Weider just put in for a bifurcated hearing. Do you understand what that means?'

'She wants to split Troy's defense from Rand's.'

'She wants to *screw* me – screw Rand. I thought we were all on the same page but she's pulling a fast one, shifting to blaming it all on my client so her little sociopath can get easy treatment. I thought you should be alerted.'

'Thanks.'

'I'm serious,' he said. 'The truth is obvious.'

'What truth is that?'

'A basically good, really stupid kid got caught up with a cold, cruel murderer. I know you've been back to 415 City, I know everyone told you that.'

I said, 'What can I do for you, Mr Lauritz?'

'I respect your expertise and want to maintain open communication. No offense about the motion to deny you access, okay? If you really want to talk to Rand, fine. He's remorseful. *Consumed* with remorse.'

I didn't answer.

'So,' he said. 'Are you going to be seeing him again?'

'I'll give you a call.'

I didn't.

He never followed up.

Three days into writing the report, I phoned Tom Laskin. 'This isn't working very well.'

'What isn't?'

'I told you at the outset that I might not be able to come up with meaningful recommendations, and that's what's happened. If you want to reduce my fee, fine.'

'What's the problem?'

'I can't produce clear data to help you with your choice. My personal preference would be juvey certification because they're kids and lacked adult capacity. But I'm not sure I'd sleep well if I was responsible for that decision.'

'Why not?'

'The act was horrendous and I doubt making them C.Y.A. wards for a few years will rehab them.'

'Are they still dangerous?' he said.

'Would they do something that bad again? On his own, Rand Duchay probably wouldn't. But if he hooked up with someone dominant and violent, it's possible.'

'Any remorse on his part?'

'He seems to have some,' I said. 'Was he thinking like an adult at the time of the murder? No. Would that change in five years, or even ten? Probably not, given his intellectual level.'

'Which is?'

I quoted the test results.

Laskin whistled. 'What about Turner?'

'Smarter – a lot smarter. He's got the ability to calculate and plan. Sydney Weider's going to claim Rand Duchay initiated the crime and her client was an innocent bystander. The forensics say that's not true, but Rand did admit striking Kristal, and his size could work against him if you didn't know better.'

'I'm still on the remorse issue,' said Laskin. 'Turner have any?'

'He talks about sin, claims to be reading the Bible, has a couple of theology students offering moral support. But I doubt there's any serious insight there. He denies he ever touched Kristal despite the fact that Kristal's skin was found under his fingernails.'

'Weider sent me an impassioned request for bifurcation. Looks like just another TODDI defense.'

The Other Dude Did It.

'Going to grant the split?' I said.

'Not unless I have to. How smart is Turner?'

'Considerably above average.' I gave him those numbers, too.

He said, 'No diminished capacity, there. Adult comprehension?'

'Intellectually, he can reason things out. But he's thirteen, which is an interesting age. There's some evidence that adolescent brains undergo changes

74

at fourteen to fifteen that lead to fuller reasoning capacity. Even with that, you know what teens are like. Rationality takes years to settle in.'

'Sometimes it never sets in,' he said. 'So you're leaning toward juvey but you don't want to put it in writing because of the enormity of the crime.'

'I don't think it's a psychological issue,' I said.

'What is it, then?'

'A judicial question. What placement would approximate justice to the greatest extent.'

'Meaning it's my problem.'

I didn't answer.

He said, 'I know teens are stupid. The problem is if we gave teen criminals special treatment, a lot of really vicious thugs would be getting off easy. And nothing in my experience matches the viciousness of this crime. They worked that poor baby over really bad.'

'I know. But you've seen Turner. He looks twelve. I'm trying to picture him at Quentin or a place like that and it's not a pretty thought.'

'Small and smart, but he murdered a two-year-old, Alex. Why the hell would a smart kid do something like that?'

'That's another question I can't answer,' I said. 'I.Q. and moral development are separate issues. Like Walker Percy said, "You can get straight A's but still flunk life."'

'Who's he?'

'A novelist and a psychiatrist.'

'Interesting combo,' he said. 'So you're telling me I've got a dumb kid and a bright little sociopath and they just happened to murder a two-year-old. Any other antisocial history for either of them?'

'Not for Rand. Everyone who knows Troy describes him as cunning, and some people at the project called him cruel. He's got a history of threatening younger kids. He's also suspected of killing stray dogs and cats, but I couldn't find any facts to back that up, so maybe the rumor mill's working overtime because of the murder. One woman implied he'd molested her daughter but refused to talk to me about it. Given his upbringing, I wouldn't be shocked if he's been abused, himself.'

I gave him a capsule of both boys' histories, including Rand Duchay's head injury during infancy. 'If you're looking for mitigating factors, you've got plenty.'

'Prisoners of biology?'

'And sociology and just plain bad luck. Neither of these two had much in the way of nurturing, Tom.'

'Which doesn't excuse what they did to that poor little girl.'

'Not in the least.'

'Have you picked up any possible motive?' he said. 'Because no one's put anything forward – including the cops.'

'From what I can tell, the abduction was impulsive. The two of them were headed to the park to smoke and drink when they saw Kristal wandering around.

They thought it would be fun to watch Kristal smoke and drink. She got sick, started to fuss, threw up, and things got out of control. There's no indication they were stalking her.'

'Bad luck for that little girl,' he said. 'Okay, so it's your basic senseless crime. I was hoping for something a little more ... psychologically illuminating. But no beef, you were up-front about no promises. Forget the b.s. about cutting your fee. When the government wants to give you money, take it ... there's nothing at all you can give me about disposition?'

'What will happen if you certify them as adults?'

'Initially, they'll get long sentences and go off to Quentin or a place like it. If I juvey them, they're off to the California Youth Authority, which, nowadays, isn't all that different from grown-up prison except the inmates are shorter. The longest they could be C.Y.A. wards would be till age twenty-five.'

'Meaning they'd be released at the peak of criminal drive.'

'You bet,' he said. 'In big-boy lockup, they'd be vulnerable to the Black Guerrilla Army and Nuestra Familia, probably run for cover to the Aryan Brotherhood. So we'd be creating a couple of little Nazis. But most of the C.Y.A. facilities are gang-ridden, too.'

'Why'd you say they'd have long sentences "initially"?'

'Because if I adult-certify, there's a good chance some higher court will lower their sentences and have them switched to lower-security facilities. Meaning they could end up with *less* time than a C.Y.A. placement. I've got the victim's family to think about. Like you said, the best we can hope for is approximating justice, and Lord knows we'll never get closure – whatever the hell that means. But there's got to be something that does the least harm.'

'I haven't seen the family in the media.'

'They've kept a low profile, but the father's called the D.A. a few times, demanding justice. No one can give him what he really wants – his kid back. And two other kids have ruined their own lives. It's a rotten situation for all concerned.'

'Beyond rotten.'

'Alex, they're so damned *young*. What the hell turned them so bad?'

'Wish I could tell you,' I said. 'The precursors are all there – bad environment, maybe bad biology. But most kids exposed to the same things don't murder toddlers.'

'No, they don't,' he said. 'Okay, send me whatever you feel comfortable putting down on paper. I'll start your reimbursement voucher churning through the system.'

10

In the end, resolution came the way it usually does once cases fade from public scrutiny: the product of backroom negotiation and the search for the least of all evils.

Five months after their arrests, in what the papers termed 'a surprise move,' both boys pled guilty and were sentenced to the California Youth Authority until they were twenty-five or until it could be proven they'd been successfully rehabilitated.

No trial, no media hoopla. No need for me to appear as an expert witness and my check from the court arrived in a timely fashion.

I talked to no one but Milo about it, pretended I was sleeping well.

Troy Turner was sent to the N.A. Chaderjian camp in Stockton and Rand Duchay ended up at the Herman G. Stark Youth Correctional Facility in Chino. The C.Y.A. promised to provide counseling for both boys and special education for Rand.

The day the deal was announced, Kristal Malley's parents were caught by a TV crew exiting the courtroom and asked for their opinion of the deal.

Lara Malley, a small, wan brunette, was sobbing.

Her husband, Barnett, a tall, raw-boned man around thirty, glared and said, 'No comment.'

The camera closed in on his face because anger's more fun for the camera than despair. He had thin, sandy hair, long sideburns, sharp features, and prominent bones. Dry-eyed; the unmoving eyes of a sniper.

'In your opinion, sir,' the reporter pressed, 'do the ages of the defendants make this an appropriate solution for closure?'

Barnett Malley's jaw flexed and he jerked his hand upward and the soundman picked up scuffling noises. The reporter retreated; Malley didn't move. The camera zoomed on his fist, frozen midair.

Lara Malley whimpered. Barnett stared into the camera for another second, grasped his wife by the arm, propelled her out of range.

Tom Laskin called me six weeks later. It was just after noon and I'd finished a session with an eight-year-old boy who'd burned his face playing with swimming pool chemicals. His parents had sued and a quack 'environmental medicine' specialist had testified that the child would get cancer when he grew up. The boy had overheard and become traumatized and it was my job to deprogram him.

'Hi, Tom.'

'Could we meet, Alex?'

'About what?'

'I'd rather talk in person. I'll come to your office.'

'Sure, when?'

'I'll be finished in an hour. Where are you located?'

He arrived at my house, wearing a camel jacket, brown slacks, a white shirt, and a red tie. The tie was limp and pulled down from an open collar.

We'd talked over the phone but had never met. I'd seen his picture in newspaper accounts of the Malley case – mid-fifties, gray hair trimmed in an executive cut, square face, steel-rimmed eyeglasses, a prosecutor's wary eyes – and had formed the image of a big, imposing man.

He turned out to be short – five-six or -seven – heavier and softer and older than pictured, the hair white, the jowls giving way to gravity. His jacket was well-cut but tired. His shoes needed a polish and the bags under his eyes were bluish.

'Pretty place,' he said, sitting on the edge of the living room chair that I offered. 'Must be nice working out of your house.'

'It has its advantages. Something to drink?'

He considered the offer. 'Why not? Beer, if you've got it.'

I went to the kitchen and fetched a couple of Grolsches. When I returned his posture hadn't relaxed. His hands were clenched and he looked like someone forced to seek therapy.

I popped the caps on the beers and handed him a bottle. He took it but didn't drink.

'Troy Turner's dead,' he said.

'Oh, no.'

'It happened two weeks ago, C.Y.A. never thought to call me. I found out from Social Services because they were looking for his mother. He was found hanging from a punching bag stand in a supply room off the gym. He was supposed to be putting equipment away – that was the job they gave him. He'd been judged too dangerous to work in the kitchen or in the vegetable garden with tools.'

'Suicide?'

'That's what they thought till they saw blood pooled on the floor and swung him around and found his throat cut.'

I've always been too good at conjuring mental pictures. The brutality of the scene – small, pale body dangling in a dark, heartless place – would visit my dreams.

'Do they know who did it?' I said.

'They're figuring it for a gang thing,' said Laskin. 'He'd been there, what, a month? Tried right away to hook up with the Dirty White Boys – an Aryan-B farm club. He was still in the initiation stage and part of the deal was jumping a Latino boy. He pulled that off ten days ago, surprised one of the smaller Vatos Locos in the shower, hit him upside the head with a heavy hairbrush and kicked the kid when he was down. The boy suffered a concussion and bruised ribs and ended up being transferred to another facility. Troy's punishment was solitary confinement for a week. He'd been back in his bunk-room for three days. The day before he died, they put him back on gym closet duty.'

'So everyone knew where he'd be at a specific time.'

Laskin nodded. 'The blood was still wet and the weapon was left at the scene – homemade shank fashioned from a toothbrush and a piece of butter knife honed to a razor-sharp edge. Whoever did it took time to wipe up his footprints.'

'Who found the body?'

'A counselor.' He finished his beer and put the bottle down.

'Want another?'

'Yes, but no.' He uncrossed his legs, held out a hand as if asking for something. 'I thought I was being compassionate by sending him to Chaderjian. Downright Solomonic.'

'I thought so, too.'

'You agreed with the decision?'

'Given the choices,' I said, 'I thought it was the best decision.'

'You never said anything.'

'You never asked.'

'The Malleys weren't happy with the decision. Mister called to tell me.'

'What did he prefer?'

'The death penalty.' His smile was queasy. 'Looks like he got it.'

I said, 'Would sending Troy to adult prison have made him safer?'

He picked up the empty bottle and rolled it between his palms. 'Probably not, but it still stinks.'

'Has his mother been located?'

'Finally. The county just authorized her for methadone and they found her at an outpatient clinic, waiting in line for her dose. The warden at Chaderjian said she visited Troy once the whole month and that was for ten minutes.'

He shook his head. 'Little bastard never had a chance.'

'Neither did Kristal Malley.'

He stared at me. 'That rolled off your tongue pretty easily. You that tough?'

'I'm not tough at all. I worked the cancer wards at Western Peds for years and stopped trying to figure things out.'

'You're a nihilist?'

'I'm an optimist who keeps my goals narrow.'

'I'm usually pretty good at coping with all the crap I see,' he said. 'But something about this one … maybe it's time to retire.'

'You did your best.'

'Thanks for saying so. I don't know why I'm bothering you.'

'It's no bother.'

Neither of us talked for a while, then he steered the conversation to his two kids in college, looked at his watch, thanked me again, and left.

A few weeks later I read about a retirement party thrown for him at the Biltmore, downtown. 'Child

Murder Trial Judge' was his new title and I guessed that would stick.

Nice party, from the sound of it. Judges and D.A.s and P.D.s and court workers lauding him for twenty-five years' good service. He planned to spend the next few years sailing and playing golf.

Troy Turner's murder stayed with me and I wondered how Rand Duchay was faring. I phoned the C.Y.A. camp in Chino, wrestled with the bureaucracy for a while before reaching a bored-sounding head counselor named DiPodesta.

'So?' he said, when I told him about the killing.

'It might put Duchay at risk.'

'I'll make a note of that.'

I asked to talk to Rand.

'Personal phone calls are limited to blood relatives and people on the approved list.'

'How do I get on the list?'

'Apply.'

'How do I do that?'

'Fill out forms.'

'Could you please send them to me?'

He took my name and address but the application never arrived. I considered pursuing it, rationalized not doing so: I lacked the time – and the desire – for long-term commitment, so what use could I be to Rand?

For the next few weeks, I scanned the papers for bad news about him. When nothing appeared I convinced myself he was where he should be.

Counseled and tutored and taken care of for the next twelve years.

Now, he was out in eight.

Wanted to talk to me.

I supposed I was ready to listen.

11

I left the house and set out for Westwood.

The restaurant was called Newark Pizza. A sign underneath the tricolor boot promised *Authentic New Jersey Pasta and Sicilian Delicacies Too!*

Lights on behind pink-and-white-checked drapes, the faint outlines of patrons.

No one waiting outside.

I walked in, got a headful of garlic and overripe cheese. Bad murals covered the sidewalls – walleyed grape pickers bringing in the Chianti crop under a bilious sun. Five round tables rested on a red linoleum floor, covered in the same checked gingham as the curtains. The rear wall was a takeout counter backed by a brick pizza oven that gave off yeasty fumes.

Two Hispanic men in stained white aprons worked the dinner crowd, which was three parties. The cooks had Aztec faces and took their work seriously.

The customers were a Japanese couple sharing a petite pepperoni pie, a young bespectacled couple trying to control a pair of wild-eyed, tomato-sauced preschoolers, and three black guys in their twenties wearing Fila sweats and enjoying salad and lasagna.

One of the countermen said, 'Help you?'

'I'm waiting for someone. Young guy, around twenty?'

He shrugged and flipped a limp white disk of dough, sprinkled it with flour, repeated the move.

I said, 'Has anyone like that been around?'

Sprinkle. Flip. 'No, amigo.'

I left and waited out in front. The restaurant was on a quiet block, sandwiched between a photocopy service and a one-story office building. Both dark for the weekend. The sky was black and, two blocks up, traffic on Pico was anemic. L.A.'s never really been a nightlife city, and this part of Westwood hibernated when the mall wasn't bustling.

The mall.

Eight years after he had brutalized Kristal Malley, Rand wanted to talk about the crime, two blocks from a mall.

I'm a good person.

If it was absolution he was after, I wasn't a priest.

Maybe the distinction between therapy and confession was petty. Maybe he knew the difference. Maybe he just wanted to talk. Like the judge who'd sent him away.

I wondered how Tom Laskin was doing. Wondered about all of them.

I stood there, careful to stay in the reflected glare of the boot sign, watching for the man Randolph Duchay had become.

He'd been a big kid, so he was probably a large man. Unless eight years of institutional food and

God knew what other indignities had stunted his growth.

I thought of the way he'd struggled to make out the word 'pizza'.

The word was two feet of tricolor neon.

Five minutes passed. Ten, fifteen.

I took a stroll up the block, watching my back for no reason except that a murderer might be looking for me.

What did he *want*?

Returning to Newark Pizza, I cracked the door, in case I'd missed him. I hadn't. This time the black guys checked me out and the cook I'd talked to got an unpleasant look on his face.

I went back outside, positioned myself ten feet up from the restaurant, waited five minutes more.

Nothing. I drove home.

My message machine was blank. I wondered if I should call Milo and ask him to check the specifics of Rand Duchay's release. Solicit a detective's guess as to what Rand had wanted and why he hadn't shown.

A quarter century of homicide work had implanted a doomsday chip in Milo's brain, and I had a pretty good idea of how he'd respond.

Once a scumbag, always a scumbag, Alex. Why mess with it?

I made myself a tuna sandwich and drank some decaf, set the house alarm, and settled on my office couch with two months' worth of psych journals. Somewhere out in the darkness a coyote ululated – a warbling, shrieking a cappella solo, part scavenger's protest, part predator's triumph.

The Glen's teeming with the creatures. They dine on the haute garbage that fills Westside trash cans, and some are as sleek and fearless as house pets.

I used to have a little French bulldog and worried about letting him out in the yard alone. Now he was living in Seattle and life was simpler.

I cleared my throat. The sound echoed; the house was full of echoes.

The howl-sonata repeated itself. Enlarged to a duet, then grew to a coyote chorus.

A pack of them, exulting in the kill.

Food-chain violence. That made sense and I found the noise comforting.

I read until two a.m., fell asleep on the couch, managed to drag myself to bed at three. By seven I was up, awake without being rested. The last thing I wanted to do was run. I dressed for it anyway, was heading for the door when Allison called from Greenwich.

'Good morning, handsome.'

'Morning, gorgeous.'

'I'm glad I caught you.' She sounded a little down. Lonely? Or maybe that was me.

'How's life with Grandma?'

'You know Gra –' She laughed. 'You don't know

her, do you? This morning, despite the fact that it's freezing, she insisted we take a walk around the grounds and look for "unique leaves." Ninety-one and she's forging through snow like a trapper. She studied botany at Smith, claims she would've gotten a Ph.D. if she hadn't "been swept into matrimony" at twenty.'

'Find anything?' I said.

'After clawing through a four-foot snowbank, I managed to produce one brown shriveled thing she found "interesting." My fingers were numb and that was with gloves on. Gram, of course, eschews hand-coverings except at lunches in the city.'

'Greatest generation. How large is the property?'

'Twelve acres, with lots of trees and rare plants she put in over the years.'

'Sounds nice.'

'It's getting a little run-down,' she said. 'And the house is way too big for her. Still clearing your consults?'

'They're clear.'

'Good for you.'

Before she left, I'd asked if she wanted me to join her for part of the trip. 'If it was up to me, Alex, you could stay the whole time, but Gram's possessive. It's a ritual with her – "special time" with each of the grandkids.'

At thirty-nine, Allison was the youngest grandkid.

'Am I keeping you from anything?'

'Not a thing,' I said, wondering if that were true.

'Consults work out okay?'

'As good as can be expected.'

'So what else is up, baby?'

I deliberated telling her about Duchay's call. 'Nothing exciting. What time does your flight arrive?'

'That's one of the reasons I'm calling. Gram asked me to extend my visit for another two weeks. It's hard to tell her no.'

'She's ninety-one,' I said.

'The rooms smell like camphor and *I* feel a hundred and twenty. I'm getting serious cabin fever, Alex. She turns in for bed at eight.'

'You could make snow angels.'

'I miss you,' she said.

'Miss you, too.'

'I was thinking maybe we can do something about it. Gram has a friend coming from St Louis tomorrow so she'll be occupied for three days. The hotels in New York are running a post-New Year's special. Big discounts and free upgrades.'

'When do you want me there?' I said.

'Really?' she said.

'Really.'

'That's great – you're sure?'

'Hey,' I said. 'I need special time, too.'

'Oh, boy,' she said. 'You don't know what you've just done for my spirits. Is there any way you could make it by tomorrow? I could take the train and be at the hotel by the time you arrived.'

'Which hotel?'

'When I traveled with my parents we always stayed at the St Regis. The location's perfect – Fifty-fifth off Fifth – and they've got butler service on every floor.'

'Nice touch, if the butler's not intrusive.'

'He won't be if we bunk in and never call him.'

'Which bunk do I get?' I said. 'Upper or lower?'

'I was thinking more in terms of share-zies.'

'I'll bring a flashlight and we'll play pup tent.'

'Alex, it's incredibly flexible of you to do this.'

'Not in the least,' I said. 'I'm acting out of pure self-interest.'

'That,' she said, 'is the best part.'

I booked a nine a.m. flight out of LAX, scrounged at the back of my closet for the gray tweed overcoat I never wore, found a similarly neglected pair of gloves and scarf, packed a carry-on, and went for a run.

Beverly Glen was seventy degrees and clear, let's hear it for winter. Weather's a trivial reason for living somewhere unless you're honest.

I set out hoping for endorphin-laced serenity. My brain had other ideas and I wondered about Rand. My body stayed tight and heavy as I huffed and kicked up dust and my brain pulled a split screen: looking out for passing cars on one side, as time flashed back on the other.

When I returned home, I called Milo's house. No answer. Then, I tried the Westside substation and asked for Lieutenant Sturgis. It took awhile for Milo to come on the line and I was still breathing hard.

'Didn't know you cared,' he said.

'Ha.'

'What's up?'

'I'm meeting Allison in New York. Tomorrow.'

He murdered a few bars of 'Leaving on a Jet Plane.' 'Where you staying?'

'St Regis.'

'Nice. The last time the department sent me to New Yawk was for that post-911 security seminar, and they vouchered me at a shitty dive in the thirties. While you're there, get me a Knicks shirt at the NBA store.'

'No prob.'

'I was kidding, Alex. The *Knicks*?'

'Optimism's good for the soul,' I said.

'So is logic. Am I correct in assuming that you called for some reason other than to boast about the superiority of your accommodations over mine?'

'You brought that up.'

'If you were really the sensitive guy you claim to be, you would've lied.'

I said, 'The St Regis has butler service.'

'I'm weeping into my case stack. Which, currently, is low. Per an interdepartmental memo, we are now experiencing an official drop in crime.'

'Congratulations.'

'Not my doing. Probably karmic crystals or chanting or the moon in scorpio-squatting or the Great Baal of Randomness . . . what's on your mind?'

I told him.

'That one,' he said. 'You didn't like working it.'

'It wasn't fun.'

'Duchay give any hint what he wanted?'

'He sounded troubled.'

'He *should* be troubled. Eight years at the C.Y.A. for murdering a baby?'

'Any professional guesses about why he didn't show?'

'Changed his mind, couldn't get it together, who knows? He's a lowlife, Alex. He was the stupid one, right?'

'Right.'

'So toss in a lousy attention span, or whatever label you guys are putting on it nowadays, in addition to his being a lowlife thrill-killer who's been thoroughly criminalized after being locked up with gangbangers for eight years. How old is he, now?'

'Twenty-one.'

'Lowlife at the height of his criminal hormone overload,' he said. 'I wouldn't take any bets on his experiencing any serious personality enhancement. I'd also not take his calls, from now on. He's probably more dangerous than he was eight years ago. Why get involved?'

'Looks like I'm not,' I said. 'Though I didn't pick up any threat or hostility over the phone. More like –'

'He's troubled, yeah, yeah. He calls you from Westwood, which isn't that far from your place. Semi-illiterate but he managed to find your number.'

'He'd have no reason to resent me.'

Silence.

'The plan was to meet him away from my place,' I said.

'That's a start.'

'I'm not minimizing what he did, Milo. He, himself, admitted hitting Kristal. But I always felt Troy Turner was the primary force behind the murder and Rand got caught up in the situation.'

'Put him in another situation and he'll get caught up again.'

'I suppose.'

'Hey,' he said. 'You called *me,* not another shrink. Meaning you were looking for hard truth, not empathy and understanding.'

'I don't know what I was looking for.'

'You craved sage detective advice and Uncle Milo's instinctual protective stance. Now that the former has been dispensed, I'll do my best to provide the latter while you're gallivanting up Fifth Avenue with a lovely lady on your arm.'

'That's okay —'

'Here's the plan,' he said. 'Though it falls well outside of my job description, I will drive by your house at least once a day, twice if I can swing it, pick up your paper and your mail, be on the lookout for shady characters lurking around the premises.'

'Gallivanting,' I said.

'You do know how to gallivant? Put one foot in front of the other . . . and just blow.'

*

At one p.m. he called back. 'When were you planning to leave for New York?'

'Tomorrow morning. Why?'

'A body showed up last night in Bel Air, dumped in some bushes near the 405 North on-ramp. White male, young, six-two, two hundred, shot in the head, no wallet or I.D. But wadded down in the little front pocket of his jeans was a piece of paper. Greasy and frayed, like it had been pawed a lot. The writing, however, was still legible and guess what it was: your phone number.'

12

I met Milo in his office on the second floor of the Westside sub-station. It's a windowless cell, formerly a utility closet, set away from the collaborative buzz of the big detective's room. There's barely room for a two-drawer desk, a file cabinet, a pair of folding chairs, and a senile computer. The station's a no-smoking zone but sometimes Milo puffs panatelas, and the walls have yellowed and the air smells like a dozen old men.

He's six-three, and when he pays attention to his diet, two-sixty. Hunched at the undersized desk, he's a cartoon.

It's a setup unbefitting a lieutenant, but he's not the typical lieutenant, and he claims it's fine with him. Maybe he means it, maybe having a second office helps – an Indian restaurant a few blocks away where the owners treat him like royalty.

The leap from Detective III to brass had resulted from leverage he'd never sought: ugly secrets unearthed about the former police chief.

The deal was that he'd get a lieutenant's salary, avoid the executive obligations that normally went with the job, and be allowed to work cases. As long as he functioned solo and stayed out of everyone's hair.

That chief was gone and the new one seemed intent on shaking things up. But so far Milo's situation had escaped scrutiny. If the current regime was as results-oriented as it claimed, maybe his solve rate would afford him some grace.

Or maybe not. A gay cop was no longer the official impossibility it had been when he'd joined the force, but he'd broken ground during colder times and would never fit in.

His door was open and he was reading a preliminary investigation report. His black hair needed a trim, cowlicks reigning, the white sideburns he called his skunk stripes bushing and trailing a half inch below his earlobes.

A spruce-green sport coat hung from the back of his chair and puddled onto the floor. His short-sleeved white shirt looked defeated, his skinny yellow tie could've passed for a mustard stain. Gray cords and tan desert boots topped off the ensemble. The unshielded ceiling bulb was vaguely pink and graced his acne-pitted cheeks with a phony sunburn.

He hooked a thumb at the spare chair and I unfolded it and sat. He handed me the prelim and some crime scene photos.

The report was the usual detached affair, recorded on the scene by Detective I S. J. Binchy. Sean was a former bass player in a ska band turned born-again Christian, a compliant kid who Milo sometimes enlisted for grunt work.

Nice kid, decent speller. The only new thing I learned was that a freeway cleanup crew had found the body at four-fourteen a.m.

The first photo was a frontal of the corpse, lying on its back, face up, as the coroner's photographer *click-clicked* from above.

Night-bleached face, hard to make out details. A close-up shot showed the gaping mouth and half-closed eyes I'd seen so many times before. Hollowness behind the irises. The right cheek was slightly convex, but it wasn't the distortion you'd see with a small-caliber bullet dancing around in the head.

A pair of lateral views revealed a dark, star-shaped entry wound, surrounded by a black halo of powder, just in front of the left ear, and a ragged exit, much larger and slightly higher on the right temple, that showcased bone and red-meat muscle and the oatmeal of brain matter.

I said, 'Through-and-through shot.'

'Coroner thinks contact shot, or just short of contact, full metal jacket, no larger than a thirty-eight, no supplementary load.'

His voice was remote. Keeping his distance from this victim.

The next photo was a close-up. 'What about these cheek abrasions?'

'He was found lying on his face, maybe he got dragged a bit during the dump. No defense wounds or tissue under his nails or any other signs of struggle. No major blood at the scene, so he was shot somewhere else.'

'He's big,' I said. 'So if there was no struggle, he was probably taken by surprise.'

'I'd ask if you recognize him, but we just got word from AFIS. The prints confirm it's Duchay.'

I reviewed the pictures, tried to look past damage and death. Rand Duchay's boyhood facial structure had been transformed by puberty into something longer and harder. His hair was darker than I remembered but that could've been the lighting. In life, he'd been a slow kid, with slack features. Death hadn't changed that, but death has a way of blunting everyone around the edges. Would I have recognized him if we'd passed on the street?

I said, 'Any fix on when it happened?'

'You know how T.O.D. is, mostly guesswork. Best guess is sometime between nine p.m. and one a.m.'

Nine was well after I'd gotten home from Duchay's no-show. Maybe he had changed his mind about the meeting. Or had his mind changed.

I said, 'Did you just happen to find out, or did you go looking for him?'

Milo stretched his long legs as far as the room allowed. 'After you called I decided to do a little research on Duchay, found out he'd been released three days ago. Four years early, good behavior.' Flaring nostrils said what he thought about that.

'I learned who he'd been released to, which took some doing. Called, got no answer, decided a thrill-killer ambling around the Westside didn't appeal to my sense of order. I left Sean a message to check prowler reports and attempted burglaries for the last three days. Then I took a drive up Westwood and hit some side streets.'

He worked his tongue inside his cheek. 'I was thinking I'd finish up at your place, you'd fix me a sandwich, I'd wish you bon voyage. Then Sean calls back, he's at the coroner, a case came in last night that looked like a whodunit and the crime scene guys missed something but the crypt attendant found it when she undressed the body. Little scrap of paper in the victim's pocket. Sean was pretty sure he recognized your number, but wanted to confirm.'

'Sean's got a good memory,' I said.

'Sean's coming along.'

'You're working the case with him?'

'He's working it with me.'

As we left, Sean Binchy stepped out of the detectives' room and hailed us. He's red-headed and freckled, in his late twenties, as tall as Milo, many pounds lighter. Sean favors four-button suits, bright blue shirts, somber ties, and Doc Martens. Old tattoos are hidden by long sleeves. Short, neat hair replaces the dreads of his music days.

'Hi, Dr Delaware,' he said cheerfully. 'Looks like you're involved in this one.'

Milo said, 'Sean, Dr Delaware's scheduled to fly

to New York tomorrow morning. I don't see any reason that should change.'

'Sure, no prob – uh, Loot, I finally got through to the folks Duchay was staying with and they had no idea he'd gone into the city to meet with Dr Delaware. He told them he was going looking for a job.'

'Where?'

'Construction site,' said Binchy. 'There's an apartment development going up not far from where they live and Duchay went to speak with the supervisor.'

'On Saturday?'

'Guess the site's open.'

'Verify that, Sean.'

'You bet.'

'What time did he leave for this alleged meeting?' said Milo.

'Five p.m.'

'Guy takes a short walk at five, doesn't come home all night, and they're not concerned?'

'They were concerned,' said Binchy. 'At seven p.m., they called Van Nuys Division to report him missing, but since he was an adult and not enough time had passed, it wasn't filed as an official M.P.'

'A convicted murderer wandering around didn't bother anyone?'

'I don't know if they mentioned that to Van Nuys.'

'Find out if they did, Sean.'

'Yes, sir.'

I said, 'Who was he living with?'

'Some people who take in troubled kids,' said Binchy.

'Duchay was an adult,' said Milo.

'Then it's troubled people, Loot. They're ministers, or something.'

'The Daneys?' I said.

'You know them?'

'They were involved with Rand's case years ago.'

'Back when he killed that little girl,' said Binchy. No rancor in his voice. Every time I'd seen him, his demeanor had been exactly the same: pleasant, unruffled, uncluttered with self-doubt. Maybe still waters did run deep. Or God on your side was the ultimate soul balm.

'Involved how?' said Milo.

'Spiritual advisers,' I said. 'They were seminary students.'

Binchy said, 'Everyone could use some of that.'

'Didn't seem to help Duchay,' said Milo.

'Not in this world.' Binchy smiled briefly.

I said, 'Both of them were murdered.'

'Both of who, Doc?'

'Rand and Troy Turner.'

'Didn't know about Turner,' said Milo. 'When did that happen?'

'A month after he was in custody.'

'So we're talking eight years in between. What happened to him?'

I described Troy's ambush of a Vato Loco, the gang-vengeance theory, the way he'd been hung in the utility closet. 'Don't know if it was ever solved.'

'A month in and he's thinking he's a tough guy,' he said. 'No impulse control ... yeah, sounds like your basic prison hit. Were he and Duchay in the same facility?'

'No.'

'Lucky for Duchay. If he'd been seen as Turner's buddy, he would've been next.'

'Duchay didn't get away clean in prison. Coroner said there were old knife scars on his body.'

Milo said, 'But he was alive until last night. Big and tough enough to defend himself.'

'Or he learned to avoid trouble,' I said. 'He got early release for good behavior.'

'That means he didn't rape or shank anyone in front of a guard.'

Silence.

Binchy said, 'I'll follow up on what exactly Van Nuys was told, Loot. Enjoy your trip to New York, Doctor.'

After he left, Milo jammed some papers into his attaché case and the two of us descended the stairs to the back of the station. We walked a couple of blocks to where I'd parked the Seville.

He said, 'Guys like Turner and Duchay *attract* bad stuff.'

'It's ironic, isn't it?' I said.

'What?'

'Rand makes it through eight years of the C.Y.A., gets out, and three days later he's dead.'

'Your feeling this, huh?'

'You aren't?'

'I pick and choose when I bleed.'

I opened the car door.

He said, 'What's really getting to you, Alex?'

'He was a stupid, impressionable kid who lost his parents in infancy, probably suffered brain damage as a baby, got raised by a grandmother who resented him, was ignored by the school system.'

'He also killed a two-year-old. At that point, my sympathies shift.'

'I can understand that,' I said.

He placed a hand on my shoulder. 'Don't let it eat at you. Go have fun in La Manzana Grande.'

'Maybe I shouldn't go.'

'Why the hell not?'

'What if I'm relevant to the case?'

'You're not. Good-bye.'

I drove home thinking about Rand Duchay's last moments. Perhaps a temple shot meant he'd been looking straight ahead, hadn't seen it coming. Maybe he'd experienced no final fireburst of terror and pain.

I pictured him lying facedown in some cold, dark place, beyond knowing or caring. Eight-year-old TV images flew into my head. Barnett and Lara Malley exiting the courtroom. She, sobbing. He, tight-lipped, smoldering. So rigid with anger he'd come close to striking a cameraman.

Demanding the death penalty.

Now both murderers of his daughter were gone. Would he find comfort in that?

Had he played a role in it?

No, that was trite and illogical. Revenge was a dish best eaten cold, but eight years between deaths was arctic. Milo was right. Damaged boys like Turner and Duchay *did* attract violence. In a sense, what had happened was the predictable termination of two wasted lives.

Three.

I checked my overnight bag, packed the toothbrush I'd forgotten, and put the house in relative order. Logging onto a weather site, I learned I'd be arriving tomorrow in the midst of a snowstorm.

Low: fifteen, high: twenty-nine. I pictured white skies and sidewalks, the flicker of Manhattan lights in our window as Allison and I holed up in a nice warm suite with butler service.

Why had Rand called me?

The phone rang. Allison said, 'Thank God, I caught you. Alex, you won't believe this.'

Strain in her voice. My first thought was something had happened to her grandmother.

'What's up?'

'Gram's friend, the one who was coming from St Louis, suffered a stroke this morning. We just got the call. Gram's taking it hard. Alex, I'm so sorry, but I can't leave her.'

'Of course not.'

'She'll be fine, I know she will, she always is – is your ticket refundable? I've already called the hotel and canceled. I'm really sorry.'

'Don't worry about it,' I said, sounding calm. No act, I was *relieved* that I wouldn't be going. What did that say about me?

'... despite the situation, I'm going to try to get out of the two-week extension, Alex. One week, tops, then I'll call my cousin Wesley and ask him to do a shift. He's a chem prof at Barnard on sabbatical in Boston, so his hours are flexible. It's only fair, right?'

'Right.'

She paused for a breath. 'You're not too upset?'

'I'd love to see you but things happen.'

'They do ... it's freezing, anyway.'

'Fifteen to twenty-nine in New York.'

'You looked it up,' she said. 'You were all prepared to go. Boo hoo.'

'Boo hoo hoo,' I said.

'The suite had a fireplace. Dammit.'

'When you come back we'll light mine.'

'In seventy-degree weather?'

'I'll buy some ice and sprinkle it around.'

She laughed. 'That's some picture ... I'll get back as soon as I can. One week, tops ... uh oh, there's Gram calling me again, what now? She wants more tea ... sorry, Alex, talk to you tomorrow.'

'Sounds good.'

'Are you all right?'

'Sure. Why?'

'You sound a little distracted.'

'Just disappointed,' I lied. 'Everything will work out.'

'Nothing like optimism,' she said. 'With all you see, how do you manage that?'

Allison had been widowed in her twenties. Her basic disposition was a good deal sunnier than mine. But I was a better faker.

'It's a good way to live,' I said.

'Oh, yeah.'

13

Monday night, I reached Milo at his house. It was just after ten and his voice was thick with scotch and fatigue.

'It's one a.m. in New York, dude.'

'I'm still on Pacific Standard.'

'What happened?'

'Allison's grandmother needed her.' I filled him in.

'Sorry about that. What's on your mind?'

'Just checking in,' I said.

'On Duchay? Turns out weekends at the construction site are for cleanup, but the supervisor said he'd never met Duchay. So either the story was bogus or Duchay was confused. Other than that, zippo to report. My working theory was that Duchay hooked up with some C.Y.A. bad guy buddy in order to do something bad. They got into conflict and the buddy did him.'

'What makes you think he was planning anything?'

'Because eight years in lockup is a Ph.D. in bad. The reason I figured a buddy was because Duchay's pattern was criminal collaboration.'

'One crime's a pattern?'

'When it's a crime like his. And you need to

consider this, Alex: The plan may have involved you. As in target.'

'Some theory,' I said.

'Step back and try to be objective,' he said. 'A convicted thrill murderer phones you out of the blue, says he wants to talk about his crime but won't give details. If it was really some confession-absolution deal, why wait eight years? He could've written you a letter. And why you? He had spiritual advisers – do-gooders who'd love to grant him absolution. The whole thing smells, Alex. He lured you out.'

'Why would he want to hurt me?'

'Because you were part of the system that sent him away for eight years. And his knife wounds say it wasn't a vacation. Nine sticks, Alex, and three had gone deep. There were scars on his liver and one of his kidneys.'

Margaret Sieff – the woman Rand had called 'Gram' – had been clear about my allegiance.

Randolph's laywer said you weren't necessarily on our side.

Maybe she'd transmitted that to Rand. Or Lauritz Montez had. He'd seen me as a prosecution tool, had gone along with Sydney Weider's petition to keep me away from the boys.

Milo said, 'Does your silence indicate I'm making sense?'

'Anything's possible,' I said. 'But he didn't sound hostile over the phone.'

'I know, just troubled.'

'Back when I evaluated him there was no hostility,

Milo. He was meek, cooperative. Unlike Troy, he never tried to manipulate me.'

'He had eight years to stew, Alex. And don't forget: He cooperated and *still* got sent to hell. You know what C.Y.A.'s like. No more status offenders and mischief makers. This year there were six murders in the system.'

'Liver scars,' I said.

'Even with that, most people would think Duchay got off easy for what he did. But try telling that to the guy who went through it. I'm thinking one very bitter twenty-one-year-old ex-con. Maybe he had plans to pay lots of people back and you were first on the list.'

'Why do you have doubts about him hooking up with a prison buddy?'

'What do you mean?'

'You said it *was* your working theory.'

'Lord, I'm being *parsed*,' he said. 'No, I haven't abandoned the basic premise. I just haven't come up with any buddies Duchay met in lockup yet. C.Y.A. guy I spoke to said he had no gang affiliations, was "socially isolated."'

'Any disciplinary problems on his record?'

'Quiet, compliant.'

'Good behavior,' I said.

'Yada yada.'

'So what's next?'

'Talk to people who knew him, try to get a fix on his movements that day. I had Sean hit every store on Westwood for three blocks north of Pico to see if anyone spotted Duchay lurking around. Nada. Same for the Westside Pavilion, so if he went in there, he didn't make an impression. Tomorrow morning I visit Reverend and Mrs Andrew Daney.'

'Reverend and Reverend,' I said. 'They were both studying to be ministers.'

'Whatever. I talked to her – Cherish, there's a name for you. She sounded pretty broken up. All those good intentions blown to bits.'

'Why'd you take the case on, big guy?'

'Why not?'

'You don't care much for the victim.'

'Who I like or don't like has nothing to do with it,' he said. 'And I am deeply hurt by your intimations to the contrary.'

'Yada freaking yada,' I said. 'Seriously, you can pick and choose. Why this one?'

'I *picked* it to make sure you're not in continuing danger.'

'I appreciate that but –'

'A simple thanks will suffice.'

'Thanks.'

'You're welcome. Try to enjoy the sunshine until Dr Gwynn returns.'

'What time are you seeing the Daneys tomorrow?'

'Not your problem,' he said. 'Sleep in.'

'Should I drive?'

'Alex, these people were advocates for the boys. That could make you not their favorite person.'

'My report wasn't a factor in the decision to certify

them as juveniles. Which, I should point out, is exactly what their lawyers were asking for. There's no logical reason for me to be targeted.'

'Strangling and beating a two-year-old wasn't logical.'

'What time?' I said.

'The appointment's for eleven.'

'I'll drive.'

I picked him up at the station at ten-thirty and took the Sepulveda Pass out to the Valley. He said nothing as we crossed Sunset and passed the spot where Rand Duchay's body had been found.

I said, 'Wonder how he got from the Valley into the city.'

'Sean's checking the buses. Probably a waste of time. Like so much of what we do.'

The Galton Street address where Drew and Cherish Daney advised spiritually was in a blue-collar Van Nuys neighborhood, a few blocks from the 405. The sky was the color of newspaper pulp. Freeway noise was a constant rebuke.

The property was fenced with redwood tongue-and-groove but the gate was open and we entered. A boxy, pale-blue bungalow sat at the front of the eighth-acre lot. At the rear were two smaller out-buildings, one a converted garage painted a matching blue, the other, set slightly back, an unpainted cement block cube. The free space was mostly pavement, broken by a few beds of draft-friendly plants edged with lava rock.

Cherish Daney sat in a lawn chair to the left of the main house, reading in full sun. When she saw us she shut the book and stood. I got close enough to read the title: *Life's Lessons: Coping with Grief*. A piece of tissue paper extended from between the pages.

Her hair was still white-blond and long, but the teased-up bulk and side-wings of eight years ago had been traded for bangs and simplicity. She had on a white, sleeveless top over blue slacks and gray shoes, the same silver chain and crucifix she'd worn that day at the jail. Most people put on weight as they get older but she had reduced to a hard, dry leanness. Still a young woman – mid-thirties was my guess – but fat's a good wrinkle filler and her face had collected some tributaries.

The same sun-bronzed complexion, the same pretty features. Noticeable curve to her back, as if her spine had bowed under some terrible weight.

She smiled without opening her mouth. Red-rimmed eyes. If she recognized me, she didn't say so. When Milo gave her his card, she glanced at it and nodded.

'Thanks for seeing us, Reverend.'

'Sure,' she said. A screen door slammed and the three of us turned toward the sound.

A girl, fifteen or sixteen, had come out of the main house and stood on the front steps holding what looked to be a school workbook.

Cherish Daney said, 'What do you need, Valerie?'

The girl's return stare seemed resentful.

'Val?'

'Help with my math.'

'Of course, bring it over.'

The girl hesitated before walking over. Her wavy black hair trailed past her waist. Plump build. Her face was dusky, round, her gait stiff and self-conscious.

When she got to Cherish Daney, she alternated between looking at us and pretending not to.

'These men are police officers, Val. They're here about Rand.'

"Oh.'

'We're all very sad about Rand, aren't we, Val?'

'Uh-huh.'

Cherish said, 'Okay, show me what the problem is.'

Valerie opened the book. Sixth-grade arithmetic. 'These ones. I'm doing them right but I'm not getting the right answers.'

Cherish touched the girl's arm. 'Let's take a look.'

'I know I'm doing them right.' Valerie's fingers flexed. She rocked on her feet. Glanced at Milo and me.

'Val?' said Cherish. 'Let's focus.' Touching Valerie's cheek, she guided the girl's eyes toward the book.

Val shook off the contact but stared at the page. We stood there as Cherish attempted to unravel the mysteries of fractions, speaking slowly, enunciating clearly, skirting the line between patience and patronizing.

Not losing her patience during Valerie's lapses of concentration. Which were frequent.

The girl tapped her feet, drummed her hands on various body parts, wriggled, craned her neck, sighed a lot. Her eye contact was hummingbird-flighty and she kept glancing over at us, shooting her gaze to the sky, then down on the ground. The book. The house. A squirrel that scampered up the redwood fence.

I'd gone to school for too long to resist diagnosis.

Cherish Daney stayed on track, finally got the girl to focus on a single problem until she achieved success.

'There you go! Great, Val! Let's do another one.'

'No, I'm okay, I get it now.'

'I think one more's a good idea.'

Emphatic head shake.

'You're sure, Val?'

Without answering, Valerie ran back toward the house. Dropped the workbook and cried out in frustration, bent and retrieved it, flung the screen door open and disappeared.

'Sorry for the interruption,' said Cherish. 'She's a terrific kid but she needs a lot of structure.'

'A.D.D.?' I said.

'It's that obvious, huh?' Now she stared at me with wide blue eyes. '*I* know who you are. The psychologist who saw Rand.'

'Alex Delaware.' I held out my hand.

She took it readily. 'We met at the jail.'

'Yes, we did, Reverend.'

'I guess,' she said, 'our paths cross at sad junctures.'

'Occupational hazard,' I said. 'Both our occupations.'

'I suppose ... actually, I'm not a minister, just a teacher.'

I smiled. '*Just* a teacher?'

'It comes in handy,' she said. 'For homeschooling. We homeschool the kids.'

Milo said, 'Foster kids?'

'That's right.'

'How long do they stay with you?' I said.

'No set time. Val was supposed to be with us for sixty days while her mother was evaluated for detox. Then her mother O.D.'d and died and all of Val's relatives live in Arizona. She barely knows them – her mom ran away from home. Top of that, they weren't interested in taking her. So she's been with us nearly a year.'

'How many fosters do you care for?'

'It varies. My husband's shopping over at Value Club. We buy in bulk.'

'What was the arrangement with Rand Duchay?' said Milo.

'The arrangement?'

'With the state.'

Cherish Daney shook her head. 'That wasn't a formal situation, Lieutenant. We knew Rand was being released and had nowhere to go so we took him in.'

'The county had no problem with his being here?' said Milo. 'With kids?'

'It never came up.' She stiffened. 'You're not going to cause problems for us, are you? It wouldn't be fair to the kids.'

'No, ma'am. It was just a question that came to mind.'

'There was never any danger,' she said. 'Rand was a good person.'

Same claim he'd made. Neither Milo nor I answered.

Cherish Daney said, 'I don't expect you to believe this, but eight years transformed him.'

'To?'

'A good person, Lieutenant. He wasn't going to be with us long term, anyway. Just until he found a job and a place to stay. My husband had made inquiries with some nonprofits, figuring maybe Rand could work at a thrift shop, or do some landscaping work. Then Rand took the initiative and came up with the idea of construction. That's where he went Saturday.'

'Any idea how he ended up in Bel Air?'

She shook her head. 'He'd have no reason to be there. The only thing I can think of is he got lost and someone picked him up. Rand could be very trusting.'

'He never phoned you?'

'He didn't have a phone,' she said.

He'd called me from a pay booth.

Milo said, 'How close is the construction site?'

'Up a few blocks on Vanowen.'

'Not very far, in terms of getting lost.'

'Lieutenant, Rand spent his entire adolescence in prison. When he got out he was extremely disoriented. His world was a buzz of confusion.'

'William James,' I said.

'Pardon?'

'Pioneer of psychology. He called childhood a blooming, buzzing confusion.'

'I probably learned that,' said Cherish. 'I took psychology in seminary.'

Milo said, 'So you kept in regular contact with Rand while he was in custody.'

'We did,' she said. 'Right after Troy died, we initiated contact.'

'Why then?'

'Initially, we were more involved with Troy because we knew him before the trouble.'

'The trouble being Kristal Malley's murder,' said Milo.

Cherish Daney looked away. Her stoop became more pronounced.

'How'd you know Troy before, Mrs Daney?'

'When my husband and I were students, part of our community service seminar involved identifying needs in the community. Our apartment wasn't that far from 415 City, so we knew its reputation. Our faculty adviser thought it would be a good place to find kids with needs. We talked to Social Services and they identified several prospects. Troy was one of them.'

'Rand wasn't?' I said.

'Rand never got his name on any lists.'

'Troublemaker lists?' said Milo.

She nodded. 'We met with Troy a couple of times, tried to get him involved with church or sports or a hobby, but we never really connected. Then, after . . . he must've mentioned us to his lawyer because she contacted us and said it would be a great time to start counseling him spiritually.'

Bible in a cell. Smooth talk about sin.

'Why didn't you connect initially?' said Milo.

'You know how it is. Kids don't always take to talking.'

She looked to me for confirmation. Before I could offer any, Milo said, 'Being arrested help Troy's communication skills?'

She sighed. 'You think we're naive. It's not that we were unaware of the enormity of what Troy had done. But we recognized that he'd also been victimized. You met his mother, Doctor.'

'Where is she?' I said.

'Dead,' she said. Snapping off the word. 'After Troy's body was ready for burial, the Chino coroner's office contacted us. They couldn't find Jane and we were the only other people on his visitor list. We contacted Ms Weider but she no longer worked for the Public Defender. Troy's body sat at the morgue until our dean agreed to donate a plot in San Bernadino where some of the faculty members are buried. We conducted a service.'

She touched her crucifix. Suddenly, tears streamed down her face. She made no effort to dry them. 'That day. My husband and myself and Dr Wascomb – our dean. A beautiful, sunny day and we watched cemetery workers lower that pathetic little coffin into the ground. A month later, Detective Kramer called us. Jane had been found under a freeway ramp, one of those homeless encampments, wrapped up in a sleeping bag and plastic tarp. Which is the way she always slept, so the other homeless people didn't think anything of it until she still hadn't budged by noon. She'd been stabbed sometime during the night. Whoever killed her wrapped her back up.'

She shuddered, pulled out the tissue paper bookmark and wiped her face.

Milo said, 'How long was that after Troy's death?'

'Six weeks, two months, what's the difference? My point is, these were lost boys. And now, Rand.'

'Any idea who'd want to hurt Rand?'

She shook her head.

'What was his mood like?'

'Disoriented, as I told you. Reeling from freedom.'

'Not happy at all about getting out?'

'To be honest? Not really.'

'Did he have any plans other than getting a job?'

'We were taking things slowly. Helping him settle in.'

'Could we see his room?'

'Sure,' she said. 'Such as it is.'

We followed her through a compact, tidy living room; a dim galley kitchen and eating area; then a low, narrow corridor. One bedroom, the master, with barely enough room for the furniture that filled it. A single bathroom served the entire house.

At the end of the hall was a windowless space, eight-foot square. Cherish Daney said, 'This is it.'

Cheap paneling covered the walls. Capped off pipes sprouted from the vinyl floor.

Milo said, 'This used to be a laundry room?'

'Service porch. We moved the washer and dryer outside.'

A framed Bible scene – Nordic Solomon and two Valkyrian women claiming motherhood of the same fat, blond infant – hung over a foldable cot. A white plastic lamp sat on a raw wood nightstand. Milo opened the drawers. Well-thumbed Bible on top, nothing in the bottom.

A dented footlocker served as a closet. Inside were two white T-shirts, two blue work shirts, a pair of blue jeans.

Cherish Daney said, 'We never even got a chance to buy him clothes.'

We walked back to the front of the house. She peered through a window. 'Here's my husband. I'd better go help him.'

14

Drew Daney came through the gateway gripping two large bags of groceries in each arm. An even larger mesh sack filled with oranges dangled from his right thumb.

Cherish took the fruit and reached for one of the bags.

Daney held on. 'I'm okay, Cher.' Dark eyes sighted us over the groceries. He stopped and placed the load on the ground.

'Dr Delaware.'

'You remember.'

'It's an unusual name,' he said, coming forward. His wrestler's frame had taken on fifteen or so pounds, most of them soft, and his thick, wavy hair was graying at the temples. He wore a beard now, a stubbly silver thing, neatly trimmed around the edges. His white polo shirt was spotless and pressed. So were his blue jeans. Same color scheme as his wife.

'Also,' he said, 'I read your report to the judge, so your name stuck in my mind.'

Cherish looked at him and went inside the house.

'How'd you come to read it?' I said.

'Sydney Weider wanted my opinion, as Troy's

124

counselor. I told her I thought it was a careful document. You didn't want to go out on a limb and say something unscientific. But you clearly weren't willing to give the boys a pass.'

'A pass on murder?' said Milo.

'At the time we were hoping for a miracle.'

'We?'

'The boys' families, Sydney, my wife, myself. It just seemed that putting the boys away forever wouldn't solve anything.'

'Forever turned out to be eight years, Reverend,' said Milo.

'Detective . . . what's your name, please –'

'Sturgis.'

'Detective Sturgis, in the life of a child, eight years is eternity.' Daney ran a hand through his hair. 'In Troy's case, a month was eternity. And now Rand . . . unbelievable.'

'Any idea who might've wanted to hurt Rand, sir?'

Daney's lips puffed. His toe scuffed one of the grocery bags and he lowered his voice. 'I don't want my wife hearing this, but there probably is something you should know.'

'Probably?'

Daney eyed the front door of his house. 'Could we find a place to talk later?'

'Sooner's better than later, sir.'

'Okay, sure, I see your point. I've got a youth council meeting in Sylmar at two. I could leave a little early and meet you in, say, ten minutes?'

'Sounds good,' said Milo. 'Where?'

'How about at the Dipsy Donut on Vanowen, a few blocks west.'

'We'll be there, Reverend.'

'Both of you?' he said.

'Dr Delaware's consulting on the case.'

'Ah,' said Daney. 'Makes sense.'

'Told you,' said Milo, as we drove away. 'You're still the opposing team.'

'And you?'

'I'm the sleuth assigned the honor of clearing Duchay's murder.'

'Want me to wait in the car while you two bond?'

'Right. Wonder what the rev wants to keep from his wife.'

'Sounds like something that would scare her.'

'Scary,' he said, 'is always interesting.'

The doughnut stand was a flimsy white booth on a cracked blacktop lot, topped by a six-foot, partially eaten doughnut with humanoid features. Brown plaster, chipped in several spots, tried to resemble chocolate. Wild-eyed merriment said the deep-fried creature loved being devoured. Three grubby-looking aluminum table-and-bench sets were scattered on the asphalt. The signage had lost a couple of letters.

DI SY DON T

Milo said, 'And here I was thinking she did.'

The place was full of customers. We went inside and breathed fat and sugar and waited in line as three harried kids bagged and served oversized fritters to a salivating throng. Milo bought a dozen assorted, finished a jelly and a chocolate in the time it took to get back to the car.

'Hey,' he said, 'it's part of the job description. And chewing's aerobic.'

'Enjoy.'

'You say that but you've got this disapproving thing going on.'

I took a hubcap-sized apple Danish out of the box and got to work on it. 'Satisfied?'

'Creative people are never satisfied.'

We sat in the Seville where he polished off a jelly-filled.

I said, 'Wonder what Rand did between six-thirty and nine.'

'Me, too. Forgot coffee, want some?'

'No, thanks.'

He returned to the doughnut shack just as the Reverend Drew Daney drove up in an older white Jeep. I got out of the car and Milo came back with two coffees.

He offered Daney the doughnut box.

Daney had added a blue blazer to his ensemble, had his hands in his pockets. 'Any crèmes?'

The three of us sat at one of the outdoor tables.

Daney found a raspberry crème, bit into it, exhaled with satisfaction. 'Guilty pleasures, huh?'

'You got it, Reverend.'

'I'm not ordained so you can just call me Drew.'

'Didn't finish seminary?'

'Chose not to,' said Daney. 'Same for Cherish. We both got involved in youth work and decided that was our calling. I don't regret it. A pulpit is usually more about internal politics than good works.'

'Youth work,' said Milo, 'as in foster care.'

'Foster care, homeschooling, coaching, counseling. I work with several non-profits – the meeting in Sylmar.' He looked at his watch. 'Better cut to the chase. This is probably nothing but I feel it's my duty to tell you.'

He finished his doughnut, wiped crumbs from his lap. 'Six months ago, Rand was transferred to Camarillo, awaiting discharge. Thursday night my wife and I drove up and brought him home. He looked as if he'd landed on another planet.'

'Disoriented,' I said, using his wife's term.

'More than that. Stunned. Think about it, Doctor. Eight years of extreme structure – his entire adolescence spent behind bars – and now he's released to a strange new world. We fed him dinner, showed him his room, and he went straight to bed. All we had was a converted service porch, but I tell you, that boy looked grateful to be in a small space again. The next morning, I was up at six-thirty as usual, went to check on him. His bed was empty, made up neat as a pin. I found him outside, sitting on the front steps. He looked worse than the previous night. Dark circles under his eyes. Really jumpy. I asked him what was wrong and he just stared at our front gate, which was wide open. I told him everything would be okay, he needed to give himself time. That only made him more agitated – he started shaking his head, really fast. Then he covered his face with his hands.'

Daney demonstrated. 'It was as if he was hiding from something. Playing ostrich. I pried his fingers loose and asked him what was wrong. He didn't answer and I told him it was important for him to let his feelings out. Finally, he told me someone was watching him. That caught me off-guard but I tried not to show it. I asked him who. He said he didn't know but he'd heard sounds at night – someone moving around outside his window. The property's small and neither my wife nor I had heard anything. I asked him what time. He said during the night, he didn't have a watch. Then he said he heard it again early morning – right after sunrise – got up and found the gate open and saw a truck driving away fast. We always close the gate, but it's just a pull-latch and sometimes if it's not shut tight, the wind blows it open. So I didn't consider that any big deal.'

'What kind of truck?' said Milo.

'He said a dark pickup. I didn't push him because I didn't want to make a big deal out of it. It just didn't seem that important.'

Milo said, 'You doubted his credibility.'

'It's not a matter of credibility,' said Daney. 'Dr Delaware, you tested Rand. Have you told the detective how severely learning disabled he was?'

I nodded.

'Now, combine that with the challenge of reentry.'

I said, 'Had you known him to fantasize about things that didn't exist?'

'Like a hallucination?' said Daney. 'No. That's not what happened Friday. It was more ... exaggerating normal events. I figured he'd heard a bird or a squirrel.'

'Now you're not sure,' said Milo.

'In view of what happened,' said Daney, 'I'd be foolish not to wonder.'

'Anything happen between Friday and Saturday night?'

'He didn't say anything more about being watched or the dark truck and I didn't bring it up,' said Daney. 'He took a walk and came back and said he'd been by a construction site and was going to go back in the afternoon to talk to the boss.'

'What time was the first walk?' said Milo.

'We eat early ... maybe eight, eight-thirty a.m.'

'What kind of job was he looking for?'

'Anything, I guess. He had no real skills.'

'C.Y.A. rehabilitation,' I said.

Daney's husky shoulders bunched. 'Don't get me started.'

Milo said, 'Sir, your wife says Rand left at five p.m.

to meet the supervisor. But the site closes down by noon.'

'I guess Rand was misinformed, Detective. Or someone misled him.'

'Why would they do that?'

'People like Rand tend to be misled.' He consulted his watch again and stood. 'Sorry, I need to get going.'

'One more question,' said Milo. 'I'm going to be contacting Rand's family. Any idea where to start?'

'Don't bother to start,' said Daney. 'There's no one. His grandmother died several years ago. Complications of heart disease. I was the one who informed Rand.'

'How'd he react?'

'Just what you'd imagine. He was extremely upset.' He glanced at his Jeep. 'I don't know if any of this was useful, but I thought I should tell you.'

Milo said, 'I appreciate it, sir. You didn't want your wife to know because . . .'

'No sense upsetting her. Even if it was relevant, it would have nothing to do with her.'

'Is there anything else that might help me, sir?' said Milo.

Daney jammed his hand in his pocket. Looked at the Jeep again. Ran a hand across the steel needles of his beard. 'This is . . . ticklish. I really don't know if I should be bringing it up.'

'Bring what up, sir?'

'Rand was found far from home, so I was

thinking, maybe that truck … what if someone *did* take him for a ride?' He tried to tug at an eighth-inch beard hair, finally managed to pincer one between his fingernails, pulled, stretched his cheek.

'A dark pickup,' said Milo. 'That ring any bells?'

'That's the thing,' said Daney. 'It does, but I'm really not comfortable … I know this is a murder investigation, but if you could be discreet …'

'About what?'

'Quoting me as the source,' said Daney. He bit his lip. 'There's a whole lot of history here.'

'Something to do with eight years ago?'

Daney pulled at his cheek again. Created a lopsided frown.

'I'll be as discreet as possible, sir,' said Milo.

'I know you will …' Daney turned as a truck loaded with bags of fertilizer drove onto the lot. Dark blue. A stick-on sign said *Hernandez Landscaping*. Two mustachioed guys in dusty jeans and baseball caps got out and entered the doughnut stand.

Daney said, 'See what I mean, pickups are all over. I'm sure it's no big deal.'

'Give it a shot, anyway, Mr Daney. For Rand's sake.'

Daney sighed. 'Okay …' Another sigh. 'Barnett Malley – Kristal Malley's father drives a dark pickup. Or at least he used to.'

'Eight years ago?' said Milo.

'No, no, more recently. Two years ago. That's when I ran into him at a True Value hardware store not far from here. I was buying parts to fix a garbage disposal and he was loading up on tools. I noticed him right away but he didn't see me. I tried to avoid him but we encountered each other at the register. I let him go ahead of me, watched him leave and get into his truck. A black pickup.'

'You two talk?' said Milo.

'I wanted to,' said Daney. 'Wanted to tell him I could never really understand his pain but that I'd prayed for his daughter. Wanted to let him know that just because I'd reached out to Troy and Rand didn't mean I didn't understand his tragedy. But he gave me a look that said "Don't go there."'

He hugged himself.

'Hostile,' I said.

'More than that, Doctor.'

'How much more?' said Milo.

'His eyes,' said Daney. 'Pure hatred.'

We watched the white Jeep drive off.

Milo said, 'Barnett Malley. It has now officially gotten messy. So how would an ambush fit the time frame – and the call to you an hour and a half after he left the Daneys'?'

'Rand could've lied to the Daneys about going to the construction site.'

'Why would he do that?'

'Because he had a meeting before the one with me and didn't want them to know about it. With Barnett Malley.'

'Why would he do that?'

'I told you he sounded troubled. If guilt was weighing him down and he was trying to prove he was a good person, who better to ask for forgiveness than Malley?'

'Daney said he was freaked out by being watched.'

'But the next morning he looked better. Maybe he'd somehow made contact with Malley, decided to take positive action. State law requires notification of victims' families when a felon's released, so Malley would've known Rand was out. What if Malley kept an eye on Rand, confronted him face-to-face during Rand's first trip to the site at eight a.m.? They agreed to meet later and Rand invented the appointment with the construction supervisor as cover.'

'Not an ambush,' he said. 'He gets in Malley's truck voluntarily, then it goes bad.'

'Rand was impressionable, not very smart, eager for absolution. If Malley came across friendly – forgiving – Rand would've been eager to buy it.'

'Okay, let's think this through. Rand hooks up with Malley around five p.m., Malley drives him into the city, drops him off at the mall, and Rand calls *you* to set up another meeting? Why, Alex?'

First time using the victim's first name. Some kind of transition had taken place.

I said, 'Don't know. Unless, Rand and Malley had made peace and Rand decided to keep the process going.'

He rubbed his face vigorously, as if washing

without water. 'Not much of a peace if Malley shot him. What, Malley dropped him off, then picked him up again?'

'Maybe Malley had more to talk about.'

'The two of them rode around together schmoozing about the bad old days, Malley decided to off him rather than let him eat pizza with you? Even if we can explain all that, the big question remains: If this is all about payback, why would Malley wait eight years?'

'Maybe he was willing to wait for both boys to get out but a C.Y.A. gangbanger beat him to Troy.'

'So he bides his time on Rand.' He drank coffee. 'According to Daney, Malley was still heated up two years ago.'

'Malley wanted the death penalty,' I said. 'Some wounds never heal.'

'Theory, theory, theory. So, now what? I intrude on a couple who lost their kid in the worst possible way because hubby gave Daney a dirty look two years ago and he drives a black pickup?'

'It could be touchy,' I said.

'It could require some serious psychological *sensitivity.*'

I took a bite of Danish. A few minutes ago it had tasted great. Now it was deep-fried dust.

'Do I have to spell it out, Alex? I'd rather you do it and I'll watch.'

'You're not worried my presence will disrupt?'

'The defense saw you as pro-prosecution, so

maybe the Malleys will remember you fondly for the same reason.'

'No reason for them to remember me at all,' I said. 'Never met them.'

'Really?'

'There was no reason to.' Funny how defensive that sounded.

'Well,' he said, 'now there's a reason.'

15

Milo phoned DMV for current licenses and registrations on Barnett and Lara Malley.

Nothing for her. Barnett Melton Malley had a Soledad Canyon address, out in Antelope Valley.

'The birth date fits,' he said. 'One vehicle, a ten-year-old Ford pickup. Black at the time of registration.'

'Soledad's forty, fifty miles from Van Nuys,' I said. 'After what they went through, I can see them wanting to get out of the city. Rural area like that, Lara would need to drive, so why isn't she licensed?'

'They're not living together and she moved out of state?'

'A tragedy like that can drive people apart.'

'I can think of a giant wedge,' he said. 'Kristal was snatched from under her nose. Maybe hubby blamed her.'

'Or,' I said, 'she blamed herself.'

As we returned to the city, Sean Binchy called in. Van Nuys Division had no record of any call from the Daneys about Rand's disappearance.

'No big surprise,' said Milo. 'He wasn't officially missing, so it wasn't filed.'

'What's the current status of your felonious friend theory?'

'Have I abandoned it completely because Barnett Malley owns a black truck? Like Daney said, plenty of pickups in the Valley. But Malley had good reason to hate Rand. I'd be an idiot to ignore him.'

'When were you planning on visiting him?'

'I was thinking tomorrow,' he said. 'Late enough to avoid the morning rush but early enough not to get tied up coming back. First, I'm gonna try to find out where he works. If I get lucky and it's somewhere closer, I'll call you.'

He scribbled in his notepad, returned it to his pocket. 'Or even luckier, some mitigating factor will emerge. Like an ironclad alibi for Malley.'

'You don't want it to be him,' I said.

'Hey,' he said. 'How about lunch? I'm thinking tandoori lamb.'

We stopped at the station first, where he cleared his messages and ran Barnett Malley through NCIC and the other criminal databases and came up empty. Same for Lara Malley.

I stayed on my feet, expecting we'd soon leave for Café Moghul. But he just sat there, eyes closed, passing the phone from one hand to the other until he called the Hall of Records downtown and asked for a clerk who owed him a favor. It took awhile to get through but once he connected, the conversation was brief. When he hung up, he looked weary.

'Lara Malley's deceased. Seven years ago, suicide by firearm. Women are shooting themselves more, nowadays, but back then it was a little unusual, right? Pills were the ladies' choice.'

'Not always, if the ladies were serious,' I said.

'Mommy cashes in a year after Kristal's murder. Enough time to see life wasn't getting any better. The Malleys ever get any therapy, Alex?'

'Don't know.'

He began punching his computer keyboard as if it was a sparring partner, logged onto the state firearms registration file. Squinted and stared and copied something down and drew his lips back in a strange, hollow smile that made me glad I wasn't his enemy.

'Mr Barnett Melton Malley has amassed quite an arsenal. Thirteen shotguns, rifles, and handguns, including a couple of thirty-eights.'

'Maybe he lives alone in a secluded area. He'd have more reason than most to be vigilant.'

'Who says he lives alone?'

'Same answer,' I said. 'If he started a new family, he'd want to protect it.'

'Angry, bitter guy,' he said. 'Loses his entire family to violence, moves out to the boonies with a stash of firepower heavy enough to outfit a militia. Maybe he's *in* a militia – one of those survivalist yahoos. Am I overreaching if I use the term "high risk"?'

'If he intended to murder someone, why would he register his weapons?'

'Who says he registered *all* of them?' He fumbled in a desk drawer, pulled out a wooden-tipped cigar, rolled it between his palms.

'The way Rand was shot,' he said. 'Contact wound, left side of the head, the killer at approximately the same height. Taken by surprise like you suggested. That conjure up an image?'

'The killer was sitting to his left,' I said. 'Close to him. As in the driver's seat of a vehicle.'

He pointed the cigar at me. 'That's the channel that switched on in *my* head. In terms of pre-meditation, maybe Malley *didn't* think it out. Maybe he started out wanting to talk to Rand. To confront the guy who'd ruined his life. We both know victims' families sometimes crave that.'

I said, 'Malley had eight years for that, but perhaps Rand's release triggered old memories.'

'Malley picks him up, drops him off, drives around and finds out he's still got unfinished business with Rand. They drive up somewhere in the hills and something goes wrong.'

'Rand wasn't articulate. He said the wrong thing to Malley and triggered big-time rage.'

' "I'm a good person," ' he said.

'I can see that coming out wrong.'

He bolted up, tried to pace the tiny office, took a single, attenuated step, reached my chair, and sat back down. I was an obstruction. My thoughts drifted to New York on a crisp, snowy day. Gallivanting.

I said, 'If Malley came armed, on the other hand, there might've been premeditation.'

'He was meeting up with his daughter's murderer. Like you said, he'd have good reason to be careful.'

'A good lawyer could make a pretty good case for self-defense.'

He tossed the cigar onto the desk. 'Listen to this, we're psychoanalyzing the poor bastard and neither of us has ever met him. For all we know, he's a pacifist Zen Buddhist vegan transcendental meditator living out in the woods in the name of serenity.'

'With thirteen guns.'

'There is that minor sticking point,' he said. 'Man, I'd love to have the techies go over that black truck of his. Love to have *grounds* for it – Alex, how about we scotch lunch. For some reason my appetite's waning.'

I said, 'Sure.'

He turned away and I left.

When I was ten feet up the hall I heard him call out, 'Eventually, we'll do the tandoori bit. I'll have my people call your people.'

He phoned that evening at seven-forty.

I said, 'What happened to your people?'

'On strike. Did more background on Malley. Eight years ago he ran his own pool-cleaning service, then it stopped a year later.'

'After Lara shot herself. Maybe he dropped out.'

'Whatever the reason, given no workplace, I figure to set out at ten tomorrow morning. The grinning fool who reads the weather on TV says warm air's coming in from Hawaii. Closest I'm gonna get to a tropical vacation. Sound good?'

141

'Want me to pick you up at home?'

'No, you're doing the psychology bit but I'm the wheelman,' he said. 'It's time to be somewhat official.'

He arrived at ten-fifteen looking as official as he was ever going to be: baggy brown suit, white shirt, putty-colored tie. The desert boots. I had on my courtroom outfit: blue pin-striped three-button, blue shirt, yellow tie. Whether Barnett Malley was a vengeance-sworn gun freak or a quietly grieving victim, wardrobe wasn't going to make a difference.

Milo grabbed a stale bagel from my kitchen and chewed at it as he drove down to Sunset then turned right, toward the 405 North. This time, he slowed and pointed out the spot where Rand Duchay's body had been found. Shrubby patch on the east side of the rise that paralleled the on-ramp. No tall trees, just ice plant and juniper and weeds. No serious intent to conceal.

The route from the dump spot to Soledad Canyon would take you right past here.

Milo spoke the obvious: 'Do your thing, dump him, go home.'

The trip was fifty-eight minutes of easy driving under blue skies. The weatherman had been righteous: eighty degrees, no smog, the air blessed by one of those faintly fruity tropical breezes that blows in all too rarely.

We passed through the northern edge of Bel Air, lush, green hills studded with optimistically perched houses. Then, the stunningly white cubes that make up the Getty Museum. It's an architectural master-piece funded by a venal billionaire's trust, housing third-rate art. Pure L.A.: might makes right and packaging is all.

Traffic stayed light all the way through the Valley. The freeway fringe shifted to the massive Sunkist packaging plant, smaller factories, big-box stores, auto dealerships. Not far east was the Daney house where Rand had slept for two nights of alleged freedom. By the time we transitioned to the 5 it was mostly us and eighteen-wheelers who had veered off onto the truck route. Three minutes later we were on Cal 14, speeding northeast toward Antelope Valley. The mountains got majestic, lush green giving way to wrinkled brown felt. The scenery off the highway was scrap yards, gravel pits, the occasional 'De-Luxe Town-Home' tract and little else. Wise people say expansion to the northeast is the future of L.A. And some day the notion of open space will be shattered. Meanwhile, the hawks and ravens do their thing overhead and the earth lies flat and still.

Fifteen degrees cooler. We closed the windows and wind whistled through the seal.

Ten miles later, Milo exited at Soledad Canyon and hooked a left away from the boomtown develop-ment of Santa Clarita and toward peace and quiet. The road climbed and curved and curled and hooked.

Isolated stands of spruce and the occasional wind-break eucalyptus hugged the west side of the highway, but the big players were California oaks glorying in their dry-earth beds, gray-green crowns shimmering in the wind. Copses of the majestic trees ran clear to the next ridge of mountain. They're tough, ancient creatures that delight in self-denial; when you spoil them with too much water they die.

As the foliage thinned, the road demanded more respect, hairpin curves wrapping around acute edges of sere mountains, spillover from rock slides pasting Milo's eyes to the road. The wind's whistle grew to an insistent howl. The big birds swooped lower, flew more assertively. Nothing to hamper them but the occasional power pole.

No sign of any other cars for miles, then a woman chattering happily on a cell phone came barreling around a blind curve in a minivan and nearly side-swiped us.

'Brilliant,' said Milo. When his breathing had settled: 'Soledad. Means loneliness, right? You'd have to like your alone time to move out here.'

A thousand feet higher a few ranches appeared, small, scrubby, desultory plots set into gullies notched off the highway and bounded by metal flex fencing. A cow, here, a horse, there. A weathered sign to nowhere advertised weekend pony rides. No stock to back it up.

'Read me the address, Alex.'

I did. He said, 'We're getting close.'

Ten miles later we came upon several private 'picnic grounds' set off the west side of Soledad Canyon Road.

Cozy Bye. Smith's Oasis Stop. Lulu's Welcome Ranch.

The numbers that matched Barnett Malley's address were burned into a blue roadside sign that announced *Mountain View Sojourn: Recreation and Pick-nicks.*

I said, 'Maybe he's not that antisocial, after all.'

Milo pulled off onto the hardpack driveway. We bumped along an oak-lined dirt path until we came to a shaky wooden bridge that crossed a narrow arroyo. The blue *Welcome!* sign on the other side was bottomed by a whitewashed plank that listed a magna carta of regulations: *No smoking, no drinking, no motor-cycles, no off-road vehicles, no loud music. Pets by individual approval only, children must be supervised, the pool is for use of registered guests only . . .*

Milo said, 'Take that, Thoreau,' and kept driving.

The entry drive ended a hundred yards later at an open paved square. To the left were more oaks – an old, thick grove – and directly in front of us were three small, white-frame buildings. To the right sat another paved area, larger and sectioned by white lines. Half a dozen trout-decaled Winnebagos were hooked up to utility lines. The backdrop was sheer golden mountainside.

We parked and got out. A shed-sized generator behind the RV lot hummed and snicked. 'Recreation and picnicking' seemed to mean a place to park, access to a bank of chemical toilets, and a few redwood tables. An in-ground pool, drained for the winter, was a giant, white, gunite bowl. Behind the swimming area, a pipe-fenced horse corral was empty and sun-bleached.

A few people, none below sixty, sat in folding chairs near their trailers, reading, knitting, eating.

'Must be a stopover,' I said.

'To where?' said Milo.

I had no answer for that and we continued walking toward the white-frame buildings. Prewar bunga-lows; all three were roofed with green tar paper and had stout casement windows and tiny front porches. The largest structure was set well back from the campgrounds. A thirty-year-old Dodge Charger, red, with chrome wheels, occupied the adjoining gravel driveway.

Staked signs shaped like pointing hands identified the other two buildings as *Office* and *Refreshments*. The sunlight made it hard to discern any internal illumination. We tried the office first.

Locked door, curtains across the windows. No response to Milo's knock.

As we headed over to *Refreshments,* its door creaked open and a tall, thin woman in a brown print dress stepped out onto the porch and positioned her hands on her hips.

'Can I help you?'

Milo put on his welcome smile as we approached

her. It didn't change the wary expression on her face. Neither did his badge and his business card.

'L.A. police.' She had a smoker's voice, sinewy, freckled arms, a scored, sun-cured face that might've been beautiful a few decades ago.

Wide-set, pink-lashed amber eyes examined both of us. Her nose was strong and straight, her lips chapped but suggestive of once-upon-a-time fullness. Permed auburn hair framed her in a way that concealed some of the wattle in her neck. White frizz near her hairline said she was due for a touch-up. Clean jawline for a woman of her age – sixty-five minimum was my guess. Katharine Hepburn's country cousin.

She tried to return Milo's card.

He said, 'It's yours to keep, ma'am,' and she folded it small enough to conceal in her hand. The brown dress was a floral jersey and it caught on the sharp bones of her shoulders and pelvis. The upper edge of her sun-spotted sternum was visible in the V-neckline. Her chest was flat.

'I used to live in L.A.,' she said. 'Back when I didn't know any better. Same question, Lieutenant Sturgis. What can I do for you?'

'Does Barnett Malley live here?'

The amber eyes blinked. 'He okay?'

'Far as I know, ma'am. Same question.'

'Barnett works here and I give him a place to stay.'

'Works as . . .'

'My helper. Doing what needs to be done.'

'Handyman?' said Milo.

The woman frowned as if he'd never get it. 'He fixes things, but it's more than that. Sometimes I feel like driving into Santa Clarita and seeing a movie, though God knows why, they're all awful. Barnett looks after the place for me and he does an excellent job. Why're you asking about him?'

'He live on the premises?'

'Right there.' She pointed to the oak grove.

'In the trees?' said Milo. 'We talking Tarzan?'

She conceded a half-smile. 'No, he's got a cabin. You can't see it from here.'

'But he's not there, now.'

'Who said?'

'You asked if he was okay –'

'I meant was he okay cop-wise, not was he okay because he was somewhere out there.' She glanced toward the highway. Her eyes said leaving the homestead was highly overrated.

'Has Barnett ever been in cop trouble, Mrs . . .'

'Bunny,' she said. 'Bunny MacIntyre. The answer is no.'

Milo said, 'So you used to live in L.A.'

'We're making small talk, now? Yeah, I lived in Hollywood. Had an apartment on Cahuenga 'cause I needed to be close to the Burbank studios.' She flipped her hair. 'Used to do stunts for the movies. Did a couple body doubles for Miss Kate Hepburn. She was way older than me but she had a great body so they could use me.'

'Ms MacIntyre –'

'Back to business, ay? Barnett's never been in *any* kind of trouble, but when L.A. cops drive all the way here and ask questions it's not because they want a nice cold drink from my Coke machine. Which, incidentally, is working just fine. I've got nachos and chips and some imported bison jerky.' She eyed Milo's waistline. 'Bison's good for you, has the saturated fat of skinless chicken.'

He said, 'Where's it imported from?'

'Montana.' She turned and walked back inside. We followed her into a single, dim room with wide plank floors and a hoop rug and the head of a large, stuffed buck mounted on the rear wall. The animal's antlers were asymmetrical, a gray tongue tip poked from a corner of its mouth, and one glass eye was missing.

'That's Bullwinkle,' said Bunny MacIntyre. 'Idiot used to sneak in and eat my garden. I used to sell fresh produce to the tourists. Now all people want is junk food. I never shot him because he was stupid – you had to take pity. One day he just dropped dead of old age on top of my Swiss chard, so I took him to a taxidermist over in Palmdale.'

She walked over to an old, red Coca-Cola machine flanked by revolving racks of fried stuff in plastic bags. A cash register squatted on an old oak table. Beside it was the jerky – rough-cut, nearly black, stacked in plastic canisters on the counter.

'Ready for that Diet Coke?' she asked Milo.

'Sure.'

'What about you, quiet guy?'

'The same,' I said.

'How much buffalo jerky? It's a buck a stick.'

'Maybe later, ma'am.'

'You notice what it's like out there? Damn oil painting, those deadbeats park all day and eat their own junk. Darn portable freezers. I could use the business.'

'I'll take a stick,' said Milo.

'Three sticks minimum,' said Bunny MacIntyre. 'Three for three bucks and with the Diet Cokes that'll be six and a half.'

Without waiting for an answer, she pressed buttons on the machine and released two cans, wrapped the jerky in paper towels that she bound with rubber bands, and slipped it into a plastic bag. 'There's no grease to speak of.'

Milo paid her. 'How long has Barnett worked for you?'

'Four years.'

'Where'd he work before that?'

'Gilbert Grass's ranch – used to be up a ways, on 7200 Soledad. Gilbert had a stroke and retired his animals. Barnett's a good boy, I can't see what business you'd have with him. And I don't pay attention to his comings and goings.'

'How do we get to his cabin?'

'Walk back behind my house – the one with no sign – and you'll see the cut in the trees. I built the cabin so I'd have some privacy. It was supposed to be my painting studio but I never got around to painting. I used it for storage. Until Barnett fixed it up nice for himself.'

16

The path through the trees was a six-foot-wide swath overhung by branches. The black Ford pickup was parked in front of the cabin.

The tiny building was raw cedar with a plank door. One square window in front. As simple as a child's drawing of a house. Propane gas tanks stood to the left, along with a clothesline and a smaller generator.

The truck's windows were rolled up and Milo got close and peered through the glass. 'He keeps it neat.'

He used a corner of his jacket and tried the handle. 'Locked. You wouldn't think he'd be worried about theft, out here.'

We walked up to the cabin. Green oilskin drapes blocked the window. A square of concrete served as a front patio. A hemp mat said *Welcome*.

Milo knocked. The plank was solid and barely sounded. But within seconds, the door opened.

Barnett Malley looked out at us. He was taller than he'd appeared on TV – an inch above Milo's six-three. Still lean and rawboned, he wore his yellow-gray hair long and loose. Fuzzy muttonchops trailed below his jaw before right-angling toward a lipless mouth. Sun exposure had coarsened and splotched his complexion. He wore a gray work shirt, sleeves rolled to the elbows. Thick wrists, veined forearms, yellowed nails clipped straight. Dusty jeans, buckskin cowboy boots. A silver-and-turquoise necklace ringed the spot just below a prominent Adam's apple.

A peace symbol dangled from the central turquoise. More aging hippie than militiaman.

His eyes were silver blue and still.

Milo showed him I.D. Malley barely glanced at it.

'Mr Malley, I don't mean to intrude, but there are some questions I'd like to ask you.'

Malley didn't answer.

'Sir?'

Silence.

Milo said, 'Are you aware that Rand Duchay was murdered Saturday night?'

Malley clicked his teeth together. Backed into his cabin. Closed the door.

Milo knocked. Called Malley's name.

No response.

We walked to the south side of the house. No windows. At the rear a single horizontal pane was set high into the northern wall. Milo stretched upward and rapped the glass.

Bird calls, forest rustles. Then: music.

Honky-tonk piano. A tune I'd always liked – Floyd Cramer's 'Last Date.' Solo piano, a recording I'd never heard.

Momentary hesitation, then the tune repeated. A flubbed note followed by fluidity.

Not a recording. Live.

Malley played the song through, then began again, improvising a basic but decently phrased solo.

The rendition repeated. Ended. Milo took advantage of the silence and knocked on Malley's window again.

Malley resumed playing. Same tune. Different improv.

Milo turned on his heel, lips moving. I couldn't make out what he said and knew better than to ask.

On our way out of the campgrounds, we spotted Bunny MacIntyre over by the RVs, talking to one of the elderly couples. Her hand went out and some bills were passed. She saw us, turned away.

'Charming rural folk,' said Milo, as we got back in the unmarked. 'Is that the theme from *Deliverance* I hear wafting through the piney woods?'

'Should've brought my guitar.'

'A duet with Barnett the Pianner Man? Was that the reaction of an innocent guy, Alex? I was hoping I could eliminate him, but just the opposite.'

'Wonder why he keeps that welcome mat in front,' I said.

'Maybe some people are welcome.' He turned the ignition key, let the car idle. 'The bloodhound part of me is itching to sniff, but the self-styled protector of victims thinks it's gonna be a shame if Malley turns out to be a murderer. Guy's life was blown to bits. I don't read the Bible, but on some level, I get the whole eye-for-an-eye thing.'

'I get it, too,' I said. 'Even though eye for an eye was never meant to be taken literally.'

'Sez who?'

'If you read the original biblical text, the context is pretty clear. It's tort law – monetary compensation for damages.'

'Did you come up with that on your own?'

'A rabbi told me.'

'Guess he'd know.' He drove out of the camp-grounds, turned onto the highway, switched on the police band. Crime was down but the dispatcher's recitation of felonies was constant.

'The possibilities,' he said, 'are dismal.'

Thursday morning, he called at eleven-fifteen. 'Time for tandoori.'

I'd just gotten off the phone with Allison. We'd managed to sneak in some personal talk before her grandmother's call for tea and comfort drew her away. The plan was for her to return in two or three days. Depending.

I said, 'What's up?'

'Let's talk about it over food,' he said. 'It'll be a test of your appetite.'

Café Moghul is on Santa Monica Boulevard, a couple of blocks west of Butler, walking distance from the station. The storefront ambience is dressed up by carved, off-white moldings and arches designed to mimic ivory, polychrome tapestry murals of Indian country scenes, posters of Bollywood movies. The soundtrack alternates sitar drones with ultra-high soprano renditions of Punjab pop.

The woman who runs the place welcomed me with her usual smile. We always greet each other like old friends; I've never learned her name. Today's sari was peacock blue silk embroidered with gold swirls. Her eyeglasses were off. She had huge, chocolate eyes that I'd never noticed before.

'Contacts,' she said. 'I'm trying something new.'

'Good for you.'

'So far, so good – he's over there.' Pointing to a rear table, as if I needed directions. The layout was four tables on each side divided by a center aisle. A group of twenty-somethings was gathered around two tables pushed together, dipping nan bread into bowls of chutney and chili paste and toasting some sort of success with Lal Toofan beer.

Other than them, just Milo. He was hunched over a gigantic salad bowl, sifting through lettuce and retrieving chunks of what looked to be fish. A cut-glass pitcher of iced clove tea sat at his elbow. When he saw me, he filled a glass and pushed it toward me.

'The special,' he said, plinking the rim of the salad bowl with his fork. 'Salmon and paneer and these little dry rice noodles over green stuff with lemon-oil dressing. Pretty healthy, huh?'

'I'm getting worried about you.'

'Get real worried,' he said. 'This is wild Pacific

salmon. The intrepid types that leap upstream when they're horny. Apparently, farmed fish are bland, lazy wimps and they're also full of toxic crap.'

'The politicians of the fish world,' I said.

He speared a piece of fish. 'I ordered you the same.'

I drank tea. 'What's going to test my digestive juices?'

'Lara Malley's suicide. Got hold of the final report from Van Nuys. Turns out the D's who worked it were the same ones who busted Turner and Rand.'

'Sue Kramer and a male partner,' I said. 'Something with an "R."'

'Fernie Reyes. I'm impressed.'

'I read their report on Kristal more times than I wanted to.'

'Fernie moved to Scottsdale, does security for a hotel chain. Sue retired and joined a P.I. agency over in San Bernardino. I've got a call in to her – here comes your grub.'

The blue-saried woman set a bowl down gently and swished off. My salad was half the size of Milo's, which was still more than ample.

'Good, huh?' he said.

I hadn't lifted my fork. He watched until I did, studied me as I ate.

'Delicious,' I said. Technically true, but tension had blocked the circuit from my taste buds to my brain and I might've been chewing a napkin. 'What's off about the suicide?'

'Cause of death was a single gunshot to the left temple, a thirty-eight. She was left-handed, so the coroner felt that supported a self-inflicted wound.'

'Through-and-through wound?'

'Yup, the bullet lodged in the passenger door. The gun was a Smith and Wesson Double-Action Perfected revolver registered to Barnett. He kept it loaded in his nightstand. His story was Lara musta taken it when he was at work, drove to a quiet spot in the Sepulveda recreational area and boom.'

'Did she leave a note?'

'If she did, it's not in the coroner's summary.'

'Was the gun returned to Malley?'

'No reason it wouldn't be,' he said. 'He was the legal owner and no foul play was indicated.'

He began shoveling fish and cubes of paneer cheese into his mouth. 'Maybe my ambivalence about Malley was misguided. His life went to hell, but looks like he coped by getting rid of everyone he blamed for Kristal's death. Starting with Lara, because she hadn't kept her eye on the kid. Then the C.Y.A. system took care of Turner. That left Rand as the last messy detail.'

'Why would he wait a full year after Kristal's death to kill Lara?' I said.

'I was being imprecise. She died seven years and seven months ago. Just one month after Troy and Rand got sent away. What's the obvious assumption?'

'Maternal grief.'

158

'Exactly. Great cover.' He pushed food around his plate. 'Malley's a weird one, Alex. The way he started pounding on that piano. I mean the smart thing to do, the cops come calling, is fake being cooperative. He does that, maybe I drop it.'

Unlikely, I thought. ' "Last Date".'

'What?'

'The song he played.'

'You're saying he was being symbolic? Rand had a last date with life?'

I shrugged.

He said, 'Guy keeps his truck locked even though he lives out in the boonies and the damn thing's sitting right in front of his cabin. Because he knows it's hard to get rid of every speck of forensic evidence. Maybe he's an old-fashioned eye-for-an-eye guy, doesn't give a shit about original biblical context.'

'Other than the similarity to Rand, was there anything iffy about Lara's suicide?'

'Nothing in Sue's report.'

'Was she a good detective?'

'Yeah. So was Fernie. Normally I'd assume they'd be damn thorough. But in this case, maybe they saw Barnett as a victim and didn't think it through.' He frowned. 'Bunny MacIntyre likes him but she didn't vouch for his whereabouts Sunday.'

He poured himself tea but didn't drink it. 'I need to get hold of the entire file on Lara before I talk to Sue. That'll be fun – reopening a case another D thinks is long-closed. Maybe I'll use the helpless approach: Here's what I'm faced with, Sue. I could use some help.'

He grabbed his fork again, held it poised over the bowl. 'So how's your appetite?'

'Fine.'

'Proud of you.'

He downed two Bengal premiums, called for the check, and was slapping cash on the table when his cell chirped Beethoven's Fifth.

'Sturgis. Oh, hey. Yeah. Good to hear from you, thanks . . . Would that be okay? Yeah, sure. Let me write it down.'

Tucking the phone under one ear, he scribbled on a napkin. 'Thanks, see you in twenty.'

Rising to his feet, he motioned me toward the exit. Some of the twenty-somethings stopped laughing and looked at him as he loped out of the restaurant. Big, scary-looking man. All that merriment; he didn't fit in.

'That was Sue Kramer,' he said, out on the sidewalk. 'She's right here in the city. Working a suicide, as it turns out, and happy to chat about Lara. So much for reading the file.'

'It's L.A.,' I said. 'Improvise.'

17

The address was in Beverly Hills, Rexford Drive, south side of the city, between Wilshire and Olympic, where apartment buildings predominated.

'That's her,' said Milo, pointing to a trim, dark-haired woman walking a champagne-colored toy poodle up the west side of the block.

He pulled up to the curb and Sue Kramer smiled and waved and gathered the dog in her arms.

'You're not allergic are you, Milo?'

'Just to paperwork.'

Kramer got in the back of the unmarked. As Milo drove away, she sniffed the air. 'That good old dirty-cuffs smell. Been awhile.'

'What're you driving now, Ms Private Enterprise? A Jag?'

'A Lexus. And a Range Rover.' Kramer was in her fifties, with a tight, leggy figure emphasized by black chalk-stripe pipe-stem pants and a tailored gray jacket over a white silk shell. Her hair was ink-black, cut short and spiked. No jewelry. Black Kate Spade purse.

'Hooh hah,' said Milo.

Kramer said, 'The Lexus I earned myself. My new husband's a financial guy. He bought me the Rover for a surprise.'

'Nice new husband.'

'Maybe the third time's the charm.' The dog panted. 'Chill, Fritzi, these are good guys – I think she's smelling scumbag back here.'

Milo said, 'My last passenger was Deputy Chief Morales. Got stuck driving him to a meeting at Parker.'

'There you go.'

Milo crossed Rexford at Olympic, turned left on Whitworth. 'How're things, Sue?'

'Things are great – pipe down, Fritz.'

'San Bernardino treating you well?'

'I could do without the smog, but Dwayne and I have a great weekend place in Arrowhead. How about you?'

'Peachy. What brings you to B.H.?'

'In the words of Willie Sutton, that's where the money is,' said Kramer. 'Seriously, it's a sad one. Divorce case, Korean couple, the usual hassles over money and custody. The husband decided to kill himself, made sure the wife found him.'

'Gun?'

'Knife. He ran a bath, got in, cut his wrists. That was after calling the ex and telling her she could have the car and the kids and all the spousal payment she'd demanded. All he wanted was for her to come by so they could talk like mature adults. She walked in, saw bloody water running all over the apartment. Coroner says suicide but his divorce lawyer hired us to make sure.'

'Iffy?' said Milo.

'Not at all, but you know attorneys. This one wants to rack up a few more billable hours before he closes the file. Which is fine with Bob – my boss. We don't make moral judgments, we just do the job. The apartment where it happened is back there, I'm supposed to watch it for a few days, see if anyone interesting goes in or out. So far, nothing, I'm going out of my mind. You did me a favor by calling.'

She leaned forward to get a better look at me. 'Hi, I'm Sue.'

'Alex Delaware.'

I reached back and we shook hands. Milo told her who I was.

'I know that name,' said Kramer. 'You evaluated Turner and Duchay, right?'

'Right.'

'Talk about sad.'

Milo said, 'Duchay's dead, Sue. That's why we're here.'

Kramer stroked the poodle. 'Really? Tell me about it.'

When he finished, she said, 'So you're thinking: If Malley's a vengeance-crazed killer, maybe he did the same to Lara.'

'I'm sure you were right on, but you know how it is when stuff comes up –'

'No need to stroke me, Milo. If the situation was reversed, I'd do the same thing.' She sat back. The dog's breathing had slowed. Kramer whispered something in its ear. 'Fernie and I did a good job on Lara. Coroner confirmed it was suicide, there was no reason to think it wasn't. Lara was what you psychologists call profoundly depressed, Doctor. Since Kristal's death, she'd lost weight, was taking medication, slept all day, refused to socialize.'

'You got this from Barnett?'

'That's right.'

'I found him a rather taciturn fellow.'

'Yeah, he did have the old Clint Eastwood thing going on,' said Kramer. 'But Fernie and I had bonded with him because we caught the two little monsters.'

'What was his reaction to Lara's death?'

'Sad, wiped out, guilty. He said he should've taken her depression more seriously, but they'd been having their problems and he'd been focusing on his work.'

'What kind of problems?'

'Marital stuff,' said Kramer. 'I didn't push. This was a guy who'd lost everything.'

'So he was feeling guilty for not paying attention to her.'

'Suicide does that. Right, Doctor? Leaves all that guilt residue. Like the case I'm working on right now. The wife hated the husband's guts, did everything in her power to squeeze him dry during the divorce. But seeing him bleeding out in that bathtub freaked her out and now she's remembering all sorts of wonderful things about him and blaming herself.'

Milo said, 'Did Barnett express any guilt about Lara using his gun?'

'No,' said Kramer. 'Nothing like that. I also talked to Lara's mother and she said basically the same.'

'She and Barnett get along?' I said.

'I got the feeling they didn't, but she never came out and said anything bad about him,' said Kramer. 'What I got from her was that Lara had really struggled after Kristal's death and she felt powerless to do anything about it, poor woman. Her name was Nina. Nina Balquin. She was devastated. How could she not be?'

'Lara was on medication,' I said. 'She get that from a family doctor?'

'Lara refused to see a therapist, so Nina gave her some of her pills.'

'Mom was depressed, too.'

'Over Kristal,' said Kramer. 'Maybe there was more. I got the sense this was a family that had dealt with a lot over the years.'

'Like what?' said Milo.

'It was just a feeling – I'm sure you've seen that, Doctor. Some families seem to live under a cloud. But maybe my opinion was colored because I was seeing them at their worst.'

'Twice,' I said.

'Talk about the pits. *I'm* getting profoundly depressed just thinking about it,' said Kramer. She laughed softly and stroked the poodle. 'Fritzi's my therapist. She loves stakeouts.'

'Walks in a straight line and doesn't talk,' said Milo. 'The perfect partner.'

'And doesn't need privacy to pee.'

Milo chuckled. 'Anything else that would be helpful, Sue?'

'That's it, guys. Those cases made me so damn sad, I couldn't wait to close both of them. So maybe I overlooked something on Lara, I don't know. But there really was nothing to indicate Barnett had anything to do with it.' She sighed.

Milo said, 'I wouldn'ta done different, Sue.'

'You really think he could've killed her?'

'You know him better than I do.'

'I knew him as a grieving father.'

'An angry, grieving father.'

'Isn't anger how men deal with everything?'

Neither of us answered.

Sue Kramer said, 'If Barnett blamed Lara for being negligent, he never said so to me. Can I see him waiting for Duchay to get out and pulling a revenge thing? I guess. I know he was happy when the Turner kid got shanked in jail.'

'He said that?' said Milo.

'Yup. I called to tell him about it. Figured it might hit the papers and he shouldn't find out that way. He listened and said nothing, there was this long silence. I said, "Barnett?" And he said "I heard you." I said, "You all right?" And he said, "Thanks for calling. Good riddance to bad garbage." Then he hung up. I have to say it creeped me out a little, because

Turner was thirteen years old and the way he died was gross. Still, it wasn't my kid he murdered. The more I thought about Barnett's pain, the more I figured he was entitled.'

'Barnett ever talk about Rand?' said Milo.

'Only before the sentencing. He said he wanted them to get what they deserved. Which I suppose they did, in the end.'

Milo stopped at a light at Doheny.

Sue Kramer said, 'I remember Turner's death making the paper, but I didn't see anything about Duchay. Was it in there?'

'Nope,' said Milo.

'Something like that, you'd think there would be coverage.'

'That would require a reporter actually ferreting something out,' said Milo.

'True,' said Kramer. 'Those guys feed off press releases.' A beat. 'Unlike us, huh, Milo? We just keep running after trouble. Sticking our fingers in holes as the world floods.'

Milo grunted assent.

Kramer said, 'I'd better be getting back, guys. Just my luck to be gone when something exciting happens. And Fritzi's due for a bathroom break.'

He circled back to Rexford.

'Drop me off in the alley out back, Milo. I left a little piece of tape at the bottom of the apartment door, want to make sure no one broke it.'

'Super-sleuth,' said Milo.

'Can't wait to close this one. When I'm finished, Dwayne's taking me to Fiji.'

'Aloha.'

'You should get some sunshine yourself, Milo.'

'I don't tan.'

'Right here's fine, big guy.'

Milo rolled to a stop behind a white-box apartment complex backed by parking slots. Stepping out, Kramer set the poodle down, leaned into his window, touched his shoulder. 'The brassocracy treating you okay?'

'They leave me alone,' he said.

'That's a brand of okay.'

'That's a brand of nirvana.'

'What do you think?' he asked me as we exited the alley and drove west on Gregory Drive.

'She did a competent job, didn't dig very deep.'

'What about that comment: the family living under a cloud?'

'Sounds like reality.'

He grunted. 'Let's find Lara's other surviving relative. See what her reality is.'

18

Nina Balquin was listed on Bluebell Avenue in North Hollywood.

Not far from the site of her daughter's suicide. Or the Buy-Rite mall, or the park where her granddaughter had been taken to be murdered.

A short drive, also, to the Daneys' house in Van Nuys.

But for Barnett Malley's escape to rural solitude, the case had tossed a narrow net.

Milo got the number, spoke briefly, finished with, 'Thanks, ma'am, will do.'

'Off we go,' he said. 'She's surprised that I want to talk to her about Barnett, not upset. Just the opposite, she's lonely as hell.'

'You picked that up in a thirty-second conversation?'

'I didn't pick up anything,' he said. 'She came right out with it. "I'm a lonely woman, Lieutenant. Any company would be welcome."'

The house was a cantaloupe orange one-story ranch on a bright, hot street. The lawn was green pebbles. A garden hose coiled loosely near the front steps, maybe for watering the elephant's ears that covered half the front wall. This sisal doormat read *DJB* over a heraldic crest. The bell chimed do-re-mi.

The woman who opened the door was petite, of indeterminate middle age, with narrow blue eyes and a glossy tension around the cheekbones that trumpeted the virtues of surgical steel. She wore a fitted orange crepe blouse over black leggings and red Chinatown slippers embroidered with dragons. Her brown hair was snipped boy-short with feathery sideburns that curled forward. Her right hand gripped a remote control. A cigarette in her left dribbled smoke that trailed downward and dissolved before it reached her knee.

She tucked the remote under her arm. 'Lieutenant? That didn't take long. I'm Nina.' Her mouth smiled but the surrounding glassy skin didn't cooperate and the expression was robbed of emotional content.

The house had no entry foyer and we stepped directly into a paneled room topped by a slanted beamed ceiling. All the wood was pickled oak, yellowed by decades. The carpet was rust plush flecked with blue, the furniture beige, tightly upholstered and newish, as if it had been plucked intact from a showroom. A paneled wet bar housed glasses and bottles and a flat-screen TV sat on the brown tile counter. The set was on. Courtroom dispute, the sound muted – people mouthing aggression; a bald, scowling judge wielding a gavel in a way that couldn't escape Freudian theory.

Nina Balquin said, 'Love that stuff, it's nice to see idiots get what they've got coming.' Aiming her remote, she switched off. 'Drinks, gentlemen?'

'No, thanks.'

'It got kind of warm outside.'

'We're fine, ma'am.'

'Well, I'm having.' She walked to the bar and poured herself something clear from a chrome pitcher. 'Make yourselves comfortable.'

Milo and I sat on one of the beige sofas. The fabric was coarse and pebbly and I felt the bumps against the backs of my legs. Nina Balquin spent a long time adding ice to her drink. I noticed a tremor in her hands. Milo was taking in the room and I did the same.

A few family photos hung lopsided on a rear wall, too distant to make out. Sliding glass doors exposed a small rectangular swimming pool. Clumps of leaves and grit floated on greenish water. Rims of concrete decking too narrow for seating comprised the rest of the backyard.

Walk out, get wet, come back in.

Nina Balquin settled perpendicular to us and sipped her drink. 'I know, it's a mess, I don't swim. Never used Barnett for the pool. Maybe I should've. He could've been good for one thing.' She drank some more.

Milo said, 'You're not fond of Barnett.'

'Can't stand his guts. Because of how he treated Lara. And me. Why are you asking about him?'

'How he treated Lara before Kristal's murder or after?'

At the mention of her granddaughter, Balquin flinched. 'You ask, I answer? Fine, but just tell me one thing: Is the bastard in some kind of trouble?'

'It's possible.'

Balquin nodded. 'The answer is he was rotten to Lara before *and* after. She met him at a rodeo – can you believe that? She went to good schools, her father was a dentist. The plan was she was supposed to go to the U. But her grades went to hell in high school. Still, there was Plan Two, Valley College. So what does she do after graduating? Gets a job at a dude ranch in Ojai and meets Cowboy Buckaroo and the next thing I know she's calling to inform me they're married.'

She gulped her drink, swished liquid in her mouth, swallowed, stuck out her tongue. 'Lara was eighteen, he was twenty-four. She watches him rope horses or doggies or whatever they rope and suddenly the two of them are at some tacky little drive-through chapel in Vegas. Her father could've ... killed them.' She smiled uneasily. 'To use an expression.'

Milo said, 'Can't blame him for being upset.'

'Ralph was *furious*. Who wouldn't be? But he never said a thing to Lara, kept it all inside. That may be why just a few years later he was diagnosed with stomach cancer.' She glanced back at the dirty pool. 'Now he's gone. *Dead*. At the time he was diagnosed we were in escrow on another house, Encino, south of the boulevard, gorgeous, huge. Thank God Ralph had decent life insurance.'

'Does Lara have siblings?' I said, still trying to make out the photos.

'My oldest, Mark, is a C.P.A. up in Los Gatos, used to be comptroller for a dot-com, he's doing fantastic as an independent consultant. Sandy, the baby, is in grad school at the University of Minnesota. Sociology. It's kind of endless for her – school; she already has one master's. But she never gave me a lick of trouble.'

She took an ice cube in her mouth, sloshed it, crushed it. 'Lara was the wild one. It's only now I'm able to get in touch with how pissed-*off* I am at her.'

'For marrying Barnett?'

'For that, for everything – for *killing* herself.' Her hand began to shake and she placed her rattling glass on an end table. 'My therapist told me suicide's the ultimate aggressive act. Lara didn't need to do that, she really didn't. She could have talked to someone. I *told* her to talk to someone.'

'Get some therapy,' said Milo.

'I'm a big fan of therapy.' She picked up the glass. 'Therapy and Tanqueray and tonic and Prozac.'

I said, 'So Lara was the rebellious one.'

'Even when she was little, you'd tell her black, she'd say white. In high school, she got in with a bad crowd – that's what messed up her grades. Of the three, she was the smartest, all she had to do was a little work. Instead, she marries *him. Vegas,* for God's sake. It was like a bad movie. He was – have you ever seen his teeth?'

During the few seconds Malley had faced us, he had never opened his mouth.

Milo said, 'Not in good shape?'

'*Trailer* trash teeth,' said Nina Balquin. 'You can imagine what Ralph thought of that.' Illustrating the contrast, she flashed a full set of porcelain jackets. 'He was lowlife, didn't have a family.'

'No family at all?'

'Every time I asked him about where he grew up, who his parents were, he changed the subject. I mean, here was this new person in our lives, doesn't it seem reasonable to ask? *Forget* it. Strong and silent. Except he wasn't strong enough to make a decent living.'

She drained her glass, steadied one hand with the other. 'We're an educated, sophisticated family – I have a degree in design and my husband was one of the best endodontists in the Valley. So who walks in? The Beverly Hillbilly.'

'Lara met him at a dude ranch,' said Milo.

'Lara's earth-shattering summer job.' Balquin grimaced. '*Here* she never made up her bed, but *there* she could clean rooms for minimum wage. She claimed she wanted to earn her own money so she could buy a more expensive car than Ralph wanted to get for her.'

'Claimed?'

'She quit after two weeks to run off to Vegas with *him*. Never got *any* kind of car until we bought her a used Taurus. She was just rebelling by going to Ojai, like every other time.'

'You said Barnett was working some kind of traveling rodeo?'

'For all I know he put stars in my daughter's eyes with *rope* tricks. I'm allergic to horses ... out of the blue she's married, informing me she wants lots of babies. Not just babies, *lots* of babies. I said who's going to pay for all those babies, and she had a ready answer. Cowboy Buckaroo was putting away his chaps and spurs, whatever, and getting himself a real job.'

Balquin snorted. 'Like I was supposed to stand and applaud. What was this great career? Working for a pool-cleaning service.'

I said, 'They were married a while before they had Kristal.'

'Seven years,' said Balquin. 'Which was fine with me. I figured maybe Lara was finally thinking straight, doing some financial planning. She got herself a job – not a great one, supermarket cashier at Vons. And Cowboy bought himself some chlorine and went out on his own.'

'You see them much?'

'Hardly at all. Then one day Lara dropped in, nervous, sheepish. I knew she wanted something. What she wanted was money for fertility treatment. Turns out they'd been trying for years. She said she'd gotten pregnant a few times but miscarried. Then nothing. Her doctor was thinking some sort of incompatibility. I knew for her to show up she'd have to want something.'

I said, 'Why was there so little contact?'

'Because that's what *they* wanted. We invited them to every family affair but they never showed up. At the time, I assumed that was his doing, but now I'm not sure. Because my therapist says I need to confront the possibility of Lara's complicity in a destructive dyad. As part of the process.'

'The process?' said Milo.

'The *healing* process,' said Balquin. 'Getting my act together. I have a chemical imbalance that affects my moods but I also need to take personal responsibility for how I react to stressful situations. My new therapist gets what loss is all about and she brought me to the point where I can take the gloves off when it comes to Lara. That's why your call was so perfect. After you called, I told my therapist we'd be talking. She thought it was karma.'

Milo nodded, crossed his legs. 'Did you give Lara the money for treatment?'

'The two of them had no health insurance. I'm not sure if fertility's even covered by insurance. I felt sorry for her, knew it was tough for her to come with her hand out. I told her I'd ask her father and she thanked me. Actually hugged me.'

Balquin's eyes fluttered. She got up and refilled her glass. 'I can get you guys something soft.'

'We're really okay, ma'am. So your husband agreed to pay for the fertility treatments?'

'Ten thousand dollars' worth. First he said no way, then of course, he gave in. Ralph was a big softie. Lara cashed the check and that was the last I heard about it. Then back to the same old routine, not returning my calls. My therapist says I have to confront the possibility that she used me.'

'What do you mean?'

'It's possible they never paid the doctor.'

'Why would you suspect that, ma'am?'

Balquin's hand whitened around her glass. 'I carried Lara for nine months and sometimes I miss her so much I can't stand to think about it. But I need to be objective for my own mental health. I always suspected those two spent the money on something else because soon after we gave it to them, they moved to a bigger place and there was still no baby. Lara said Barnett needed space for his piano. I thought what a waste, all he played was country-western songs and not very well. Kristal didn't arrive until years later – when Lara was twenty-six.'

'That must have been something,' I said.

'Kristal?' She blinked some more. 'A cutie, a beauty. From the little I saw of her. Here I was, a grandma, and I never got to see my grandchild. Lara had choices but I know *he* had a role in it. He isolated her.'

'Why?'

'I don't know,' she said. 'That man never once

uttered a pleasant boo-hoo to any of us. Despite our feelings about the marriage, we tried to be nice. When they got back from Vegas we threw them a little party, over at the Sportsman's Lodge. The invitation said "Business attire." *He* came in dirty jeans and one of those cowboy shirts – with the snaps on it. His hair was all long and unkempt – my Ralph was a real dapper guy, you can imagine. Lara used to love dressing up, but not anymore. She wore jeans just as filthy as his and a cheap-looking little halter tank top.'

She shook her head. 'It was embarrassing. But that was Lara. Always keeping things lively.'

'Ma'am,' said Milo, 'would it be too painful to talk about the suicide?'

Nina Balquin's eyes floated upward. 'If I said yes, would you drop it?'

'Of course.'

'Well, it *is* painful, but I *don't* want you to drop it. Because it wasn't my fault, no matter what anyone says. Lara made choices her whole life, then she ended her life with a horrible, stupid, rotten *choice*.'

'Who says it's your fault?' I said.

'No one,' she said. 'And everyone, implicitly. Lose a child to an accident or an illness, everyone feels sorry for you. Lose a child to suicide and people look at you as if you were the most horrible parent in the world.'

'How did Barnett react to the suicide?'

'I wouldn't know, we never spoke about it.' Her

eyes clenched and opened. 'He had Lara cremated, never had the decency to have a service. No funeral, no memorial. He cheated me – the *bastard*. Can't you tell me what he's suspected of? Is it something to do with drugs?'

Milo said, 'Barnett used drugs?'

'Both of them smoked pot. Maybe that's why Lara couldn't get pregnant – isn't that supposed to do something to your ovaries or whatever?'

'How do you know about their drug usage?'

'I know the *signs*, Detective. Lara was a pot-head when she was in high school. I never saw any evidence she'd stopped.'

'The bad crowd she fell in with,' I said.

'Bunch of spoiled kids,' she said. 'Driving around in their parents BMWs, booming that music and pretending they were ghetto. Neither of my other two went for that nonsense.'

'You figure Lara continued using after she was married.'

'I know she did. The few times I visited their apartment – the few times they let me in – everything was a mess and you could *smell* it in the air.'

Milo said, 'Did they ever use anything stronger than marijuana?'

'Wouldn't surprise me.' Balquin eyed him. 'So this *is* about drugs. Is Barnett pushing?'

'Have you known him to sell drugs?'

'No, but I'm being logical. Don't users become pushers to pay for their habit? And all those guns he keeps – Lara wasn't raised with that, we never had so much as a BB gun in our home. All of a sudden they've got rifles, pistols, horrible stuff. He kept them out in the open, in a wooden case – the way sophisticated people display books. If you're not doing something shady, why do you need all those guns?'

'Ever ask him?'

'I mentioned it to Lara. She told me to mind my own business.'

I looked for bookshelves in her front room. Nothing but pickled oak paneling and the photos on the back wall.

She said, 'Lara used one of his guns to shoot herself. I hope he's happy.' Her hands tightened into fists. 'If he is a pusher, I hope you catch him and put him away forever. Because the last thing my daughter needed was another bad influence.'

She scraped an incisor with a fingernail, raised her glass to her lips, and drank slowly but steadily. Finished off the refill without taking a breath.

Milo said, 'Is there anything else you'd like to tell us, ma'am?'

'I shouldn't say this but . . . oh, what the hell, she's gone and so is Kristal and I need to concentrate on rebuilding my own life.' She tightened her face again, held the tension so long that even the refashioned muscles of her cheeks and chin gave way.

'I always wondered if drugs had something to do with Lara losing sight of Kristal. She insisted it was only for a second, the store was crowded and she turned her head and she was gone. But doesn't dope slow your reflexes?'

Milo uncrossed his legs. He took his pad out but didn't write.

Nina Balquin said, 'It's a terrible thing to say about your own child, but how else can you explain it? I raised three kids, and as a toddler Mark was a hellion, all over the place, you couldn't get him to sit still. But I never *lost* him. How do you just *lose* a child!'

Her voice had risen to a near scream. She plopped back heavily, massaged her left temple. 'Damn cluster headache … the last thing I'd want to do is blame my daughter, but objectively … maybe that's why Lara felt guilty enough to do what she – oh, *spit it out, Nina*! Maybe that's why she *killed* herself!'

Both her hands began shaking violently. She sat on them, shut her eyes. A high-pitched keen made its way from behind closed lips.

Milo said, 'We know this is hard, ma'am. We appreciate your being so frank.'

Nina Balquin opened her eyes. Her expression was vacant.

'Insight,' she said, 'can be a bitch.'

As Milo thanked her, I walked to the back of the room and looked at the photos. A couple in their thirties with two kids under ten – the accountant son and his family. A woman who resembled Lara Malley, wearing a cap and gown. Heavier face than

Lara's, red hair curling from under the mortarboard. Sister Sandy.

No image of Lara, but below her sibs hung a cheaply framed, three-by-five snapshot of Kristal. Infant photo – less than a year old from the way she needed support to sit up. Wearing a pink cowgirl dress and matching hat. Bucking broncos and cacti in the background, a tiny moon above the plains, airbrushed slick. Probably one of those kiddie-photo outlets. The kind you find in every mall.

Smiling baby girl, chubby, rosy-cheeked. Big brown eyes engaged the camera. Moisture on her chin – teething drool.

Nina Balquin said, 'I got that when I dropped in on them and brought Kristal a Christmas present. They had a stack. I had to *ask* for that one.'

We left her standing in her doorway, new drink in her hand.

Milo drove away, muttering, 'Sometimes *my* crazy family doesn't seem so bad.'

I said, 'Mom hates Barnett's guts but she never considered that he might've murdered Lara.'

He said, 'That woman's so fragile I kept waiting to pick up shards. Wonder how she'll cope if we find out Barnett's a much badder guy than she imagined.'

He chose surface streets over the freeway, took Van Nuys Boulevard north and connected to Beverly Glen. As we curved through the canyon, he said,

'Just like Malley's neighborhood, huh? Except for gazillion-dollar houses, tennis courts, foreign cars, a lot more greenery, and no trailer parks.'

'Perfect match,' I said.

'Anything Balquin say illuminate Malley psychologically?'

'If she's credible, he isolated Lara from her family, was close-mouthed about his origins, used dope. We know the part about gun-hoarding is true. Toss in the way he reacted to us and there's potential for ugly.'

'Don't guys who isolate their wives also abuse them?'

'It's a risk factor,' I said. 'If Malley's basic approach to life was us against the world, Kristal's murder would've buttressed that.'

'The world's a rotten, dangerous place so stay armed and vigilant.'

'And strike back. What interests me is Nina's suspicion that Lara was negligent due to drugs. That's a tough place to get to when it's your own kid. No matter how much therapy you have.'

'There's Barnett's reason for blaming Lara. Even though he's also a doper.'

'Lara was the mom,' I said. 'Mothers always get blamed. After Troy and Rand were sent away, Lara and Barnett started examining their own lives. Here's a couple who had trouble conceiving. Finally, they produce a child only to have her ripped away in the worst manner possible. Talk about stress on a relationship. Maybe tension escalated to unbearable, the wrong things got said. A history of isolation and drugs and abuse would've added more heat. Maybe Lara stopped putting up with the abuse.'

'Got too assertive with the cowboy.' He aimed a finger gun at the windshield. 'Kapow.'

'Kapow, indeed.'

19

For most of the ride back to the city, Milo waded through LAPD bureaucracy in order to get hold of the complete file on Lara Malley's suicide.

I let my mind run, ended up in some interesting places.

He pulled up in front of my house. 'Thanks. Onward. Somewhere.'

'Are you in the mood for more speculation?'

'What?'

'Nina Balquin suspects Malley was involved in the dope trade. If that's true, he'd be likely to know unpleasant people. The kind who'd be able to get something done behind bars.'

He twisted and faced me. 'The hit on Troy Turner? Where'd *that* come from?'

'Free association.'

'Turner was written up as a gang thing. He assaulted a Vato Loco.'

'And maybe it even happened that way,' I said.

'Why wouldn't it be righteous, Alex?'

'Why would a thirteen-year-old kid hang in a supply closet for an hour bleeding before anyone noticed?'

'Because C.Y.A.'s a mess.'

'Okay,' I said.

He shoved the seat back violently and stretched his legs. 'Malley puts a hit on Turner a month into Turner's sentence but waits eight years to take care of Rand?'

'That is problematic,' I said.

'Sure is.'

'I can offer an explanation but it would be broad conjecture.'

'As opposed to wild speculation?'

'Malley craved immediate vengeance for his daughter's death. He saw Troy Turner as the primary killer so Troy paid quickly. After that satisfaction, Malley's rage subsided. It's possible he hadn't even decided that Rand deserved the ultimate penalty. But the two of them got together and something went wrong.'

'Malley does his own wife quickly but cuts Rand eight years of slack?'

'If he blamed Lara for Kristal's death, that was a whole different level of rage.'

'You only kill the one you love? I don't know, Alex. It's a big jump.'

'Lara's own *mother's* still angry at her. There was a picture of Kristal in her house but none of Lara. Put yourself in Barnett's place. All those years of infertility and she blows it big time.'

'I guess,' he said.

'There'd also be a practical reason not to hit Rand immediately after Troy. Both boys dying so close together would set off suspicions about revenge. Lara was different, there was no reason to assume her death was anything other than suicide.'

'Sue didn't suspect. And she was a smart cop. Maybe . . .'

'If Malley did kill Lara and managed to fool the coroner and the cops, that implies cunning and planning. Which is consistent with an ability to delay gratification. So is Malley's lifestyle – ascetic. Perhaps he mulled Rand's fate for years, decided to check out the quality of Rand's atonement.'

'You flunk you die,' he said. 'Thirty-eight revolver. Cowboy gun . . . still, eight years is a helluva long time to wait.'

'Maybe the eight years were broken up by periodic contact – an extended testing period for Rand.'

'Malley visited Rand in prison? Spent face time with the punk who killed his kid?'

'Face time or letters or phone calls,' I said. 'You've seen it, victims and offenders making contact after the disposition. The initiative could've come from Rand. He wanted to unload his guilt and made the first move.'

'You see Malley responding to that? We're not talking Mr Touchy-Feely.'

'Eight years changes people. And just because he hoards guns doesn't mean he's not hurting.'

'That sounds like a defense brief.' The police band burped. His hand shot out and switched it off. 'Guess I'd be a putz not to check out Rand's visitors' list. Which, given the fact that C.Y.A.'s a *big* mess, isn't gonna be simple. As long as I'm churning paper, I'll also try to learn what I can about Turner's death. And let's not forget the joy of excavating Barnett Malley's personal history.'

'Always happy to brighten your day.'

'Hey,' he said. 'It's more than I had before you started free *associating*.'

Five messages on my machine. Four junkers and Allison, sounding cheerful.

'I'm free! Seven a.m. flight tomorrow on JetBlue. I should arrive in Long Beach by ten-thirty.'

I reached her cell. 'Got the good news.'

'Dropped a whole lot of guilt on cousin Wesley,' she said. 'My Ph.D. put to practical use. He gets in from Boston tonight. I'm packed and ready to go.'

'How did Grandma take it?'

'There were a few genteel sniffs but she's saying the right things.'

'Seven a.m. flight in New York means a drive in the dark from Connecticut.'

'Got a car picking me up at three-thirty,' she said. 'Does that tell you how motivated I am? The day after I arrive I've got patients, but if you have time tomorrow, we could have some fun.'

'Fun is good,' I said. 'I'll pick you up.'

'I booked a car in Long Beach, too.'

'Unbook it.'

'Ooh,' she said. 'Tough guy.'

*

At nine p.m., my service called. I'd downed a sandwich and a beer, was ready to kick back with some journals.

'It's a Clarice Daney, Doctor,' said the operator.

'Cherish Daney?'

'Pardon?'

'I know a Cherish Daney.'

'Oh, could be, this is Loretta's handwriting – yeah, that could be it, Doctor. You want me to hold her number or give it to you? She said it was no emergency.'

'I'll take it.'

She clicked me in.

'Oh,' said Cherish Daney. 'Sorry, I was just going to leave a message. They didn't need to interrupt your evening.'

'No problem. What's up?'

'I was actually trying to reach Lieutenant Sturgis, but they told me he's out of town. So I thought of calling you. I hope that's okay.'

Out of town?

'It's fine. What's on your mind, Ms Daney?'

'After you left I realized I didn't get a chance to talk much about Rand. My husband spoke to you but there's something I thought I should add.'

'Please.'

'Okay,' she said. 'This is probably nothing, but I thought you should know that Rand was really upset the entire time. More than upset. *Highly* agitated.'

'Your husband said he was afraid.'

'Did Drew say why?'

I remembered Daney's protectiveness. Decided she was an adult and that I cared more about her reaction. 'He said Rand thought someone had prowled near his window at night. In the morning Rand spotted a dark truck driving away from your house and for some reason that worried him.'

'The dark truck,' she said. 'Drew told me all that, but I'm referring to something different. Something heavy on Rand's mind right *before* he was released. It actually started a few weeks before. I wanted to open Rand up but felt I should take it slow because of all he'd been through.'

'Open him up,' I said.

'I'm not a psychologist, but I do have a certificate in spiritual counseling. The nonverbal signs were all there, Doctor. Lack of concentration, drop in appetite, insomnia, general restlessness. I put it down to prerelease jitters, but now I wonder. And it began well before we got Rand home, so I don't think it had anything to do with being stalked by a truck.'

'Can you tell me more about it?' I said.

'As I said, he'd been jumpy for a while. But when we picked him up in Camarillo, he looked awful. Pale, shaky, really not himself. During the drive home we stopped off to get some gas and my husband went to the men's room and Rand and I had a few minutes alone. By that time, he was barely able to sit still. I asked him what the matter was but he didn't answer. I decided to be a *little* persistent and finally he said there was something he wanted to talk about. I asked what and he hemmed and hawed and finally he said it was about what had happened to Kristal. Then he started to cry. Which made him real embarrassed, he started gulping back his tears and forcing himself to smile. Before I had a chance to probe, Drew was back with the drinks and the snacks and I could tell Rand didn't want me to say anything. I planned to follow up over the weekend, but somehow the timing was never right. I so wish I had, Doctor.'

'Something about what happened to Kristal,' I said. 'Any idea what?'

'My assumption was he needed to unload. Because he'd never really dealt with what had happened. During our visits he had expressed some remorse. But maybe now that he could see freedom on the horizon, he was getting to a place where he could take a higher level of responsibility.'

'Such as?'

'Integrating his atonements into his consciousness. Perhaps by making proactive gestures.'

'I'm not sure I follow.'

'I know,' she said. 'This must sound like gobbledygook to you. And I'm not sure I understand it myself. I guess I can't help but think there was *something* Rand wanted to say that he hadn't said before. Whatever it was, I'm *kicking* myself for not prying it out of him.'

'Sounds like you did more for him than anyone else did.'

'That's kind, Doctor, but the truth is, with all the

other fosters, there are so many demands on my attention. I should have reacted more ... affirmatively.'

'Are you saying Rand's guilt had something to do with his murder?'

'I don't know what I'm saying. To be honest, I'm feeling pretty foolish right now. For bothering you.'

'No bother,' I said. 'What had Rand told you before?'

'At first, he claimed he didn't remember a thing. Maybe that was even true – you know, repression. Even if it wasn't, the psychodynamic would be the same, right, Doctor? The enormity of his transgression was just too much for his soul to bear, so he closed up and marshaled his defenses. Am I making sense?'

'Sure,' I said.

'I mean, it was all that boy could do just to get through each day. They claim it's a juvenile facility but it's not that at all.'

'There were old scars on Rand's body,' I said.

'Oh, I know.' Her voice broke. 'I heard about each assault but was never allowed to visit him when he was in the infirmary. When we got home he changed into fresh clothes and I took the old ones to wash. When he slipped off his T-shirt, I had a quick look at his back. I shouldn't have been shocked, but it was hideous.'

'Tell me about the assaults.'

'The worst was when he was jumped by some

gang members and stabbed several times for no reason at all. Rand wasn't a fighter, just the opposite. But did that stop them?'

'How seriously was he hurt?'

'He ended up in the infirmary for over a month. Another time he was surprised from behind and hit on the head while taking a shower. I'm sure there were other incidents he didn't talk about. He was a big strong boy, so he recovered. Physically. After the stabbing, I complained to the warden but I might as well have spit into the wind. The guards beat the inmates, too. Do you know what they call themselves? Counselors. They're hardly that.'

'Those types of experiences could make someone jumpy,' I said.

'Of course they could,' she said. 'But Rand had adjusted, it wasn't until his release approached that the symptoms began. He was an amazing person, Doctor. I don't know if I could've coped with eight years of that place and not gone crazy. If only I could've guided him better ... One thing about working with people, you constantly get reminded that only God is perfect.'

'Did you visit Troy as well?'

'Twice. There wasn't much time, was there?'

'Did Troy ever express any guilt?'

Silence. 'Troy never got the chance to grow spiritually, Doctor. That child didn't have a chance in the world. Anyway, that's what I wanted to tell you. Whether it's relevant, I don't know.'

'I'll pass it along to Detective Sturgis.'

'Thanks . . . one more thing, Dr Delaware.'

'What's that?'

'Your report on the boys. I never got a chance to tell you at the time, but I thought you did a very fine job.'

Rick Silverman answered at Milo's house. 'I'm out the door, Alex. Big Guy flew to Sacramento a couple of hours ago.'

'Where's he's staying?'

'Somewhere in Stockton, near some youth prison. Got to run, car crash, multiple traumas. I'm off-call but the hospital needs extra docs.'

'Go.'

'Nice talking to you,' he said. 'If you speak to him before I do, tell him I'll handle Maui.'

'Vacation plans?'

'Allegedly.'

20

Fun.

A woman's body curled next to yours, inhaling her skin, her hair.

Cupping your hand over the swell of hip, tracing the xylophone of ribs, the knob of shoulder.

I propped myself up and watched Allison sleep. Absorbed the rhythm of her breathing and followed the slow fade of the flush that had spread across her chest.

I got out of bed, slipped on shorts and a T-shirt, and made my escape.

By the time she wandered into the kitchen wearing my ratty yellow robe, I'd made coffee and checked my service for messages and thought a lot about Cherish Daney's call.

Rand wanting to talk about Kristal. Same thing he'd told me.

No, that wasn't quite right. He had mumbled and I'd raised the topic and he'd agreed.

Opening him up.

Allison mumbled something that might've been 'Hi.' Her gait was unsteady and her black hair was loose and unruly in that nice way really thick hair can pull off. She blinked a few times, struggled to keep her eyes open, made it over to the sink, ran the tap and wet her face. Cinching the robe's belt tight, she patted herself dry with a paper towel, shook her head like a puppy.

Gaping yawn. Her hand reached her mouth belatedly. ''Scuse me.'

When I took her in my arms she fell against me so heavily I wondered if she'd dropped back to sleep. In heels, she's no giant. Barefoot, she barely reaches my shoulder. I kissed the top of her head. She patted my back, a curiously platonic gesture.

I steered her to a chair, filled a mug with coffee, put some ginger cookies on a plate. She'd bought them weeks ago. They'd never been opened. I keep telling myself to learn some serious cooking skills, but when I'm alone it's whatever's easy to fix.

She stared at the cookies as if they were some exotic curiosity. I placed one at her lips and she nibbled, chewed with effort, swallowed with a gulp.

I got some coffee in her and she smiled up at me woozily. 'What time is it?'

'Two p.m.'

'Oh . . . where'd you go?'

'Just here.'

'Couldn't sleep?'

'I had a catnap.'

'I passed out like a wino,' she said. 'I don't even know what time zone I'm in . . .'

Her eyes swung to the mug. 'More? Thanks. Please.'

Half an hour later, she was showered, made-up, hair combed flat down her back, wearing a white linen shirt, black slacks, demi-boots with heels too thin to support a chihuahua.

She hadn't eaten since tea with Grandma the previous afternoon and wondered aloud about protein. The choice was mutual and easy: a steak house in Santa Monica that we frequented when we needed quiet. Dry-aged beef, good bar. Also, the place we'd first met.

The air outside was a brutal seventy-five and we took her black Jaguar XJS because it's a convertible. I drove and she kept her eyes closed during the trip, rested a hand on my thigh.

Glorious day. I wondered about the weather in Stockton.

I'd been there once, years ago, on a court-ordered evaluation. It's a nice aggie town south of Sacramento, in the heart of the San Joaquin Valley, with a river port. That far inland, all those flat fields, it had to be hotter.

By now, Milo would be sweating, probably cursing. Thinking about Maui?

The case that had drawn me to Stockton was for Family Court. A recently divorced Croatian taxi driver had absconded with his three children only to be picked up three months later outside Delano, trying to rob a convenience store while using the kids as lookouts. Sentenced to ten years, he settled himself in jail and demanded joint custody and regular prison visits. The fact that the mother was a meth addict who started riding with outlaw bikers gave his claim enough substance to nudge the legal machinery.

I'd done my best to protect the kids. A stupid judge had wreaked havoc with that . . .

Allison's hand left my knee and pressed against my cheek. 'What're you thinking about?'

Robin had always hated hearing about the ugly stuff. Allison loves it. She carries a little gun in her purse, but my impulse is always to shield her.

'Alex?'

'Yes?'

'It wasn't a trick question, dear.'

We were a block from the restaurant. I started talking.

Brief interruption as we ordered a T-bone for two and a bottle of French red.

She said, 'It sounds as if Mr and Mrs Daney don't communicate that great.'

'Why do you say that?'

'Mister keeps a secret from Missus and tells you about Rand's fear of being stalked, the dark truck. All of which seems well founded, Rand *was* murdered. But Missus minimizes that and points you in another direction.'

'She really didn't point me anywhere,' I said. 'Mostly recited a bunch of psychobabble.'

'Her guilt about not "opening him up." She actually used those words?'

I nodded.

'Is she some kind of therapist?'

'She's got some sort of certificate in spiritual counseling.'

'In the future everyone will be *doing* therapy, so there'll be no time for anyone to *get* therapy. Maybe I should retrain in veterinary medicine.'

'You'd consider that after meeting Spike?'

'You love Spike like a brother. Admit it.'

'Do the names Cain and Abel ring a bell?'

She laughed, poured more wine, grew thoughtful. 'It sounds as if Rand was this woman's project and she figured she could heal him. Now that he's dead, she's tormenting herself that he was harboring a deep, dark secret that should've been brought to light. Which may be true, he implied the same thing to you. The big question is, Was his secret relevant to his murder? Doesn't sound as if Ms Daney has anything of substance to say about that. She's basically preoccupied with her own guilt.'

'So why'd she try to reach Milo?'

'To feel she's done her civic duty.' She played with my fingers. 'On the other hand, Rand called *you* for a reason, and a few hours later he was dead.'

The food came.

Allison said, 'You have no idea what Rand wanted to talk about?'

'He ended by saying he was a good person. I figured he was after some kind of absolution.'

'Makes sense, we're not that dissimilar from priests.'

'What puzzles me,' I said, 'is why he'd reached out to me. My role in the case was pretty minimal.'

'Maybe not to him, Alex. Or maybe he simply wanted to square things with everyone related to the case. Which would certainly include Kristal's father. Who happens to drive a black truck.'

'Full circle to Barnett,' I said.

'What do you know about this guy?'

'Lara's mother is certain he and Lara were dopers, suspects Barnett might've sold dope. She also says Barnett isolated Lara, which got me thinking about abuse. He lives out in the boonies, stockpiles guns.'

'Sounds like a charmer.'

'Lara's mom also wondered out loud if Lara could've been high when she lost Kristal.'

'Lost her,' she said. 'That sounds like misplacing your keys.'

We finished dessert and coffee, took a long time metabolizing. Allison fought for the check, finally won. A flush sparked her cheeks.

'It's good to have you back,' I said. 'Even if you won't let me pay.'

'Good to be back . . . something bothers me, Alex.

I can see Lara getting high being an issue for her husband. But why would Rand care – or even know about that?'

I had no answer for that.

She played with my sleeve. 'Am I being a bore? Sorry, you've piqued my curiosity.'

'Anything but. Go on.'

'This was supposedly a random crime, right? The boys never knew Kristal before they abducted her.'

'They said they just happened to spot her wandering around by herself. Why?'

'It seems odd,' she said. 'A little girl in a mall, all those shoppers. You'd think she wouldn't get very far before someone intervened.'

'Post-Christmas sales,' I said. 'Everyone was out for a bargain. Maybe no one noticed because there wasn't an obvious struggle. To a casual observer it could've looked like a couple of teenagers babysitting a younger sib.'

'I suppose,' she said.

'What's bothering you?'

'Kristal was two, right?'

'A month shy.'

'That's a peak period for separation anxiety. Why wouldn't there be a struggle?'

'Some kids are more trusting than others,' I said.

'And some neglected and abused kids show no stranger anxiety at all. Was there any indication of child abuse?'

'The autopsy didn't reveal any old breaks or scars

and the body was well-nourished. I suppose that if Nina's claims about drugs and isolation are true, there could have been some level of neglect.'

'How close did the Malleys live to the mall?'

'About half a mile.'

'So Lara probably shopped there often.'

'She did.'

'How far were they from the housing project?'

'Around the same distance. You're thinking the boys knew Kristal even though they claimed they didn't?'

'They hung out at the arcade, would've had opportunity to see her. Perhaps they'd noticed Lara's attention span lapsing before, had even talked to Kristal when she took her eyes off her. That would've made it easier for them to take her.'

'Premeditation,' I said. 'The boys plotted the whole thing beforehand and they lied about that because it would've made them look worse? You think that was what plagued Rand?'

'Or just the opposite, Alex. Rand told you he was a good person. He was trying to *minimize* his guilt, and what better way to do that than to pin the bulk of the blame on others? Troy, for one. But also *Lara,* because Rand had seen her let Kristal wander off before. It's certainly nothing Lara would ever admit, but it could've plagued her, contributed to her depression and her suicide. All of which Barnett had put behind him. Until Rand brought it up. Talk about pushing buttons.'

My digestion had come to a halt and steak sat in my gut. 'Rand wasn't bright, I suppose he could've read the signals wrong, been that clumsy. You have a fertile mind.'

'I'm just thinking out loud, sweetheart. Like you do.'

'What a fun couple we are,' I said.

'We really are, Alex. Anyone can talk about stupid stuff.'

21

'Unseasonably warm,' said Milo. 'Unlike the reception I got at Chaderjian.' His broad back rounded as he stuck his head inside the fridge.

He'd been back from Stockton for an hour, had driven straight to my house, announced that the airlines were out to starve him. A loaf of bread and a jar of peanut butter were already out on the counter. He'd drunk half a carton of milk without bothering to use a glass.

'You're running low on provisions,' he said, voice muffled by enamel. 'The lack of jelly, jam, preserves, or reasonable facsimile is inexcusable.'

'Want some potato chips and a cupcake in your school lunch, junior?'

'Hnh.' He foraged, straightened, massaged his sacroiliac with one palm. 'This will have to do.' His big hand concealed whatever he carried to the counter. He set it down next to the bread.

Carton of peach yogurt. Something else Allison had brought over . . . had to be weeks ago.

'It could be bad,' I said.

'So am I.' Flipping the lid, he sniffed, frowned, spooned gobs of glossy, beige stuff into the sink, flushed with a spurt of tap water that spotted his tie.

Another sniff. 'Jam at the bottom's still good.' A spoonful of orange goop landed on a slice of bread. Peanut butter got slathered on another slice and he slapped the two halves together. Folding the sandwich double, he ate standing up.

'*Bon appétit.*'

'No French, don't have the patience, today. *Mon ami.*'

'No cooperation from C.Y.A.?' I asked.

'You'd think,' he said, 'that wardens and all those other prison types would be simpatico with cops, seeing as we're both committed to the public safety.' He wiped his lips. 'But you'd be wrong. Our job's putting bad guys away, they're chronically over-crowded, get buckets of shit tossed in their faces and all sorts of other indignities. So their goal is moving miscreants *out*. They made me feel like a germ, Alex.'

'No counseling?' I said.

'What?'

'That's what they call C.Y.A. guards. Counselors.'

He laughed. 'There was a squirrelly feel to the place, Alex. Lots of silence, no mistaking the tension. Later, reading the local paper, I found out there's all sorts of rumbling about an investigation of the whole C.Y.A. system by the legislature. Too many dead wards. Top of that, their record-keeping's even worse than the department's. But all was not lost — got any more yogurt?'

'*Mi* fridge *es su* fridge.'

'Now it's Spanish? Go get a gig at the U.N.'

'Talk about miscreants.'

He created a second concoction using honey as the sugar source, consumed it at a more measured pace.

Four gulps, sitting down.

'Say what you want, but sometimes gluttony pays off,' he said. 'I hadn't had a thing to eat since the night before, the dive I was staying at didn't have room service, and by the time I got outside, I was feeling pretty mean. First place I spotted was a bar and grill two blocks from the prison. Bartender got the kitchen to microwave a plate of spareribs, and we started talking. Turns out he used to work as a prison cook, left seven years ago.'

'A year after Troy's murder.'

'Ten months to be exact. He remembered Troy's murder clearly, was there when they took the body out. Couple of *counselors* carried it right through the kitchen out to a loading dock. Didn't even bother to wrap it, just put the kid on a board and used belts to keep him from sliding off into the soup. Bartender said Turner didn't look much bigger than a plucked turkey, was about the same color.'

He strode to the fridge, pulled out a beer, popped the top, sat back down.

I said, 'Bartender had a good eye for detail.'

'It helped that there was no love lost between him and the prison. He claims they fired him for no good cause. His other clear memory is that there was a prime suspect for the murder. Not a Vato Loco, an independent freelance knife-boy named Nestor Almedeira. The V.L.s and the other gangs used him and guys like him when they wanted to keep a low profile. And guess what? Said prince got out a few months ago and his last known address is right here in L.A., the Westlake District.'

'Almedeira ever work for nongang clients?'

'As in Barnett Malley? Who knows? As far as I can tell, Malley never visited. Ditto for Rand. All Troy got was three personals, one from his mother and two from Drew and Cherish Daney. No phone logs were kept.'

'What put Nestor Almedeira in Chaderjian?' I said.

'He knifed two other kids to death in MacArthur Park when he was fifteen. Served six years for manslaughter and got out.'

'Two dead kids is manslaughter?'

'It is when they're packing blades themselves and their sheets are as bad as the guy who did them. Nestor's P.D. claimed self-defense and got it pled down.'

'And Nestor promptly went freelance in prison,' I said.

'So what else is new? Bartender said Nestor was a *very* bad boy. Short fuse, everyone thought he was nuts. I guess that squares with the way Troy got done.'

'Nestor have a drug connection?'

'Heroin.'

'If Malley was selling, they could've known each other.'

He ambled back to the fridge, retrieved the milk carton, finished it.

I said, 'Heading over to Westlake soon?'

'I was thinking now. Nestor got himself a job at a food stand on Alvarado. Ain't that a pretty thought? Bloody hands stuffing your chimichangas?'

An L.A.-bound tourist plugging 'Westlake' into one of those computer-map services could get confused.

There's Westlake Village, on the far western edge of the Valley, a wide-open bedroom community of meticulous industrial parks, high-end shopping centers, tile-roofed vanilla houses perched prettily on oak-studded hills, and multiacre horse ranches. People with money and scant interest in urban pleasures move to Westlake Village to get away from crime and congestion and smog and people not like them.

All of which abounds in the Westlake *District*.

Set just west of downtown and named after the man-made water feature created from the swamp that was once MacArthur Park, Westlake has the population density of a third-world capital. Alvarado's the main drag and it's crammed with bars, dance halls, check-cashing outlets, discount stores and fast-food joints. A few of the once-grand apartment buildings erected in the twenties remain, sprinkled among the hideous postwar instaboxes that pushed out history and architecture and destroyed Westlake's identity as a high-rent destination. Some of the structures had been sectioned and resectioned into dorm-style rooming houses. Official residency statistics didn't begin to explain things.

For a couple of decades after its birth, the park was a pretty place to go on Sunday. Then it became as safe as Afghanistan, overrun with dopers and dealers, strong-arm specialists and pedophiles and wild-eyed people who talked to God. Wilshire Boulevard bisects the green space and a tunnel connects the halves. Walking through the gray, graffitied conduit used to be life-threatening. Now murals have covered the gang braggadocio, and the mostly poor Hispanics who populate the district picnic near the water's edge after church on Sunday and hope for the best.

Milo had taken Sixth Street from its inception at San Vicente. He made a left and traveled south onto Alvarado. The thoroughfare was crowded, as it always is, intersections teeming with pedestrians, some purposeful, some aimless. Better to be out-doors, sucking in grimy air, than sitting alone in the single, fetid room you share with eight strangers.

The unmarked crawled along with the traffic. Spanish on the signs, cut-rate merchandise hawked on the sidewalk. Plastic bags of fruit and bunches of carnations dyed in unnatural tones were displayed by small, cinnamon-skinned men who'd bargained with death to get over the border. Behind us was the park.

Milo said, 'Is it melting in the rain?'

'Not much rain in awhile,' I said.

'Melting in the smog, then … well, look at *that*.' He cocked his head toward the passenger window.

I turned and saw nothing out of the ordinary. 'What?'

'A heroin deal just went down in front of that photography studio. Lowlifes not even bothering to hide it – okay, here we are.' He pulled up in the red zone. A line of people curled at the takeout window of Taqueria Grande. The building was blue stucco chipped white at the corners. An expansion would've made it the size of a single-car garage.

Milo said, 'I'd like to see *Taqueria Pequeña*,' adjusted his harness holster, slipped on his jacket, and got out.

We waited in line. The smell of pork and corn and onions blew through the window and out to the curb. The prices were good, the portions benevolent. Customers paid with soiled dollar bills and coinage and counted their change carefully. Two people worked the stand, a young man at the deep fryers and a short, round, middle-aged woman handling the public.

The fry cook was twenty or so, thin and sharp-chinned. He wore a blue bandanna on his head. What was visible of his hair was clipped to the skin and tattoos explored his arms. All around him, grease arced and spattered. No screen guards, and I could see airborne specks land on his arms and face. It had to hurt. He worked steadily, remained expressionless.

The customer in front of us collected his tamales

and rice and *agua de tamarindo* and we stepped up. The round woman had her hair pinned up. The makeup she'd put on that morning was doing battle with sweat. Her pencil poised without looking up. *'Que?'*

Milo said, 'Ma'am,' and showed her his I.D.

Her smile was slow to settle in. 'Yes, sir?'

'I'm looking for Nestor Almedeira.'

The smile closed up instantaneously, like a sea anemone reacting to being prodded. She shook her head.

Milo eyed the man in the bandanna. 'That's not him?'

The woman shifted to one side and peered around Milo's bulk. Several customers had queued up behind us but now they were drifting away. 'Carlos.'

'Could we see Carlos's I.D., please?'

'He got no driver's license.'

'I'll see whatever he has, ma'am.'

She pivoted and shouted something in Spanish. Bandanna tensed up, drew his hand away from the fryer, and eyed the back door.

Milo said, 'Tell him if he's not Nestor, there'll be no problem. Of any sort.'

The woman shouted louder and the young man froze. She covered the four feet between them with three choppy steps, talked and gesticulated and held out her hand. The young man drew a yellow scrap of paper out of his pocket.

The woman took it and handed it to Milo. Western Union receipt verifying that Carlos Miguel

Bermudez had wired ninety-five dollars and fifty-three cents to a money-transfer office in Mascota, Mexico. The date of the transaction was yesterday.

Milo said, 'That's all he's got?'

'He not Nestor,' said the woman.

'Nestor got fired?'

'No, no.' The woman's eyes got heavy around the lids. 'Nestor got dead.'

'When?' said Milo.

'Few weeks ago,' said the woman. 'I think.'

'You think?'

'Nestor din't show up much when he was alive.'

'How'd you find out he's dead?'

'He sister tell me. I give him the job because I like her, nice girl.'

'How'd Nestor die?'

'She don't say.'

'How long did Nestor work here – officially?'

She frowned. 'Maybe a month.'

'Bad attendance, huh?'

'Bad attitude.' Another glance behind us. No customers. 'You no want to eat?'

Milo returned the yellow scrap to her and she slipped it into her apron. Carlos the cook was still standing around, looking nervous.

'No, thanks,' said Milo. He smiled past her. Carlos bit his lip. 'What's Nestor's sister's name, ma'am?'

'Anita.'

'Where does she live?'

'She work at the *dentista* – up three blocks.'

'Know the dentist's name?'

'Chinese,' she said. 'Black building. You wanna drink?'

Milo ordered a lemon soda and when she tried to comp him, he left a five on the counter and made her smile.

By the time we got back in the unmarked, the lunch line had resumed.

22

Drs Chang, Kim, Mendoza, and Quinones practiced in a one-story building veneered with shiny black ceramic tile. White graffiti stuck to the bottom of the facade like food-fight pasta. The sign above the door said, *Easy Credit, Painless Dentistry, Medi-Cal Accepted.*

Inside was a waiting room full of suffering people. Milo marched past them and tapped the reception window. When it opened, he asked for Anita Almedeira.

The Asian receptionist lowered her glasses. 'The only Anita we have is Anita Moss.'

'Then I'd like to speak with her.'

'She's busy but I'll go see.'

The waiting room smelled of wintergreen and stale laundry and rug cleaner. The magazines in the wall rack were in Spanish and Korean.

A pale woman in her late twenties came to the reception desk. She had long, straight black hair, a round face, and smooth, sedate features. Her pink nylon uniform skirt showed off a full, firm figure. Her nametag said *A. Moss, Registered Dental Hygienist.* Lovely white teeth when she smiled; the job had its perks.

'I'm Anita. May I help you?'

Milo flashed the badge. 'Are you Nestor Almedeira's sister, ma'am?'

Anita Moss's mouth closed. When she spoke next it was at a near whisper. 'You've found them?'

'Who, ma'am?'

'The people who killed Nestor.'

Milo said, 'Sorry, no. This is about something else.'

Anita Moss's face tightened. 'About something Nestor did?'

'It's possible, ma'am.'

She looked out at the waiting room. 'I'm kind of busy.'

'This won't take long, Ms Moss.'

She opened the door and walked through, approached an old man in work clothes with a collapsed jawline and an eye on the racing form. 'Mr Ramirez? I'll be with you in one minute, okay?'

The man nodded and returned to the odds.

'Let's go,' said Anita Moss, sweeping across the room. By the time Milo and I reached the exit, she was out of the building.

She tapped her foot on the sidewalk and fooled with her hair. Milo offered to seat her in the unmarked.

'That's all I need,' she said. 'Someone seeing me in a police car.'

'And here I thought we were camouflaged,' said Milo.

Anita Moss started to smile, changed her mind. 'Let's go around the corner. You drive a bit and I'll catch up with you and sit in the car.'

The unmarked had taken on heat and Milo rolled down the windows. We were parked on a side street of cheap apartments, Anita Moss sitting stiffly in the back. A few women with children strolled by, a couple of stray dogs wove from scent to scent.

Milo said, 'I know this is hard, ma'am –'

'Don't worry about me,' said Moss. 'Ask what you need to.'

'When was your brother murdered?'

'Four weeks ago. I got a call from a detective and that's all I've heard about it. I thought you were following up.'

'Where did it happen?'

'Lafayette Park, late at night. The detective said Nestor was buying heroin and someone shot him and took his money.'

'Do you remember the name of the detective who called you?'

'Krug,' she said. 'Detective Krug, he never gave me his first name. I got the feeling he wasn't going to put too much time into it.'

'Why's that?'

'Just the way he sounded. I figured it was because of the type of person Nestor was.' She straightened her back, stared at the rearview mirror.

'Nestor was an addict,' said Milo.

'Since he was thirteen,' said Moss. 'Not always heroin but always some kind of habit.'

'What else besides heroin?'

'When he was little, he huffed paint and glue. Then marijuana, pills, P.C.P., you name it. He's the baby in the family and I'm the oldest. We weren't close. I grew up here but I don't live here anymore.'

'In Westlake.'

She nodded. 'I went to Cal State L.A. and met my husband. He's a fourth-year dental student at the U. We live in Westwood. Dr Park's one of Jim's professors. I'm supporting us until Jim gets out.'

'Nestor got out of the Youth Authority three months ago,' said Milo. 'Where did he live?'

'First with my mother and then, I don't know,' said Anita Moss. 'Like I said, we weren't close. Not just Nestor and me. Nestor and the whole family. My other two brothers are good guys. No one understood why Nestor did the things he did.'

'Difficult kid,' I said.

'From day one. Didn't sleep, never sat still, always destroying things. Mean to our dog.' She wiped her eyes. 'I shouldn't be talking about him like this, he was my brother. But he tortured my mother – not literally, but he made her life miserable. Two months ago she had a stroke and she's still pretty sick.'

'Sorry to hear about that.'

She frowned. 'I can't help thinking Nestor living with her contributed to it. She had a history of high blood pressure, we were all telling Nestor to go easy on her, don't stress her out. You couldn't tell him anything. Mom wasn't naive. She knew what Nestor was up to and it really upset her.'

'Drugs.'

'And everything that goes with that lifestyle. Out all night, sleeping all day. One week he'd be working at a car wash, then he'd get fired. He'd just disappear without a word, then he'd show up at Mom's with way too much money. My mother was a religious person, she had a real problem with money you couldn't explain.'

She plucked at her badge. 'One time he threatened my husband.'

'When did that happen?' I said.

'Maybe a week after he got out. He showed up at our place late at night and demanded we let him crash there. Jim offered him money but wouldn't let him come in. Nestor got mad and grabbed Jim's shirt, really got in Jim's face. He told him he'd be sorry. Then he spit on Jim and left.'

'You call the police?'

'I wanted to but Jim didn't. He thought Nestor would calm down. Jim's a really even person, nothing fazes him.'

'Did Nestor calm down?'

'He didn't bother us again and a week later he showed up at the office and begged me to forgive him. He claimed he was clean, this time he was going to go straight, he needed a real job. I know a woman who runs a food stand down the block and I asked her if she'd give him a chance. She agreed but he screwed that up.'

'How?'

'Bad attitude, poor attendance. Now I don't even go there for lunch.'

'Being Nestor's sister was a challenge,' I said.

She exhaled and pulled at an eyelash. 'Why are you asking me all this now?'

Milo said, 'Do you have any idea where Nestor was living right before he died, and who he was hanging around with?'

'Not a clue,' said Moss. 'Soon after he got out, he bought some nice clothes. I figured he'd sold some dope. A few weeks later he was back living with Mom and the fancy clothes were gone.'

'We're looking into something Nestor might have done when he was locked up. Maybe he talked about it.'

Silence.

'Ma'am?'

'Oh,' said Anita Moss. 'That.'

She sat back against the seat cushion. Ran her hand over her eyes. 'I tried to do something about it.'

'About what, ma'am?'

'You're talking about the little white kid, right? The kid who killed that baby girl.'

'Troy Turner,' said Milo.

Anita Moss's shoulders tightened. A fisted right hand drummed the seat. '*Now* you're here?'

'What do you mean, ma'am?'

'Right after Nestor told me about it I *tried* to tell the authorities. But no one listened.'

'Which authorities?'

'First, at Chaderjian. I phoned them and asked to speak to whoever was in charge of solving crimes that take place in the prison. I spoke to some therapist, counselor, I don't know. He listened to me and said he'd get back but he never did. So I called the cops – Ramparts station because Nestor lived here. They said it was Chaderjian's jurisdiction.'

Her eyes blazed.

Milo said, 'I'm sorry, ma'am.'

'I called because Nestor was scary. He was living with Mom, I didn't want him doing anything crazy.'

Her eyes were wet. 'It was *hard* to tell on him. He *was* my brother. But I had to think of Mom. No one cared then, and now Nestor's dead and you're here. Seems like a waste of time.'

'What exactly did Nestor tell you?'

'That he was a hit man at Chaderjian. That he got paid to hurt or kill people and that he'd killed a bunch of kids in the prison.'

'When did he tell you this?'

'Not long after he got out – a couple of days after. It was my brother Antonio's birthday and we were at my mom's, trying to have a family dinner, my brothers and their families, Jim and me. Mom wasn't feeling well, she really didn't look good, but she made a beautiful dinner. Nestor showed up late, with expensive tequila and a dozen Cuban cigars. He insisted all the guys go outside and smoke. Jim doesn't touch tobacco so he refused but my brothers went out on the balcony. Soon after my oldest brother Willy came in and said Nestor was running his mouth about all kinds of crazy things, violent things, and he didn't want Mom to hear, *I* should quiet Nestor down.'

She frowned.

'You handled Nestor better than anyone,' I said.

'I was the only one willing to confront him and he never got hostile with me. Maybe because I'm a girl and I was nice to him even when he was a wild little kid.'

'So you went to talk to Nestor.'

'He was smoking this gigantic cigar, making all this stinky smoke. I told him to blow it the other way, then I said stop talking trash. He said, "I'm not talking trash, Anita, I'm talking *real*." Then he gave this bizarre smile and he said, "It's kind of a Christian thing." I said what do you mean and he said, "Hanging dudes up and letting them bleed is making 'em like Jesus, right? That's what I did, Anita, I didn't have no nails but I tied up a dude and cut him and made him bleed."

'It made me sick. I told him to shut up, he was grossing me out and if he couldn't behave himself he should leave. He kept going on about what he'd done, like it was really important for him to talk about it. He stayed on the Christ thing, saying he was like Judas, got twenty pieces of silver to do the job. Then he said, "But he was no Jesus, he was the Devil in a little white kid's body, so I did a good thing." I said what are you *talking* about and he said the dude he hung up was some little white kid who killed another little white kid. Then he pulled something out of his pocket and showed it to me. It was an I.D. card from Chaderjian, just like Nestor's but with another kid's picture on it.'

'Troy Turner.'

'That was the name on the badge. I said you could get that anywhere. Nestor went nuts, said, "I did it, I did it! Hung the dude up and made him bleed, look him up on your computer, smart girl, there's gotta be something there."'

A tremor ran down the center of Anita Moss's throat. 'He'd made me sick to my stomach. Mom had cooked this beautiful dinner, all her beautiful food and I felt like it was all coming up. I yanked the cigar out of Nestor's mouth and ground it out with my foot. Then I told him to shut up, I meant it, and went back inside. Nestor left and didn't return, which was fine with everyone. That night, trying to sleep, I couldn't stop thinking about that kid's picture on the badge. He looked so *young.* Even with Nestor's always bragging and lying, he freaked me out. 'Cause of the details.'

'What details?' said Milo.

'He insisted on telling me how he did it. How he'd followed that little boy for days. "Hunted the dude like a rabbit." He learned Troy Turner's routine, finally cornered him in a supply room off the gym.'

Her face crumpled. 'Talking about it *now* makes me sick. Nestor said he hit him in the face to subdue him. Then, he ...' She gulped again. 'That night, after Jim fell asleep, I got out of bed and went on the computer and plugged in Troy Turner's name. Found a short article in the *Times* and a longer one from a paper near Chaderjian. What they both said matched everything Nestor told me. Maybe Nestor didn't do it, maybe he just heard about it and got that badge somehow.'

I said, 'Knowing Nestor, you believe he could've done it.'

'He was proud of it!'

'Nestor said he'd been paid to kill other boys,' said Milo. 'Did he mention any other names?'

She shook her head. 'Troy Turner was the only one he wanted to talk about. Like that had been a real big accomplishment for him.'

'Because Troy was notorious?' I said.

She nodded. 'He said that. "Dude thought he was a stone killer but I killed his ass."'

'Did he say how much he'd been paid?'

Anita Moss shook her head. Lowered her eyes. 'I came to hate Nestor, but talking about him like this ...'

'Did Nestor ever talk about who paid him, ma'am?'

She kept her head down, spoke softly. 'All he said

was that it was a white guy and the reason was Turner had killed a baby.'

'Did he give you any details about this white guy?' said Milo.

'No, just that. I told the exact same thing to that counselor. When he didn't call back, I phoned the police. No one cared.'

Her lips folded inward. She shook her head back and forth.

'That boy,' she said. 'That picture. He looked so *young*.'

23

Milo and I sat in a rear booth of a coffee shop on Vermont just north of Wilshire, drinking Cokes, waiting for Ramparts Detective Philip Krug. Krug had been in his car when we reached him and he welcomed the opportunity for lunchtime company.

The locale was his choice, a big, bright, half-empty place with puce-colored vinyl booths, cloudy windows, and the outward profile of a toy rocket ship.

He was twenty minutes late and I used the time to raise the issues Allison had brought up.

Milo said, 'The premeditation thing's interesting, but I don't see where it takes us. Rand wanting to feel less guilty by blaming Lara could be important. If he tried it on Malley. What do you think about Nestor's bragging?'

'Sounds authentic. He knew all the details,' I said.

'I was thinking about the white guy hiring him.'

'Revenge hit. It fits.'

He looked at his Timex.

I said, 'Troy bragged, too, when I interviewed him in jail. Said he had plans to be rich.'

'You're thinking he had hit-man fantasies, too?'

'I don't see him planning for the Ivy League. Maybe he saw Kristal as career practice.'

'Goddamn little *savages*. What do you *do* with them?'

Phil Krug was a compact man in his forties with thin red hair and a copper-wire mustache so thick it extended farther than his crushed nose. He wore a gray suit with a navy shirt and a pale blue tie. The waitress knew him and said 'The usual?' before he had a chance to sit down.

Krug nodded at her and unbuttoned his suit jacket. 'Nice to meet you guys. Tell Elise what you're having.'

We ordered burgers. The waitress said, 'Phil orders his with blue cheese.'

Krug said, 'That's "the usual."'

Milo said, 'Sure.'

Nonconformity seemed impolitic. I said, 'Ditto.'

In between bites of cheese-slathered ground chuck on an undistinguished bun, Krug discussed the little he'd learned about Nestor Almedeira's murder. Unknown assailant, no leads, granules of heroin on the dirt near the body.

A single head-shot, close proximity, through-and-through temple wound, coroner's guess was a .38, no bullet recovered and no casing, so the killer had picked up or used a revolver.

I side-glanced at Milo. Expressionless.

'Lafayette Park,' he said.

Krug wiped cheese from his mustache. 'Let me tell you about Lafayette Park. Coupla months ago I got called for jury duty, civil case, they hear them over at the courthouse on Commonwealth, which is right near the park. I knew I'd be disqualified but I had to show up and wait and do all that good citizen stuff. Lunch break comes and the clerk reads off this prepared statement telling all the jurors where to eat. Then she goes into this speech about never going into Lafayette Park, even during the day. We're talking a courthouse yards away swarming with law enforcement, and they're saying don't step foot inside.'

'That bad,' I said.

'It sure was for our boy Nestor,' said Krug. 'So what's the connection to West L.A.?'

Milo told him about Rand Duchay and Troy Turner's murders, but left out Lara Malley's suicide and the similarities between the shootings.

'I remember that one, snatched little baby,' said Krug. 'Depressing, glad it wasn't mine. So maybe Nestor was the hit boy on Turner, huh?'

'He claimed he was to his sister.'

'She never mentioned that to me.'

'She told C.Y.A. right after Nestor bragged about it, got no interest, phoned Ramparts, same deal.'

'She probably talked to some clerk,' said Krug. 'We don't always get the sharpest knives in the drawer ... they do that, the idiots. Brag. How many you solve that way? Plenty, right?'

'Plenty,' said Milo.

'So what are you thinking, someone went on a revenge kick and hit the other baby killer? With all those years in between? What's it been, ten?'

'Eight,' said Milo.

'Long time,' said Krug.

'It's a problem, Phil, but there're no other leads.'

'I've been figuring Nestor as your basic dope thing. Patrol officers I.D.'d him as a bottom-feeder with a bad disposition, he was working Lafayette and MacArthur and the streets.'

'Bottom-feeder user?'

Krug pantomimed a bellpull. 'Bingo. His arms and legs were full of tracks and there was dope in his blood. You know what it's like when they get to that point. They're just selling to stay healthy.'

Milo nodded. 'How much heroin was in him?'

Krug said, 'Don't remember the numbers, but it was enough to get him high. The way I figure, being numbed out made him easier to kill. They found a knife on him but it never got out of his pocket.'

'The killer feeds him, then does him?' said Milo.

'Or Nestor fed himself and ran into bad luck. If I was out to get a guy like Nestor, that's how I'd do it. And a guy like Nestor would have enemies.'

'Bad disposition.'

'The worst,' said Krug, 'but we never picked up any specific street talk on who he pissed off.'

'Where was he living?' said Milo.

'Dump on Shatto, pay by the week. You could

go there but you'd find nothing. Nestor's total belongings fit into one box and there was nothing interesting. Maybe the coroner still has it but you know the storage problems at the crypt. My guess is it got tossed.'

'Nestor's sister said he showed her Turner's I.D.'

'It wasn't in his stuff.'

'What was?'

'Clothes, needles, spoons, crappy clothing.'

'Anyone at his crib have anything to say?'

'You're kidding, right?' said Krug. 'We're talking transients and a clerk who does the blind-dumb-deaf bit.'

Krug took a bite of his burger. 'Excellent, huh? One thing the French are good for is cheese … anyway, whatever bragging Nestor might've done in the past, his crowing days were over.'

He reached in his pocket and brought out a post-mortem shot of a hollow-cheeked visage. Matted hair, sallow complexion, death-glazed eyes bottomed by gray pouches. Patchy facial hair came across as a gray skin rash.

Like his sister, Nestor Almedeira had a round face. Bad living had wiped out any other resemblance to her.

I motioned for the picture and took a closer look. Nestor had been the baby of the family, but he looked ten years older than Anita. His head had been tilted by the morgue photographer to give a view of the entrance wound. Left temple, black-and-ruby hole sharpened by stellate skin shredding and framed by a pointillist ring of powder.

Milo said, 'Was he sitting when he was shot?'

'Right on the park bench,' said Krug. 'Your kiddie killer was sitting, too?'

'Maybe in a car. Anything happening on the case, Phil?'

'You're about it,' said Krug, finishing his burger and wiping his lips. 'Be sure to let me know if you learn anything. Be nice to close this one, even if no one else gives a shit.'

'No family agitation,' said Milo.

'You met the sister. She thinks Nestor was scum. Family wasn't making any moves to claim the body, coroner had to keep bugging them. Finally, one of the brothers paid for the mortuary to pick it up.'

Krug waved and the waitress brought the check and placed it in the center of the table. He took some time cleaning his mustache, pulled a steel toothpick from his shirt pocket and worked it around his gum line.

'So.' He smiled.

Milo picked up the check.

Krug said, 'You made my day,' and sauntered out.

When the waitress came by for payment, Milo said, 'We'll have coffee.'

She glanced disapprovingly at the completed bill. 'I'll have to re-total.'

Milo handed her a wad of bills. 'Keep it.' She

flipped through the money and winked. 'On the house.'

As she returned to the counter, he said, 'If Malley was the white man who paid Nestor to hit Troy Turner, Nestor was an obstacle that had to be cleared up. On the other hand, Nestor had a big mouth, and for all those years at C.Y.A. he never gave Malley up.'

'Because he wanted to get out,' I said. 'But once he was free – and stoned – his inhibitions dropped. He bragged to Anita, so there's a good chance he talked to other people. The problem is, they were probably people who didn't care.'

'Other junkies and losers,' he said. 'To them he'd be just another fool shooting off his mouth. Anita did care and tried to report it and everyone shined her on.'

Milo pulled on his upper lip. 'Another proud moment for the department. . . . Nestor's crime scene sounds a lot like Rand's. And Lara's. Okay, that makes Malley suspect-of-the-week.'

'There's another unnatural death we should think about. Jane Hannabee was killed a few months after Troy. When I interviewed her she predicted Troy's death. Said his notoriety would make him a desirable target. From what Anita said, that's exactly how Nestor saw him.'

'You think Hannabee figured out who paid to kill Troy?'

'Or she was eliminated out of revenge because she spawned Troy,' I said.

'You destroy my family, I destroy you. Man, that's cold.'

'So is shooting your own wife six months after she's lost her only child and faking it as suicide.'

His forehead creased. 'Hannabee wasn't shot.'

'Neither was Troy,' I said. 'Because Troy was behind bars and with all of C.Y.A.'s problems, they keep firearms out. Shooting someone in a homeless encampment in the middle of the night would be possible but extremely reckless. Hannabee's murder was so stealthy it wasn't discovered for hours. She was pulled out of her sleeping bag, cut, slid back in, rewrapped in plastic.'

'You're saying signature doesn't matter to Malley.'

'He's not governed by a structured compulsion because his goal isn't sexual satisfaction. His goal is housecleaning. Whatever gets the job done.'

'Alex, if Malley's really done all these people, he's still a serial killer. Guess Rand's grandmother's the lucky one, dying of disease.'

The coffee arrived. The waitress set Milo's mug down with exquisite caution, leaned over and flashed a triangle of freckled chest. Tight wrinkles tugged at her cleavage. She lingered for a second before straightening.

'Anything else?' she said with a song in her voice.

'Nope, we're fine, Elise.'

'You're very kind,' she said.

'So they tell me.'

*

We headed back to West L.A., taking Sixth again. Milo slowed to glance at Lafayette Park. Trees, lawns, benches, a few men sitting, a couple of others walking. The courthouse on Commonwealth loomed. Who'd have thought so much threat resided in empty, green space.

He said, 'Anyone approaching the campgrounds where Malley lives from either direction on Soledad would be spotted easily. There's nowhere to hide on the road, so forget surveillance. Not that surveillance would tell me anything. Doesn't sound as if Malley's gonna go pub-crawling and blab to lowlife friends.'

He rubbed his face and made an abrupt lane shift that evoked frenzied honks. 'Yeah, yeah,' he muttered.

The honker's Toyota whipped in front of us. On the rear bumper was a *War Is Not the Answer* sticker.

Milo growled. 'It got rid of slavery in America and Nazis in Germany.'

I said, 'If Malley's still active in the drug trade, he might leave the campsite periodically.'

'Unless I can watch him, how the hell do I find that out?'

'Maybe his boss is more aware of his comings and goings than she let on.'

'Bunny the stuntwoman? Think there's more than a work relationship, there? I sensed something personal going on.'

'Maybe. She made a point about not keeping tabs

on Malley. Which was an answer to a question you didn't ask.'

'The lady protesting too much?' he said. 'If she is Barnett's love-interest, questioning her further is only going to alert him. I'm gonna call the coroner about Nestor's belongings, check out his dump on Shatto despite what Krug said. Anita was right about Krug. He doesn't give a shit. I also know a Ramparts uniform who might be able to turn me on to some street junkies, maybe I'll get lucky and find out Nestor blabbed to someone else. Better check into Jane Hannabee's death, too. Big-time fun, huh?'

'Can you handle more complication?'

'What doesn't kill me, makes me stronger.'

'If Malley's anger extends to everyone he perceives as having been on the boys' side, and killing Rand rekindled his rage, the Daneys could be in jeopardy. If Malley was outside Rand's window that night, he could've been spying on them as well.'

He thought about that. 'Yeah, they should probably be warned, but it's tricky. What if they go over to Malley's place and try to talk things out? Being all spiritual and positive about basic human goodness and all that. If we're right about what happened to Rand, heartfelt discussion with Cowboy Barnett is not a prescription for longevity.'

'Warn them not to have contact with him,' I said.

'Think I can compete with God?'

'Good point,' I said. 'Cherish, especially, might try

to talk things out. She fancies herself a therapist.'

'God bless the God-pushers. You like feel-good religion, Alex? Inherent blessedness of the human spirit, eternal forgiveness, the certainty of an afterlife where all is bright and airy?'

'Everyone needs comfort.'

He laughed angrily. 'Give me that *old*-time religion, bro. And I ain't talking rousing hymns and babbling in tongues. My childhood was nuns who smacked my hands raw and priests stoked by guilt and hellfire and blood sacrifice.'

'Blood sacrifice sells movies,' I said.

'Sells entire civilizations.'

'Optimism's for wimps?'

'Hey, it's great if you can swallow it,' he said. 'Blind Faith 101.'

After dropping me back at my place, Milo leaned out the passenger window. 'Has my resolute negativity brought you down? Because there's something you can do for me while I'm up to my neck in Nestorania.'

'Sure.'

'How about *you* warn the Daneys? Be psychologically sensitive and hold back if you sense they're gonna do something stupid. And as long as we're putting out warnings, what about the boys' lawyers – talk about getting on Malley's wrong side. Remember their names?'

'Sydney Weider for Troy, Lauritz Montez for Rand.'

'That just rolled off your tongue. The case stayed with you.'

'Until Rand called, I thought I'd forgotten about it.'

'So much for optimism, pal. Anyway, feel free to schmooze with them, too. I hate talking to lawyers.'

24

Monday, I called the Daneys' home. No one answered, so I turned to Sydney Weider and Lauritz Montez.

Weider was no longer at the Public Defender's and I found no home or office listing for her. Lauritz Montez was still a P.D. but he'd moved uptown to the Beverly Hills office.

He answered his own extension, just the way he'd done years ago. This time, my name evoked silence. When I asked him if he'd heard about Rand, he said, 'Oh . . . you're the psychologist. No, what about him?'

'He was murdered.'

'Shit,' he said. 'When?'

'Nine days ago.'

His voice went flat as lawyer's wariness took over: 'You didn't call just to inform me.'

'I'd like to talk to you. Could we meet?'

'What about?'

'It would be better in person,' I said.

'I see . . . when were you thinking?'

'Sooner's better than later.'

'Okay . . . what is it now, four-thirty, I've got paperwork but I need to eat. Know where the Bagel Bin is on Little Santa Monica?'

'I'll find it.'

'Bet you will. Five sharp.'

The place was New Age Deli: glass cases of smoked fish and meat and all the right salads, but the stainless-steel/vinyl ambience was autopsy room. Maybe that was honest; lots of creatures had died to feed the early-dinner throng.

I arrived on time but Lauritz Montez was already at the counter ordering. I hung back and let him finish.

His hair was now completely gray but remained long and ponytailed. The same waxed mustache fanned across his bony face; the chin fuzz was gone. He wore a wrinkled cream linen suit, a pink button-down shirt, and a bottle-green bow tie. Two-tone olive suede and brown leather wingtips graced narrow feet; the left shoe tapped the floor rapidly.

He paid, got an order slip, turned, nodded.

'You look pretty much the same,' he said, motioning me toward the single open table.

'So do you.'

'Thanks for lying.'

We sat and he began arranging the salt and pepper shakers and the sugar bowl into a tight little triangle. 'I did some checking and found out Rand's a West L.A. homicide case but no one will tell me anything. You must be wired right into the cops.'

'I'm consulting on the case.'

'Who's the detective?'

238

'Milo Sturgis.'

'Don't know him.' He studied me. 'Still a prosecution groupie, huh? How long was Rand out of
custody before he got killed?'

'Three days.'

'Jesus. How'd it happen?'

'He was shot in the head and dumped near the
405 North in Bel Air.'

'Sounds like an execution.'

'It does.'

'Any physical evidence?' he said.

'You'd have to ask Detective Sturgis.'

'Such discretion. What do you want from me?'

A kid in a paper hat and an apron brought his
order. Sliced pumpernickel bagel, baked salmon,
sides of coleslaw and baked beans, Styrofoam cup
of tea.

I said, 'There are no real suspects, but there is a
hypothesis. And speaking of discretion –'

'Yeah, yeah, sure. So you work full time for the
other side?'

'The other side?'

'The righteous bunch that sits on the other side of
the courtroom. Are you a resident prosecution expert
or just a freelance?'

'I do occasional consultations.'

'Have Freud, will travel?' He lined up his utensils
perfectly parallel to his plate. Removed a sugar packet
from the bowl and squared a folded corner before
slipping it back in. 'What's the hypothesis?'

I said, 'They're looking at Kristal Malley's father.'

He said, 'That guy. Always thought he hated my guts. You really think he'd be that nuts?'

'Can't say.'

'Isn't it your job to say when people are nuts?'

'Don't know Malley well enough to diagnose,' I said. 'Never met him during my evaluation and haven't spoken to him since. How about you?'

He stroked his mustache. 'Only time I ever saw him in person was at the sentencing.'

'But you feel he hated your guts.'

'I don't feel, I know. That day in court, I was up at the bench doing my thing, returned to the defense table and caught him glaring at me. I ignored it but kept getting that itchy feeling at the back of my neck. I waited until the D.A. starting blabbing before I turned around, figuring Malley's attention would be shifted. His eyes were still on me. Let me tell you, if they were guns, I wouldn't be here.'

'He owns real guns,' I said.

'So do I,' said Lauritz. He flicked his bow tie. 'Surprised?'

'Should I be?'

'I'm a bleeding heart subversive.' His mustache lifting was the sole indication he'd smiled. 'But as long as the law says I can own bang-bangs, I will.'

'Self-defense?'

'My dad was military and the one thing we did together was blast away defenseless animals.' He massaged his left eyebrow. 'I was actually good enough to qualify for my college team.'

'Have you been threatened because of your work?' I said.

'Nothing explicit, but it's an edgy job so I stay on the edge.' He removed another packet, smoothed its edges, passed it from hand to hand.

'Law begets order,' he said. 'And a shitload of *dis*-order. I stopped fooling myself a long time ago. I'm part of the system so I triple-lock my doors at night.'

'Did Malley ever do more than glare at you?'

'No, but it was a heavy-duty glare. *Serious* rage. I didn't blame the guy. His kid was dead, the system's set up to be us-them and I was them. He didn't scare me and I'm not scared now. Why should I be? All this time's passed and he never made a move on me. Do the cops seriously think he killed Rand?'

'It's just a —'

'I know, hypothesis.' He wiped salt grains from the top of the shaker. 'I suppose you know Troy Turner was murdered, too.'

I nodded.

'Think there's a connection?' he said.

'Troy was killed a month into his sentence,' I said.

'And this is eight years later. Yeah, if I was Malley and wanted to do the revenge bit, I'd have finished the job quickly. It's something I thought about when I heard about Turner's death. I got concerned for Rand, called his warden and asked for a special watch. The jerk said he'd look into it. Definitely bullshitting me.'

'When you called were you thinking about Barnett Malley?'

'Maybe,' he said. 'But even in general terms, I was thinking Rand would make a good trophy for some testosterone-laced sociopath out to make his rep.' He looked down at his food but didn't touch it. 'Anyway, I appreciate the warning, but if I got freaked out about every victim's family member going after me I'd be a basket case.'

He held his hands out, palms up, steady. 'See, no anxiety.'

Just compulsively organized table items.

I said, 'You're in Beverly Hills now. Must be a different level of offenders.'

'B.H. is more than just celebrity shoplifters. We handle a lot of West Hollywood's felony cases, so, no, I'm not sleeping at the wheel.'

'Didn't mean to imply you were.'

He took a long time assembling a salmon and cream cheese sandwich. Picked out capers one by one and imbedded them around the outer edge of the bagel's whitened, bottom half. Inspecting his handiwork, he closed the sandwich but didn't eat.

I said, 'How much contact did you have with Rand after he went away?'

'I called him a couple of times,' said Montez. 'Then I moved on. Why?'

'He phoned me the day he died, said he wanted to

242

talk about Kristal but wouldn't give details over the phone. We made an appointment and I showed up but he didn't. A few hours later, he was found — dead. Any idea what could've been on his mind?'

He played with the sandwich on his plate, nudging it with his thumb until it sat dead center. When he looked up, his jaw was taut. 'This isn't really about warning me, is it? It's about pumping me for information.'

'It's both,' I said.

'Right.'

'We're not in an adversarial position, Mr Montez.'

'I'm a lawyer,' he said. 'In my world everything's adversarial.'

'Fine, but now we're on the same side.'

'Which is?'

'Getting some justice for Rand.'

'By locking his killer up?'

'Wouldn't that be a good start?' I said.

'In your world,' he said.

'Not in yours?'

'You want to know something?' he said. 'If the cops do find whoever shot Rand and the P.D.'s office gets the case, I'd be happy to take it.'

'Even if the shooter turns out to be Barnett Malley?'

'If Malley accepted me, I'd do my best to keep his ass out of prison.'

'Pretty detached,' I said.

'Survival skills go beyond guns,' said Montez.

243

'When you represented Rand, did you sense he was holding back about anything?'

'He was holding back about *everything*. Wouldn't communicate with me, basically he played mute. No matter how many times I told him I was on his side. It could've been frustrating but the script had already been written. I never got a chance to bring in my own shrink because of the plea deal. Sure, I would've liked to know what was going on in that kid's head. Which I didn't get from your report. That was a masterpiece of omission. All you said was that he was stupid.'

'He wasn't bright,' I said, 'but there was plenty going on in his head. I thought he felt remorse and I said so. I doubt your expert would've come up with any profound abstractions.'

'Just a dumb kid? Bad seed?'

I said nothing.

'Yeah, I sensed remorse, too,' he said. 'Unlike his compadre. Now *that* one was a piece of work. Evil little bugger, if Rand hadn't gotten involved with him, his life could've turned out a whole lot different.'

'Troy was the main killer,' I said. 'But Rand admitted hitting Kristal.'

'Rand was a dumb, passive follower who hooked up with a cold little sociopath. In a trial, I would've emphasized the follower angle. But like I said, nothing would've mattered.'

'The script.'

'Exactly.'

'Who wrote it?'

'The system,' he said. 'You don't murder a cute little white kid and walk away.' His hand brushed over his butter knife. Adjusted the angle of the handle. 'Weider claimed she wanted to mount a team defense. I was so green I bought it. That tells you something about the system, doesn't it? One year out of law school and Rand got me as his one-man army.' He waved a finger. 'Justice for all.'

'Why'd she change her mind?'

'Because all she wanted to do was pump me for information. Once we got to court, she was going to pull a switcheroo and dump all over my client. Her prelim motions emphasized Rand's size and strength, she had all this expert research data showing low I.Q. sociopaths were more likely to turn violent. If it had gone to trial, Turner would've been morphed into some frail little dupe who'd been physically intimidated by Rand. Anyway, we were spared all that. The case went down easy.'

'Not for the Malleys,' I said.

He showed me his palm. 'I can't think in those terms. And if Barnett Malley doesn't understand that, I'm ready for him. Nice seeing you again, Doctor.'

I stood and asked if he knew where I could find Sydney Weider.

'Going to warn her, too?'

'And pump her for info.'

Montez pulled out a pair of sunglasses, held the lenses up and used them as mirrors. One end of his bow tie had drooped lower than its counterpart. He frowned and righted it.

'You can probably find her,' he said, 'on the tennis court or the golf course or sipping a Cosmopolitan on the country club terrace.'

'Which country club?'

'I was speaking metaphorically. I have no idea if she belongs to any club but it wouldn't surprise me. Sydney was rich then, so she's probably richer now.'

'Rich girl playing at the law?' I said.

'Good insight, you must be a psychologist. The first time you met Sydney she'd be sure to let you know where she was coming from. Swinging the Gucci purse, letting drop all the relevant data in machine-gun monologue. Like you were a student and she was teaching Introductory Sydney.'

'She talked about her money?'

'About her daddy the film honcho, her husband the film honcho, all the industry parties she was "compelled" to attend. The sons at Harvard-West-lake, the house in Brentwood, the weekend place in Malibu, the Beemer and the Porsche on alternate days.' He mimed a finger-down-the throat gag.

'When did she leave the P.D.'s office?' I said.

'Not long after the Malley case closed, as a matter of fact.'

'How soon after?'

'Maybe a month, I don't know.'

'Think it had anything to do with the case?'

'Maybe indirectly. Her name got into the paper

and soon after she got a fat private practice offer from Stavros Menas.'

'Mouthpiece of the high and mighty,' I said.

'You've got that right. What Menas does is more P.R. than criminal defense. Which makes him the perfect L.A. guy. *He* alternates between a Bentley and an Aston Martin.'

'Does she still work for him? She's got no office listing.'

'That's 'cause she *never* worked for him,' he said. 'The way I heard it, she changed her mind and retired to a life of leisure.'

'Why?'

He glanced down at his food. 'Couldn't tell you.'

'Burnout?'

'Sydney didn't feel deeply enough to burn out. She probably just got bored. With all her money there was no reason for her put up with all the shit. When I first heard she quit, I figured she was going to try to get a movie deal out of the case. But it didn't happen.'

'You figured because her husband's a film exec?'

'Because she's like that. Manipulative, out for herself. She'd fly to Aspen for the weekend on a private jet, be at work Monday in a Chanel suit and try to sound convincing about fighting for justice for some dude from Compton. By lunchtime, she'd be dropping names about who sat next to her at The Palm.' He laughed. 'I'd like to think she's not real happy, but she probably is.'

'Did you hear any specific rumors about a movie deal?' I said.

'I do know that she wrangled to get the case.'

'How?'

'By kissing up to the boss. The way it works at the P.D. is whoever's top of the list gets the next client. Unless the boss handpicks someone for a specific case. I know for a fact that Sydney wasn't next up on Troy Turner because the guy who was told me he'd been bumped. He wasn't bitching, he had no stomach for high-profile bullshit. The way he phrased it was "The bitch did me a favor."'

'Was she qualified?'

Montez clicked his teeth together. 'I'd like to say no, but yeah, she was smart enough. By that time she had three, four years under her belt and her win-loss record was as good as anyone's.'

'Three or four years out of school?' I said. 'I remember her as older.'

'She was older. After she passed the bar she got married, did the mommy bit, waited until the kids were older.' He wiped his mouth and folded his napkin. 'When you see her, give my regards.'

'I will.'

'I was kidding.'

I phoned Milo's desk from the car. He was out and I asked for Detective Binchy.

Sean said, 'Hey, Dr Delaware.'

'Could you get me an unlisted address?'

'I don't know, Doc, it's kind of against regulations.'

'Milo asked me to talk to this person, so in a sense I'm a police surrogate.'

'A surrogate . . . okay. I guess. You're not going to shoot anyone, are you?'

'Not unless they piss me off.'

Silence.

He said, 'Ha. Okay, hold on.'

Lauritz Montez's rant about Sydney Weider's lifestyle had cited houses in Brentwood and Malibu but maybe that had been metaphorical, too. Or, she'd defied his rich-get-richer expectations and downsized.

Her listed residence was a smallish, single-story ranch house on La Cumbre Del Mar, on the western edge of Pacific Palisades. Sunny street cooled by Pacific currents, seven-figure ocean view, but by no means palatial. Splintering redwood siding striped the white stucco front. Half-dead sago palms and droopy ferns backed a flat lawn spiked with crabgrass. A shaggy old blue-leafed eucalyptus created gray litter on the grass. The driveway was occupied by a dented, gray Nissan Pathfinder filthy with gull shit.

As I walked to the door, I could smell the Pacific, hear the slow breathing of rustling tide. No one answered my knock or two bell pushes. A young woman across the street opened her door and observed me. When I faced her, she went back inside.

I waited awhile longer, took out a business card, wrote a note on the back asking Sydney Weider to call me, and dropped it in the mail slot. As I returned to my car, she came walking up the block.

She had on green sweats and white sneakers and dark glasses, walked with a stiff gait that threw her hip out at an odd angle. Her hair was chopped short and she'd let it go white. She was still thin but her body looked soft and loose-jointed and ungainly.

I stepped out to the breezeway in front of her house. She saw me and stopped short.

I waved.

She didn't react.

I stepped toward her and smiled. She thrust her arms in front of her torso in a sad, useless defensive move. Like someone who'd seen too many martial arts movies.

'Ms Weider –'

'What do you want?' Her lawyer's voice was gone, tightened by fear-laden shrillness.

'Alex Delaware. I worked on the Malley –'

'Who are you?'

I repeated my name.

She stepped closer. Her lips fluttered and her chin quaked. 'Go away!'

'Could we just talk for a minute? Rand Duchay's been murdered. I'm working with the police on the case and if you could spare –'

'A minute about what?' Ratatat.

'Who might've killed Rand. He was shot last –'

'How would I know?' she yelled.

'Ms Weider,' I said, 'I don't want to alarm you, but it might involve your personal safety.'

She clawed the air with one hand. The other was balled tight, flat against her flank. 'What are you talking about? What the hell are you talking about?'

'It's possible –'

'Go away go the fuck away!' Shaking her head frantically, as if ridding it of noise.

'Ms Weider –'

Her mouth gaped. No sound for a second, then she was screaming.

A gull harmonized. The same neighbor from across the street stepped out.

Sydney Weider screamed louder.

I left.

25

The haunted look in Sydney Weider's eyes stayed with me during the drive back home.

I went to my office and played Search Engine Poker. Thirty hits came up for 'Sydney Weider' but only one was related to her work on *People v. Turner and Duchay.* A paragraph in the *Western Legal Journal,* dated a month prior to the final hearing, speculating about the ramifications for juvenile justice.

Weider had been quoted predicting there'd be plenty of 'ground-breaking consequences.' No words of wisdom from Lauritz Montez. Either he'd declined to comment or no one had asked his opinion.

The remaining citations preceded Weider's assignment to the P.D. by years. An obituary for Weider's father listed him as Gunnar Weider, a producer of low-budget horror flicks and, later, episodic TV. Sydney was listed as his only survivor and as the wife of Martin Boestling, a CAA film agent.

The *Times* used to run a social page before political correctness took over. I logged onto the archives and found notice, twenty-eight years ago, of the Weider-Boestling nuptials. The Beverly Hills Hotel, Sydney had been twenty-three, her groom, two years older. Big wedding, lots of Faces in attendance.

I plugged in Boestling's name. A few years after marrying Sydney he had left CAA for ICM, then William Morris. After that, he took a business affairs post at Miramax, where he'd stayed until a year before the Malley murder, when he resigned to start MBP Ltd., his own production company.

According to the press release in *Variety,* the new firm's emphasis would be on 'quality, moderately budgeted feature films.' The only MBP credits I could find were three made-for-TV cheapies, including a remake of a sitcom that had been stale in its first incarnation.

Lauritz Montez had talked about a script. Had there been a real one and had Boestling gone out on his own to peddle it?

To my mind, the Malley case had nothing to offer cinematically – no happy ending, no redemption, no character development – but what did I know?

Maybe it would've worked as a quickie cable stinker. I searched some more. As far as I could tell, no one, Martin Boestling included, had done the project.

The other hits were mentions of Sydney and Martin at fund-raisers for the predictable causes: Santa Monica Mountains Conservation League, Save the Bay, The Women's Wellness Place, Citizen's Initiative for Gun Control, The Greater L.A. Zoo Association.

The single photo I found showed the couple at a Women's Wellness benefit. Weider looked the way

I remembered her from eight years ago: sleek, blond, haute coutured. Martin Boestling was dark, stocky, pitched forward like an attack dog.

She'd always been a fast talker but now her cool, deliberative demeanor had given way to manic speech patterns and ragged fear. From private jets and a Porsche/Beemer combo to a bird-splotched Nissan.

Did only one car in the driveway mean Boestling was away at work? Or was Weider living alone?

I phoned Binchy. Now he was out, but Milo was in.

I recounted the talk with Montez, the welcome I'd received from Weider, her house, her car.

'Sounds like an unhappy woman,' he said.

'Jumpy woman and I made her jumpier. Scared the hell out of her.'

'Maybe she doesn't want to be reminded of her former life. Getting poorer can do that to you. Not that I'm weeping, she's still living in the Palisades.'

I said, 'Can you find out if she and Boestling split up?'

'Why?'

'Her getting poorer. And I got the feeling she lived alone.'

'So?'

'Her reaction was bizarre.'

'Hold on.' He went off the line, came back several minutes later.

'Yeah, they're divorced. Filed seven years ago

and closed three years after that. That's as much as I can get without driving downtown. Three years of drawn-out legal battle couldn't be fun and maybe she didn't get what she wanted. Now here's my show-and-tell: Went over to Nestor Almedeira's dump on Shatto. All the roaches you can stomp. Like Krug said, no one remembers Nestor ever existing. After some prodding, the clerk thought *maybe* Nestor *sometimes* hung out with another junkie named Spanky, but he had no idea what Spanky's real name was. Male white, twenty-five to forty-five, tall, dark hair and mustache. Possibly.'

'Possibly?'

'The hair *coulda* been dark blond or maybe reddish or reddish brown. The mustache *coulda* been a beard. Clerk's about five-two, so I'm figuring anyone would look tall to him. At eight a.m. his breath reeked of booze, so don't buy stock on his advice. Nestor's belongings are nowhere to be found. I asked around about Krug and he's got a rep as a lazy guy. I'd bet he never bothered to go through Nestor's treasures, gave the other junkies in the place time to do the vulture bit on Nestor's dope kit, whatever else they figured they could use or sell. The rest probably got tossed.'

'Including Troy Turner's prison I.D.,' I said. 'No street value in that. Or maybe Nestor carried it on him and the killer took it as a souvenir.'

'If the motive was hushing Nestor, that's a real good bet. Wouldn't it be nice if I could get a warrant for Cowboy Barnett's cabin and the damn thing's sitting in a drawer? Next item: Jane Hannabee. Central can't seem to find her murder book, one of the D's who worked the case is dead and the other moved to Portland, Oregon. I'm waiting for his callback. I did manage to locate the coroner's report on Hannabee, they're supposed to be faxing it any minute. Last but not least, I background-checked the old stunt gal, Bunny MacIntyre. She's an upright citizen, has owned the campsite for twenty-four years. Anyway, that's my life. Suggestions?'

'With no dramatic leads, I'd follow up on Sydney Weider.'

'Back to her? Why such a big deal?'

'You had to be there,' I said. 'The way she went from wary to panicked. Also, she angled for the case eight years ago and Montez voiced a half-joking suspicion that she and Boestling wanted to make a movie about it. I know none of that ties together, but she twanged my antennae.'

'You wanna talk to the ex, it's fine with me. What about the Daneys? How'd they react to being warned?'

'They weren't in.'

'Okay,' he said. 'Let's do this: You give the Daneys another try and – ah, here's the coroner's fax on Hannabee falling through the slot ... looks like lots of paper, let me check it out, if anything interesting comes up, I'll call you.'

*

I made two more attempts at the Daney residence. The phone kept ringing.

No machine. Considering all the foster kids they cared for, that seemed odd.

At a quarter to six, I called Allison at her office.

'One more patient, then I'm free,' she said. 'Want to do something different?'

'Like what?'

'How about bowling?'

'Didn't know you bowled.'

'I don't,' she said. 'That's why it's different.'

We drove out to Culver City Champion Lanes. The place was dark and black-lit, throbbing with dance music, and crowded with skinny, young, hair-gelled types who looked like reality show rejects. Lots of drinking and laughing and ass-grabbing, twelve-pound balls guttering, a few clackering hits.

Every lane taken.

'Studio night,' said the pouch-eyed, middle-aged attendant. 'Metro Pictures has a deal with us. They toss the slaves a perk once a month. We make out good on booze.' He eyed the cocktail lounge on the alley's north end.

'Who are the slaves?' said Allison.

'Messengers, gofers, assistant directors, assistants to assistant directors.' He smirked. 'The *industry*.'

'How long does it last?' I said.

'Another hour.'

'Want to wait?' I asked Allison.

'Sure,' she said. 'Let's play that machine where you try to fish out cool prizes.'

I spent five bucks moving a flimsy robotic claw around a pile of twenty-cent toys, trying in vain to snag a treasure. Finally a tiny pink fleece troll-like thing with a dyspeptic smile managed to get an arm caught in a pincer.

Allison said 'How cute,' dropped it in her purse, and touched her lips to mine. Then we entered the lounge and took a booth at the back. Red-felt walls, moldy carpeting so thin I could feel rough cement underneath. This far from the lanes, the technopop was reduced to a cardiac throb. Allison ordered a tuna sandwich and a gin and tonic and I had a beer.

She said, 'What mischief have you been up to?'

I caught her up.

'The eight-year lag stayed in my mind,' she said. 'How about this: The fact that Rand was being released set something off in Malley. Does he use amphetamines or coke?'

'Don't know.'

'If he does, that could prime his rage further. He'd know about Rand's release, right?'

'At least thirty days before,' I said. 'So life stress made him do it?'

'We see it all the time with substance abuse patients. People fighting impulses and bad habits and doing fine. Then something hits them and they backslide.'

Murder as a bad habit. Sometimes it boiled down to that.

26

Monday night, I slept at Allison's. She had six Tuesday patients and I left just before eight. During the drive home, I tried the Daneys' house again. Still no answer.

Family vacation with the foster kids? Home-schooling meant their schedule was flexible, so maybe.

Or had they encountered something non-recreational?

I drove through Brentwood and into Bel Air, turned off Sunset onto Beverly Glen. Passing the road that leads up to my house, I continued north into the Valley.

Galton Street was peaceful, a guy watering his lawn, a couple of kids chasing each other, birds flittering. The noise from the freeway was a chronic, distant throat-clearing. I came to a stop half a block up from the Daney property. The redwood gate was shut and the fence blocked out everything but a peak of roofline.

I recalled how crowded the lot had been by three buildings. No room for parking, any vehicles would have to be out on the street. Drew Daney's white Jeep wasn't in sight. I had no idea what Cherish drove.

I nudged the Seville forward, searched for a black truck or anything else that seemed wrong. A dark pickup was parked two houses up.

Black? No, dark blue. Longer than Barnett Malley's truck, with an extra seat, twenty-inch tires and chrome rims.

Plenty of trucks in the Valley.

I came to a stop ten feet from the gate, was about to turn off the engine when a small, beige car pulled away from the curb across the street and raced past with as much pep as four cold cylinders would allow.

Toyota Corolla, lots of dents and pocks, a few Bondo patches on the doors. I caught a split-second glimpse of the driver.

Long-haired blond woman, both hands gripping the wheel. Cherish Daney's eyes were fierce.

She drove to the corner, came to a rolling stop, turned right, sped off.

A bit of a head start but four cylinders wouldn't be much challenge.

Morning traffic was thin and I picked her up easily, hurrying west on Vanowen. Using a slow-moving camper as a shield, I kept my eye on the little car's sagging bumper as it approached the Ventura Freeway East.

She chugged up the on-ramp, lost momentum climbing, and slowed. I pulled ahead of the camper, drove to the bottom of the ramp, and waited until she made it over the hump. If a cop saw me, I'd have some explaining to do.

But no cops in sight. Very few people in sight. The Corolla finally disappeared from view and I shot forward.

Cherish Daney merged nervously into the slow lane, swerved a bit as she switched to the center. One hand to her ear; talking on a cell phone. She needed a half mile to build up to seventy-five miles per, maintained that speed on the route through North Hollywood, past Burbank and into Glendale, where she exited at Brand Boulevard.

Maybe this was nothing more than a shopping trip at the Galleria and I'd feel foolish.

No, the mall wasn't open this early. The look I'd seen on her face said she wasn't thinking about bargains.

I stayed two vehicles behind the Corolla on Brand and drove south.

Past the Galleria. One mile, two, two and a quarter.

Suddenly, without signaling, Cherish Daney yanked the Corolla's wheel and bumped up into the parking lot of a gravel-roofed coffee shop called Patty's Place. A banner on the window promised *Breakfast Special: Best Huevos Rancheros in Town!* Below that: *Dip Into Our Never-Empty Coffeepot! Our Hotcakes Are Flappelicious!*

Despite all that culinary temptation, Glendale appeared skeptical – only three other vehicles sat in the wide, sunny lot.

Two compacts. A black pickup.

Cherish pulled up alongside the truck. Before she got out, Barnett Malley was at her side. He had on the same outfit I'd seen at his cabin plus a wide-brimmed leather hat. Yellow gray hair streamed over his collar. His thumbs were hooked in his belt and his long legs bowed.

Cowboy Buckaroo.

Cherish Daney was all city girl: fitted yellow top, black pants, high-heeled black sandals. Her white blond hair, loose in the car, was now pinned in a chignon.

The two of them moved toward one another, seemed about to touch, stopped just short of contact. Without exchanging a word, they walked toward the restaurant, in perfect step. When Malley held the door open for Cherish, she glided past him without hesitation.

Used to it.

They stayed in there just short of an hour and when they left he held her elbow. My diagonal watch-spot afforded a clear view of Patty's Place, but I was too far away to make out facial expressions.

Barnett Malley held Cherish's car door open, waited until she got behind the wheel before entering the black pickup. She drove away, continued south on Brand, and he followed soon after. I was third in the convoy, hanging a block behind.

They drove to a Best Western near Chevy Chase

Boulevard. Through the motel's glass facade two levels of rooms were visible above a bright aqua pool.

Barnett Malley went in and Cherish Daney waited in her car. Seven minutes passed before she got out of the Corolla, glanced around, tamped her hair. The Seville was one of many cars in the motel lot and this time I was close enough to pick up nuance.

Tight face. She licked her lips repeatedly. Glancing at her watch, she patted her hair again, tugged at her blouse, ran a finger across her lower lip. Inspecting the digit, she rubbed it against a trouser leg. Then she locked her car, took a deep breath, threw back her shoulders, and marched grimly toward the motel's entrance.

Thinking about sins of the flesh? Or had the concept lost its punch?

She reemerged alone forty-five minutes later. Still tense, slightly hunched, the way she'd been the first time I'd met her. Arms clamped close to her body. Racewalking to the Corolla, she backed out, sped away.

I let her go and waited.

Malley appeared after nine minutes. His hat was in his hand, his walk was loose and easy, and he smoked a long, thin cigar.

I followed him onto the 134 West. A mile or so later, he switched to the 5 North; when he got on Cal 14 twenty miles later, I lowered my speed and put a couple of eighteen-wheelers between us. He was pushing eighty-five and the next twenty-three miles were consumed like fast food. When he got off at the Crown Valley exit, I kept going, took the next exit, got back on the freeway, and headed back toward L.A.

Like Milo had said: This was his turf, nowhere to hide.

I was home by one p.m. My cell calls to Milo's house had been answered by his machine. He wasn't at his desk.

Allison would be working for another couple of hours. The plan was we'd get together at five, maybe see a movie. I fed the fish, tried to relax, got on the phone again.

Milo said, 'Hey.'

'Malley does leave his house,' I said. 'All he needs is a bit of motivation.'

I told him what I'd seen.

He said, 'This changes everything.'

27

At two p.m. Milo strode through the front door that I'd left open. Grabbing an orange juice carton, he said, 'I need fresh air.' We went down to the pond.

'I was trying to be well-adjusted,' he said. 'As in sniff the petunias. Rick was off so we went walking in Franklin Canyon, then grabbed some brunch at Urth Café. All the beautiful folks, and me for contrast.' He touched his gut. 'Whole grain waffles – kind of takes the fun out of overeating.'

He tipped the juice carton to his lips.

I said, 'Sorry to spoil your leisure.'

'What leisure? Rick got called to stitch up a kid who fell out of a tree and the whole time I was thinking about the case and faking mellow.' He tossed food pellets at the water, muttered, 'Come to Uncle Milo.' The koi swarmed and splashed. 'Nice to be appreciated.'

He gulped until the juice was gone, kneeled and picked a few leaves out of the mondo grass that rims the pond rocks. Ground them to dust between his fingers before sitting down. 'Malley and Cherish doing the nasty. Good old reliable human frailty.'

'It fits what Allison said about the Daneys not communicating well. With Cherish's skepticism about the black truck. She was downplaying Barnett as a suspect.'

'Diverting attention from her boyfriend,' he said. 'How do you think the two of them got together?'

'Had to be something related to Kristal.'

'They were on opposite sides of the aisle.'

'Love is strange,' I said.

'What, they passed each other in the hallway and clicked? From everything we've heard, Malley despised anyone on the defense team.'

'Apparently anyone but Cherish.'

He scratched his nose. 'Think it's been going on for eight years?'

'It's not brand new,' I said. 'They were comfortable with each other.'

'Good old Cherish, woman of the cloth. Meanwhile the cowboy's cherishing *her* in some sleazy motel.'

'It was actually a pretty nice place,' I said. 'AAA certification, swimming pool –'

'Yeah, yeah, and water beds that bounce to the rhythm of misbegotten passion. What is it with these religious types, Alex?'

'There're plenty of decent religious folk doing good works. Some people are attracted to religion because they're struggling with forbidden impulses.'

'And others see it as a way to make a buck. How much does the county pay to take care of foster kids?'

'It used to be five, six hundred a month per ward.'

'Not a way to get rich,' he said.

'Five hundred times eight kids is four thousand a month,' I said. 'Which wouldn't be chump change to a divinity school dropout. Especially if it was supplemented by other income.'

'Daney's other jobs. What'd he call them – nonprofits. He runs around to churches while wifey does some motel-schooling.'

'Plus, they might be getting supplementary fees. I'm not versed in the welfare regs, but there could be a homeschooling allowance. Or extra money to take care of kids with A.D.D.'

'So they could be raking in decent dough.' He rolled his jaw. 'Okay, Cherish and Malley are a love connection. What does that say about the murders, if anything?'

'The only thing I can think of is that Troy had three visits before he was killed. One from his mother, two from the Daneys. Theoretically, Cherish could've made contact with Nestor Almedeira.'

He put down the bag of fish food. Loosened a shirt button, slipped his hand under the fabric, rubbed his chest.

'You okay?' I said.

He turned toward me. 'Reverend Blondie acting as Malley's emissary to arrange the hit? She poses as a thirteen-year-old's spiritual support and sets him up to be cut like a hog? Jesus, that would make her a four-plus monster.'

'It's a hypothetical. It's just as logical to assume Barnett knew Nestor from the drug trade.'

'And Cherish is just a plain old adulteress.' Another chest rub.

I said, 'Itch?'

'Self-administered cardiac massage. If Cherish and Malley didn't hook up during the six months it took for the boys to be sentenced, when would they have the opportunity?'

'They used to live pretty close to each other.'

'What, a chance meeting at Kmart? One look at Cherish and Barnett goes from enraged dad to lover boy?'

I shrugged.

'Okay, let's put that aside and think about the next body: Lara. That could still be what we theorized – Malley blamed her for Kristal, their marriage was falling apart. But toss in a new girlfriend and you beef up the motivation. Wonder if there was any life insurance out on Lara.'

'If there was Malley didn't use it to finance the good life.'

He jotted in his pad. Picked up the bag and tossed more pellets to the fish.

I said, 'The new girlfriend wouldn't have to be Cherish.'

'Barnett's a ladies' man?'

'He looked pretty jaunty exiting the motel and you felt there was chemistry between him and Bunny MacIntyre. Cherish, on the other hand, seemed pretty tense.'

'The cowboy's a player,' he said. 'Sure, why not.

MacIntyre's crack about not keeping tabs on his comings and goings was gratuitous bullshit. You saw the layout there. He drives his truck through the trees and she's not gonna notice? Next d.b.: Hannabee. Though I'm still not convinced she's part of it. Cherish making it with Barnett spin that in any new way?'

'The Daneys were providing support to Jane during the trial. Cherish might have known where Jane slept at night.'

'The fixer, again. Okay, for argument's sake, Cherish is a charter member of the Very Bad Girls Club. What does that say about the case the city's actually paying me to work on?'

'It points to another setup,' I said. 'If Cherish is dirty, Drew was telling the truth about Rand hearing noises under the window, seeing the black truck. Barnett Malley went after Rand because Rand knew something about Kristal's murder that threatened him. Something Rand told Cherish because he trusted her.'

'She goes and rats him out to her boyfriend. What would Rand know, eight years later, that threatened Barnett?'

'The obvious answer is Barnett had something to do with his daughter's death.'

'The boys beat and choked Kristal, no one debates it. Why would Barnett have had anything to do with that?'

'Don't know.' The two of us sat staring at the fish

that I'd put in the pond because I thought it would help me relax. Once in a while, it does.

Milo said, 'Even if there is something to that, why eight years later. What are we talking about? One of those recovered memories?'

'Or a young man making sense of something that had confused him for years. Rand could have come to it long before his release, but who would he tell? The prison staff was unresponsive, they never even followed through on teaching him to read. His only confidante was Cherish. But his trust was misplaced.'

'Once he was out, he thought of someone else,' he said. 'A guy with a Ph.D. who'd been fair and warmhearted and objective.'

He looked at me. 'The meeting he never made. Maybe that was the point of killing him.'

We walked back up to the house, popped a couple of beers, and sat at the kitchen table.

Milo finished his bottle and put it aside. 'How's this for ugly, Alex: What if Cherish and Malley didn't meet at the trial. They were getting it on *before* Kristal's murder. She wanted to marry him, needed to get rid of the competition. As in his existing family. So she found herself a little killer for hire and started with the offspring.'

'Cherish paid Troy to murder Kristal?'

'She knew Troy from before. She's into psychology, went looking for a cold-eyed little psychopath and found one. Troy told you he was gonna get rich.

Cherish strung him along by promising to get him out early, with some pot of gold at the end of the goddamn rainbow. Instead, she got him bumped. Six months later, phase two: Lara goes down.'

'Lara was shot with Barnett's gun,' I said.

'So either Barnett did her himself, or Cherish, being his girl, had ample opportunity to pick the thirty-eight out of the collection. My bet's on them both being dirty. Remember how pissed Nina Balquist was about Barnett cremating Lara instead of holding a funeral? Why be in such a rush unless you had something to hide? And if Barnett abducted Rand, he'd have to know what was going on.'

'The only problem is,' I said, 'it's eight years later and Cherish and Barnett aren't married. Why would they go through all that for the sake of an illicit affair?'

'Hey,' he said, 'relationships are tough. The passion cooled, whatever.'

'Not enough to stop the motel trysts.'

'Okay, they discovered that hot-bedding it is more fun than going domestic. Or Cherish doesn't want to give up all that county money and the income from Drew's moonlighting. Divorce usually hurts the woman, right? Look at Weider. Cherish keeps the house, the kids, the holy-roller persona, and has her fun on the side.'

'Could be,' I said. 'It sure fits with Allison's guess about premeditation. Troy was paid and brought Rand along as backup. Rand wasn't in on it from the beginning, but somehow he figured it out.'

He rubbed his face hard. 'Still, it's a tough one, pinning Kristal on Barnett. Here's a guy waited years to be a father. He went so far as to borrow money for fertility treatment.'

'Nina Balquin suspects the money was never used for treatment.'

'Barnett and Lara must've done something, Alex. They had a kid. If Cherish is Little Miss Hitler I can see her trying to eliminate the other chimp's baby. But Barnett doing his own kid for her?'

I heard the question but my brain was somewhere else. His mention of Nina Balquin had flashed me back to her house. The rear wall.

I said, 'Oh, my.'

'What?'

'Kristal's baby photo. Her eyes. Big and brown. Barnett's blue-eyed and so was Lara. I remember seeing her in court, she had huge, gray-blue eyes that she was constantly wiping because she was always tearing up. Two brown-eyed parents can produce a light-eyed child but the opposite's only remotely possible, through spontaneous mutation.'

'Kristal wasn't the cowboy's kid?'

'It wasn't until six years after they borrowed the money that Lara got pregnant.'

'Lara got herself a different kind of fertility treatment.' His smile was vicious. 'Both of them fooling around but Lara left evidence and Barnett couldn't handle it.'

'Barnett dominated and isolated Lara,' I said.

'Another reason for her to go looking for love elsewhere. Any husband would be enraged by his wife having another man's baby, but someone like Barnett — asocial, bad temper, gun freak — would've been especially prone to a violent reaction. He punished Lara twice. First by eliminating the fruit of her infidelity, and when that didn't put out the fire in his belly, he got rid of her. And if he needed encouragement, Cherish was there to egg him on.'

'Pillow talk,' he said. '"I've got a solution, honey." Yeah, makes sense, doesn't it?'

'It makes stomach-crawling sense.'

'So how did Rand figure it out?' he said.

'He must've recalled something from the time of the murder,' I said. 'Spotting Cherish with Troy shortly before the abduction. Or seeing Cherish and Barnett together. For all we know one of them went to the mall that day to make sure everything went down smoothly. Or Barnett's involvement was more direct. Lara said she only turned her head for a minute before Kristal disappeared. What if someone Kristal knew and trusted lured her away?'

'Come to Daddy,' he said. 'Then Daddy hands her over to Troy and Rand. Jesus ... and Rand came to all this spontaneously, after years of sitting behind bars?'

'Rand knew he was behind bars because he'd been part of something terrible. Isolation and maturation got him ruminating. He began to assess his share of the guilt. To try to feel like a good person. Barnett and Cherish had no reason to worry about him because he hadn't been in on the plot. Until he began talking to Cherish. Troy, on the other hand, was an immediate threat, and was eliminated quickly.'

'What's the name of that seminary she went to?'

'Fulton.'

'Any idea where it is?'

I shook my head. 'According to Cherish, Troy's buried there. She convinced the dean to donate a plot.'

'Oh, I'll bet she did.' He laughed and cracked his knuckles. 'Cherish is a word I use to descri-ibe . . .'

'On the other hand,' I said.

'What?'

'It's a great house of cards, but all we really know about Cherish is that she's sleeping with Barnett Malley.'

His face got hard. 'So we find out more. That's what life's all about, right? Broadening one's horizons.'

28

I walked Milo to his car. 'Was Kristal buried or cremated?'

'You're thinking DNA.'

'If you ever get a sample from Barnett, it would answer the paternity question.'

'Let me tell you about DNA in the real world. We used to send stuff to the sheriff's crime lab, but they're backlogged till the next millennium, and they can't get the county to pay for the latest equipment so they sometimes have to send stuff out. Department recently contracted with Orchid Cellmark in New Jersey, but it's a priority game: sexual homicides first, then rapes, then crimes against minors. The quickest you can get something back is two to four months. And that's after you get your requisition approved by the pencil pushers. In this case, if Kristal was buried, I'd need an exhumation order, which could take even longer than DNA analysis, especially with no consent from the surviving relative. Going that route would also mean letting Malley know he's under suspicion.'

'Just a thought,' I said.

'On the other hand, maybe the coroner kept something from Kristal's autopsy and I can send that to Cellmark ... I'll head over to the crypt, see if they can find something. Ciao.'

I returned to the house in order to educate myself about foster child reimbursement in L.A County, and to learn more about Fulton Seminary.

The first assignment was easy. I phoned Olivia Brickerman at home. She's a professor in the Department of Social Work at the gracious old university across town, a battle-toughened veteran of the ground war that is California's social services system, the widow of a chess grandmaster, a frizzy-haired fireplug old enough to be my mother and one of the smartest people I've ever encountered.

She said, 'You only call when you want something.'

'I'm a bad son.'

She laughed, finished with a gasp.

'You okay?' I said.

'As if you care.'

'Of course –'

'I'm on my feet, darling. Which is a positive sign, considering. So how's it going with Dr Snow White?'

'Allison?'

'The ivory skin, the black hair, the soft voice, all that gorgeous? The analogy's obvious. Am I overstepping boundaries, here?'

'Allison's fine.'

'And Robin?'

'Robin's in Seattle,' I said.

'Which begs the question.'

'Last time I spoke to her she was doing well, Olivia.'

'So that's it?' she said.

I didn't answer.

'I'm a terminal yenta, Alex. Slap my wrist. Seattle, eh? The Genius and I used to go there. Before the computers and the coffee. The Genius could row a boat pretty well, we used to go out on Lake Washington . . . Robin still with Voice-boy?'

'Yup.'

'Mr Tra La La,' she said. 'She brought him by a few months ago for Sunday brunch. Unlike other people who can't find the time.'

'Allison and I took you to dinner at the Bel-Air.'

'Don't quibble. What I'm getting to is that I didn't care for him.'

'Robin does.'

'He's too quiet,' she went on. 'Aloof, if you ask me. Not that anyone has.'

'I'm always open to your wisdom, Olivia.'

'Ha. So what do you need to know?'

'How well does the state pay for foster care?'

'I was hoping for more of a challenge, darling. First of all, the state mandates foster care and sets up basic fees but each county distributes the funds. Counties also have the discretion to supplement the state. Traditionally, they've been tight with the purse strings. The rates vary but not much. Which county?'

'L.A.'

'The other thing you need to know is that, officially, foster parents aren't paid. A stipulated amount is allocated per child and the custodial adult gets to disburse it.'

'Meaning foster parents are paid,' I said.

'Exactly. The basic rate varies with the age of the child. Four hundred twenty-five a month to five ninety-seven. Older kids get more.'

'I'd assume just the opposite,' I said. 'Babies require more care.'

'You'd be thinking logically, darling. This is the government. No doubt some number cruncher set up a formula based on pounds of flesh.'

'What age group gets the max?'

'Over fifteen. Twelve through fourteen gets five forty-six, and so on down to the babies who get four twenty-five. Which doesn't pay for a lot of formula and diapers. Quite often it's family members who take the kid in and apply as kinship guardians. That what we're talking about, here?'

'No, these are nonrelatives,' I said. 'Can the basic rate be supplemented?'

'Wards with special needs get extra payments. Right now the max is a hundred seventy a month. That's through Children's Services, but there are other bureaucracies you can tap if you know how to play with paper. The system's full of goodies.'

'Would kids with A.D.D. be considered special needs?'

'Absolutely. It's a recognized disability. Is there

any point in my asking you why you want to know all this?'

'There are some people under suspicion,' I said. 'Milo wants to know if they're getting rich at the public trough.'

'Dear Milo. Has he lost weight?'

'Maybe a little.'

'Meaning no. Well, I haven't either. You know what I say to constitutionally skinny people? Go away. Anyway, if you want you can give me names of these suspicious individuals, when I get back to the office I'll run them through the computer.'

'Drew – probably Andrew – and Cherish Daney.' I spelled the surname and thanked her.

'Cherish as in I love you?'

'As in.'

'Except maybe she loves money too much?'

'It's a possibility.'

'Anything else you want to tell me?'

'How many foster children can one family care for?'

'Six.'

'These people have eight.'

'Then they're being naughty. Not that anyone's likely to notice. There's a shortage of what the state feels are decent homes and very few caseworkers to look into details. If nothing terrible happens, no one pays attention.'

'What comprises a decent home?' I said.

'Two parents, middle class would be great but not

necessary. No felony record. Optimally, someone's working but there's also someone in the home to supervise.'

'The Daneys fit the bill on all accounts,' I said. 'Does the state pay for homeschooling?'

'Same answer: It depends on how you fill out the forms. There's a clothing allowance, a supplemental clothing allowance, all sorts of health care surcharges that can be tapped. What's up, darling? Another one of those scams?'

'It's complicated, Olivia.'

She sighed. 'With you it always is.'

Fulton Seminary offered one degree, a master of divinity. According to its website, the school's curriculum emphasized 'scriptural, ministerial, and public service aspects of professional evangelical training.' Students were allowed a range of 'intellectual concentrations' including Christian Leadership, Evangelical Promotion, and Program Supervision.

Several paragraphs were devoted to the school's philosophical underpinnings: God was perfect, faith in Jesus superseded all actions, humans were depraved until saved, worship and service were essential elements of fixing a world in dire need of repair.

The campus sat on three hilly acres on Glendale's northern rim. A fifteen-minute ride to the motel on Chevy Chase.

I scrolled through pages of photos. Small groups of clean-cut, smiling students, rolling lawns, the same glass-fronted sixties building in every shot. No mention of an on-site cemetery.

The faculty numbered seven ministers. The dean was Reverend Doctor Crandall Wascomb, D.Theol., Ph.D., LL.D. Crandall's picture made him out to be around sixty, with a thin face below a high, smooth dome of brow, silver-white hair that covered the top of his ears, and crinkly eyes of the exact same hue as his powder blue jacket.

I called his extension. A woman's taped voice told me Dr Wascomb was out of the office but he really cared about what I had to say. 'Please leave a detailed message of any length and repeat your name and phone number at least once. Thank you and God Bless and have a wonderful day.'

My message was short on details but I did toss in my police affiliation. There was a good chance I'd made it sound more official than it was, but Dr Wascomb's training prepared him for minor transgressions.

Repeating my name and number, I hung up, reflecting on human depravity.

Just after nine p.m., Dr Crandall Wascomb called while I was out with Allison. My service operator said, 'Such a nice man,' then she gave me the number. Different from his office. It was nearly eleven but I phoned anyway and a soft-voiced woman picked up.

'Dr Wascomb, please?'

'May I ask who's calling?'

'Dr Delaware. I'm a psychologist.'

'One second.'

Seconds later, Wascomb came on, greeting me as if we were old friends. His voice was a lively tenor that conjured a younger man. 'Do I understand correctly that you're a police psychologist?'

'I consult to the police, Dr Wascomb.'

'I see. Is this about Baylord Patterman?'

'Pardon?'

A beat. 'Never mind,' he said. 'How can I help you?'

'Sorry to bother you so late, Doctor, but I'd like to talk to you about a Fulton alumna.'

'Alumna. A woman.'

'Cherish Daney.'

Pause. 'Is Cherish all right?'

'So far.'

'So she's not a victim of something terrible,' he said, sounding relieved.

'No. Is there some reason you'd think that?'

'The police aren't generally messengers of hope. Why are you concerned about Cherish?'

'I've been asked to learn about her background –'

'In what context?'

'It's a bit complicated, Dr Wascomb.'

'Well,' he said, 'I certainly can't talk to you over the phone about something complicated.'

'Could we meet face-to-face?'

'To talk about Cherish.'

'Yes.'

'I must tell you, I have nothing but good things to say about Cherish. She was one of our finest students. I can't imagine why the police would want to learn about her background.'

'Why didn't she finish her degree?' I said. *And who's Baylord Patterman?*

'Perhaps,' said Wascomb, 'we should meet.'

'I'll be happy to come to your office.'

'My office calendar's quite full,' he said. 'Let me leaf through my book ... it appears as if I have one opening tomorrow. One p.m., my usual lunch break.'

'That would be fine, Dr Wascomb.'

'I wouldn't mind getting away from campus,' he said. 'But it has to be somewhere close, I've only got forty-five minutes ...'

'I know a place,' I said. 'A bit south of you on Brand. Patty's Place.'

'Patty's Place ... haven't been there in ages. Back when the school was undergoing remodeling I'd sometimes meet there with students – did you know that, sir?'

'No,' I said. 'I just like pancakes.'

Baylord Patterman pulled up five hits on Google. A Burbank-based attorney, he'd been arrested a year ago for running an insurance fraud ring that set up phony traffic accidents. The bust resulted when a fender bender on Riverside Drive turned into an air-bag disaster that killed a five-year-old girl.

284

Patterman, his hired drivers, a couple of crooked chiropractors, and assorted clerical staff were charged with vehicular homicide. Most were pled down to white-collar crimes. Patterman ended up with a conviction for involuntary manslaughter, was disbarred, and sentenced to five years in state prison.

The Fulton Seminary connection appeared in two of the citations: Patterman was the son of a founding trustee of the school and a continuing donor to the cause. Dr Crandall Wascomb was quoted as being 'unaware and appalled' by his benefactor's dark side.

If he was sincere, I felt sorry for him. All those years pushing virtue and he was going to be disappointed again.

29

My week for coffee shops.

Patty's Place smelled of butter and eggs, meat on the grill, pancake batter, the soap-and-water breeze that accompanied a cheery young Latina waitress name-tagged Heather who said, 'Anywhere you like.'

The restaurant was half-filled with serious eaters of retirement age. Big portions, tall glasses, grease on chins. To hell with the food nazis. My presence brought down the median age by a decade. I took a booth with a view of the entrance and Happy Heather brought me a mug of dangerously hot coffee unspoiled by pretentious labeling.

Dr Crandall Wascomb showed up at seven after one, tugging at the knot of his tie and smoothing his white hair. He was short, very thin, wore black-rimmed eyeglasses too wide for his knife-blade face. He had on a brown herringbone sport coat, a white shirt, lighter brown slacks, and tan loafers. His bright blue tie stood out like a nautical spinnaker.

When his eyes found mine I gave a small wave. He came over, shook my hand, sat down.

The hair was shorter and sparser than in his official photo. His smooth dome was scored by parallel lines.

I guessed him at seventy or so. He blended right in with the clientele.

'Thanks for meeting with me, Dr Wascomb.'

'Certainly,' he said. 'Do you have preset notions about evangelical Christians, Dr Delaware?'

'When I judge people it's by behavior not belief.'

'Good for you.' His eyes didn't move. Bluer than in the photo. Or maybe they'd absorbed some of the necktie's intensity. 'I assume you checked into the Baylord Patterman issue.'

'I did.'

'I won't offer excuses but I will explain. Baylord's father was a fine man, it was he who helped us get started. That was thirty-two years ago. I'd come out from Oklahoma City, worked in the petroleum supply business before going back to school. I wanted to make an impact. Gifford Patterman was that rare man of wealth with an open, warm heart. I was naive enough to think the same applied to his son.'

Heather arrived, pad in hand.

Wascomb said, 'It's been a long time since I've been here. Are the flannel cakes still fabulous?'

'They're awesome, sir.'

'Then that's what I'll have.'

'Full stack or half?'

'Full, butter, syrup, jelly, the works.' Wascomb flashed cream-colored dentures. 'Nothing like breakfast in the afternoon to make the day seem young.'

'Something to drink, sir?'

'Hot tea – chamomile if you have it.'

'And you, sir?'

'I'll try the flannel cakes, too.'

'Good choice,' said Heather. 'You're gonna love your meal.'

Wascomb didn't watch her leave. His eyes were on his napkin.

I said, 'Baylord Patterman let you down.'

'He let Fulton down. The investigation into his activities gave us a black eye because we were the largest beneficiary of his filthy lucre. You can imagine the reaction of some of our other major donors.'

'Race to the exit.'

'Stampede,' said Wascomb. 'It hurt. We're a small school, operating on a shoestring budget. I call us the seminary that does more with less. The only reason we're able to survive is that we own the land the school sits on and maintenance costs are just about covered by a good Christian woman's will. Baylord Patterman's grandmother.'

His tea arrived. Pressing his hands together, he bowed his head and uttered a silent grace before sipping.

'Sorry for your problems,' I said.

'Thank you. We're getting our head above water. Which is why I chose to meet you here rather than at the school. I simply can't afford any more bad publicity.'

'I have no intention of giving you any.'

He studied me over his tea. 'Thank you. I'm going

to deal openly with you because I'm an open person. And frankly, there's no longer any privacy. Not in the computer age. But that doesn't mean I can talk freely about a former student without that student's permission. Not without good reason.'

Holding on to his cup, he sat back in the booth.

I said, 'What would be a good reason?'

'Why don't you tell me what you're after?'

'I'm limited in what I can say, too, Dr Wascomb. There are certain details the police keep to themselves.'

'So this is a homicide case?' He smiled at my surprise. 'I took the liberty of researching you, Dr Delaware. Your consultations to the police seem to center on homicide. That shocked me. I can't imagine Cherish involved in anything criminal, let alone homicide. She's a gentle person. As I told you, one of our finest students.'

'But she didn't finish her degree.'

'That,' he said, 'was most unfortunate. But it had nothing to do with her.'

I waited.

Wascomb looked over at the counter. Heather was standing around, talking to the cashier.

'Doctor?' I said.

'Cherish's misfortune was somewhat similar to mine,' said Wascomb. 'Vis-à-vis Baylord Patterman.'

'She had something to do with the accident scandal?'

'No, I was speaking analogously. The Bible issues

repeated exhortations against keeping bad company. Cherish and I failed to heed those warnings, but I was the teacher and she was the student, so I suppose some of her error lies at my door.'

'Cherish got blamed for something a friend did.'

'Cherish was put in an uncomfortable position through no fault of her own.'

Heather brought our food. 'Here it is, guys!'

Wascomb smiled up at her. 'It smells wonderful, dear.'

Her left eyebrow cocked. 'Enjoy.'

He uttered a silent grace, then cut his stack of hotcakes in half, sawing straight through to the bottom. Rotating the plate, he sliced again, then once more until the pile had been sectioned into eighths. Lauritz Montez would approve.

Montez and Wascomb had both chosen to minister to sinners. I supposed they couldn't be blamed for seeking the illusion of an orderly world.

Wascomb ate with such enjoyment that it seemed a shame to interrupt him. I worked on my own plate, finally said, 'Who was Cherish's bad friend?'

He put his fork down. 'This is absolutely necessary for your investigation?'

'I can't answer that until I know, Doctor.'

'Appreciate your honesty.' He wiped his lips, removed his glasses, touched his temples with his fingertips. 'Not a friend. Her husband.'

'Drew Daney.'

Slow nod.

'How'd he get her in trouble?' I said.

'Oh,' said Wascomb, as if the memory made him weary. 'I had reservations about him early on. We're small and chronically short on funds, we need to be selective in who we accept. Our typical student is an honors graduate of a respectable Bible college, trained in the evangelical tradition. Cherish was such an individual. She graduated first in her class from Viola Mercer College in Rochester, New York.'

'And Drew?'

'Drew claimed to have attended a very solid school in Virginia. In truth, he dropped out of high school. That was the extent of his education.'

'He lied on his application.'

'He falsified transcripts.' Wascomb sighed. He pushed his plate away, one-third eaten. 'No doubt you think I'm a gullible fool. Or slipshod. Without sounding overly defensive, I would like to stress that this was an aberration. The vast majority of our graduates are out in the world doing the Lord's work in an exemplary manner.'

'Drew must've been good to fool you.'

He smiled. 'That's very kind, sir. Yes, he did say the right things, seemed well-grounded in Scripture. As it turns out, his religious experience was limited to serving as a counselor at several Christian summer camps.'

'He learned the jargon,' I said.

'Exactly.'

'When did all this come out?'

'Seven and a half years ago.'

Precise memory. Six months after Kristal Malley's murder.

I said, 'What caused you to look into his background?'

'Someone else looked into his background,' said Wascomb. 'A very angry man who claimed that Drew was committing adultery with his wife.' He winced. 'A claim that turned out to be true.'

'Tell me about it.'

He shook his head. Pushed his plate away. 'There are issues of respect, here. For innocent people involved —'

'A half year before you found out about Drew, he and Cherish were involved in a murder case as part of their community service work for Fulton. Counseling a boy who'd killed a toddler. I'm sure you recall that, Dr Wascomb.'

He blinked twice, started to speak, stopped himself.

'Sir?'

'That poor little girl.' His voice had gone hoarse. 'There's more to that? After all this time?'

'One of the boys who murdered Kristal Malley has been murdered himself.'

Wascomb winced. 'Oh, my. Then I suppose I need to be forthright.' He clicked his dentures. 'Drew committed adultery with one of the lawyers on that case. A defense attorney.'

'Sydney Weider.'

Nod. 'It was her husband who barged into my office with medical reports, raving about the school, my incompetence, how could I train a person like that, I was a hypocrite, all "Bible freaks" were nothing but hypocrites.'

He looked away from me. 'I'm afraid I've lost my appetite.'

'Sorry,' I said. But not sorry enough to drop it. 'We're talking about Martin Boestling. A movie producer.'

'A *loud* man. At the time I thought him crass. After some consideration – after the shock wore off – I considered what he'd endured and felt compassion for him. I called him, tried to apologize. He was gracious, as far as that went.'

'What he'd endured,' I said. 'More than adultery.'

He stared.

'You said Boestling brought medical reports. As in lab tests?'

Slow nod. 'His own and his wife's.'

'He'd been infected with something. AIDS?'

'Not that bad,' said Wascomb, 'but bad enough. Gonorrhea. His wife had given it to him and Boestling claimed Drew had given it to her.'

Wascomb shook his head. 'The implication, of course, was promiscuity. I took a closer look at Drew, learned of his lies, and expelled him. We've had no contact since then.'

'And Cherish left with him,' I said. 'Because she was a dutiful wife?'

'Because she was ashamed. As I said, we're a small community.' He fooled with his fork. 'How is Cherish, nowadays? Are they still together?'

'They are.'

'Has Drew repented?'

'I couldn't say.'

'I always hoped she'd find peace ... now you're here asking questions about her.'

'They may come to nothing, sir.'

'Is she ... has she maintained herself as a woman of character, Dr Delaware? Or has Drew's influence polluted her soul?'

If you only knew. I said, 'From what I can tell, she continues to do good works.'

'And him? What's he up to?'

'The same.'

His eyes got flinty. 'There's a lesson for you, Dr Delaware. Judging behavior isn't always sufficient. It's what's beneath the surface that matters.'

'How do you measure that, sir?'

'You don't,' he said. '*We* don't.'

He got up to leave. '*God* does the measuring.'

'One more question, Dr Wascomb. Cherish told me Troy Turner was buried on the grounds of your school.'

He placed a hand on the table, as if needing support. 'That's partially true.'

'How so?'

'Cherish asked me – begged me. We've got a small cemetery in San Bernardino. For faculty and indigent individuals recommended by donors and other trust-worthy people. We view it as a community service.'

'Cherish qualified as a trustworthy person.'

'She still does, Dr Delaware, unless there's something you tell me that suggests otherwise.'

I didn't answer.

He said, 'Affording that boy hallowed ground was compassion for the sinner. After some deliberation I felt it would be appropriate. We provided the boy with a service.'

'Who attended?'

'Cherish and myself and my wife.'

'Not Drew.'

'Drew, as well,' he said. 'He wanted to lead the service. I decided to do it myself.'

'What about Troy's mother?'

'No,' said Wascomb. 'Cherish said she had tried to reach the woman but was unable. I remember the day. Late spring, nice weather, the air was clean. Small coffin, it barely made a sound as they lowered it into the ground.' He placed money on the table.

I said, 'On me.'

'No, I won't hear of it.'

'Split check, then.'

'All right.' He smiled at me.

'Sorry if this was upsetting, Dr Wascomb.'

'No, no, you're doing important work.' He turned to leave, stopped. Touched my shoulder. 'The boy did a terrible thing, Dr Delaware, but you'd never know it to look at that coffin.'

30

Heather came by and eyed Wascomb's uneaten food. 'Do you want a doggy bag?'

'No, thanks.'

She followed Wascomb's slow walk out the door. 'He barely touched his food. Is he okay?'

'He's fine.'

'Is he your dad?'

'No,' I said. I handed her the total plus ten bucks. 'Keep the change.' Big smile.

'Were you working yesterday?'

'Here?' she said. 'I think so. Yeah, yesterday I was here.'

'Working two jobs?'

'Three. Here, KFC after five, and then Thursday and Friday nights I babysit for an emergency room doctor at Glendale Memorial.'

'Tough schedule.'

'That's what my dad says. He keeps bugging me to quit something and have some fun.' She stuck her tongue out. 'I'm saving up for fashion school.'

'Good for you,' I said. 'Yesterday morning, around nine, did you notice a couple who came in for breakfast? She had long blond hair; he was tall and wore a leather cowboy hat.'

'Them,' she said. 'Sure. I served them. I remember him because he reminded me of this actor my dad used to like. Peter . . . Peter something.'

'Fonda?'

'That's it. There's this real old movie my dad watches over and over. It's got Jack Nicholson in it but he's a lot younger and skinnier.'

'*Easy Rider.*'

'Uh huh. Jack and some other guy and the other guy – Peter – they're like biker hippies.' She giggled. 'Peter's kind of a cutie if you go for that retro hippie thing. That's what that guy – the guy with the hat – reminded me of.'

'Retro.'

'Lost in the sixties. His hair was like down his back and his shirt had *snaps* on it. Which gave me an idea for a dress. Cowboy Punk thing.'

'Original.'

'Thanks. How come you're asking about them?'

'I work with the police.'

Her eyes got huge. 'You're a cop?'

'Consultant.'

'Wow,' she said. 'They did something nasty?'

'They're just people we're interested in.'

'Like witnesses?'

'Something like that. Is there anything you remember about them?'

'Not really. They didn't talk much.'

'To each other?'

'To each other or me. I'm a real motormouth, like

you can't tell. I'm always talking to the customers, it makes them feel you're interested in them and it pays off in the tips department. Didn't work with those two, they just sat there, like they were having a fight.'

'They eat?'

'They ordered but only he ate. Bacon and eggs. She asked for a sweet roll and milk but she didn't touch it – like that old guy you were with. I figured there wouldn't be much payoff and I was right. Ten percent tip, which is *old*. She paid.'

'Overhear any conversation?'

'There wasn't any that I saw.'

'Have they been here before?'

'Once before,' she said. 'Last week. Lauren served them. It was dinnertime and I was going off shift.'

'When last week?'

'Let's see.' She pressed a finger to her lower lip. 'Lauren works Tuesdays and Thursdays and Fridays and it wasn't Friday because I'm off Friday and it wasn't Tuesday because she called in sick Tuesday because her boyfriend got tickets to the Jason Mraz concert.' She stopped for breath. 'Had to be Thursday.'

'Around what time?'

'Five-ish. Wow, so this is like an investigation?'

'Uh-huh.'

'You can't tell me what they did?'

'Sorry, Heather.'

'Cool, I understand.'

'So they've only been here twice.'

'That's all I saw.'

'How long have you been working here?'

'Three years, off and on.'

'How'd they act on Thursday?'

'The same. That's how I remember. Lauren said they didn't talk, just sat. He ate, she didn't.'

'Ten percent tip.'

'Eight percent, actually.' She grinned. 'I guess it's my charm.'

I thanked her and gave her another ten.

'Oh, wow, you don't have to,' she said, but she made no effort to return the money. 'If you want I can keep an eye out and if they come in again I'll call you.'

'I was just going to ask.' I handed her my card.

'Psychologist,' she said. 'Like crazy criminals, Hannibal Lecter stuff?'

'It's not always that exciting.'

'My sister went to a psychologist. She was pretty screwed up, had some real bad friends.'

'Did it help her?'

'Not really. But at least she moved out and I don't have to listen to a bunch of yelling.'

'Guess you'd call that partial success,' I said.

'Yeah,' she said absently. As she drifted back to the register, I saw her re-count her money.

I got back on the 134 West, checked for messages when traffic slowed.

One from Olivia Brickerman. I exited the freeway

on Laurel Canyon, drove to Ventura Boulevard, found a spot across the street from an adult motel, and called her office.

'Your Mr and Mrs Daney are pretty good at the paper game,' she said. 'They total about seven grand a month fostering. They've been taking in kids for just over seven years, haven't made any attempt to hide the fact that they're exceeding the limit by two wards. That tells me they're vets who know the system's broke. Mrs Daney has also applied for certification as an educational therapist, which would entitle her to additional treatment money. Generally, that requires some sort of teaching credential but there's been some loosening of the regs due to shortages of providers. This help?'

'Very much. How badly is the system broken?'

'The geniuses in the state legislature just turned down a request for more caseworkers and the counties are already severely shorthanded. Meaning no one checks anything. A couple more things about the Daneys: They always foster teenagers with learning disabilities. What I found really interesting is that all their wards have been females. Which is unusual, there's no shortage of boys in the system.'

'Can foster parents pick and choose age and sex?' I said.

'There's supposed to be mutual consent between the agency and the caregiver. In the best interests of the child.'

'So you can ask for a girl.'

'Alex,' she said, 'right now, if you're white and middle class and don't have a criminal record, you can ask for just about anything and get it.'

I thanked her and asked for a list of the Daneys' wards.

She said, 'All I've been able to find is the last few years. I'll fax it to you soon as I get off. Regards to Allison. I hope I wasn't too cheeky with the Snow White stuff.'

'Not at all,' I said. 'Brilliance has its privileges.'

'You flatter me, darling.'

The only Martin Boestling I found listed in the phone book was a 'confectionery dealer' on Fairfax Avenue. Unlikely, but it was an easy drive over Laurel Canyon.

The Nut House turned out to be a double storefront a block north of the Farmer's Market/Grove complex. The *Parking in Rear* sign kept its promise and I found a space next to a green van with the store's name, address, and website under a giant cashew that resembled an eyeless grub. A locked screen door covered an open delivery arch. I rang the bell and a heavy, kerchiefed woman in her sixties peered out, turned the bolt, and trod back wordlessly toward the front of the store.

The space was one big room lined with bins of candy, coffee, tea, rainbow-hued desiccated things, equally garish jellied morsels, and nuts. At least a dozen varieties of almonds. A sign said *No Peanuts Here, Allergic People Don't Worry.*

The shoppers, all female, strolled the aisles and scooped goodies into green bags rolled from overhead spools. The green-aproned man at the register was mid-fifties, round-shouldered, and stocky with dark wavy hair. His face looked as if it had argued with a wall and lost. His hands were outsized and blocky and he bantered easily with two women checking out. In the Internet photo I'd found, he'd been tuxedoed, arm in arm with Sydney Weider. She'd changed a lot. Martin Boestling hadn't.

I scooped smoked almonds into a bag, waited until the shop was quiet, and approached.

Boestling rang up the sale. 'You'll like these, an Indian family in Oregon does the smoking themselves.'

'Great,' I said, paying. 'Mr Boestling?'

His eyes narrowed. 'Why?'

'I'm looking for a Martin Boestling who used to produce films.'

He transferred the almonds to a paper bag, slid it across the counter, started to turn away.

I showed him my police I.D.

He said, 'Police shrink? What's this all about?'

'I consult to –'

'And now you're at The Nut House. How apropos.' His eyes aimed at the woman behind me in line. 'Next.'

I stepped aside, waited until she checked out.

Martin Boestling said, 'Anything else I can do for you, purchase-wise?'

'It's about Sydney Weider,' I said. 'And Drew Daney.'

His big hands became flesh cudgels. 'What is it *exactly* that you want?'

'A few minutes of your time, Mr Boestling.'

'Why?'

'Daney's the subject of an investigation.'

Silence.

'It could be serious,' I said.

'You want dirt.'

'If you've got any.'

He waved the kerchiefed woman over. 'Magda, take over. An old friend just dropped in.'

We walked up Fairfax, found an unoccupied bus bench, sat down. Martin Boestling had forgotten to remove his apron. Or maybe he hadn't.

He said, 'Sydney was a bitch from hell, he was a fucking bastard, end of story.'

'I know about the gonorrhea.'

'Know how big my dick is, too?'

'If it's relevant I can probably find out.'

He grinned. 'You'd think it *would* be relevant, size mattering and all that. I married Sydney because she was smart and rich and good-looking and loved to screw. Turned out, she was making a fool out of me from the day we tied the knot.'

'Promiscuous.'

'If she had showed restraint, you could've called her promiscuous. Day of the wedding, she screwed one of my so-called friends.' He began ticking his finger. 'The pool boy, the tennis pro, the fish tank guy, bunch of lawyers she worked with. It was only later, after the divorce, that people started to come up and tell me, phony sympathy in their eyes. *Sorry, Marty, we didn't want to make waves.* I could never prove it but I'm convinced she screwed some of her clients, too. You know the kind of clients she worked with?'

'Indigent.'

'Murderers, robbers, scumbags. Think about that: She's keeping long office hours in order to spread her legs for lowlife while I'm hustling to support her in the style to which she'd become accustomed. I hated the industry, stayed with it because I was desperate to impress her. Know where we met?'

'Where?'

'Your investigation didn't carry you that far back? We met at the Palisades Vista Country Club where her family belonged and I was working my way through the U. as a towel jockey. Spritzing rich people with bottled water while they turned like chickens on a spit. Should've known how it was going to be when Sydney left her rich boyfriend in the dining room so she could do me in a cabana. We dated off and on for a while, until I graduated and got a job in the mailroom at CAA and convinced her to marry me.'

I said, 'Was it her idea for you to go into the industry?'

'I had a B.A. in English, which is about as useful

as a second appendix. It sounded interesting and I was good at it. Mostly, I did it for Sydney. I was crazy about her.'

He plucked at his apron. 'Her old man got me the mailroom gig but I earned the right to stay. Worked like a galley slave and took abuse from the worst people you'll ever meet. I produced more than all the Ivy League dilettantes who were doing it for fun, climbed fast, was making serious money while Sydney finished at the U. School-wise she was always smart, graduated summa, took a break to have the kids, then we all moved to Berkeley so she could attend Boalt Law School. I stayed down in L.A., flew up on weekends to be with her and the boys. I had it down to a science, the four p.m. Friday into Oakland to avoid the fog, return late Sunday. The boys turned out good, considering. They both hate her. It didn't take long for the marriage to go sour – we were bored with each other. But no one else's marriage seemed any better so I didn't think anything of it.'

'Until the lab report,' I said.

'The lab report came later. What blew everything up was I caught her doing Daney. In my house, my bed, my robe and slippers on the chair.' He laughed. 'Total cliché. I had a meeting over at Fox TV on a script. The moron in charge cut it short because she heard my demographic wasn't right. Meaning my projects were aimed at I.Q.s higher than that of a rutabaga. I was expecting a longer meeting, brought along the writer, poor schmuck. So I'm out of there in ten minutes, in a not-so-good mood, decided to go home, take a swim and a *shvitz* in the brand-new sauna I put in. When I get home, I hear moaning and groaning from upstairs and go into the master suite – which I just paid a fortune to remodel, let me tell you, our place in Brentwood was state of the art. The door's wide open and Sydney and that pissant are doing the two-headed goat.'

His voice had risen loud enough for passersby to notice. Smoothing his apron, he cracked his knuckles. 'I yell, Sydney opens her eyes. Then she closes them and keeps *going*. I rush over and I'm hitting Daney on the back and neck and *he* wants to get off her but she's got a leg-lock on him. I'm pounding him on the back, his head, anywhere I can land a punch and he's struggling to get free but Sydney still won't let him. Finally she finishes and shoves him off and the bastard grabs his clothes and runs out of there like his nuts are on fire.'

He laughed until his eyes got wet. 'I can laugh at it now. Even feel sorry for the idiot.'

I smiled.

'Mr Subdued Reaction,' he said. 'Remind me not to put you in the audience. Anyway, that's the story.'

'Any idea how long they'd been carrying on?'

'No, because we never talked about it. Sydney locked herself in the bathroom, took a shower, when she came out I was ready to fight. She breezes past, gets in her car and leaves. She stayed out all night, luckily the boys were away at school. I sat there like a lox, waiting for her, finally got myself a room at the Hotel Bel-Air. A few days later, pus started coming out of my dick. But I got her good. Guess how?'

'Something financial.'

'The pre-*nup*. Which *her* old man put in for *her* sake. The deal was she got to keep all the assets she came into the marriage with. Only problem for Sydney was the old man made some real bad investments and emptied her trust fund. Her sole assets were *zippo* leaving only our joint assets. Which wasn't as much as either of us thought because we were living way beyond our means. For me it was no big deal, my dad worked for a living – the nut business. I used to put it down for not being glamorous, till I learned about the industry.'

'Sydney had trouble coping,' I said.

'Sydney was a spoiled bitch who became a lawyer for status and *fulfillment*. After we split, she tried to get herself a private practice job but it didn't work out. Meanwhile, the divorce lawyers are looting whatever's left. Her mother finally died and left her enough to get herself a place in the Palisades along with a small monthly allowance. The zip code's right but it's a dump and she doesn't maintain it. She was always hyper, now I hear she's downright manic.'

He looked to me for confirmation. I said, 'What happened to her private practice job?'

'Ah, that,' said Boestling, smiling. 'Unfortunately, her boss received a copy of that pesky lab report. So did every other serious criminal defense firm in town.

Now, who'd do something so vengeful?' He yawned.

'And you told Daney's seminary about him.'

'I figured I was doing the Lord's work. Thanks for the memories, Doc. Time to get back to real life.'

'You said Daney should have thanked you.'

'Damn straight he should've. I got Sydney and him meetings with some serious people.'

'To make a film?'

'No, to make Polish sausage, yeah a film. A feature, not TV. Sydney made a *big* point of that, her attitude was always I was TV so I was low on the food chain. Her project was going to be *stars* and a substantial *shooting* budget. The two of them thought they had the greatest story ever told. But who did they come to when they wanted references?'

'Was the story the Kristal Malley murder?' I said.

'Yup,' said Boestling. 'Two kids kill another kid and go to jail. Not exactly *Titanic*.'

'Whose idea was it?'

'Can't say for sure, but my bet is Daney was your typical delusional jerk and he infected Sydney.' He snickered. 'Along with other things.'

'You know for a fact that he gave her the clap?'

'Or it was one of the other five thousand dicks she rode. He's the one I saw, so I'm putting a face on it – so to speak.' He shrugged. 'For all I know it was the other kid's lawyer, some Latino guy.'

'Lauritz Montez,' I said. 'She slept with him, too?'

'For sure.'

'How do you –'

'When Sydney first started on the case, she did nothing but bad-mouth Montez. Stupid, no experience, an albatross who was going to drag her down. Then, a couple weeks in, she started taking late meetings with him. *Lots* of late meetings. Working on a joint defense. I bought it until I caught her with that scumbag Daney and finally stopped being the densest moron in the galaxy. The only joint defense going on was when Montez tucked his dick back in his pants.'

I said nothing.

Boestling said, 'Just another waltz down memory lane. Now if you –'

'Did Sydney say anything about the Malley case that you thought was unusual?'

'This is about *that*? After all these years?' he said. 'What's Daney suspected of?'

'Can't get into details. Sorry.'

'One-way conversation.'

'Unfortunately.'

'Well, unfortunately for *you,* all Sydney told *me* was that her client was a murderous little monster and there was no way she was going to get him off. Seen her recently?'

'I tried to talk to her a few days ago. She got very upset –'

'And went nuts on you and started screaming, right?'

'Right.'

'Good old Sydney,' he said. 'Freaking out was

always her technique. In court she was real controlled, but outside, anyone tried to disagree with her she'd just blast out with this wall of Indy 500 noise. At me, the boys, her parents.' He shook his head. 'Amazing what I put up with. My second wife was a different story. Mellow, couldn't be sweeter. Dead in the sack, though. Eventually, I'll find the right combination.'

He got up and headed back toward his store. I walked with him, pressed for more details about the movie.

'Never saw a script. Never got involved directly. Don't forget, I was just a *TV* guy.'

'You were good enough to set up meetings,' I said.

'Exactly.' He scratched his chin. 'I did all kinds of stupid things back then. Had a little substance-abuse problem that clouded my judgment. I'm talking to you in the first place because my sponsor says I need to be honest with the world.'

Same thing Nina Balquin had said. How much of what passed for honesty nowadays was atonement?

I said, 'I appreciate that.'

'I'm doing it for myself,' said Boestling. 'Should've been a lot more selfish when it counted.'

I drove to Beverly Hills and caught Lauritz Montez exiting the court building on Burton and Civic Center. The double-wide briefcase he toted dragged at his right shoulder as he headed for the rear parking lot.

'Mr Montez.'

An eyebrow lifted but he never broke step. I caught up.

'What now?'

'A reliable source tells me you and Sydney had more than a business relationship.'

'And who might that be?'

'Can't say.'

No answer.

I said, 'Tell me about Sydney's movie ambitions.'

'Why would I know anything about that?'

'Funny,' I said. 'You didn't say "what movie?"'

We entered the lot and he walked to a ten-year-old gray Corvette, put his case on the ground. 'You're getting annoying.'

'Judge Laskin's retired but he's got friends. I'm sure the judiciary and the bar association would be thrilled to know how you comported yourself during a major case.'

'Is that a threat?'

'Heaven forbid,' I said. 'Then again, maybe you'd rather file indictment forms in Compton for the next twenty years.'

'You're a real piece of work,' he said, keeping his voice low. 'My money says LAPD has no idea what you're doing.'

I held out my cell phone. 'Speed-dial five.' Which would've connected him to my dentist.

He didn't take it. A Beverly Hills cop drove past us in a brand-new Suburban. One officer, all that curb weight. Gas economy doesn't mean much in 90210.

I pocketed the phone.

Montez said, 'What do you really want?' His voice wavered on the last two words.

'What you know about the movie and anything else you can tell me about Sydney and the Daneys.'

He backed away, positioned himself between the Corvette's scoop-nose and the parking lot wall.

'The Daneys,' he said, smiling coldly. 'Always figured them for your typical Jesus freak hypocrites, and I was right.'

'Right, how?'

'Daney was doing Sydney any way he wanted.'

'How'd you find out?'

'Saw her going down on him in her car. In the parking lot, after dark. Asked her about it the next day and she screamed at me to fuck off and get out of her life.'

'Which parking lot?'

'County jail.'

Same place she'd offered her baby blue BMW for the interview with Jane Hannabee. 'High-risk behavior,' I said.

'That was the thrill for Sydney.'

'So Daney broke the eighth commandment,' I said. 'What made his wife a hypocrite?'

'C'mon,' said Montez. 'She had to know. Sydney and Daney were hooking up all the time, how *couldn't* she know?' He worked his lips as if to spit, wiped his mouth with the back of his hand. 'She rubbed me the wrong way. Psychobabble-spouting airhead. The only one she cared about was Troy, I couldn't get her to even talk to Rand. You really care, you reach out to everyone.'

'Why'd you want her involved?'

'Character reference.'

'Why'd she favor Troy?'

'They both did. Because they knew Troy from before,' he said. 'He was one of their do-gooder projects at 415 City. Which shows you how effective they were.'

'Rand wasn't a project.'

'Rand never got into big-time trouble until he met up with Troy, so he never had the benefit of their wise counsel. Not that it would've made a difference, like I told you.'

'The script.'

'If you don't believe there's a script for everything, you don't deserve that Ph.D.'

'What happened with the real script?'

'Sydney's movie? What do you think? *Nothing* happened. This is L.A.'

'What was the story line?'

'How would I know?'

'Never read it?'

'No way, this was top secret. Don't even know if there was a script.' He pulled out a remote and disarmed the Corvette's alarm. Moving around me, he opened the door.

'What was there?'

He didn't answer.

'Suit yourself,' I said and clicked open my phone.

He said, 'All I saw was a summary, okay? A *treatment* Sydney called it. Only reason I knew about it was I found it in her desk when I was looking for matches.' Tiny smile. 'I like to smoke afterward.'

'You and she got it on at the office?'

'Those cheap government desks are good for something.'

'What did the treatment say?'

'The names were changed but it was basically Kristal Malley. Except in her story, the boys had been manipulated by the kid's father into killing her.'

'What was his motive?'

'It didn't say, we're talking two paragraphs. Sydney came back from the john, saw me reading, tore it out of my hand, and did the old scream bit. I said, "Interesting theory, maybe we can use it for real." She freaked out and kicked my ass. Literally, she kicked me.' He rubbed his rump. 'She had on these pointy pumps, it hurt like hell.'

'So the treatment was written before the case closed.'

'Before the formal sentencing, but everyone knew how it was going to go down.'

I said, 'Whose idea was the deal?'

'Sydney proposed it, Laskin accepted. She lied and told him I'd agreed. I ended up agreeing anyway, because I thought it was the best I could do for Rand.'

'Get the boys started on their sentence and party with co-counsel,' I said.

'It wasn't like that,' he said. 'That night – her desk – was after we'd done the bulk of our work. That's when Sydney and I really started getting it on. Before that, it was only minor stuff. We kept it outside the office.'

'Motels?'

'None of your business.'

'In her car?'

'You want to be a judgmental prick, go ahead. It's no crime to have fun.'

'Fun till she started kicking you.'

'She was insane,' he said, 'but let me tell you. She had her talents.'

31

'Nymphomaniac,' said Milo. 'To use a quaint old term.'

He blew cigar smoke into the air. The way the air felt today, he was cleansing it. 'Not that I'm nostalgic for quaint old terms. Having borne the brunt of such.'

'"Queer" is common parlance now,' I said.

'So's "niggah" if you're Snoop Dogg. Try it on some dude at Main and Sixty-ninth and see how many giggles you get.'

Smoke rings floated upward, wiggled and dissip-ated. We were two blocks from the station, walking slowly, thinking in silence, talking in bursts.

'So everyone's screwing everyone,' he said. 'Literally and otherwise. You think Weider's story line pinning it on Malley was fiction? Or did she and Daney latch onto something eight years ago? Like Malley not being Kristal's father. Like Troy telling Weider that Malley had put him up to it.'

'Montez jokingly suggested to Weider that they use it as a red herring and she freaked out. Maybe that was more than keeping her hot idea under wraps.'

'She's got exculpatory evidence but conceals it.

Because her main goal isn't defending Troy, it's cutting a film deal. Cold. As in what passes for morality in Hollywood.'

I said, 'If Weider needed to rationalize, she could've. Malley pulled the strings but the boys did the actual murder and were going down for a long time, no matter what. She said as much to Marty Boestling. Her advice to Troy would've been keep quiet, I'll get you out of jail quickly and you'll be rich. That would explain his fantasy of wealth.'

'Troy was a streetwise little thug, Alex. Think he'd buy it?'

'He was also a thirteen-year-old with no future,' I said. 'Kids flock to Hollywood every day believing in Rich and Famous. Still, because he was a kid, his patience couldn't be relied on indefinitely. Maybe Troy's death wasn't Malley's doing, after all.'

He bit down on the cigar. Choppy smoke created a jagged halo. Picking a scrap of tobacco from his tongue, he spat and frowned. 'Weider was a P.D.; she'd have known how to connect to a guy like Nestor Almedeira.'

'Maybe so would Daney,' I said. 'Working with disadvantaged youth. He and Cherish *both* visited Troy.'

'Daney was the white guy Nestor talked about, not Malley? Jesus.' Puff puff. 'Yeah, it could go that way as easily as Cherish being Jacqueline the Ripper. Especially 'cause I've got no real evidence for *either* scenario.'

He dropped the cigar, ground it out on the sidewalk, waited until the butt cooled, and pocketed it.

'What a good citizen,' I said.

'Enough dirt in this city. So how would Rand's murder fit with a Weider-Drew thing?'

'Same as with a Cherish-Barnett thing. Rand was never in the loop so he was allowed to live. Somehow, he figured out the truth behind Kristal's death and made himself a target.'

'The truth being Malley's revenge, because he wasn't Kristal's daddy.'

'That seems to be the constant,' I said. 'Any progress on the DNA?'

'Filled out a requisition, waiting to hear from the muck-a-mucks. I'd still like to know how and when Cherish started sleeping with Barnett. But now maybe we know the why: payback for Drew screwing around.'

'Makes sense. The waitress at Patty's said Cherish and Barnett had only been there once before and she's been working there for years. Cherish chose Patty's because she knew it from her seminary days – Wascomb used to meet there with students. But the two of them could have other spots.'

'Their main *spot* was the motel. I'll go by there and see what the clerks have to say.'

'Another possibility,' I said, 'is Cherish snitched Rand out to Drew, not Barnett.'

'She's cheating on Drew. Why would she confide in him?'

'She didn't have to confide, just mention that Rand seemed really nervous, was dropping hints about Troy. Because she suspected that Drew played a role in *Troy's* murder and if she could get him to eliminate Rand, it would save Barnett the trouble.'

'Dutiful girlfriend posing as a dutiful wife,' he said. 'That's manipulation elevated to an art form. Wascomb said she was a spiritual girl.'

'Wascomb hasn't learned the fine points of cynicism.'

He took out another cigar, left it in its plastic wrapper, and rolled it nimbly from finger to finger. Nifty little trick; I'd never seen it before.

'There's another manipulation to think about,' I said. 'Drew's story about the black truck was the reason we started looking seriously at Barnett Malley. But given what we've learned about him, we need to consider that he was playing us.'

'Not afraid of Malley, just wanting to point us in Malley's direction.'

'Unfortunately for Drew, it got us looking closely at him.'

'Three dead kids,' he said. 'Maybe two teams of murderers.'

We turned a corner. 'Alex, now I'm thinking I need to take Jane Hannabee more seriously as a related crime. If Troy told his mommy about the movie and she wanted in, that would've made her a problem for Sydney and Drew.'

'An addict down on her luck,' I said, 'she'd definitely want in.'

'We were saying Cherish coulda known where Jane slept, being Jane's spiritual adviser, but the same applies to Drew.' He jammed his hands in his pockets. 'This is growing like cancer. You ever find out how much the Daneys are sucking from the county tit?'

'Seven thou a month.'

'Not bad for a coupla defrocked mopes.'

I said, 'With some of it illegal. Olivia said no one enforces the regulations but it could be a wedge if you need one. I asked her to fax over the names of all the kids they've fostered. Drew's got a history of falsifying documents. Maybe he's been naughty in other ways.'

'Good thinking. What about Hot Pants Weider? Think I should confront her?'

'Boestling and Montez both said the way she went off at me was her usual approach to conflict. All you've got on her is hearsay adultery and she doesn't practice law, so any threat of disbarment would be empty.'

'I could still embarrass her.'

'After the way Boestling humiliated her I don't imagine there'd be much self-esteem left to threaten.'

'All the more so,' he said. 'Hit her when she's down.'

'You could try it.'

'But you wouldn't.'

'Not now,' I said. 'Too little bang for the buck.'

'Then who's my target?'

'Not who,' I said. 'What. Paperwork.'

I walked him to the lot across the street from the station where he retrieved his unmarked and followed me home. Passing me up at Westwood Boulevard, he got there first.

The fax from Olivia sat in my machine. One page of names and social security numbers, birth dates, periods of foster care.

Twelve girls, between the ages of fourteen and sixteen. Eight were still living with the Daneys. One name was familiar. *Quezada, Valerie.* The restless, resentful girl Cherish had tutored in math. Cherish leading her through the steps, the essence of patience. Moments later, Cherish's tears when she talked about Rand . . .

The list covered only a twenty-five-month period. Olivia's handwritten note at the top said, *This was as far back as I could get. The Geniuses' archival system is a mess. Maybe permanently.*

Milo said, 'Let's start by cross-referencing the four who no longer live with them.'

'To what?'

'Worst-case scenario, for starts.' He phoned the coroner, asked to speak with 'Dave,' and said, 'No, not today, but I'm sure I'll get there eventually. And get me a better mask, next time, I'm no stranger to decomposition but ... yeah, nothing like water damage. Listen Dave, what I need is just a record-check ... yeah, I know, hearing my voice makes your day.'

Five minutes later we got the callback from Coroner's Investigator David O'Reilly: None of the four names matched the crypt's roster of unnatural deaths. Milo phoned the Hall of Records, got the runaround before hooking into county records and the roster of natural deaths.

He put the phone down. 'They all seem to be alive. Our bit of good cheer for the day.'

I thought: They could've died outside of L.A. County. 'What next?'

'Any ideas?'

'You could try to locate them, see if they've got anything to say about the Daneys. I'd focus on these two, who are still minors. Maybe life got better for them and they no longer need fostering. On the other hand ...'

'I like that,' he said. 'Constructive pessimism.'

Olivia gave us a contact at D.C.S. and we had the data by three p.m.

Leticia Maryanne Hollings, seventeen, was still a state ward, living with a 'kinship guardian' – an aunt in Temecula. No one answered the number and Milo filed it for future reference.

Wilfreda Lee Ramos, sixteen, was no longer on

the foster list. Her last known contact was a twenty-five-year-old brother, George Ramos.

Phone listing for him but no address. City of residence was *'L.A., Ca.'* Occupation: *'Student.'* The 825 number made the U. a good bet.

I tried it. Inactive. A phone call to the university registrar revealed two George Ramoses currently enrolled. One was an eighteen-year-old freshman. The other, twenty-six, was a first-year law student, and that was all I could learn.

Milo got on the line, pushed his credentials, couldn't cadge any more out of the clerk. Same thing at the law school office.

We drove to campus, parked on the north end, walked to the school, where Milo bantered with an amiable white-haired secretary who said, 'You just called. Unfortunately, the answer's the same. Privacy regulations.'

'All we want to do is talk to Mr Ramos, ma'am.'

'Ma'am. Just like in a cowboy movie,' she said, smiling. 'I'm sure that's true, Lieutenant, but don't forget where we are. Can you imagine how many of these people would love to file a suit for breach of privacy?'

'Good point,' he said. 'Would it help if I told you Mr Ramos isn't in trouble but his sister could be? I'm sure he'd like to know. Ma'am.'

'Sorry. I wish I could help.'

He relaxed his shoulders. Deliberately, slowly, the way he does when he's struggling to stay patient.

Big smile. He pushed back hair off his forehead and pressed his bulk against the counter. The secretary moved back instinctively.

'Where are the first-year students, right now?'

'They should be out of ... jurisprudence class. Maybe out on the lawn.'

'How many are we talking about?'

'Three hundred seven.'

Milo said, 'Male Hispanic. You guys doing better with your minority admissions or will that narrow it down?'

'He's not real Hispanic-looking,' said the secretary.

Milo gazed at her. She blushed, leaned forward, whispered, 'If someone was real tall, they'd be easy to spot.'

Milo smiled back. 'We talking basketball, here?'

'Maybe a guard.'

Long, slow strides carried George Ramos across the lawn in an awkward but purposeful trajectory. Like a wading bird – an egret – making its way through a marsh. I put him at six-six. Pale and balding and stooped, carrying a stack of books and a laptop. Whatever hair he had left was medium brown and fine and streamed over his ears. He wore a blue V-neck sweater over a white T-shirt, pressed khakis, brown shoes. Tiny-lensed glasses perched above a beak nose. Young Ben Franklin stretched on the rack.

When we stepped in front of him, he blinked a

couple of times and tried to pass us. When Milo said 'Mr Ramos?' he stopped short.

'Yes?'

Badge-flash. 'Do you have a moment to talk about your sister, Wilfreda?'

Behind his glasses, Ramos's brown eyes hardened. His knuckles bulged and whitened. 'You're serious.'

'We are, sir.'

Ramos muttered under his breath.

'Sir?'

'My sister's dead.'

'I'm sorry, sir.'

'What in the world led you to me?'

'We're looking into some foster children and –'

'Lee committed suicide three months ago,' said Ramos. 'That's what everyone called her. *Lee.* If you knew anything about her, you'd know she hated "Wilfreda."'

Milo kept silent.

'She was sixteen,' said Ramos.

Milo said, 'I know, sir.' It's rare for him to have to look up at anyone. He didn't like it.

Ramos said, 'What kind of parents would name someone Wilfreda?'

The three of us found a bench on the west side of the lawn.

George Ramos said, 'What do you want to know?'

'Lee's experiences in foster care.'

'What, a scandal?'

'Maybe something like that.'

'Her experiences,' said Ramos. 'For Lee, foster care was a lot easier than being at home. Her father – my stepfather – is a fascist. Those preachers she lived with didn't give her any supervision. Custom-order for someone like Lee.'

'What do you mean?' said Milo.

'Lee was rebellious in the womb, did her own thing no matter what. She got pregnant when she was in foster care, had an abortion. The coroner told us that after the autopsy. The preachers talked a good case but my feeling is they collected the money and let Lee run wild.'

'Which coroner told you this?'

'Santa Barbara County. Lee was living in Isla Vista, with some dopers, when she . . .' Ramos removed his glasses and rubbed his eyes.

'This was after she got out of foster care,' said Milo.

Ramos nodded. 'The fascist finally allowed her to come home on condition she stick to all his rules. She was home for two days before she ran away. The fascist said she should live with the consequences of her own behavior and my mother has always been totally under his thumb. So no one went looking for Lee. We found out where she'd been staying after she died. Some crash pad in Isla Vista, ten kids living like animals.'

I said, 'The fascist isn't your father but you and Lee had the same last name.'

'We don't. Her name's Monahan. When he got so fed up with her that he made her a ward of the state, he burned her clothes and locked her out and told her she was no longer his daughter. She said fuck you and started calling herself Ramos.'

'Sweet guy,' said Milo.

'Real peach,' said Ramos, cracking his knuckles. 'She phoned me from Isla Vista, wanted me to have her name changed legally. I told her I couldn't do it because she was a minor and she hung up on me.'

I said, '"Ramos" is listed on state documents.'

Ramos laughed. 'The state doesn't know its ass from a crater on the moon. There's little about the system that doesn't need changing.'

Milo said, 'That why you're in law school?'

Ramos stared at him myopically. 'That's a joke, right?'

Milo smiled.

'Sure, I'm breaking my butt for a lifetime of mindless bureaucracy and shitty pay,' said Ramos. He laughed. 'When I get out I'm going corporate.'

We talked to him for another quarter hour. I ended up doing most of the talking because the topic had slid into my bailiwick.

Wilfreda Lee Monahan/Ramos had exhibited severe learning disabilities and a history of disruptive behavior as long as her brother could remember. George Ramos's father had died when he was five and a few years later his mother married a former marine who thought raising kids was a variant of boot camp.

For Lee, adolescence had meant promiscuity, drugs, and mood swings so severe I was willing to bet they resulted from more than substance abuse. By fourteen, she'd made two suicide attempts – overdose cries for help. Cursory attempts at counseling followed, along with a flood of recrimination at home. When her father found her having sex with a boy in her bedroom, he kicked her out.

George Ramos wasn't aware of any notable problems during her six months under the Daneys' care, but he admitted, with downcast eyes, that he had never visited her.

Lee Ramos had left foster care a month before turning sixteen. On her birthday, at midnight, she'd stayed home while her roommates went out to party. Shortly after, she cut her wrists with a rusty box cutter, lay down on a ratty mattress, and quietly bled to death.

32

Talking about his sister had left George Ramos pale and worn.

Milo apologized for intruding. Ramos said, 'You're just doing your job,' and stared at the grass.

I said, 'Did you have any contact with the Daneys?'

'I called them once after Lee died. Don't ask me why. Maybe I thought they'd care.'

'They didn't?'

'I spoke to the wife – Charity, Chastity, something like that –'

'Cherish.'

'That's it,' he said. 'She broke down, sobbed, got damn near hysterical. Maybe I'm cynical but I thought it was a little over the top.'

'Putting on an act?' said Milo.

'They only had Lee for a few months and obviously they didn't do a very good job.'

'You tell her that?'

'No,' said Ramos. 'I didn't – wasn't in a mood to talk.'

'Cherish do anything to make you think she was faking her grief?'

'No, but who knows?' said Ramos. 'Who knows about anything?'

'Ever speak with her husband?'

'Nope, just her.' Ramos stood and snatched up his books and his laptop.

I said, 'Did Lee ever hint around about getting pregnant?'

Ramos's long face turned sad. 'Don't you guys get it? We didn't *talk*.'

He let the books dangle, clutched his laptop to his chest, and bird-walked away. Other law students continued to stream out, some chatting in tight little groups, a few preoccupied loners forging their own trails.

Milo got up and stretched. 'I just creaked.'

'Didn't hear a thing.'

'So the Daneys take on too many wards but don't supervise. Fits with moral laxity.'

'It does.'

'Ready to go?'

I stayed on the bench.

'Alex?'

'What if?' I said.

He sat back down.

A group of students passed us. When they were gone, he said, 'What evil thoughts have seized that brain of yours?'

'George Ramos assumes Lee got pregnant on the street. It could've happened in-house. Literally.'

'Daney?'

'He was the only male in the house. Which, come

to think of it, is a haremlike situation. All those teen-age girls from troubled backgrounds. Maybe there's a reason the Daneys ask for female wards.'

'Oh, man.'

'We know Daney's a fraud and an adulterer, and we've just raised suspicions about his involvement in murder. Impregnating a minor under his care doesn't seem out of character. He'd have been sure to terminate the pregnancy, which fits with Lee Ramos's abortion. It could also explain her suicide. We're talking about an extremely troubled girl whose relationship with her father was hostile. She'd be looking for a compassionate substitute. The state found her one but if he betrayed her, then had her sweep away the evidence, that would've been traumatic.'

'Surrogate incest.'

'Precisely the kind of violation that could have led to serious depression.'

'Slashing her arms on her birthday,' he said. 'If it was suicide.'

'You're thinking it wasn't?'

'I'm letting my imagination run free.'

He phoned the Santa Barbara coroner, spoke to the forensic pathologist who'd conducted Lee Ramos's autopsy, did a lot of listening, hung up shaking his head.

'Doesn't seem to be any doubt about suicide. She locked herself in the room from the inside, put on music, the only window was painted shut. No sign of struggle, no defense wounds, just deep longitudinal gashes on her arms – serious intent. Beforehand, she polished off a pint of Southern Comfort and swallowed a bottle of Valium. If the razor hadn't done it, the dope would've. The kids she lived with said she'd been really down for the last few weeks. They'd tried to get her to go party with them – it was for *her* birthday. Lee begged off at the last moment, said she was feeling sick.'

My eyes got tight. A girl I'd never met. 'Birthday suicide,' I said. 'Unable to face another year.'

Milo put his weight on the back of the bench, showed me the back of his head, folded his arms across his chest. A breeze ruffled the trees behind us. The grass responded a few seconds later.

'She always had some cash, so the roomies suspected she'd been turning tricks. Sixteen years old. It doesn't get that way overnight, does it?'

Before I could answer, he shot to his feet, marched away slapping his notepad against his thigh. Nothing avian about *his* walk.

Bear on the prowl. Definitely a bear.

I followed, not sure what I was.

We returned to the car and cruised along the campus's eastern periphery.

I said, 'Daney works the system. I wonder if he'd dip into his own pocket for an abortion.'

Milo slowed. 'Bastard knocks up a ward and bills

332

the state? He's been getting away with everything else, sure, why not?'

'It's one thing,' I said, 'that we could elevate from theory to fact.'

Olivia said, 'Officially, the files are confidential, so I'm not sure you could use it in court.'

'Let's see if there's anything to use,' I said.

'Your call, darling. It could take some time.'

'You're always worth waiting for.'

'Oh, yes,' she said. 'My girlish allure.'

My cell squawked as we drove up the Glen, a mile before my house. 'Some time' had been five minutes.

'Nothing under "Ramos,"' Olivia said, 'but the termination of Wilfreda Lee *Monahan's* pregnancy was indeed billed to the taxpayers. The provider's in North Hollywood. The Women's Wellness Place.'

She recited an address on the six thousand block of Whitsett. Short ride from the Daneys' house, more of that same tight net.

'Did an adult accompany her?' I said.

'That wouldn't be in there. State supreme court nixed parental consent back in 1998.'

'Even with her being in foster care?'

'Even with. In fact, with the girl already on the rolls, billing would've been a cinch, just toss another code into the mix. Codes, plural. Looks like she also got a full physical, ob-gyn checkup, pregnancy counseling, and AIDS education.'

'Thorough,' I said.

'Sounds like major league chutzpah at play here.'

'You don't want to know, Liv. Would you do me a favor and run another name through? Leticia Maryanne Hollings, seventeen years old.'

'Another one,' she said. 'So it's worse than chutzpah.'

Leticia Hollings's abortion had taken place a month before Lee Monahan's. Same comprehensive billing.

Same clinic.

The Women's Wellness Place stuck in my head but I couldn't say why. I asked Olivia to cross-reference the two girls who'd left the Daneys and had reached majority.

One, a girl named Beth Scoggins, now nineteen, had also terminated a pregnancy at the Women's Wellness Place. Two years ago, when she'd been a foster ward.

Olivia said, 'This is getting yucky.'

I told Milo about Scoggins. His eyes blazed and I could hear his teeth grinding as he snatched the phone. From the soft, gentle way he thanked Olivia, you'd never have known.

We pulled up in front of my house and I rushed ahead of him into my office.

Thirty-eight hits for Women's Wellness Place. Most citations referred to legitimate programs at major hospitals. Three matched the North Holly-wood clinic.

The first explained my déjà vu.

I'd come across it before, researching Sydney Weider. Fund-raiser, eight years ago. Weider and Martin Boestling among the donors. Publicity photo taken during better times.

The other two citations were dated two years later, also parties to finance the 'compassionate, non-profit programs' of the clinic. No mention of Weider or Boestling; by then they'd split up and dropped several social rungs.

What the two hits did offer was a roster of Women's Wellness's professional staff.

Alphabetized list. A name as blatant as a scar, sandwiched among M.D.s and Ph.D.s, chiropractors, counselors, art therapists, massage specialists.

Drew Daney, M.Div., Pastoral Consultant.

The growling noise behind me raised the short hairs on the back of my neck.

'"*I do some work with nonprofits,*"' Milo said. 'Sure you do, dude. You're a regular fucking saint.'

'Maybe he gets a kickback,' I said. 'Percentage of total billings. An additional incentive to get them pregnant and terminated.'

'Additional?'

'Something like that is never just about money.'

We moved to the kitchen and I brewed coffee.

'At the very least, this guy's abusing young girls,'

said Milo. 'If he's done everything we've wondered about, he's a dimestore Manson. Problem is I can't do a damn thing about it because officially I'm not allowed to have access to the girls' medical files. Even *with* the files there's no proof Daney was responsible for the pregnancies.'

'As a psychologist, I'm obligated to report abuse,' I said. 'The rules of evidence don't apply.'

'How much proof do you need in order to report?'

'The law says suspicion of abuse. What that means is unclear. Every time I've tried to get clarification – from the medical board, my lawyer, the state psych association – I've failed. I know colleagues who've gotten into trouble for reporting and those who've been screwed because they didn't.'

'The law's an ass,' he said, bypassing the coffee and getting a beer from the fridge. 'One thing puzzles me, Alex. Even with kickbacks, Daney getting all those girls pregnant would be dangerous. Be easier to get them birth control, or use some himself, than risk their telling someone.'

'They haven't told yet,' I said. 'Or maybe they did and no one listened.'

'The poor Ramos kid.'

I nodded. 'Even if Daney didn't murder anyone else, if he was the father of her child, he's responsible, on some level, for her death.'

He popped his beer but didn't drink. 'So how do I find out?'

'How about this: I could try to talk to Leticia

Hollings and Beth Scoggins. Couch it as a general inquiry into foster care. If they mention or hint about being exploited, I'll have a clear obligation to notify the police.'

'Any police in particular?'

'In a pinch, you'll do.'

He smiled weakly. 'The problem is, Alex, if you approach them as a police surrogate, the confidentiality thing will still get in the way of a criminal investigation.'

'Not necessarily,' I said. 'I began as a police consultant but veered off to independent research.'

'Thought that was a cover story.'

'It could be real.'

He looked up. 'How so?'

'I learned about Lee Ramos's suicide working with you and got intrigued on an intellectual level.'

'Intrigued about what?'

'The relationship between foster care and suicide. The articles I published years ago on stress and abuse would make it a natural.'

'You still do research?'

'Haven't for a while, but I'm a full professor and full professors get to do what they want.'

'When did you get promoted?'

'Last year.'

'You never mentioned it.'

'No big deal,' I said. 'It's a clinical appointment. What it boils down to is once in a while they ask me to supervise an intern or a grad student, serve on an ad hoc committee, or read a research proposal.'

'You get paid for that?'

'No,' I said. 'It's my way of giving back.' I formed a halo with my hands and held it over my head.

'What a guy,' he said. 'You don't look a day over associate professor.'

His phone beeped. 'Sturgis. Oh hi ... yeah, long time ... you're kidding. That's great. Thanks a mill. I owe you big time.'

Wide smile. Long time since I'd seen that.

'That was Coroner's Investigator Nancy Martino, R.N. She found tissue samples from Kristal Malley's autopsy stored in a cooler. Kidney and stomach sections. Some of it looks degraded but there might be enough for analysis. They'll hold it until I give them the word.'

'Congratulations,' I said.

'For what it's worth.' His smile died.

'Now what?'

'What's the DNA really gonna do, Alex? Confirm what we already know from the eye color: The cowboy wasn't Kristal's daddy. What it *won't* accomplish is get me any closer to Malley for Rand. Or to Daney for whatever bad stuff he did.'

He tapped a calypso beat against the beer bottle. 'Two bad guys, no leads, life is beautiful.'

'Better than no bad guys.'

'How comforting,' he said. 'You must be a therapist.'

33

I copied down Leticia Hollings's phone number in Temecula and Milo got Elisabeth Mia Scoggins's last-known address from the DMV in Santa Monica; it matched a phone book listing for Scoggins, E.

Chucking his beer bottle, he saw himself out.

Beth Scoggins lived in an apartment on Twentieth Street near Pico. Low-rent section of the beach city, but the thought that she'd achieved some sort of independence was encouraging.

It was seven-fifteen p.m. Allison's office was on Montana, the high-rent north end of Santa Monica. I knew she was booked with patients until nine but her usual dinner break was at eight. If I managed to set up a meeting with Beth Scoggins, maybe I'd have time to drop in later. . . .

Mr Halo.

A young woman picked up the phone, sounding wary.

'Ms Scoggins?'

'This is Beth.'

I gave her my name and my title, asked if she'd be willing to talk about her experiences in foster care.

'How'd you *find* me?' she said.

Panic in her voice made me want to back down. But that might scare her more. 'I'm doing research –'

'Is this . . . is this some kind of rip-off?'

'No, I really am a psychol –'

'*What* research? What are you *talking* about?'

'I'm sorry if –'

'What re*search*?'

'The stresses of foster care.'

Silence.

'I consult to the police and a young woman who was cared for by the same people who cared for you was found –'

'*Cared* for? Is that what you said? *Cared* for? What's your name?'

I told her.

Scratching sounds; copying it down.

'Ms Scog –'

'You shouldn't be calling me. This is wrong.'

Click.

I sat there feeling dirty. Plenty of time to drop in on Allison now, but I was in no mood to be social. Logging onto my med school computer account, I ran an Ovid search on suicide and foster care, found no objective studies, only suggestions that kids taken out of their homes were at risk for all kinds of problems.

Gee thanks, academia.

I thought of calling Beth Scoggins back. Couldn't see any way that wouldn't make things worse. Maybe tomorrow. Or the day after. Give her time to consider . . .

By eight I was starting to feel the need to eat. Not hunger, more like an obligation to keep my blood sugar up. Maybe I'd be useful to someone.

As I was contemplating canned soup versus tuna, Robin called.

The sound of her voice tightened my scalp.

'Hey,' I said. Eloquent.

'Am I interrupting something?'

'Not at all.'

'Okay,' she said. 'There's no easy way to tell you this, Alex, but I felt it was the right thing to do. Spike's not doing so great.'

'What's the matter?'

'Age. He's got arthritis in his hind legs – you remember the left one was always a little dysplastic? Now it's really weak. Also, his thyroid function's low and his energy level's flagging, I have to put medicine in his eyes, and his night vision's just about gone. All the other tests are normal except for a slight enlargement of his heart. The vet says it's understandable, given his age. For a Frenchie, he's a real old guy.'

The last time I'd seen Spike, he'd hurled his twenty-six pounds three feet in the air and come down insouciant. 'Poor little guy.'

'He's not the same dog you'd remember, Alex. Lies around most of the day and he's gotten pretty passive. With everyone, even strange men.'

'That's a switch.'

'I just thought you should know. He's getting good care, but ... no buts. That's it. I thought you should know.'

'Appreciate it,' I said. 'Glad you found a good vet up there.'

'I'm talking about Dr Rich.'

'You're back in L.A.?'

'Have been,' she said. 'For a month.'

'Permanently?'

'Maybe ... I don't want to get into that. I can't honestly say how much longer Spike's got. This seems better than calling you one day with bad news and have you not prepared.'

'Thanks,' I said. 'I mean it.'

'If you'd like, you can come see him. Or I can bring him over sometime.' Pause. 'If Allison doesn't mind.'

'Allison wouldn't mind.'

'No, she's sweet.'

'How are you doing?' I said.

'Not great.' A beat. 'Tim and I are over.'

'I'm sorry.'

'It's for the best,' she said. 'But this really isn't about that, it's about Spike, so if you do want to see him ...'

'I'd like to if you think it would be helpful for him. Last time I dropped by he was pretty eager to have you to himself.'

'That was ages ago, Alex. He's really not the same dog. And deep down he loves you. I think competing

342

with you for my attention gave him a reason to get up in the morning. The challenge of another alpha male.'

'That and food,' I said.

'I *wish* he still stuffed his face. Now I have to coax him ... the funny thing is, he never paid much attention to Tim one way or the other ... no hostility, just ignored him. Anyway ...'

'I'll get by soon,' I said. 'Where are you living?'

'Same place,' she said. 'In the physical sense. Bye, Alex. Be well.'

Eeny meeny miny mo made it canned soup. Chicken noodle. The decision shouldn't have taken fifteen minutes. I was opening the can when the phone rang.

Allison said, 'Hi, it's me. Got a problem.'

'Busy? I was thinking we could get together, but tomorrow's fine.'

'We *have* to get together,' she said. 'Now. *That's* the problem.'

I was at her waiting room twenty minutes later. The space was empty and softly lit. I pushed the red button next to the sign that said *Dr Gwynn* and she emerged.

No hug, no kiss, no smile – and I knew why. Her hair was tied up and the day had eaten most of her makeup. She ushered me to the small side office usually occupied by her assistant.

Perching on the edge of the desk, she twisted a gold bracelet. 'She says she's ready.'

'Your patient,' I said. 'I still can't believe it.'

'Believe it,' she said. 'Five months of therapy.'

'Can you tell me how she came to you?'

'I can tell you everything,' she said. 'She gave me carte blanche. Not that I'll use it, because in her present state she can't be trusted to make optimal decisions.'

'I'm sorry, Ali –'

'She was referred by one of the volunteer counselors at the Holy Grace Tabernacle. She'd been searching for therapy, took some wrong turns, finally found someone with the good sense to refer out. She's a resilient kid and on the surface she's been doing okay. A research study would rate her as doing *great* because there's no substance abuse and she's gainfully employed – works at The Gap. She owns a fifteen-year-old clunker that usually starts and shares a one-bedroom apartment with three other girls.'

'You see her pro bono?'

'There's no such thing as free,' she said. 'I don't sell delusions.'

Allison volunteered once a week at a hospice. Was one of the few busy Westside therapists who saw patients at deep discount.

That, I supposed, made Beth Scoggins's presence a bit more than coincidence.

'The first three months were spent earning her

trust. Then we started dancing around the issues. The history of abandonment was obviously crucial but she was resistant. Wouldn't talk about foster care either, other than to say it hadn't been fun. I'd gotten more directive the last few weeks but it's been a drawn-out process. Her next appointment wasn't for four days but an hour ago she put in an emergency call. Agitated, crying, I've never heard her like that, she's always been a restrained girl. When I finally calmed her down, she told me someone claiming to be a psychologist had called her out of the blue, a research project on foster care. It confused her and scared her, she didn't know what to think. Then she told me the caller's name.'

She crossed her leg. 'She broke speed limits to get here, Alex. Began to unload before she sat down.'

'What a mess. I'm sorry, Ali —'

'On balance, maybe it'll turn out to be positive.' Her eyes met mine. Blue, cool, direct. 'Are you really conducting research?'

'Of sorts.'

'Of sorts as in Milo stuff?'

I nodded.

She said, 'That's what I was afraid of. You felt deception was absolutely necessary?'

I told her what we'd come to suspect about Drew Daney. Lee Ramos's pregnancy, abortion, and suicide. The trail of deceit and betrayal that had led me to Beth Scoggins.

'I'm sure that made it seem exigent,' she said.

'Right now I've got an extremely vulnerable nineteen-year-old in my office. Ready?'

'Do you think that's a good idea?'

'You assumed it was a *great* idea before you knew she was my patient.'

'Allison –'

'Let's not deal with that now, Alex. She's waiting and I've got another patient in forty minutes. Even if I *didn't* think it was a good idea, at this point I can't dissuade her. You opened up some kind of Pandora's box and she's a very persistent young woman. To the point of obsession, at times. I haven't tried to quash that because at this stage of her life persistence might be adaptive.'

She slid off the desk. 'Ready?'

'Any guidelines?' I said.

'Lots,' she said. 'But nothing I need to spell out for you.'

Beth Scoggins sat stiffly in one of Allison's soft white chairs. When I entered, she flinched, then she held her gaze steady. Allison made the introductions and I held out my hand.

Beth's was narrow, freckled, cold. Nails bitten short. A hangnail caught on my flesh momentarily as she pulled away.

I said, 'Thanks for meeting with me.'

She shrugged. Her hair was straw clipped in a page. Worry lines tightened a narrow mouth. Wide, brown eyes. Analytic.

Salesgirl at The Gap, but tonight she wasn't making use of the employee discount. Her navy suit looked like vintage poly. A size too large. Grayish stockings encased skinny legs. Blue flats with square toes, blue plastic purse on the floor next to her. A string of costume pearls settled on her chest.

Costuming herself as a dowdy, middle-aged woman from another decade.

Allison settled behind her desk and I took the other white chair. The cushions were warm and smelled of Allison. The position placed me three feet from Beth Scoggins.

She said, 'Sorry for hanging up on you.'

'I'm the one who should apologize.'

'Maybe you did me a favor.' She glanced at Allison. 'Dr Gwynn said you work with the police.'

'I do.'

'So what you told me, about research, it wasn't true?'

'It's possible that I may look into the general topic of foster care, but right now I'm focusing on some specific foster parents. Cherish and Drew Daney.'

'Drew Daney abused me,' she said.

I glanced at Allison. Allison's eyes were on Beth. It brought back my intern days. Talking to patients while being evaluated by supervisors behind one-way mirrors.

Beth said, 'He started off being really nice and moral. I thought I'd found someone honest.'

Her eyes turned blank. Then they came back into

347

focus and shifted toward Allison. 'Should I give all the background?'

'Whatever seems right, Beth.'

Beth breathed in deeply and squared her shoulders. 'My father left my mother when I was eighteen months old, he's some kind of roofer but I don't know much about him and I don't have any brothers or sisters. My mother moved from Texas to Willits – that's up north – then she left *me* to raise horses in Kentucky when I was eight. I have severe learning disabilities. We were always fighting over school and everything else. She always told me I was a hard kid to raise and when she moved away I figured it was my fault.'

Her knees pressed together, glossy-silver knobs in gray nylon.

'She always liked horses. My mother. Liked them better than me and I'm not just saying that. I used to think it was because I gave her problems. Now I know she was lazy, just wanted an animal that was easy to train.'

34

Beth Scoggins stopped talking and stared at the ceiling.

Allison said, 'Hon?'

Beth lowered her head and nudged the purse on the floor with one shoe. Deep breath. Her tale of abandonment continued in a soft, flat voice.

Cared for by a widowed maternal grandmother who eked out a living running a thrift shop. Passing through school without learning much. Discovering boys and dope and alcohol and truancy at twelve, a habitual runaway by her thirteenth birthday.

'Grandma got mad but she always took me back. The cops said she could declare me incorrigible but she figured she had to be a responsible person.'

If she'd been my patient, I might've suggested that her grandmother cared about her.

This wasn't therapy.

What was it?

'The last time, I ran all the way to Louisville. Took the bus and hitched and I finally found her after a week. My mom. She had different hair, had got skinny, was married to another horse groom and they had a baby, real cute, a little girl. Amanda. She didn't look a thing like me. My mother was like freaked because I showed up. She couldn't believe how big I got. She said I could stay. I hung around for a few days but I don't like horses and there was nothing for me to do, so I came back. Grandma got liver disease from her drinking and died and they collected her junk from the shop in boxes and took it away. Some people from the state wanted to talk to me but I got out of there.'

She went silent again.

A history not unlike Troy's and Rand's. They'd murdered a child. This young woman was struggling to make it. Coming along nicely, until a stranger called.

Allison said, 'You're doing great, Beth.'

Beth's freckled hands gathered skirt fabric. 'I went all the way up to Oregon, then back to Willits. Some people were coming down to L.A. to see a concert at the Anaheim Pond, they said they'd get me tickets. They didn't but I was here so I stayed. In Hollywood. I met some other people.'

She blinked several times. 'I ended up at a shelter in Glendale run by this church school. They assigned me to Mrs Daney and she was nice, her hair reminded me of my mom's. She said I could leave the shelter and move in with her, she had other girls, everyone was cool, I just couldn't use drugs. I moved in and it was okay except there was too much praying and the other kids were mostly Mexican. Mrs Daney was homeschooling everyone, had all these books and lesson plans. I was seventeen, hated school. Mrs

Daney said you should do something, so I ended up being Mr Daney's assistant. That meant I'd go with him when he went to all these places and help out.'

'What kind of places?' I said.

'Sports programs, churches, church camps. He drove around doing jobs.'

'Church jobs?'

'Sometimes he'd lead prayers or grace,' she said. 'Mostly he was like a camp counselor or a coach. Or he'd teach Bible. He did it because he needed the money.'

'He told you that?'

'He said that after he gave up a career as a minister he didn't make enough money to do just one job. Said all the foster money went to the kids. They did feed us pretty good and we always had clean clothes even though it was mostly cheap stuff. I was being his assistant for about a month when he started to abuse me.'

She stared at the carpet.

Allison said, 'You can stop any time.'

Beth chewed her lower lip. 'I think what he did was put something in my Seven-Up, a roofie or something.'

'He drugged you?' I said.

'I'm pretty sure. We were in the car, driving home from some camp, and it was late and he said he was hungry. We stopped at a Burger King and he bought a cheeseburger for himself and two Seven-Ups. After I drank mine, I started to feel sleepy. When I woke up, we were parked somewhere else, some road, real dark. I was in the back of the car now, and he was next to me and my pants were off and I knew from the smell that we did it.'

She bent forward, as if in pain. Two breaths.

'After that we started doing it pretty regularly. He never asked, just pulled over in the car and led me to the backseat. He held my hand and opened the door for me and talked nice and didn't hurt me. It was always real quick, which made it kind of like nothing. Sometimes he said thank you. It's not like it was ... I mean ... I wasn't feeling much those days.'

Moisture collected in the corners of her eyes. 'I guess I thought he cared about me because sometimes he asked if I felt okay, was it good, could he do anything to make it better.'

She fingered her beads. 'I lied and said it was great. A few months after we started I was late for my period. When I told him is when he started acting weird.'

Two hands filled with fabric, gathered her skirt above her knees. She smoothed it down quickly. Patted her eyes with her fingers.

'Weird, how?' I said.

'Like part of him was happy but part was freaking out.'

'Happy about ...'

'Getting me pregnant. Like he was ... he never said "Great, you're pregnant," but there was something

... the way he looked at me. Like he was ... Dr Gwynn?'

'Proud of himself?' said Allison.

'Yeah, proud of himself. Like look what *I* did.'

'But there was also the angry part.'

'Exactly, Dr Gee. Like look what *you* did, stupid. He called it "the problem." It's your problem, Beth, but I'm going to help you fix it. I said maybe I'm just late, that happened before.' Her eyes shifted to the floor. 'What I didn't tell him was that I was pregnant before, years ago, but I lost the baby – it wasn't really a baby, just a little glob of blood, I saw it in the toilet. This was in Portland, the people I was hanging with took me to a free clinic. I got scraped out and it hurt like cramps. I didn't want to do that again unless I was sure. He wouldn't listen.'

Allison said, 'He demanded that you fix your problem.'

'He said we can't afford to wait, Bethy. That's what he called me, Bethy, I hated it but I didn't want to hurt his feelings.'

She turned toward Allison. 'Dumb, huh?'

'Not at all, Beth. He manipulated you into thinking he was kind.'

Beth's eyes got wet. 'Yes, exactly. Even when he talked about fixing my problem, he was patient. But he wouldn't let me disagree. Put a finger on my lips when I tried to say let's wait. 'Cause I didn't want to be scraped again. Anyway, the next day, he told Mrs Daney we were going to a sports night out somewhere far. In Thousand Oaks, I think. Instead we went to this place, a clinic, that was close to the house. It was nighttime and the place looked closed but the doctor was like come on in. She put me in a room and I got aborted really quick.'

'Remember the doctor's name?' I said.

'She never said. She had an accent. Short and dark, kind of . . . not fat but . . . thick, you know? Like she'd have a hard time wearing fitted jeans, would need relaxed fit? There was no one there with her but she moved real quickly, everything went real quick. Afterward, Drew was hungry and we went out for doughnuts. I had some cramps but they weren't so bad. A few days after that, he stopped taking me to the nonprofits and he got another girl to be his assistant. A new one, she'd just been there a couple of days. I guess I felt jealous. For sure I was real bored so I took some money out of his wallet and went to Fresno. I met some new people. Dr Gee? I'm thirsty.'

She finished two cups of water. 'Thanks, that was refreshing.' To me: 'You can ask me questions if you want.'

'Do you remember the name of the girl who became Mr Daney's new assistant?'

'Miranda. Don't know her last name. She was younger than me, maybe sixteen. Mexican, like I said, most of the girls were Mexican. She thought she was street but she was just spoiled – had attitude. When she became his assistant, she was like, I'm all *that*.'

She twisted and faced Allison: 'Maybe I should've told her, Dr Gee. What being an assistant was. But even though she was just there a few days she was mean to me and I figured if she was all that, she could handle it.'

'You had a lot to deal with. It wasn't your responsibility to protect anyone else,' said Allison.

'I guess ... also, like you were saying before, I didn't really figure out it was abuse. I thought it was ...'

'Attention.'

Beth faced me. 'I had no feelings back then, it felt like attention.'

Tears trickled from her eyes and she turned back to Allison. 'What you said last week, Dr Gee? Everyone looks for someone to attach to? I guess that was it.'

Allison walked around her desk and stood next to Beth. Beth held out her hand and Allison took it.

'I'm okay. Really ... sir – Doctor – you can ask questions.'

'You're sure?' I said.

'Yeah.'

Allison patted Beth's arm and returned to her seat.

I said, 'Do you think Mrs Daney knew what Mr Daney was doing?'

'I don't know. He was always lying to her. About little things, like it was fun to fool her.'

'What kind of little things?'

'Buying doughnuts and candy and hiding them in his Jeep. He'd be like, "Cherish doesn't want me to spend money on junk food, but we won't tell her, huh?" Then he'd wink. Like I was part of the ... scheme, I guess you'd call it. But then he didn't share the doughnuts and the candy. He was like, "You've got to keep that fantastic figure, Bethy."'

She laughed. 'Like I was some supermodel. Mrs Daney was the strict one. Making all the rules, making the kids do their lessons. She could be a little bossy. I figured she didn't have much fun.'

'Why's that?'

'She was stuck in the house, cooking, cleaning, while he was driving around to all his nonprofits. He told me, "Cherish doesn't like to have fun." Then he'd be like, "I'm so glad I've got you, Bethy, because you're so beautiful and young with that gorgeous figure and you *do* know how to have fun." Then, he'd go off on some religious stuff.'

'He talked about religion?'

'Like a sermon in church. Like "Fun's not a sin, Bethy. God made a beautiful world and if we don't enjoy it, *that's* the sin, Bethy."' She smiled. 'That was usually right before he'd unzip his pants. It was like he had to ... convince himself what he was doing was okay with God.'

She waved a hand impatiently. 'He'd go off on these long stupid speeches about God and fun. About God not being a God of vengeance like in the

Old Testament. God was basically this cool guy who wanted everyone to have fun.'

The Creator as party animal. Hollywood would love it.

Beth Scoggins emitted a ragged laugh. 'It was like he had to convince *himself* he was a nice person. Then I got pregnant and it was like, "*You've* got a problem." I think he enjoyed it.'

'Enjoyed what?'

'Getting me aborted. On the ride over he was real quiet, but when it was over he was in a *great* mood. Let's go out for doughnuts. Like the whole thing was *fun*.'

I asked her if she remembered the name of the abortion clinic.

'Woman's something.'

'The Women's Wellness Place?'

'Yeah, that's it. They had all these posters about AIDS and safe sex and making smart choices.'

'Did the doctor do anything besides the abortion?'

'Like what?'

'Blood tests, a general checkup.'

'No, nothing. Like I said, she was real fast. Something for the pain before, then scrape scrape, it's over, here's some Midol if it starts to hurt.'

She shivered. 'Kind of spooky, no one was there, most of the building was dark. And I was by myself. Drew handed me over to the doctor and left. He was parked out on the street when I came out.'

'Did you go back for a follow-up visit?'

'Uh-uh,' she said. 'I took the Midols, that's it. Drew offered me some different pills, I think they were Demerol. I didn't take them. I'd been pretty clean and sober since they put me in the shelter.'

Except for a Rohypnol to get things going. 'Beth, do you know if he abused any other girls besides Miranda and you?'

'I never saw anyone, but probably. 'Cause he was like ... there was no nervousness. It was like something he was *used* to, you know? And he had only girls in the house. Why are you investigating him?'

I turned to Allison. She said, 'It's okay.'

'A girl he cared for committed suicide.'

Beth's eyes remained steady. 'How?'

'She cut her wrists.'

'That's terrible,' she said. 'That would hurt.'

I asked if there was anything else she wanted to know.

'Nope.'

Thanking her again, I got up and shook her hand. No warmer.

Allison said, 'I'll be back in a sec, hon,' and walked me out. It was nearly nine and passersby strolled Montana Avenue.

'As far as I'm concerned,' she said, 'I've got no obligation to report because she's nineteen. He's a monster but that's not my problem right now. She may change her mind but in the meantime I insist you don't bring her into any police investigation.'

'No argument.'

She touched my hand. Her lips looked parched. 'I need to get back in there. We'll talk later.'

'I can come back when you're through.'

'No,' she said. 'I'm bushed and I've still got two more patients. Tomorrow's pretty heavy, too. I'll call you.'

I leaned in to kiss her.

She squeezed my hand and offered her cheek.

35

Back at my office, I found the citations I'd printed for the Women's Wellness Place.

The only full-time physician was the medical director, Marta A. Demchuk, M.D.

Four hits for her. The oldest, six years ago, was a state medical board listing of doctors facing legal prosecution or ethical censure. The charge against Demchuk was billing fraud.

Six years ago, but she was still in practice. No answer at Milo's house but I connected with his mobile.

'Out on the town, big guy?'

'If the town's Van Nuys,' he said. 'Just got finished talking to a creepy little lady doc about the specifics of her gynecology practice.'

'Marta Demchuk?'

Silence. 'What the *hell*? If you were hiding in a corner, I didn't see you.'

I recounted Beth Scoggins's story.

He said, 'Allison's patient? Talk about karma.'

'Unfortunately, she won't be available for follow-up.'

'Why?'

'Allison's protecting her.'

'Maybe you could –'

'I can't.'

Silence. 'Okay.'

I said, 'How'd you get onto Demchuk?'

'The more I thought about that clinic the worse it started to stink. Daney gets minors aborted there, the bills are probably padded, and he's listed on the board with a fake divinity degree. I ran the same search you did, found out who the boss was and that she was brought up on fraud charges. I did a little more background, learned she's Ukrainian, had to take the licensing exam three times before she passed. So now I'm figuring some Russian scam and I call a guy I know at the medical board. From what I can tell, abortion's always been Demchuk's thing, she started doing it the minute she got licensed. First at other clinics, also run by Ukrainians, then she started her own place nine years ago.'

'Women's Wellness.'

'The main wellness is hers,' he said. 'It's strictly Medi-Cal, she's into high volume, rakes it in.'

'She claims to be nonprofit. All those fund-raisers.'

'What that means is Demchuk filed as a nonprofit and lists herself as an employee. She takes a huge salary, and the clinic never makes it into the black. What got her in trouble six years ago was sloppy record-keeping that led to some duplicate billing. She claimed clerical error, ignorance of what her staff was doing, got a sixty-day suspension of Medi-Cal billing privileges.'

'Slap on the wrist,' I said. 'The right friends?'

'Her husband's a big-time immigration lawyer, contributes to politicians.'

'Hence the fund-raisers.'

'Hence. I dropped in on her an hour ago. She's pulling seven figures but the décor's plain-wrap.'

'That probably tugs at contributors' heartstrings,' I said. 'You found her working late?'

'The lights were on and Demchuk's Mercedes was the only vehicle in the parking lot. I woulda kept going except I noticed another vehicle parked up the block. White Jeep.'

'Daney was *there*?'

'Extremely there. Chilling in the front seat, eating something, and from the way his head was moving, listening to music. I circled around and positioned myself half a block down. Twenty minutes later Demchuk comes out with a girl who's walking kind of shaky. Daney gets out of the Jeep, puts his arm around the kid, guides her in, and they drive away. I recognized her. The girl Cherish was trying to teach math.'

'Valerie Quezada. Sixteen years old with A.D.D.'

'Obviously he likes them young and vulnerable. The thing is, her body language said she liked him, too. Putting her head on his shoulder. Before she got in the Jeep, she kissed his hand. And this is right after she's had an abortion.'

'Beth Scoggins said his manner was gentle,

solicitous, flattering. Until she got pregnant, then he got stern and broke it off with her.'

'Well, he hasn't broken it off with Valerie yet. Meaning even if I could find a way to talk to her, she'd clam up. Now you're telling me Scoggins won't cooperate. I'm stuck.'

'Beth said a girl named Miranda was her successor. Anything like that on the foster list?'

'I'll check tomorrow,' he said. 'So, Allison's not impressed by the magnitude of this asshole's offenses?'

'Allison's got to think about Beth Scoggins's mental health in the short run,' I said. 'Also, right now, I don't hold much sway.'

'Why not?'

'She saw me in another light and didn't like it.'

'What light's that?'

'Deceptive.'

'A woman who still thinks men don't lie?' he said. 'Thought she dug all the police stuff.'

'Until it got too close,' I said.

'You really think it's useless to talk to her again? Maybe in a coupla days?'

'I'll play it by ear. Eventually, Beth might decide to go public. Right now Allison feels it would be too much to handle.'

'*Eventually* Daney's gonna knock up more girls.'

I didn't answer.

He said, 'Fine. Anyway, after Daney drove away, Demchuk stayed outside and lit up a cigarette. White

363

coat and she's puffing away. I decided to take the risk, walked up on her in the dark, flashed the badge, scared the hell out of her, she drops her smoke, gets ashes all over the coat. But she recovered pretty fast, got cagey, told me she had nothing to say, headed back inside. I followed her and she yapped about civil liberties and made empty threats and I postured right back and eventually we ended up finding some common ground. Because she doesn't care for Daney either. Says he's a greedy fellow.'

'He gets a kickback? She admitted that?'

'She claims *nyet,* that was never part of the plan, it was just a mutually convenient situation. It started when she put his name on the advisory committee at Sydney Weider's request. Something about Weider wanting him to have credibility for a movie deal. Soon after that, he started bringing her girls.'

'Demchuk ever suspect he was more than a concerned foster parent?'

'She denied it, but come on, all those abortions?'

'All?'

'The agreement we came to was that when I busted Daney I'd do my best to keep Demchuk's name out of it. In return, she had to document every Daney ward whose pregnancy she's terminated and be forthcoming with other information as requested. She had it right there in the computer and printed it out for me. Nine girls in eight years.'

'My God,' I said.

'Like you said, Drew's underage harem. This guy's beyond bad news.'

'He's got the perfect victim pool living under his roof. Abandoned girls with low self-esteem, learning problems, probably histories of sexual activity. He impregnates them deliberately, gets a kick out of destroying the fetus. And the taxpayers pay for everything.'

'Without getting into the whole when-does-life-begin thing, Alex, he's basically a prenatal serial killer, right? What's the thrill?'

I thought about that. 'Create and destroy. Playing God.'

'Nine girls,' he said. 'And not one of them has complained.'

'He's gentle – seductive, not coercive. Ties it in with the whole paternal intimacy thing. When he moves on to another girl, they think it's their fault. Beth admitted being jealous. She dealt with it by escaping.'

'That place of his,' he said, 'main house, converted garage, and that weird-looking cinder-block building? Lots of construction for a small lot. I was figuring dorms for the kids. But who knows what goes on there. No way *Cherish* couldn't know, right?'

'Beth says Drew delighted in going around Cherish. From petty stuff like eating doughnuts on the sly to leaving her with the scut work while he took his "assistants" out on the road.'

'Okay,' he said, 'maybe that worked for a while, but she finally caught on.'

'And started sleeping with Barnett Malley.'

'Her own brand of sin.'

I said, 'How did Daney's greed come into the picture with Demchuk?'

'He'd been hinting around for a while about getting a cut of the action. Demchuk lent him money to put him off – small amounts he never repaid, she figures three, four grand total. Recently, though, he's gotten pushier. Coming out and asking for his share, outright. Insisting he's her best "referral source." Implying he might go elsewhere. Demchuk's not the sharing type. And Daney's timing couldn't be worse because Demchuk's ready to retire, wants to sell the clinic. She was figuring she'd buy him off with a screw-you payment. I told her selling the place wasn't gonna be easy when all the bad stuff about Daney came out. Made that sound more imminent than it is. Demchuk tried to stay cool but I could tell I shook her. That's why she was willing to deal him off. As in handing over Valerie Quezada's aborted fetus.'

'She keeps them?'

'No, she tosses them in the trash out back, which is a health code violation. I had her fish it out and put it in dry ice, then I brought it over to the coroner's to be stored with Kristal Malley's tissue samples. Which is where I am now, breathing in the aroma of decomposition and drinking county coffee. No word on my DNA requisition yet, but now it looks like I'll have another package to send to Cellmark. We get Daney's DNA in the fetus, I've got a gift for the Juvey Sex Crimes unit they just started downtown.'

'You're bringing them into it?'

'Not yet,' he said. 'Not until I get closer to Daney for murder. But the pedophilia thing could turn out to be good leverage.'

'How long can you sit on it?'

'Eight girls living on Galton Street bothers my sleep, but I can't risk screwing things up by moving without evidence. First order of business is to get DNA from Daney. Any suggestions about how to approach it?'

'Arrange a meet by playing his ego. You've bought into his suspicions of Barnett Malley but Malley remains a mystery man; ask him if he has any other suggestions.'

'That part's true. Still researching Malley and can't come up with a damn thing. Okay, a face-to-face with Dynamic Drew. Then what? Swipe his tooth-brush for the sample?'

'That's the easy part,' I said. 'He likes doughnuts.'

36

Rain fell the next morning, and the temperatures dropped into the high fifties. L.A. finally auditioning for winter. When Milo pulled the unmarked into the Dipsy Donut lot at ten a.m., the sky had closed and Vanowen Boulevard smelled of wet laundry.

Drew Daney was there, drinking coffee at the same aluminum table. Exact position he'd occupied the first time – a man of patterns.

He had on a brown corduroy car coat, rested his denim haunches on newspaper he'd spread to soak up dampness from the bench. When he saw us, he smiled and waved.

Warm smile. It spread his stubbly silver beard. His eyes crinkled.

This was the face of evil. He could've served as a model for a tool supply catalog.

Milo pumped his hand as if they were longtime buddies. 'Morning. Not hungry?'

Daney winked. 'Waiting for you guys.'

'How about I get us an assortment?'

'Sounds good, Lieutenant.'

Milo left and I sat down opposite Daney. My assignment, should I choose to take it, was to check out nonverbal cues and whatever 'psych stuff' I came up with.

'Way I figure, Alex, having you along will play to his ego. Make him feel like a peer ... even though you're peerless.'

I watched Daney's teeth disappear as his smile shifted to a close-mouthed one. 'Thanks for meeting with us on such short notice.'

'Hey, anything I can do to help.' Under his car coat he wore a spotless yellow polo shirt, tight across his broad chest. Well-developed musculature. His complexion glowed and his eyes were clear.

Picture of vitality; sometimes – too often – good things happen to bad people.

I said, 'How's your wife doing?'

The question made him blink. 'In terms of?'

'Rand's death. She seemed pretty affected.'

'Of course she was,' he said. 'We all are. It's a process – healing.'

'Your foster kids were affected?'

'Definitely. Rand wasn't with us long, but he was a presence. You know what it's like.'

'Dealing with death?'

'That and kids in general,' he said. 'The developmental stages they go through.'

'What's the age range of your wards?'

'They're all adolescents.'

'There's a challenge.'

'You bet.'

'Is that by choice?'

'We're masochists,' he said, chuckling. 'Seriously, a lot of people don't want the baggage teens bring to the table, so Cherish and I figured that's where our efforts would be best spent.' Boyish shrug. 'Sometimes I wonder, though. It can feel like temporary insanity.'

'That I can believe.'

He looked over at the doughnut stand. Crowded, just like the first time.

I said, 'Rand wasn't that long out of his teens. That could also be an issue for your kids.'

'Sure,' he said quickly, but his eyes told me he wasn't tracking.

'Perceived similarity,' I went on. 'There's a whole bunch of data on how it relates to empathy.'

'If it could happen to him, it could happen to me?' he said. 'Sure, makes total sense. But what I was referring to are the core issues they're wrestling with. Sense of identity, establishing autonomy. And, of course, they think they're immortal.' Wry smile. 'We did, at that age, right? All that stuff we kept from our parents.'

I forced my own smile. Trying not to think about what this guy did to young girls' autonomy.

A thirteen-year-old bleeding out in a prison supply room.

I said, 'Thank God my parents never knew some of the things I did.'

'You were a wild guy?' he said, shifting closer.

Engaging me with those warm dark eyes. As if I were the most important person on earth.

Return of the teeth.

Charisma. The most skillful psychopaths know how to play it like a guitar. Sometimes the smartest ones get to the top of the corporate ladder or the highest rungs of elected office. In the end, though, shallow theatrics are often counterbalanced by laziness and sloppiness.

Doing someone else's wife in the marital bed.

Writing and shopping a thinly described screenplay and expecting it to make you an overnight millionaire.

Impregnating minors for a hobby and billing the state for their abortions.

For all his wizardry at manipulation, Daney was miles from where he wanted to be, the lifestyle he'd glimpsed after hooking up with Sydney Weider: Brentwood, Aspen, private jets, red carpet fantasies. All that upscale pillow talk fevering his brain.

Look at me look at me look at me!

Eight years later, instead of all that, he was a middle-aged guy running around singing camp songs and trying to cadge money from Dr Marta Demchuk.

Fool's move; Demchuk was tough and Daney's smarmy mojo worked only on the weakest of victims.

He flexed a thick wrist, ran his hand through his thick, wavy hair.

I said, 'I was never wild enough to get into serious trouble, but I had my moments.'

'I'll bet you did.'

'How about you?'

He hesitated for a moment. 'Nah, I was a good boy. Maybe too good.'

'Choir boy?'

'I was brought up thinking fun meant good deeds.'

'Preacher's kid?'

'You guessed it . . .' A shadow darkened his face.

Then a larger shadow, bearish, tinted the aluminum table pewter.

Daney turned to see Milo looming behind him, holding a greasy cardboard box. 'Fresh out of the fat.'

'Smells yum, Detective.'

Milo let him have the first pick.

Jelly-filled. Just like last time.

As he chewed with obvious pleasure, I told myself to turn off the analysis, maybe he just loved jelly-filled doughnuts.

He wiped his beard, took another bite. 'Aren't these just the best?'

Milo said, 'Guilty pleasures, Rev,' and swallowed a mouthful of cruller.

I got to work on a maple-glaze. Cars drove in and out of the lot. The air got warmer. A flock of pigeons flew over from across Vanowen and began exploring the leavings. Milo tossed them a crumb and they flittered like paparazzi.

Daney said, 'There's your good deed for the day.'

We laughed.

Just a bunch of guys, stuffing their faces with junk food, on a damp day in the Valley.

Milo said, 'So have you come up with any insights, Rev?'

Drew Daney scanned the doughnut box, picked out a pink thing topped with chocolate sprinkles. 'You haven't been able to learn anything at all about Malley?'

'I wish. Guy seems to be a cipher.'

'Guess that fits,' said Daney.

'With what?'

'If he had a history of antisocial behavior, he'd want to cover his tracks.'

'Well,' said Milo, 'if there are serious tracks, we'll uncover them.'

'That sounds pretty confident, Lieutenant.'

'We usually get to the bottom of things. It's just a matter of how long it takes – hand me that chocolate thing.'

The box was within Milo's reach but Daney stretched to comply. 'Anyway,' he said, 'after you called last night I spent some time thinking about why Malley would get so violent after all these years. The only thing I can think of is that Rand became some sort of threat to him. Or Malley perceived Rand that way. Now, that would mean the two of them communicated somehow, so I looked at my phone bill to see if Rand made any calls over the weekend. He didn't. So unless he spoke to Malley from prison, or used a pay phone, I don't know what to tell you.'

'Where's the pay phone closest to your house?' said Milo.

Daney's eyes shifted to the left. 'You're able to check them?'

'Sure.'

'Well,' said Daney, 'I think there's one a few blocks that way.' Pointing east. 'I never really paid attention. Nowadays, with cell phones, who uses pay booths?'

'People with no money,' said Milo.

'Hmm . . . guess so.'

I said, 'Seems to me the "where" isn't important. It's the "what" we're after. What Rand *told* Malley.'

Daney put his pink doughnut down. 'That was speculation on my part. Because you asked me to speculate. For all we know, Malley simply went nuts after he heard Rand was getting out. Old wounds, opening.'

'Or wounds that never healed,' said Milo. 'The way he looked at you in that hardware store.'

'True,' said Daney. 'That *was* pretty intense. Still . . .'

'Any sign of the black truck?'

Daney shook his head. 'But I'm gone a lot.'

Milo turned away, seemingly distracted. Daney watched him, then returned to his pink doughnut but didn't eat.

I let the silence grow for a while before saying,

'For argument's sake, let's go with the assumption that Rand told Malley something that set him off. What do you think it could've been?'

Daney said, 'Hmm ... I guess it wouldn't have been anything malicious. And I can't see Rand being confrontational. He was basically a nice kid.'

He waited for Milo's reaction to that. None followed.

'The only thing I can think of,' he went on, 'is there was some sort of miscommunication.'

'Such as?' said Milo.

'I'm not sure what I mean,' said Daney. 'Like I said, this is all theorizing.'

'Understood,' said Milo. 'But give it a try, 'cause we've got nothing else.'

'Well,' said Daney, 'when we brought Rand home, he was clearly troubled. Like I told you. The only explanation I can come up with is lingering guilt. Maybe he tried to get some closure by meeting Malley face-to-face and apologizing.'

'Or Malley accosted Rand and demanded an apology,' I said.

'Sure. That, too.'

Milo said, 'That makes more sense to me, Rev. Malley follows Rand when he leaves your house to go to the construction site, gets him in the truck, either by convincing him he's friendly or at gunpoint. Then something – could be an apology demanded by Malley, or something else – goes haywire. What do you think, Doc?'

I said, 'Makes sense.'

Daney said, 'Rand's verbal skills were poor, Detective. I can see him saying the wrong thing, phrasing something in a way that would spark Malley's rage. I mean, isn't that how so much crime originates?'

'Miscommunication?'

'Two guys in a bar,' said Daney. 'An argument gets out of hand? Isn't that a big part of police work?'

'Sure,' said Milo.

Daney took a bite of the pink doughnut. Ate half and put it down. 'There is something else. Kind of far-fetched but as long as we're theorizing . . .'

'What's that?'

Daney hesitated.

'Sir?'

'This goes way back, Detective. To the boys' hearings. I was spending a lot of my time on the case because the defense asked me to be there as support. Cherish and I attended everything and I got to look at the evidence.'

'Something about the evidence was off?' said Milo.

'No, no, nothing like that. What I'm getting at is in my field you learn to observe. People, their reactions. Kind of like what you do, Doctor.'

I nodded.

'I'm a little uncomfortable getting into this,' said Daney. 'It's nothing I'd want to sign my name to, and I really wouldn't be comfortable going on record as the source. But if you could confirm it independently . . .'

He broke off. Scratched his beard. Shook his head. 'Sorry for waffling, but it's . . .'

He slung his jaw, shook his head. 'I don't know, maybe it's not a good idea.'

Milo said, 'We're in bad shape on this one, Reverend. *Anything* you can tell us would be helpful. And if it's something I can confirm independently, I promise you I will.'

'Okay,' said Daney. 'First, let me say that I never brought this up because the boys had clearly done the crime. That isn't to say I didn't think they deserved compassion. But everyone had suffered enough, there was simply no point.'

He reached for another doughnut. Chose blindly and extracted an apple turnover. Holding the pastry in one hand, he watched as flakes of dough snowed on the table.

'Eye color,' he said, barely audible. 'Little Kristal had brown eyes. I'd never have noticed, but in the evidence packet were photos of that poor little girl. In life and in death. The postmortem shots I couldn't bring myself to look at. The others were baby pictures, the prosecution was going to use them to build sympathy. Emphasizing how small and cute she'd been . . . that's neither here nor there. The point is I saw those photos, but at that time the fact that Kristal's eyes were brown didn't mean much. Until I noticed that both Lara and Barnett had pale eyes. Hers were blue or green, I'm not sure. His are definitely blue. I'm no geneticist, but I've learned enough science to know that brown eyes are dominant and light-eyed parents usually can't have dark-eyed kids. I had my suspicions, but like I say, there was no reason to open that can of worms, who would it help? But last night, after you called and asked me to give the case some serious thought, I went on the Internet to confirm and it's highly unlikely – close to impossible – for two blue-eyed parents to produce a brown-eyed child.'

His speech had grown rapid and the last few words had tapered to whispers, inaudible. Gulping air, he exhaled and put the turnover down. 'I'm not out to slander anyone but . . .'

'Kristal wasn't Malley's kid,' said Milo. 'Whoa.'

'It's the only logical conclusion, Lieutenant. And that could be the source of Mr Malley's rage.'

'Kristal was nearly two,' said Milo. 'You'd think Malley would've figured it out.'

'He struck me as an unsophisticated person. He worked rodeos or something like that.'

'Rodeos?'

'Riding, roping, or at least that's what I heard,' said Daney. 'From the defense.'

'Sounds like Ms Weider did her background research.'

'You bet. She was extremely hardworking and thorough. I was glad when she got the case.'

'You were involved before she got the case?' I said. 'I thought she brought you on as a support-person.'

'Just the opposite, actually,' said Daney. 'I brought

her on. Not officially, but I had a hand in it.'

'How so?'

'I knew Troy from working with him at 415 City. I also knew Ms Weider from some other youth work I'd done. My seminary had a program, working with inner-city teens, trying to get them involved in summer activities. In the course of that, I developed some contacts with the Public Defender's Office, because that's where so many of our kids ended up. I knew several of the P.D.s, but thought Ms Weider would be perfect for the boys. Because she *was* so thorough. I called her and asked if she could help out. She said there was a system in place but she'd see what she could do.'

'As a favor to you.'

'Partly,' said Daney. 'To be honest, the case attracted her because it was high-profile. She was pretty ambitious.'

'And then she asked you to stay on for support,' said Milo.

'Exactly.'

'You ever tell her about the eye color thing?'

'No, like I said, I didn't see the point.'

Milo exhaled. 'Wow ... that's a bombshell, all right. Thank you, Rev.'

'I don't like telling tales, but ...'

'So you're figuring Rand knew Kristal wasn't Malley's kid and mentioned it to Malley.'

'No, no,' said Daney. 'I hadn't taken it that far.'

'But it coulda happened that way.'

'No, I honestly don't think so, Lieutenant. How would Rand know?'

'Same way you did. He noticed.'

Daney shook his head. 'Rand just wasn't that observant. But even if he did know, there'd be no reason to throw it in Malley's face.'

'What, then?'

'What I'm getting at – and this is *really* out there – is maybe Barnett Malley wasn't a total victim.'

Daney flinched, pushed the turnover away. 'I feel like I'm ... wading into something and I'm really not comfortable. Sorry.' Pushing up a corduroy sleeve, he peered at a black-faced sports watch. Milo placed a hand on his arm. Flashed that lupine smile. Daney stiffened for a second. Dropped his shoulders, shot us a look of misery.

'I've got that sinking feeling, guys, like when you've gone too far, you know?'

I said, 'You're saying Malley found out Lara had cheated on him, built up a whole lot of rage, and decided to act out against Kristal.'

'I don't want to say more,' said Daney. 'Because I'm scared and not ashamed to admit it.'

'Scared of Malley?' said Milo.

'A lot of people depend on me, Detective. That's why I don't skydive or ride a motorcycle or go mountain climbing.'

'Miss all that?'

'Not anymore,' said Daney. 'Now, I really need to get going –'

I said, 'It's a whole new way of looking at it, Milo.' To Daney: 'Did Malley know Troy and Rand before the murder?'

'I wouldn't know,' said Daney.

'Lara went to the mall frequently and so did the boys. So there'd be opportunity for Barnett to see them, as well.' I turned back to Milo: 'They hung out at that arcade. Maybe Malley was into video games, too. Being an unsophisticated guy.'

Both of us stared at Daney.

He said, 'It's possible.'

Milo said, 'Troy and Rand *never* mentioned knowing Malley? After they got arrested?'

'Troy definitely didn't,' said Daney. 'I wasn't talking much to Rand, he was pretty nonverbal back then. Right, Doctor?'

'You bet,' I said. 'But I always got the feeling he was holding back.'

'Defensive,' he said. 'Yes, I sensed the same thing.'

'Frustrating.'

'I tried to open him up,' said Daney, 'but not being a psychologist, I didn't want to step into uncharted territory. In the end, it didn't matter because the case got settled optimally. Or so I thought.'

'What do you mean?' said Milo.

'Look what happened to Troy. And to Rand.'

'I hear what you're saying, Rev. About Rand not being perceptive. But if he really knew Malley had some culpability, would he hold on to it for eight years?'

'Maybe,' said Daney, 'he was confused.' He stood quickly. 'I'm sorry, this is getting way too complicated and there's nothing more I can tell you. If it ends up helping you, great. But please keep my name out of it.'

He ran his hands over his shirt, as if brushing off dirt.

Milo got up and faced him, used his height to advantage. 'Absolutely, sir. I wouldn't lose too much sleep because, to be honest, I don't see any way of pursuing any of this.'

Daney stared up at him.

Milo said, 'Like you said, too speculative.'

Daney nodded. 'Good luck.' He pivoted and began to walk away.

'I mean the only time it would ever be relevant,' said Milo, 'is if we got solid, physical evidence on Malley and put him behind bars. Then we'd ask you to give a deposition.'

Daney stopped. Weak smile. 'If that happened, Detective, I'd be happy to do my part.'

37

Milo watched as the white Jeep drove away. 'Wish there was a shower nearby.'

He took an evidence bag out of his attaché case, gloved up, sealed Daney's coffee cup, and slipped it in. Into a second bag went the half-eaten pink doughnut.

I said, 'He snarfed that right before he graced us with his reluctant insights on eye color. His appetite peaked because he was aroused by the game.'

'Letting us know the cowboy wasn't Kristal's daddy. Thinking he's being subtle.'

'It was a dual thrill: He gets to be the hero of the story, granting you vital information. And he heightens the focus on Malley.'

'All that frighty-dighty about mean old Barnett, but right off he's telling us Malley's antisocial, covered his tracks.'

'That could've been more than a diversion strategy,' I said. 'Attributing his own behavior to Malley, consciously or otherwise.'

'He's covered some tracks of his own.'

'The lies didn't start with his seminary application. The image he pushes is Fun Guy with a Sensitive, Spiritual Side. While you were ordering he told me he was a well-behaved kid, brought up in the church. Be interesting to know what his childhood was really like.'

He stashed the bags in the case. 'Time for some serious digging. Be nice if it's more productive than my research on Malley. Can't find any insurance policies on Lara or Kristal, the cowboy seems to be using his real name and social security number, has no arrest record, no military record, no real estate ownership. I was able to trace his birth records to Alamogordo, New Mexico, but the local law doesn't remember him and there are no Malleys living there now. Maybe I'm missing something, there are all these new computer tricks the department doesn't have . . .'

He snatched his phone from the table, punched in a number, and asked for Sue Kramer.

Two seconds later: 'Nancy Drew? It's Joe Hardy. Listen, I don't know what your schedule's like but . . . did it? Excellent . . . listen, Sue, all those things you private hotshots can do that I can't . . . the high-tech stuff . . . yeah, exactly, I need a couple guys looked into . . . him and also the spiritual adviser – Daney . . . let's just say he's become interesting . . . the usual and anything else you can think of . . . sooner's better than later, I'll pay you personally . . . no, no, send me a full bill . . . I mean it, Sue . . . okay, fine, but send something . . . thanks, have a nice day, hope the winds are good.'

Clicking off, he said, 'Her B.H. surveillance just

ended. She spotted the Korean widow going into the apartment, found the lady praying at some kind of shrine, crying how much she loved hubby, why'd he have to go kill himself. So the suicide stands and Sue'll start digging tomorrow when she gets back from a little R and R.'

'The winds,' I said. 'Sailing?' Thinking about his brief fling as a P.I., during a suspension from LAPD. The rise in income. The plague of tedium. When the department took him back, he had raced home like a trained pigeon.

'Sailing on her new boat,' he said. 'Over the bounding main.'

'Ever miss private enterprise?'

'The lack of red tape and paramilitary rigidity? The chance to make serious money? Why the hell would I miss that?' He stared at his phone, clicked it shut. 'That comment Daney made about my sounding pretty confident. What was that, a taunt?'

'Or fishing for information. Or both,' I said. 'He was clearly fishing when he steered the conversation to the topic of pay booths. Your line about being able to trace pay calls made his eyes jump.'

'Yeah, I noticed that.'

'Rand called me from a pay booth but Daney would have no way of knowing that unless he was there.'

His eyes compressed to surgical incisions. 'Daney was with Rand the day he died.'

'Or nearby, watching Rand make the call,' I said. 'Which got me thinking: What if he made up the story about the black truck to divert attention from the fact that it was *him,* not Barnett who followed Rand? Cherish told us he wasn't home that afternoon.'

'Off at one of his nonprofit gigs.' He passed his phone from hand to hand. Tapped the table. Rubbed his face.

Finally, he said, 'Daney did Rand, not Malley.'

'The only reason we focused on Malley is because Daney pointed us in that direction.'

'That and Malley's mother-in-law said he was a scumbag dope dealer who was rough on Lara.'

'A scumbag dope dealer with no arrest record or known aliases who uses his own social security number,' I said. 'Who registers his guns legally. In a sense, Nina Balquin was a character reference for Malley. She hates his guts but she's never suspected him of murdering Lara.'

He slipped the phone in his pocket. Ungloved and grabbed a bear claw and chewed, spewing crumbs. 'There's still the eye color issue. Malley had to know he wasn't Kristal's daddy.'

'Maybe Daney's right about him being too unsophisticated to figure it out. But even if he did know, unless we find something psychopathic in his background, it's a long stretch to killing a toddler.'

'Unlike Daney, who we know to be an *extremely* bad boy.'

I nodded. 'It's also possible Malley knew about Kristal's paternity and didn't care.'

He put down the bear claw. 'Guy has no problem

raising someone else's kid? That's a stretch of another kind.'

'The Malleys had fertility problems for years. Lara eventually got pregnant but what if the fertility problem was Barnett's and he came to accept the idea of a surrogate?'

'He let some other guy go to stud with Lara?'

'Or Lara slept with someone and got pregnant and Barnett accepted it. If Balquin's dope suspicions are on-target, Lara and Barnett could've gotten into some alternative behaviors. Promiscuity, swinger parties. Or just plain old infidelity.'

'She gets knocked up at an orgy and Barnett says keep it? That's pretty damn tolerant, Alex.'

'You're probably right. But in any event, now that we know the truth about Daney's character, we can't ignore him for Rand. He hasn't been directing us to Malley out of civic obligation.'

He gave the bear claw another try. Grimaced and put it aside.

I drank coffee. It sloshed in my stomach. Burned like drain cleaner when my thoughts uncoiled. 'Daney fed us another tidbit he shouldn't know about. Malley riding the rodeo. He claims Sydney Weider told him and maybe she did. But I read all the court documents and it never came up. In fact, my sense was Weider wasn't paying any sort of attention to the Malleys. Daney's playing us, Milo. And screwing up, in typical psychopath fashion, because he's too clever for his own good.'

'Daney did Rand,' he said, looking off into the distance. 'No reason why it doesn't fit.'

'Something else: Whether or not the boys knew Lara or Barnett is an open question. But one of them sure knew Daney. Troy was a budding psychopath. Daney's the fully-developed version. Put them together and there's no question who'd pull the strings.'

'Daney got Troy to do Kristal?'

'And now he'll help you "solve" the case.'

'Man,' he said, 'you are full of evil thoughts.'

'So I've been told.'

He said, 'Guess it's like those firebugs who return to the scene and rescue people. Or one of those Munchausen mommies racing to resuscitate their kids.'

'It fits Daney's act,' I said. 'Image is important to him. Outwardly, he's a man of faith, a tireless youth worker, caretaker of downtrodden teens. While you were ordering, he spun off a bunch of psychobabble, told me he and Cherish chose adolescents to foster because no one else wanted them. If I didn't know better, I'd have bought it. Meanwhile, he's cheating the government, seducing minors, and impregnating them intentionally. Getting off on having the pregnancies terminated and trying to snag a share of the fees.'

'What a prince ... at least when the DNA match comes through, we've got him for kiddie rape on Valerie Quezada.' He shook his head. 'One reinterview and *he's* our new Hitler. What does that say for Cherish's guilt or innocence?'

'Don't know. Their relationship's a big question mark.'

'I can buy Daney as a scumbag,' he said. 'But speaking of questions marks, what was his motive to have Kristal murdered?'

'Kristal survived,' I said.

'Survived what?'

'Survived period. Daney has a thing about his progeny living and breathing.'

'Daney was Kristal's daddy? Where'd that come from?'

'More of the ugly in here.' I tapped my forehead. 'Think about it: Daney's kick is playing God. Generating life and terminating it. We know his sexual exploits went beyond teenage wards – Sydney Weider. Why not other married women? And why not play the pregnancy game with them, too? Your remark about a prenatal serial killer was on-target. And serials need increasing amounts of stimulation.'

'From fetus to full-term victim,' he said.

'There are mothers like that,' I said. 'Get pregnant repeatedly but can't tolerate parenthood. Fathers, too. How many cases have we heard where the boyfriend or daddy shook the baby too hard. We always assume it's an impulsive thing, poor anger control. But maybe not. It sure happens with primates. Chimp moms defend their babies from aggressive daddies all the time.'

'I create, I destroy . . . except that seducing vulnerable teens is one thing, Alex. Getting a married woman pregnant means a whole lot of carelessness on all accounts.'

'Hole in the condom, or some other trick. Beth Scoggins thinks Daney drugged her. Maybe he did that routinely. And in a sense, married women would be *easier* targets than teenage girls. Because convincing them to terminate would be a cinch. Until Daney met up with a married woman who resisted. Because *she'd* been yearning to have a baby for a long time.'

'Lara,' he said.

'Daney's got brown eyes. He'd like us to think he's Mr Observant, but he didn't chance upon the genetic angle.'

'And now he's throwing it in my face with all that phony reluctance. Oh, man.'

I reached over and tapped his attaché case. 'Long as you're at it, I'd suggest a few other DNA tests.'

We took the 101 to the 5 South, headed for the Mission Street exit. Milo drove way too fast, seemed distracted. 'If Malley's innocent, why wouldn't he talk to me?'

'The system failed him, he's a burnout ... I don't know. The same logic could be twisted in his favor: If he was hiding something would he want to get you suspicious?'

'I guess,' he said. 'But I'm still not comfortable dropping him. Even if Daney does turn out to be Kristal's daddy.'

'Hey,' I said, 'an open mind's a terrible thing to waste.'

He laughed. Gripped the wheel and fed more gas, glanced back at the case on the backseat. 'All of a sudden there're all these possibilities. I have a confession: If Daney did everything you think he did, I have encountered a level of bad that creeps me out.'

'So you're human.'

'Only on alternate days.' He took another look back at the case. The unmarked stayed in lane. 'Either way,' he said, 'the motive for Rand's the same, covering up the truth about Kristal. But there's still the problem of how Rand found out. And the fact that Kristal was nearly two, talk about your late-term abortion. If Daney has this psycho lust to destroy his own sperm, why would he wait that long?'

'Maybe he kept working on Lara to terminate. She got angry, refused, broke off their relationship. Daney had to step aside but he couldn't accept losing. He kept fantasizing. Plotting. Found a thirteen-year-old he could hire to kill.'

'Lara shopping at the mall, the boys hanging at the arcade.'

'Another possibility,' I said, 'is that Lara's relationship with Barnett grew progressively rockier and she decided to leave him. Because she had her own fantasies.'

'Hooking ol' Drew.'

'The guy who'd come through biologically. But putting pressure on Drew would've been a fatal error.'

'He puts a hit on the kid. Does Lara, too.'

'Or she really was a suicide. She had an inkling of why Kristal had been killed, couldn't come forward because it would have implicated her. Her depression deepened and she killed herself.'

'Head-shot in a car?' he said. 'Same as Rand? To me that says they were both murdered by the same person.'

'Or whoever shot Rand imitated Lara's suicide.'

He knuckled his temple, made an abrupt lane change, put on more speed. 'Daney's character notwithstanding, Malley's the one with the guns and it was one of those that killed Lara. And he's also got a thing for other guys' wives.'

He slapped the dashboard. 'How 'bout this for a screenplay: The Malleys weren't the only ones swinging. They met Drew and Cherish at a swap party. Drew and Lara parted ways but Malley and Cherish are still doing it.'

I considered that. 'It might help explain Barnett accepting Lara's pregnancy. If it was the product of a group scene, the threat would be depersonalized.'

'It takes a village,' he said. 'Whatever the case, no way I'm scratching the cowboy off my list.'

We parked in the coroner's lot and entered the north building. Milo talked to Dave O'Reilly, a thin, red-faced, white-haired man with a keen, searching intellect, and asked for Kristal Malley's tissue samples and Valerie Quezada's aborted fetus.

'You just dropped Quezada off,' said O'Reilly. 'Something come up?'

'You don't want to know.'

'I'm sure I don't. Okay, I'll call down and have them put it in a refrigerator bag and a Styrofoam biohazard box.'

'All official,' said Milo. 'I like that.'

'I like tall, skinny brunettes with big natural boobs.'

We returned to the car. Milo put the box in the trunk, along with the attaché case, and started up the engine. A white coroner's van pulled around from the back of the building and cruised through the lot before turning toward Mission.

He said, 'Wonder what police work was like in the rubber hose days.'

'You and Daney alone in a room?'

'Me and anyone I damn well *want* alone in a room.' He bared his teeth. 'Think Daney was telling the truth about knowing Weider before the murder?'

'Why would he lie?'

'Puffing up his chest, more hero-of-the-story crap,' he said. 'Making like he's got big-time contacts at the P.D., masterminded the whole defense.'

'Easy enough to check out,' I said. 'And if he was telling the truth about working with inner-city teens, I'd be interested in one particular delinquent other than Troy.'

'Nestor Almedeira.'

'And the dedicated lawyer who stood up for his rights.'

Not that easy to check out.

We sat in the coroner's lot and Milo phoned the Public Defender's Office. Several transfers later, he ended up with a supervisor. I watched as amiability morphed to wheedling, then deteriorated to veiled threats. He hung up growling.

'All I want is what would be in a normal court record if Nestor wasn't a juvenile and the file wasn't sealed. I can get it eventually if I fool around long enough at the Hall of Records, but it's gonna take time. Stonewalling bastards. They hate cops and everything else that's good and true.'

'Try Lauritz Montez,' I said.

'He likes cops?'

'He's vulnerable and weak-willed.'

The call to Montez's Beverly Hills office was answered by a tape.

I took the phone, punched 411, and asked for the number of Dr Chang's dental office on Alvarado. There's nothing more effective with a doctor's staff than having a doctorate. I had Anita Moss on the line within seconds.

'How may I help you, Doctor?'

'Ms Moss, I was with Detective Sturgis the other day –'

'*With* him? You're not a cop?'

'I'm a psychologist. I consult to the police –'

'I'm sorry, I'm busy –'

'Just one question and I'll be out of your way: Which attorney represented Nestor on the manslaughter charge?'

'Why?'

'It could be important. We'll find out anyway, but you could make things easier.'

'Okay, okay. A blond lady,' she said. 'With a funny name – Sydney something.'

'Sydney Weider.'

'She put a lot of pressure on my mom to attend every hearing, even though my mom wasn't in good health. She ordered her to sit where the judge could see her, and cry a lot. Told my mom she'd have to take the stand when it came time for Nestor to be sentenced and lie about what a good son Nestor was and then cry a whole bunch more. Coaching her as if Mom was stupid. As if Mom wasn't crying all the time, anyway.'

'She put on an aggressive defense.'

'I guess,' she said. 'I always felt she was doing it more for herself – to win, you know? If she cared about my mother, she wouldn't have bossed her around like that. It didn't matter anyway. Nestor was guilty, they did this plea-bargain thing. Which was okay with me. I didn't want my mom to have to cry for strangers.'

'Was a man named Drew Daney involved with Nestor's case?'

'It sounds familiar, but . . .'

'A divinity student and youth worker –'

'Oh, yeah, him. The church guy,' she said. 'A few months before Nestor killed that dealer he got sent to some drug rehab program and the church guy worked there. Did he do something wrong? 'Cause that would surprise me.'

'Why?'

'Him I liked. He seemed real sincere about wanting to help Nestor. Wrote a letter to the judge for Nestor.'

'Puts everything in place, doesn't it?' said Milo, driving out of the lot.

'Daney visits Troy in Stockton,' I said. 'Uses the opportunity to drop in on Nestor and set Troy up.'

'Meanwhile, Rand's over in Chino. Think that's the reason Daney left him alone? No juvey hit man planted there?'

'More likely Rand wasn't a threat. Until he was.'

He got back on the freeway. 'You in the mood to ply your trade?'

'With who?'

'A crazy woman.'

38

Sydney Weider opened her front door wearing a soiled white T-shirt with a Surfside Country Club flying dolphin logo over her left breast, gray stretch athletic shorts, and bare feet. Up close, her face was pallid, scored vertically by wrinkles that began at the corners of her eyes and tugged her mouth down. Her legs were white, varicosed, her feet hangnailed and grubby around the ankles.

She opened her mouth in surprise.

Milo said, 'Ma'am,' and showed her his badge.

She slapped him hard across the face.

As he hauled her out to the unmarked, cuffed her, hissing and twisting, a *snick* sounded from across the street and a woman ran out of a pretty, black-shuttered Colonial.

Same neighbor who'd watched Weider scream at me a few days ago.

'Here we go,' muttered Milo. 'Where's the damned video camera?'

Weider growled and slammed her head into his arm and tried to bite him. He held her at arm's length. 'Open the door, Alex.'

As I did the woman from across the street sped toward us.

Late thirties, blond ponytail, shapely in tight black pedal pushers and a sea-green tank top. Grace Kelly facial definition. Sydney Weider in a younger, happier time.

She looked furious; let's hear it for Neighborhood Watch.

As she got closer, Milo said, 'Ma'am –'

'Good for you!' she said. 'That bitch screams at all the children and *terrifies* them! She makes everyone's lives miserable! What'd she do to finally get you to take some *action*?'

Sydney Weider spat in her direction. The gob landed on the sidewalk. The woman said, 'You're disgusting. As always.'

Before Weider could respond, Milo pressed down on her head, managed to get her into the car, and slammed the door. His face was flushed.

'What'd she finally do?' the woman repeated. 'You people said there was nothing you could –'

'Can't discuss that, ma'am. Now if you'd please –'

Thump thump thump as Weider kicked the window.

The ponytailed woman said, 'See? She's insane. I've got a list for you. Give me your fax number.'

'She's been that big of a problem?' I said.

'*Everyone* will rejoice when she's gone. We'll have a frickin' block party. A child touches her lawn, she steps out and screams at the top of her lungs. Last month, she threw a kitchen knife at Poppy and

Poppy's not one of those aggressive shar-peis, he's sweet as can be, ask anyone, they'll tell you. She runs up and down the street, talks like a banshee – she's insane, believe me, totally insane. I'm sure everyone on the block will be happy to give you a report or a deposition or whatever.'

Milo said, 'Appreciate it, ma'am.'

'Good riddance,' said the woman, glaring through the window. Sydney Weider lay on her back, feet up. She began kicking the window again. Barefoot, but hard enough to make the glass shudder.

The woman said, 'You should hog-tie her. Like on *Cops*.'

As we drove away, other doors opened but no one emerged.

Sydney Weider screamed wordlessly and resumed kicking the window. Milo stopped the car, parked, retrieved a set of plastic ties from the trunk, and defended himself against Weider's gnashing jaws and vicious feet as he fought to bind her ankles. I got out and held Weider's heels. Yet another divergence from accepted psychological practice.

Finally, he managed to flip her on her stomach, pull the ties snug. She writhed and foamed at the mouth and butted her head against the door as the car pulled away. Potty-mouth tirade; all those years in law school spent parsing and composing elegant phrases wasted.

I felt sorry for her.

*

When Milo reached Sunset, she turned silent. Panting, then snuffling, filled the car. I glanced back. Still flat on her belly. Eyes closed, inert.

I figured he'd take her to the jail at the Westside station, but he drove east through the Palisades and turned in to Will Rogers State Park.

A little-girl voice from the back said, 'I used to ride horses here.'

'Good for you,' said Milo.

Moments later: 'What did I do to make you so angry?'

'How about assaulting an officer?'

'Oh . . . ,' she said. 'I'm sorry I really am I don't know what happened I just you scared me I thought you were sent by my husband to torment me one of those process servers he won't let go one Halloween he sent a process server dressed up as a goblin and I opened the door for trick or treat and this goblin threw court papers at me and when I threw them back he grabbed me made contact with my arm that was real assault believe me much worse than what I did I'm an attorney I know what assault is when I see it listen I really didn't mean to hit you I was defending myself you really scared me.'

No pause for breath. The neighbor had talked about Weider's racing up and down the block. I remembered her as a fast talker and Marty Boestling had called her manic.

The only marathon was in her head.

'Really,' she said. 'I know now what I did I see it clearly and I'm so so so so sorry.'

We parked in the nearly empty lot that faced the polo fields.

'No horses anymore everything goes to shit in this city please,' said Sydney Weider. 'Just take off these things I hate to be restrained I really hate it.'

Milo switched off the engine.

'Please please I promise to behave appropriately.'

'Why should I trust you, Sydney?'

'Because I'm an honest person I know I acted irrationally but I already explained that to you it's my ex he never stops he won't give up making my life a living hell.'

'How long's he been doing that?' I said.

'At least the foot thingies please? They hurt they're bending my legs in a not-good way I'm constricted it's hard to breathe.'

Milo got out and undid the plastic ties, sat her up, careful to maintain distance from her teeth.

Weider smiled and flipped her hair and looked pretty for a pathetic second. 'Thank you thank you you're a doll thanks so much now how about the cuffs too?'

Milo returned to the front seat. 'So how long's your ex been tormenting you?'

'Always but what I'm talking about is since the divorce seven years seven long years of nonstop torture that's after he robbed me blind took everything my father left me my father was a film producer one of the top guys in Hollywood and that bastard knew where everything was kept he looted me looted me like something from the Watts riot we used to have a house cars Angelo Donghia furniture Sarouk rugs you name it we had a great life on the surface –'

'How come Mr Boestling's so angry?'

'What do you think he's a Jew,' said Weider. 'Vengeful eye for an eye they don't let go until you're sucked dry.'

'What's he want revenge for?'

'For my being superior for my being . . . it's complicated he'll never be happy he's consumed. About what? About making me pay and pay and pay for those people it's all about money he libels me tells everyone I'm crazy manic-depressive just because my energy's superior to his he could never –'

She stopped abruptly. 'You. The psychologist. You can tell I'm fine.'

Her eyes were bright with madness.

I said, 'Sure.'

Milo's eyelids vibrated. The mark Weider had left on his cheek had started to fade.

She smiled again. 'There you go you know about that kind of thing you tell this very kind police individual I'm an attorney a wife a mother did it all raised two beautiful boys you should see the deal Microsoft offered them both of them but they didn't take it they have their own software to develop why should someone else get rich on their accomplishments?'

I said, 'Despite all that Marty Boestling's being vengeful.'

'Mindlessly vengeful he's a nothing –'

'Maybe,' Milo broke in, 'finding you with Drew Daney wasn't a real fun experience for him.'

Weider's mouth hung open. She sank back down. 'You are blaming me for his inadequacies do you think if he could ... wait you talked to him are you really police are you from him a process ser –'

'No!' Milo bellowed. 'I'm an LAPD lieutenant who couldn't give a rat's ass about your marriage or your sex life. I *am* interested in talking about Drew Daney.'

Weider twitched, rolled her shoulder, looked out at the polo field. 'What about him?'

'What kind of guy is he?'

'What kind of guy is he scum pond scum the black stuff *under* pond scum –'

'You two have a lover's quarrel?' said Milo.

'Ha. Hahahahaha. There was no lover no love no lovemaking this was straight you know what he was nothing to me none of them were.'

'Who?'

'Don't pretend Marty didn't tell you he told you did he also tell you he got it started he was the one who liked watching me with other guys it only became a problem when I started to act independently meaning when he wasn't watching did he tell you that did he?'

'Like I said, Sydney, your sex life doesn't inter –'

'Right right you want to talk about Daney all Daney was to me was a male organ and not a big one at that you want to know about him I'll tell you he's a loser and a liar thought he was so smart thought he could get me to play his game.'

'What game was that?'

'You tell me you're the LAPD lieutenant why would anyone want to do anything so stupid you tell me that?'

'What was stupid?'

'Sticking a pin in the condom I always used condoms always bought them myself because when men think with the little head they're retarded and no way was I going to get messed up that way no way and I don't like the pill it's supposed to be good for your skin but it messed up mine gave me adult-onset acne and my mother died of cancer so who needs that so it was always rubbers.' Slow spreading smile. 'With tickly things.'

'How'd you know Daney poked holes in one?'

'Found him that's how he sneaked off into the bathroom,' she said, 'he thought I was dressing up in the tacky things he bought over at Trashy Lingerie costumes all that stupid cliché stuff like I was going to dress up for him ha no way so I was already out of my bathroom he was in Marty's bathroom and heard him messing around in there and walked in on him said what the hell do you think you're doing he made up some lame story about testing out a sample to see if it was strong to be extra careful I saw that I bitch-slapped him –'

She stopped.

Milo said, 'He got you mad.'

'Wouldn't you be mad if there was someone sneaking around on you doing that?' Weider laughed. 'Not that he was getting off the hook I opened a new one made sure it was fine and had him put it on in front of me made jokes about maybe I should've gotten a size small believe me that slowed things down fine with me I set the tone he never had me I had him.'

'Did that end the relationship?' said Milo.

'What relationship he was a tool what ended it was Marty being a loser screwing up a pitch meeting and coming home early and finding us not that I cared about Marty it was the way he reacted Daney just scurrying off with his you know what tucked between his legs.' She flipped her hair. 'My motto no wimps no losers no complications.'

'How'd Daney react to your breaking it off?'

'Called me kept calling me finally he gave up.'

I said, 'Why do you think he punctured the condom?'

'You tell me you're the psychologist,' said Weider.

'Could he have wanted to get you pregnant?'

'No because he didn't like kids.'

'He told you that?'

'Sure more than once he said his wife wanted them

she couldn't have them he said no way he didn't want the hassle.'

'He confided in you.'

'He talked about everything I couldn't get him to shut up what'd he do anyway?'

'You never asked him to explain why he'd tried to puncture the condom?'

'I told you he gave me that stupid story and I hit him upside the head I didn't care what his story was the main thing was do things my way.' Another hair flip. 'I don't think it was pregnancy per se I think it was sperm.'

'Pardon?'

'S-P-E-R-M he thought his was the elixir of the gods he'd go off on these long speeches about his you-know-what and how it was the magic wand of the future you could create cities countries continents with a teaspoon he'd get like that after he had his glorious three minutes all he wanted to do afterward was raid my refrigerator and blab.'

'Magic sperm,' said Milo.

'He was really into it really weird obsessive what's that other word – fixated that's a psychological term right that's what you guys call it fixated.'

I nodded.

Milo said, 'Daney had a sperm fixation.'

'Want to know what I think about Daney I think he was a fixation sperm egomaniac everything about him was so so important he even started thinking he was an attorney thought he could tell me how to run my case believe me that didn't last long I put him in his place.'

I said, 'The Malley case?'

'He watched too many movies had all these ideas these bad TV movie ideas like cross-examine the cops until they wore themselves out or shift the blame to the kid's father so there'd be reasonable doubt I said shutup this isn't Perry Mason the little bastards were caught with the body they admitted they did it I'll get the best deal for them but they're going away and that's what happened.'

'Daney wanted to blame Barnett Malley.'

'He said I should dig into Malley's background and find out if Malley and the mother were getting along and if there was some sort of conflict I could suggest Malley hated the wife and the kid hired those two little bastards to kill the kid I said you're insane that's the stupidest thing I ever heard of he said not if Troy backs it up I could talk to Troy Troy trusts me Troy would say anything I tell him to because we have rapport –'

'Daney knew Troy that well?'

'He knew him from working as a youth worker that's a laugh a youth leader who doesn't like kids he kept trying to convince me with his stupid story finally I threatened to stop sleeping with him told him what you're asking me to do is suborn perjury you idiot the facts are clear the best we can hope for is extenuating circumstances rough childhood abuse neglect all that if you can find me some abuse some real abuse I'll go to the damned judge with that but otherwise stay out of it – can you take off these cuffs?'

Milo said, 'Going to behave?'

'Haven't I?'

'You haven't had much choice, Sydney.'

'Even without cuffs what's my choice you're three times my size in your arms I'm a little girl.'

Hair flip.

Milo said, 'One screwup and they go back on.'

'Fine I get it you're the boss the man you call the shots.'

He made another trip to the backseat. Sydney Weider said, 'Ahh it's like Joni Mitchell said you don't know what you got till it's gone so why all these questions about Daney he finally do something real stupid?'

Milo walked around the car, got in back, and sat next to her. 'As opposed to small-time stupid?'

'Exactly he was always small-time stupid.'

'How exactly did you meet him?'

'Another case,' she said. 'Another little psychopath Daney doing his youth work bullshit he calls offers to help any way he can I figured why not maybe he could put a letter in the kid's file for sentencing.'

'Same thing he did for Troy,' I said.

'That's the way it is at the P.D. ninety-five percent of what we did was process guilty people and angle for the best deal –'

'Remember the name of the other little psychopath?'

'Some Latin junkie he shot some other junkies downtown I got it pled down to manslaughter Nestor something ... Almodovar, that's it, Nestor Almodovar.'

Milo didn't correct her. 'Daney wrote a letter for Nestor.'

'Your basic character reference Nestor was a good kid rough childhood extenuating circumstances blah blah blah.'

'And Daney just happened to be working on another of your cases?'

'No no no,' said Weider, 'Daney called me asked me to defend Troy at first I didn't want to do it because believe me I was putting in the hours who needed the hassle but he kept working on me telling me I was the smartest D.P.D. in the office which happened to be true then I figured why not it could be interesting.'

'How so?' I said.

'Interesting –' Weider repeated. Then she stared at me, went silent, twisted her mouth nonstop, as if compensating for the lack of sound.

Milo said, 'Interesting as in high-profile. As in getting your name in the paper.'

Weider turned toward him. 'Why shouldn't I get some of the good ones you put in the hours why not get a little coverage?'

'And a movie deal,' said Milo.

Weider did the open-shut thing with her mouth again. More panting, more lip acrobatics. She snapped her head away from Milo and stared out the window. 'That was after the case resolved nothing illegal about that it happens all the time.'

'Was the movie your idea or Daney's?'

'His,' she said, too quickly. 'He used to say look at Marty such a total loser but he's driving a Mercedes and lunching at the studio commissary even though with all that opportunity he still couldn't produce anything better than grade C made-for-TV crap.'

'Daney figured he could do bet –'

'He figured if he had Marty's opportunities he'd own a studio.'

'Delusions of grandeur,' said Milo.

'Doesn't stop anyone else in Hollywood,' said Weider. 'I could tell you stories besides I knew why he was talking himself up like that.'

'Why?'

Smug smile. 'To get himself hard that's what he'd do when he had problems he'd talk himself up and put Marty down that's what it's all about for men out-dicking the other guy.'

'Still,' I said, 'you took the movie idea seriously.'

'What do you mean?'

'Didn't you and Daney take meetings?'

'Everyone takes meetings you stop taking meetings the industry shrivels up like Daney's you-know-what when he got nervous.'

'Everyone takes meetings but so did you.'

'Yeah I went I took it as seriously as anything else

why not what was there to lose do you guys have anything to drink I'm really thirsty.'

'Sorry, no,' said Milo.

'Damn I'm parched that's why I hate ...' Her head dropped. Staring at her legs.

'What do you hate?'

'Pills dope poison I refuse to take anything to hell with stupid doctors the best thing for stress is activity work off the toxins speaking of which I'm starting to feel really confined could we walk a little take a little stroll –'

Milo said, 'Who set up the meetings?'

'I did Daney tagged along thinking he was smooth –'

'Not Marty?'

'Marty gave us some names big deal I already knew them from my father he had a Rolodex to die for don't listen to anything Marty tells you he's nuts –'

'Do you have a copy of the treatment?' I said.

'No why would I?'

'Ever register it with the Writers' Guild?'

'No why would I?'

'Isn't that basic procedure?'

'If you care,' she said. 'I lost interest after a couple of meetings you could tell from the reaction it was going nowhere fast that's the way it is in the industry you're insta-hot or insta-not stupid mistake my one mistake.'

'What was that?'

'Letting Daney write it he put in the same old crap he'd wanted me to use with Troy.'

'Blaming Barnett Malley,' I said.

'Blaming Barnett Malley but kicking it up to an absurd level now Malley was some kind of serial killer obsessed with power and control and body parts.'

'Sounds a bit like Daney himself,' I said.

'Hey,' she said, merrily. 'You must be some kind of shrink.'

39

Milo said, 'I'll take you home, Sydney.'

'I'm still thirsty could we stop somewhere?'

'If I pass a place, I'll get you a Coke.'

'How about Joya Juice there's one near my house.'

As we left the park, she turned silent and fidgety.

I said, 'What was your impression of Cherish Daney?'

'Drew said she was a real religious type wanted kids a whole bunch of them a brood was the term he used but she couldn't have any she was sterile it was an issue.'

'Not having kids?'

'Adoption she finally accepted she couldn't have her own decided she wanted to adopt was really obsessed with adopting even a kid from China Bulgaria Bolivia one of those places he didn't want it didn't want the commitment I said what about foster kids that way she gets to play mama then they leave and you're off the hook and you get paid.'

'Drew like the idea of fostering?'

'He loved it said brilliant Syd you're a genius that's what he called me *Syd* extremely irritating big burr in the saddle but he kept doing it a real loser when we get to Joya I'd like something with pineapple in it okay?'

She directed him to the juice bar, just north of Sunset, in Palisades Village. He left her cuffed and went inside.

Women who looked like Weider were all around. She sank down and lay flat on the rear seat. I asked her about Barnett Malley but she claimed to know nothing about him.

'No impressions?'

'Why would I he was the other side?'

'Daney's theories never got you curious?'

'That was bullshit.'

'What about Malley riding the rodeo?'

'What are you *talking* about?'

Milo returned with a giant cup and a straw. She sat up and said, 'Take off the cuffs I need to hold it.' He leaned into the car and held the straw to her mouth. She said 'Oh c'mon,' but drank greedily, cheeks deflating. When she stopped for a breath, a speck of froth remained on her lower lip. Milo wiped it off.

She looked up at him with fear. 'Please let me hold it.'

'No more problems?'

'I promise really.'

'Gonna avoid issues with the neighbors?'

She smiled. 'What do you care about that you're a big-issue guy it's Daney you're after obviously he's done something serious but I don't even care what.'

'No curiosity?'

'I don't live in the past the past is like a dead body just keeps rotting and stinking may I have another sip please and can you please take off the damned cuffs?'

'You and Drew don't talk anymore?'

Hoarse laugh. 'Haven't talked to that loser in seven years what do you think I'm going to call him tell him you were here that'll be the day if he ever tried to get near me I'd cut off his you-know-what.'

'Bet you would,' said Milo. He freed her hands and handed her the cup. She sipped, remained docile and silent during the ride back to her house.

When we got there, Milo helped her out of the car. She stood looking at her front door as if she'd never seen it before. Milo took her by the elbow and walked her up the drive. Halfway there, he hung back. She stopped, flipped hair, flashed teeth, said something that made him smile. Stood on her tiptoes and pecked his cheek.

He watched as she walked to her door, stood there as she crossed the threshold. Returned shaking his head.

I said, 'What was the joke?'

'The – Oh, that. She said "You're sending me off like a little birdie out of the nest chirp chirp chirp."' He jammed the key in the ignition. 'It caught me off guard. For a second, she seemed kinda cute.' He frowned. 'That kiss. I need to wash my face.'

*

A block later, he said, 'She's completely nuts but everything she told us fits. What do you think of Daney's sperm-obsession?'

'All part of his me-obsession. What interests me is that right from the beginning Daney wanted to focus blame on Malley. Why would that be unless he knew Malley before Kristal's murder and had some reason to resent him? I brought up the rodeo to Weider and she looked at me as if *I* was crazy. So Daney lied about hearing it from her. He knew Barnett eight years ago or did research.'

'Maybe the swinger's scene, like you suggested.'

'Or a tamer possibility,' I said. 'Now that we know we've got two couples with infertility problems.'

'A clinic,' he said. 'They met at a damned fertility clinic?'

'Weider said Cherish had "finally" given up on having her own children. That implies she had tried to conceive for a while. That had to include medical treatment.'

'Chatting in the waiting room, the old misery loves company bit.'

'Until Drew and Lara took the friendship a step further,' I said. 'The two spouses who just happened to be fertile. It's possible neither of them knew that and Lara's pregnancy caught them by surprise. Drew had to figure she'd terminate because of the repercussions with Barnett. But she refused. Having a baby meant more to her than her marriage.'

'All of a sudden the Malleys are having a baby and the Daneys aren't.'

'Leaving Cherish with a whole lot of frustration and anguish. Three guesses who she'd vent to.'

'She gets on Drew's case, pushes for more fertility treatment.'

'Which would be expensive and a monumental hassle for something Drew didn't want in the first place. Either he agreed and it didn't work, or he refused. In either case, Cherish switched her goal to adoption. Became obsessed with it.'

'Idiot thinks he's the cleverest guy in the world and all of a sudden his life's getting knotted up because of a problem *he* helped create. Talk about insult added to injury.'

'So he decided to eliminate the source of the insult,' I said. 'Turned Kristal into an object lesson for Cherish. "See the joy babies bring, hon?" At the same time, he was able to play out his God fantasy and free himself of any future demands from Lara. And as long as he was cleaning house, why not get a movie deal out of it?'

He hunched and scowled and gripped the wheel, as relaxed as a student driver. Salt air blew through the car's open windows. Charming neighborhood. How long before Sydney Weider imploded?

Milo said, 'Cleaning house permanently. Kristal, then Troy because he killed Kristal, then Nestor because *he* killed Troy. And Lara either because she wanted to get serious with him or she had figured out he had something to do with Kristal's death.'

'Jane Hannabee, too, because Daney couldn't be certain Troy hadn't said something to his mother.'

'And now Rand ... think Drew did any of them himself or were they contract deals?'

'Whoever did Lara did Rand. My money's on Daney for those. Hannabee could've gone either way.'

'Six bodies,' he said. 'And there's something I neglected to mention. I checked for any Mirandas on Daney's foster list. Nothing close.'

'Why would Daney take in a ward and not bill the state?'

'Why, indeed.'

'Oh,' I said.

'Now how the hell am I going to prove any of it with no evidentiary connections?'

I had no answer.

'Yeah,' he grumbled. 'I was afraid you'd say that.'

He dropped me home at one-forty p.m. Allison hadn't called my cell and there were no messages on my machine.

In five minutes, she'd be between patients. I watched the clock, had a cold cup of coffee, phoned her office when the big hand touched the nine.

'Hi,' she said. 'I'm in the middle of something, promise to call as soon as I can.'

'Emergency?'

'Something like that.'

'We're okay?'

Silence. 'Sure.'

It was seven-thirty when I heard from her.

'Emergency resolved?'

'This morning Beth Scoggins went into a changing room at work and locked herself in. It took awhile before anyone noticed. When they found her she was sitting on the floor, curled up, sucking her thumb. She was unresponsive, had wet her pants. The manager dialed 911 and the ambulance took her to the U. They gave her a physical and a tox scan, then some psych residents tried out their interview skills on her. Finally, she let someone know I was her therapist and an attending psychiatrist called me. It was him I was talking to when you phoned. I canceled my afternoon patients and went over there, just got back to the office.'

'How's she doing?'

'Still regressed but she's starting to talk. About things she never talked about before.'

'More about Daney or –'

'I can't get into it with you, Alex.'

'Sure,' I said. 'Allison, if I had anything to –'

'She's obviously been sitting on a mountain of issues – a volcano. I was probably too laid-back, should've worked harder at opening her up.'

Same thing, nearly word for word, that Cherish Daney had said about Rand.

This was different. Allison was trained. Cherish had been running with scissors.

Out of her element.

Or maybe not.

My head flooded with what-ifs.

I said, 'I'm sure you handled it optimally.' That came out hollow.

'Whatever. Listen, I've got to phone all those cancellations, rearrange my schedule, extend my hours, then go back to the hospital. It's going to be awhile before we can ... socialize. Don't even suggest to Milo that he'll ever have access to this girl.'

'It's not an issue.'

'I know what's at stake, Alex, but we're on opposite sides on this one. I'm sorry, but that's the way it has to be.'

Three hours later, she was at my door, dangling her car keys. Her hair was tied up in a careless way I'd never seen before, black as the night sky behind her. One of her stockings sported a run from knee to mid-calf, the polish on some of her nails was chipped, and her lipstick had faded. A picture I.D. badge was clipped to the lapel of her black cotton suit. Temporary privileges, Department of Psychiatry. Her eyes, always deep-set, were captives in fatigue-darkened sockets.

She said, 'I haven't meant to be distant. Though I still have problems – big problems – with the whole deception thing.'

'Have any dinner yet?'

'Not hungry.'

'C'mon in.'

She shook her head. 'Too tired, Alex. I just wanted to say that.'

'Come in anyway.'

Her chin trembled. 'I'm exhausted, Alex. Won't be good company.'

I touched her shoulder. She edged past me as if I were an obstacle. I followed her into the kitchen, where she tossed the keys and her purse on the table and sat staring at the sink.

She refused food but accepted hot tea. I brought a mug with some toast.

'Persistent,' she said.

'So I've been told.' I took a chair across from her.

'It's ridiculous,' she said. 'I've had patients go through worse than this. A lot worse. I think it's a combination of this particular patient – maybe I let the countertransference get out of hand – and your being involved.'

She raised the mug to her lips. 'When I met you, what you do ... it turned me on. The whole police thing, the whole heroic thing – here was someone in my profession doing more than sitting in an office and listening. I never told you this, but I've had hero fantasies of my own. Probably because of what happened to me. I guess I've been living *through* you.

On top of that you're a sexy guy, no question. I was a sucker.'

What 'had happened' to her was sexual assault at age seventeen. Warding off attempted robbery and gang rape years later.

She eyed her purse and I knew she was thinking about the shiny little gun. 'What you do *still* turns me on, but this has been a rude awakening. I'm realizing that maybe there are aspects of it that aren't healthy.'

'Like deception.' And holding down a woman's ankles so a detective can hog-tie her.

Her eyes turned the color of gas jets. 'You flat-out lied to her, Alex. A girl you didn't know, with no consideration of the risks. I'm sure most of the time it's no big deal, just a fib in the service of law enforcement and no one gets hurt. This time ... maybe in the long run it *will* be good for her. But now ...'

She put the mug down. 'I keep telling myself if she was this close to the edge she would've been tipped over eventually. Maybe it's my ego that's wounded. I got caught unawares....'

I touched her hand. She didn't touch back.

'Deception's okay for Milo, I understand the kind of people cops come into contact with. But you and I took the same licensing exam and we both know what our ethics code says.'

She freed her hand. 'Have *you* thought it through, Alex?'

'I have.'

'And?'

'I'm not sure my answer's going to make you happy.'

'Try me.'

'When I see patients in a therapeutic setting, the rules apply. When I work with Milo, the rules are different.'

'Different how?'

'I'd never hurt anyone intentionally, but there's no promise of confidentiality.'

'Or truthfulness.'

I didn't answer. No sense mentioning the man I killed a few years ago. Clear self-defense. Sometimes his face came to me in dreams. Sometimes I manufactured the faces of his unborn children.

'I don't mean to attack you,' said Allison.

'I don't feel attacked. It's a reasonable discussion. Maybe one we should've had earlier.'

'Maybe,' she said. 'So basically, you compartmentalize. That doesn't wear on you?'

'I deal with it.'

'Because bad people sometimes get what's coming to them.'

'That helps.' I worked hard at keeping my tone even. Saying the right things though I did feel attacked. Thinking about six bodies, maybe seven, no obvious solution. Thinking about Cherish Daney in a way that I couldn't let go of.

Allison said, 'Is deception a big part of what you do?'

'No,' I said. 'But it happens. I try never to grow glib, but I rationalize when I have to. I'm sorry about what happened to Beth and I'm not going to make excuses. The only lie I told her was that I was researching foster parenting in general. I don't see that as a factor in her breakdown.'

'Getting *into* the whole issue precipitated her breakdown, Alex. She's an extremely vulnerable girl who should never have been drawn into a police investigation in the first place.'

'There was no way to know that.'

'Exactly. That's why we learned about discretion and taking our time and thinking things through. About doing no harm.'

'Witnesses are often vulnerable,' I said.

Long silence.

She said, 'So you're fine with all this.'

'Would I have approached Beth directly if I'd known she was going to decompensate? Of course not. Would I have taken another approach – like going through you? You bet. Because a lot is at stake, even more than I've told you, and she was a potential source of crucial information.'

'What more is at stake?'

I shook my head.

'Why not?' she said.

'There's no need for you to know.'

'You're mad so you're doing a tit for tat.'

'I'm not mad, I want to keep you from the bad stuff.' *The way I used to keep Robin.*

424

'Because I can't hope to understand.'

I thought you did. But it's too much ugly.

'There's just no reason for you to get involved, Allison.'

'I'm already involved.'

'As a therapist.'

'So I just run off and do my therapy thing and keep my nose out of your business?'

That would simplify things.

'It's one of the ugliest cases I've ever worked on, Ali. You already spend your days soaking up other people's crap. Why would you want more soul pollution?'

'And you? What about your soul?'

'Such as it is.'

'I won't accept that it doesn't affect you.'

Unborn children . . .

I didn't answer.

She said, 'You can handle it, but I can't?'

'I don't ask you about patients.'

'That's different.'

'Maybe it really isn't.'

'Fine,' she said. 'So now there's a new taboo in our relationship. What binds us together? Hot sex?'

I pointed to the toast. 'And haute cuisine.'

She worked at a smile. Got up and took the mug to the sink, where she emptied and washed. 'I'd better be going.'

'Stay.'

'Why?'

I walked behind her, slipped my arm around her waist. Felt her abdominal muscles ripple as she tensed up. She removed my hand, turned, and looked up at me. 'I've probably put some kind of wedge between us. Maybe I'll wake up tomorrow and feel like a first-class idiot, but right now I've still got some righteous indignation burning in my belly.'

I said, 'The higher stakes are six murders, maybe seven. If you include the girl who succeeded Beth as Daney's assistant. She seems to have vanished and she's not on the foster rolls.'

She stepped out of my arms, braced herself against the counter, and stared out the kitchen window.

'Plus a toddler,' I went on. 'Two teenage boys, three women, a mentally challenged young man. And so far, no way to prove any of it.'

She lowered her head into the sink, heaved and dry-retched.

I tried to hold her as she shuddered.

'Sorry,' she whimpered, pulling away. Splashing water on her face, she dried it with her sleeve. Snatched up her purse and keys, left the kitchen.

I caught up as she opened the front door. 'You're exhausted. Stay. I'll take the couch.'

Her lips were parched and tiny blood spots freckled her cheeks. Petechiae from the strain of vomiting. 'It's a nice offer. You're a nice man.'

'I'd like to be a good man.'

Her eyes shifted. 'I need to be alone.'

40

I returned to the kitchen, chewed on the toast I'd made Allison, and thought about what had just happened.

Tomorrow I might also wake up feeling rotten. If I slept at all. Right now I was glad to be alone, reunited with the possibilities that had flooded my head.

It was eleven-fifteen. I figured Milo wouldn't be sleeping much either. And if he had drifted off, too damn bad.

'What time is it?' he rasped.

'Cherish Daney told me she tried to open Rand up, wished she'd been more effective. For his sake. But what if she had another motive? What if she found out what Drew had done, wanted Rand to come forward about Drew's involvement in Kristal's murder?'

He let out a couple of barking coughs, cleared his throat. 'Good evening to you, too. Where'd all this come from?'

'You've been saying all along Cherish had to know something. Maybe she had suspicions but was able to deny them until she finally came upon something blatant.'

'Like what?'

'Trophies. Someone with Drew's control obsession might very well keep some. He got a kick out of sneaking around Cherish, a hidden cache would be great fun. But arrogance leads to carelessness. Maybe he slipped up and left something for her to find. Or all those trips with "assistants" got her suspicious and she started to snoop around the house. If she's anything but a monster herself, finding hard evidence of Drew's crimes would horrify her. She'd also be scared on a selfish level: If the truth ever came out, she was sure to come under suspicion as an accomplice. One way to deal with all that would be to come forward with evidence of her own and bail. Having Rand corroborate Drew's involvement in Kristal's murder would be a big step in that direction.'

'Daney molests and murders for years and she's Little Miss Clueless until now?'

'Nothing we've learned so far says she did anything worse than exceed the foster limit. Beth Scoggins said she filled her days cooking, cleaning, and teaching. My bet is she kept busy so as not to think.'

'Not to mention seven grand a month.'

'For Drew it was the money,' I said. 'Maybe for her, too. But she drives an old heap and lives simply. Plus you saw how she worked with Valerie. Patient, despite Valerie's resentment.'

'The dutiful hausfrau,' he said. 'Meanwhile Drew's out doing his sperm thing ... I'm still not convinced she's squeaky clean, but fine, let's run with it. She wants Rand to rat out Drew, does therapy with him, then what?'

'She fails. The most common errors unqualified therapists make are moving too fast and talking too much. Toss in Cherish's anxiety and she'd have come on way too strong. She needed Rand to "see" that Drew had contracted Troy to kill Kristal. Whether or not he had.'

'She tried to plant it in his head?'

'It started during prison visits. Hinting around, hoping to set off a spark in Rand's head. Rand was a submissive personality, impressionable, so perhaps he actually recalled something – seeing Drew talk to Troy shortly before the murder, an offhand comment by Troy about Drew. Or he thought he did. Because an adult mastermind would be welcome news for *him*. Reduce his own culpability.'

' "I'm a good person." '

' "I'm a good person because *Daney* was behind it and *Troy* was his henchman and *I* was in the wrong place at the right time." Cherish could've even presented it to him that way.'

'If he bought it, why didn't he open up?'

'Eight years in jail, being beaten and stabbed and left to fend for himself, had taught him to be wary. Nevertheless, the idea Cherish planted took root and it terrified him: He'd be living under the roof of the devil who'd ruined his life. *That's* why he was so anxious when he was released to the Daneys.'

'Then why'd he go there in the first place?'

'He had no immediate alternatives. No family, no resources, no grasp of what the world outside prison was like. He also had to be careful not to set off Drew's suspicions with a sudden shift in plans. But I'll bet he intended to get out of there as soon as possible. As soon as he could get someone to listen.'

'You.'

'Cherish's eagerness could have made him even more wary. Lauritz Montez had defended him by the numbers. He sure wouldn't view the D.A. or the police as sympathetic. That left me.'

'Modesty, modesty,' he said. 'So he gives the Daneys a phony story, walks away, somehow makes it over the hill, calls you from Westwood.'

'I don't think he made it over the hill alone. He couldn't keep his anxiety under control and Drew *did* catch on that something was wrong. Drew was out of the house when Rand left. He could've been nearby, watching Rand. Or he called in and Cherish told him Rand had gone to the construction site. That fed Drew's suspicions because he knew the site was closed Saturday except for cleanup. He went after Rand, spotted him, picked him up in the Jeep.'

'And took him into the city? Why?'

'To allay Rand's fears,' I said. 'Rand's shuffling along, disoriented, looking for a pay phone, or just trying to clear his head. Daney cruises by, all smiles, says hop in, let's grab a bite. Caught off guard, Rand would've felt forced to comply, so as not to appear nervous. Daney drove over the hill and disarmed

Rand further with small talk. Dropped him off at the entrance to Westside Pavilion with some pocket change, told him to have a good time, he'd pick him up later. No one from the mall remembers Rand, he may never have gone in. This was a dull, confused kid who'd grown up behind bars. It would have been like dropping him on Mars.'

'Why would Daney go to all that trouble? Why not drive him somewhere secluded and kill him right off?'

'Daney had his suspicions, but at that point, Daney wasn't sure killing Rand was necessary. Another Kristal-related death might set off a whole chain of events he couldn't control. Which is exactly what happened. After he dropped Rand off, he stuck around to watch. Saw Rand walk away from the mall, watched him head for the phone booth. Rand was agitated when he called me, his body language would've been easy to read. When Rand left the booth, Drew went after his quarry.'

'Picking him up again,' he said. 'This time it would have to be at gunpoint, Rand wouldn't have gone willingly.'

'Drew's deviousness can't be discounted. I can see him using a phony story – Cherish had suddenly taken ill, they needed to get home fast. Maybe Rand figured that if he didn't show up at the pizza place, I'd sound some kind of alarm and someone would come to his aid.'

If so, he'd overestimated me.

Milo said, 'Okay, one way or the other, he gets back in the Jeep and Drew drives somewhere secluded – the dump site says it was probably up into the foothills of Bel Air. Rand, not knowing the city, doesn't catch on that Drew's taken a detour. Drew finds a spot, pulls over. Then what?'

'Rand was big and strong, so Drew needed to avoid a physical struggle by keeping it friendly. He'd prepared by opening the Jeep's passenger window. Came across calm, paternal, even spiritual. Rand was probably looking straight ahead, scared and confused but fighting to maintain calm, when Drew pressed the gun against his temple and pulled the trigger. Drew had plenty of time to wipe down the Jeep and look for the bullet. Then he cruised back to Sunset after dark, drove to the on-ramp, made sure no one was watching, and dumped the body. The next day, he probably washed the Jeep. But there still might be some kind of transfer – blood, powder residue, tiny bone fragments.'

'Good story, Alex. Great story, makes perfect sense. But clever plots don't earn warrants.'

'You've already got grounds for a warrant,' I said. 'Drew's statutory rapes. Get the downtown juvey team interested, toss the house, include the Jeep in the paperwork.'

'For that I need DNA to prove what Daney did to Valerie,' he said. 'Or one of the other girls coming forward.'

'You saw him with Valerie at the clinic.'

'I saw him waiting and picking her up. It's suggestive but not probative. Any progress on Beth
Scoggins?'

'No.'

'Just like that.'

'Just like that.'

'Allison's adamant?'

'Let's leave it at "just like that,"' I said.

Silence. 'Any other suggestions?'

'Isolate Cherish and talk to her. Don't mention the
murders right off, tell her you know about Valerie's
abortion and that you suspect Drew was the father.
She might be willing to acknowledge her suspicions
about the molestations or even go all the way and
talk about Kristal.'

'If she's so intent upon clearing herself, why didn't
she come forward after Rand was murdered?'

'Like Rand, she's living under the same roof with
Drew. Maybe she's worried she doesn't have enough
evidence to ensure he'd be put away.'

'Makes sense,' he said. 'But we've left something
out: Cherish and Malley. If he's her squeeze, why
wouldn't she tell him? And if she did, why didn't
he cooperate with me? Something's still wrong with
the picture, Alex. I'm not ready to put Barnett or
Cherish on the good-guy list.'

'We *know* what list Drew's on and he's living with
eight underage girls. Then there's Miranda.'

'I am not unaware of the exigencies.'

'Didn't mean to imply you weren't.'

433

'Let me sleep on this. So to speak. In the morning, I'll get Binchy to watch the Daney house really early, which ain't gonna be a snap, Galton Street being so quiet. If Cherish leaves first, Sean'll follow her and hand her off to me. If Drew leaves, Sean'll stay on him and I'll pay Cherish a little visit.'

'Either way, let me know.'

'You might very well be there.'

41

The doorbell, followed by spirited knocking, woke me at seven a.m. My clouded brain knew what was happening: Allison had come by before work, wanting to make up.

I stumbled out of bed, padded to the door in my boxers, flung it open with a welcoming smile.

Milo stood there, wearing a tired green blazer, gray cords, yellow shirt, brown tie. In one hand was a box of Daffy Donuts, in the other two extra-large cups of the same outlet's coffee. He squinted at me as if I were a rare and unsavory species.

'Revenge?' I said.

'For what?'

'Last night's wake-up call.'

'Huh – oh, that. No, I was just dozing in the chair. Stayed up till three, working over a bunch of scenarios.'

He stepped past me. I left him in the kitchen and put on a robe. When I returned, the box was open, revealing a jarringly vivid assortment of fried things. Milo's paw was wrapped around a coffee. He'd made admirable progress on a bear claw the size of a puppy.

Same thing he'd ingested during the second meeting with Drew Daney and I said so.

'Yeah, I was inspired,' he said, spewing crumbs.

'Give grease its due.' He pointed at the other cup. 'Drink and awaken, lad.'

'Daffy instead of Dipsy?'

'My local purveyor, indie outfit. I'm doing my bit for free enterprise.'

I sipped the coffee, tasted copper and dishwater and something vaguely javalike. Fighting the urge to spit, I said, 'Decide on any new scenarios?'

'No, I've decided to go steady with the one you gifted me with: Cherish tried the shrink bit, moved too fast, scared the hell out of Rand, Drew caught on.' He stuffed what was left of the bear claw in his mouth. Sugary lips twisted upward. 'Here I was thinking all that *pacing* you therapy folk do – all those months of "Uh huhs" and "I hear you's" – was to keep the payment rolling in.'

'Here *I* was thinking cops didn't always sacrifice their pancreases to sucrose.' I yawned. 'Are we off somewhere this morning or is there more to talk about?'

'We're off when Sean calls.'

'When's that?'

'I told him to start watching the house at seven and touch base hourly. Finish your coffee, get cleaned up and dressed.'

'Two out of three ain't bad,' I said, and left the cup on the table.

When I got back he was sprawled in the living room, cell phone to his ear, nodding and pumping his left leg. 'Thanks, great, really great.' Snapping the phone shut, he stood. 'You still look half-asleep.'

'You don't,' I said. 'What's fueling you?'

'The remote possibility that things could fall into place. That was Sue Kramer, God bless her. She was up with the birds, too, following leads in other time zones. If I were of the hetero persuasion I'd betroth her.'

'She's already married.'

'Picky, picky. Anyway, she found out a few things about both our boys. Let's get going, I'll tell you in the car.'

He asked me to drive and when I started up the Seville, his head dropped onto his chest. As I took the Glen toward the Valley, he snored with gusto. At Mulholland, his head shot up and he began reciting as if there'd been no lull.

'The cowboy was born in Alamogordo, like I said. Moved to Los Alamos when he was ten because the ranch where his dad worked shut down and Pops got a janitorial gig at the nuke lab. The family lived there for ten years. One sib, an older sister, married with kids, works for the city of Cleveland. After high school, Barnett did a couple of years as truck driver, then he got a job with Santa Fe P.D.'

'He was a cop?'

'Worked patrol for eighteen months until a couple of complaints about undue force brought him and the department to a mutual understanding.'

'He quit, no prosecution.'

He nodded. 'After that, there were some years when he reported no income, as best as Sue can tell, he drifted around as a laborer. He got on the dude ranch circuit ten years ago, moved to California. After he got married, he switched to swimming pool maintenance. Other than a short temper with suspects when he was twenty-one, he's got nothing iffy in his background. The surface impression seems to be all of it: a taciturn loner whose life hasn't turned out so great.'

'As opposed to Daney.'

'Reason *he* was hard to trace is he changed his name. He was born Moore Daney Andruson, is five years older than he claims on his driver's license. Grew up in rural Arkansas, one of seven kids, at least three of whom have ended up in prison for violent crimes. His folks were itinerant preachers on the hillbilly circuit.'

'The part about growing up in the church was true,' I said.

'More like growing up in revival tents. With reptiles. His daddy was one of those rattlesnake handlers, religious rapture supposed to protect him against venom. Until it didn't.'

'How'd Sue find all this out?'

'Despite being a scumbag the name change was legal and Daney *has* been reporting income with the IRS, on and off since he was eighteen. His credit history as Moore D. Andruson bottomed out twelve years ago. Lots of unpaid bills, a couple of bank-ruptcies.'

'Wonder why he bothered to file returns,' I said.

'He didn't have much choice. His early jobs were salaried, required withholding, SSI, all that good stuff. Now that he bills the state, there's different paperwork required.'

'What kind of jobs are we talking about?'

'Guess.'

'Youth work.'

'Camp counselor, substance abuse counselor, substitute teacher, Sunday school teacher, gym coach, always in small towns. He put bogus degrees on his applications and that eventually got him kicked out of three jobs in three different towns. After that, he tried suburbia, drove a school bus for a girls' preppie academy in Richmond, Virginia.'

'What a surprise.'

'That's where he met Cherish. He was Drew Daney by then. She'd gotten a degree from Bible college, was teaching retarded kids at another school.'

'He's got no southern accent,' I said. 'More re-invention. His employers discovered his phony credentials *after* they'd hired him. Meaning they got suspicious about something else and checked him out.'

'No doubt, but no one's being free with the details. Sue had to work just to get them to admit they knew him.'

'Meaning they kept it in-house. Anyone report the credentials scam?'

'Nope, they just sent him packing.'

'To his next victim.'

'So what else is new?' he said. 'He did manage to acquire a police record, but not the type that would get entered in NCIC or any other national file. Indecent exposure pled down to a misdemeanor trespassing in Vivian, Louisiana; bad checks settled by reimbursement, no jail time, in Keswick, Virginia; sexual assault in Carrol County, Georgia. That one was dismissed. Sheriff said he knew Andruson did it but the girl he was accused of seducing had cerebral palsy and could barely talk. They figured she wouldn't make the grade as a witness, wanted to spare her the ordeal.'

'Moral of the story: go for the vulnerable.'

'I asked Sue to find what she could on that missing girl, Miranda. Gave her Olivia's number. Talk about your meeting of the minds.'

Out of his jacket pocket came tinny music. No more Beethoven, some sort of Latin beat. He reached in and extricated his cell phone. It kept tangoing as he checked the caller's number. He had reprogrammed the ring. I'd thought it was mostly kids who did that.

'Sturgis . . . yeah, hi. No, there's no parking on the property. I'm sure, Sean. You're positive you didn't miss anything? Well, that definitely complicates things . . . hope not . . . yeah, yeah, check all that out, our E.T.A.'s fifteen, twenty, I'll call you unless you learn something earth-shattering.'

Click. 'Sean's been in place since six forty-five. Neither Daney's Jeep nor Cherish's Toyota are in sight. Ditto for Malley's black truck. The gate's closed so he can't tell if anyone's home. No sight or sounds of any kids, but he's a hundred feet up. I told him to list the plates of any cars on the block and run them.'

'Both gone, separate cars,' I said.

'Maybe they went for doughnuts. Why don't you drive a little faster?'

I sped over the canyon, raced through morning traffic, finally reached Vanowen just after eight. Milo got back on the phone and asked Binchy about the vehicle registrations. 'No, keep going ... no, no ... hold on, repeat that one ... interesting. Okay, stay there until we show up. Thanks mucho, lad.'

'Something come up?' I said.

'Cream-colored Cadillac DeVille parked right in front of the house,' he said. 'And guess who pays the sticker fees.'

The Reverend Dr Crandall Wascomb looked as if his faith had been tested and he wasn't sure he'd passed.

He opened the gate within seconds of Milo's pounding, stepped back, stunned.

'Dr Delaware?'

Milo's badge made his shoulders drop. Not dismay, relief. 'Police. Thank goodness. Cherish called you, as well?'

'When did she call you, sir?' said Milo.

'Early this morning,' said Wascomb. 'Just after six.'

His white hair floated above his brow and he had dressed haphazardly: heavy gray cardigan buttoned out of sequence so that it bunched mid-chest, white shirt with one bent collar point, maroon tie knotted well short of his neckline. Behind his black-framed glasses, his eyes were watery and uncertain.

'What did she want, Reverend?'

'She said she needed my help immediately. Mrs Wascomb's not well and I keep the phone in the hallway rather than at bedside so as not to wake her. The ring got me up, but at that hour I assumed it was a wrong number and didn't get out of bed. When it rang again, I answered and it was Cherish, apologizing for disturbing me. She said something had come up, implored me to come to her house as soon as I could. I tried to get her to explain. She said there was no time, I simply needed to believe her, hadn't she always been a faithful student.'

Wascomb blinked. 'She had been.'

I said, 'Was she distraught?'

'More like . . . anxious, but in an efficient way. As if she was faced with a sudden challenge and was rising to the occasion. I wondered if one of the children, or Drew, had taken ill. I asked her again what was wrong and she said she'd tell me when I showed up. If I'd come. I said I would and went to get dressed. Mrs Wascomb had stirred and I told her I was having one of my insomnia episodes, she should go back to sleep. I instructed the housekeeper to keep an eye on her, got myself presentable, and drove over.'

His eyes compressed as they traveled from Milo to me. 'When I arrived, the gate was open but no one was in the house. The front door had been left unlocked so I assumed Cherish wanted me to come straight in. The house was empty. I looked around, came back out. I was growing quite alarmed. Then a young woman came out of there.'

He cocked his head toward the pair of outbuildings. Converted garage painted pale blue to match the house. Off to the side, the odd-looking cement block cube.

The door to the cube was ajar.

'I left it open so the girls wouldn't feel confined,' said Wascomb. 'There's only one window and it's bolted shut. Two of them were in that other building, the blue one, but I assembled them all in one place until help arrived.'

'Have you called for help?' said Milo.

'I was thinking about who to call when you arrived. There doesn't seem to be any crisis, other than Cherish and Drew not being here.' Another look at the block structure. 'None of them appear to know what's going on, but perhaps she didn't want to worry them.'

'Them being the kids.'

'Yes, the flock.'

'The flock?'

443

'That's how Cherish referred to them in the instructions.'

'What instructions?'

'Oh, dear,' said Wascomb. 'I'm getting ahead of myself, this has all been so ...' From a pocket of the cardigan he pulled two sheets of paper folded to postcard size.

Milo unfolded them, read, jutted his lower jaw. 'Where'd you find this, sir?'

'When I looked around the house, I peeked into the bedroom and saw it on the desk.' Wascomb licked his lips. 'I noticed it because it lay in the center of the desk, atop a piece of blotting paper. As if she wanted me to see it.'

'Was it folded?'

'No, flat. It really seemed as if she'd intended for me to read it.'

'Anything else on the desk?'

'Pens, pencils,' said Wascomb. 'And a strongbox. The type banks use for safety deposit. That, of course, I didn't touch.'

Milo handed the papers to me. Two pages of neat, forward-slanting cursive.

The Flock: Instructions for Daily Care

1. *Patricia: Lactose-sensitive (soy milk in the fridge). Needs special help with reading and penmanship.*
2. *Gloria: Ritalin 10 mg. before breakfast, 10 mg. before dinner, self-esteem issues, doing well in all remedial areas but needs a lot of explicit verbal encouragement.*

3. Amber: Ritalin 15 mg. before breakfast, 10 mg. before dinner, Allegra 180 mg. as needed for hay fever, penicillin allergy, shellfish allergy, doesn't like meat but should be encouraged to eat some chicken; math, reading, penmanship . . .

Milo said, 'Looks like she's been preparing to be gone for a while.'

Wascomb said, 'Cherish was always an organized student. If she did leave for an extended period, I'm sure her reason was sound.'

'Such as?'

'I couldn't tell you, Lieutenant. But I do have the utmost respect for her.'

'As opposed to Drew.'

Wascomb's jaw set. 'I'm sure the doctor has told you of our problems with Drew.'

'He's gone, too,' said Milo.

'They are husband and wife.'

'You think they left together.'

'I don't know what to think, sir,' said Wascomb.

'When Cherish called she mentioned nothing about going away, Reverend?'

'No – Is it lieutenant? No, she didn't, Lieutenant. I fully expected her to be here when I arrived. If Cherish didn't call *you*, sir, may I ask why you're here?'

'Protecting and serving, Reverend.'

'I see,' said Wascomb. 'Will you be needing me any further? I'd be happy to pledge Fulton's support for the children, in the short term. However –'

'Could you stick around a bit?' said Milo. 'Show me that strongbox?'

'It's right on the desk, Lieutenant. I should be getting back to Mrs Wascomb.'

Milo's hand alit on Wascomb's sleeve. 'Stay for a short while, Reverend.'

Wascomb smoothed down his hair to no effect. 'Of course.'

'Appreciate it, sir. Now let's tend to the flock.'

The interior of the cube was twelve feet square, with a red cement floor and block walls painted a pinkish beige. Three wood-frame double bunks were set up against the sidewalls, two on the left, one on the right. A white fiberglass booth in the far right-hand corner was labeled *toilet*. Flower stickers decorated the door.

A sliver of wall space hosted three double-decker dented metal lockers. An *L.A. Unified School District Surplus* sticker was at the bottom of one, *Practice Spontaneous Acts of Kindness* on another.

The solitary window was set into the back wall, screened and bolted. The pane was wide enough to let in a funnel of diffuse, dusty light. Animal-print curtains had been parted. The view was the rear wall of the property and the black tar roofline of a neighbor's garage.

Beneath the windowsill sat a squat, six-drawer chest. Stuffed animals shared the top with tubes and bottles and jars of cosmetics. Off to the side, a stack of Bibles.

Eight girls sat on the three bottom bunks, wearing pastel-colored pajamas and fluffy white socks.

Eight pairs of teenage eyes took us in. Narrow age-range; my guess was fifteen to seventeen. Six Hispanic girls, one black, one white.

The room smelled of hormones and chewing gum and face cream.

Valerie Quezada sat at the front of the rear left-hand bunk. Fidgeting, rolling her shoulders, playing with the ends of her long, wavy hair. Two other girls moved restlessly. The others sat quietly.

Crandall Wascomb said, 'Morning, young ladies. These are the police and they're very nice. This gentleman is a police *lieutenant* and he's here to help you, both these gentleman want to help you ...' He flashed us a helpless look and trailed off.

Milo said, 'Hi, there.'

Valerie pointed a finger. 'You were here already.'

Milo cued me with a tiny movement of his head.

I said, 'Yes, we were, Valerie.'

'You know my *name*.' Accusatory.

Some of the girls tittered.

I said, 'Where's Cherish, Valerie?'

'Left.'

'When did she leave?'

'When it was dark.'

'Around what time?'

Her stare told me the question was absurd.

No clock in the room, no radio, no TV. Light from the window would be the sole arbiter of time.

The room was clean – spotless, the cement floor freshly swept. Each of the six bunk beds was set up identically with two smallish white pillows and a white top sheet folded over a pink blanket.

Blankets tucked military-tight.

I didn't see Wascomb ordering the girls to make their beds. They had a routine.

I said, 'Anyone else have any idea what time Cherish left?'

A couple of head shakes. Neatly groomed heads. The girls appeared to be well-nourished. How often did they leave the property? This room? Were meals taken in the main house, or eaten here? Did home-schooling extend to occasional outings? Maybe that's why no one had answered the phone when I'd called a few days ago. Or ...

What did it do to your sense of reality to inhabit this tight, sterile space?

'Anyone want to take a guess?' I said.

Valerie said, 'They don't know nothing. It was me saw her leave. Only.'

I walked closer to her. More giggles. 'Did you talk to her, Valerie?'

Silence.

'Did she say anything at all?'

Reluctant nod.

'What did she say?'

'She had to go out, someone would take care of us.'

One of the other girls elbowed her neighbor. Valerie said, 'You got a problem?'

'I ain't got no problem.' Quick retort, but meek voice.

'You better not.'

Wascomb said, 'Now, let's keep everything calm, young ladies.'

Milo said, 'What about Mr Daney? When did he leave?'

'Drew left before,' said Valerie.

'Before Cherish?'

'Yesterday. She got mad at him.'

'Cherish did?'

'Uh-huh.'

'What was she mad about?'

Shrug.

I said, 'How could you tell she was mad?'

'Her face.' Valerie looked to the other girls for confirmation. Pointed at a bespectacled girl with thin straight hair. The girl began making squeaky noises with her tongue against her teeth. Valerie's glower failed to stop her. My smile did.

I said, 'So Cherish was mad at Drew.'

Valerie stomped her foot. 'Trish?' Pointing at a pretty, long-legged girl with boyish hair and a fine-boned face marred by acne.

Short for 'Patricia.' *Lactose-sensitive. Special help with reading and penmanship.*

She didn't answer.

Valerie said, 'You can tell she's mad from her face. *Say* that.'

Trish smiled, dreamy-eyed. Her pajamas were sky blue with white eyelet borders.

'Say it,' demanded Valerie. 'Her *face*.'

Trish yawned. 'She never got pissed at me.'

'Just at Drew,' I said.

Another girl said, 'He didn't come home last night, prolly that made her mad.'

I said, 'She didn't like when he didn't come home.'

'Nope.'

'Was that often?'

Shrug.

Valerie twisted a thick rope of black hair around her finger. Let it uncoil and watched it drop past her waist.

I turned back to her. 'Was it once a week? Something like that?'

She gazed up at the mattress inches from her head. Rolled her shoulders and tapped her fingers and beat out a rhythm with one foot.

'Valerie?'

'Time to shower,' she said.

'Where do you shower?'

'The other place.'

'The main house?'

'The *other* place.'

'The building next door.'

'Uh-huh.'

I tried Trish again. 'Did Drew go out a lot?'

'He was here except when he went out.' To Valerie: 'Like when he went out with *you-u*.' Slowly spreading smile.

Valerie's eyes flashed.

Trish said, 'Tell him. You went out all the *time*. That's why you always *need* to shower.'

Valerie got up from the bunk and charged her. Trish waved her long arms uselessly. I got between them, pulled Valerie away. Soft middle but her arms were tight and her shoulders were granite lumps.

'It's like true,' said another girl.

Yet another opined, 'He went out with you all the time, you *gotta* shower.'

Voice from a bunk across the room: 'You get to sleep in the other place.'

'You get to shower whenever you want.'

''Cause you dirty.'

Val grunted and fought to free herself from my grasp. She was sweating and the moisture flew off her face and hit mine.

'She freakin' out.'

'Like she always does.'

Trish said, 'He takes you out all the *time*!'

Valerie let loose a string of obscenities.

Wascomb shrank back.

Trish said, 'She gets up at night and walks around like a . . . like a . . . vampire thing. That's how she saw Cherish.'

'She wakes us up. It's good she's in the other place.'

'Tell 'em, Monica. You sleep in the other place now, too.'

The sole white girl, pug-faced and strawberry blond, stared at her knees.

'Monica goes out.'

'Monica gots to shower.'

'Bitch!' screamed Valerie. She'd stopped struggling but shook her fist at one group of girls, then the others. Her eyes were hard, dry, determined. 'Shut up!'

'Admit it, Monica! You gots to shower!'

'He take you out, too, Monicaaaa!'

Monica hung her head.

'Admit it, Monicaa!'

Individual comments coalesced to a chant. *'Admit it! Admit it! Admit it! Admit it!'*

Monica began crying.

'Fuck youuu!' screamed Valerie.

Wascomb said, 'That kind of language really isn't –'

'*You* the fucker,' said Trish. 'You and Monica fuck him every night and then you shower.'

'*Valerie fucks! Monica fucks! Valerie fucks! Monica fucks!*'

Wascomb braced himself against the wall. His skin had turned chalky. His mouth moved, but whatever he was saying was swallowed by the noise.

Val lunged and nearly broke free.

Milo came over and the two of us steered her out of the cube.

The chanting continued, then faded. Behind us, Crandall Wascomb's voice, thin and tremulous, filtered out into the morning air. '... some prayer. How about Psalms? Does anyone have any favorites?'

42

I led Valerie to a lawn chair outside. The same chair Cherish Daney had occupied the first time we'd been here. Solemn and weepy, reading a book about coping with loss.

Her grief had seemed genuine. Now I wondered what she was really crying about.

'I want to take a shower.'

'Soon, Valerie.'

'I want hot *water*.' She bounced her knees together, tickled one. Looked up at the sky. Scrunched her mouth. Glanced back at the block building, now silent. 'It's my fuckin' water, I want it. The bitches can't use it up.'

'I'm sorry they did that, Valerie.'

'*Bitches.*' She lifted a twist of hair from her shoulder, ran it across her mouth, licked.

I said, 'You know more than anyone. Do you have *any* idea where Drew and Cherish went?'

'I *told* you.'

'You said Drew left before and that Cherish was mad.'

'Yeah.'

'But where'd they go, Valerie? It's important.'

'Why?'

'Cherish is mad at him. What if she went to yell at him?'

'He's okay,' she said. 'He goes places.'

'Like where?'

'Places.'

'What kinds of places?'

'Nonprofits.'

'He takes you to nonprofits.'

Silence.

I said, 'You help him and the other girls are jealous.'

'Bitches.'

'He trusts you.'

'I *get* it.'

'Get what?'

Silence.

'You get it so you help him,' I said.

'Uh-huh.'

'What do you get?'

Long silence.

'Valerie? What do you –'

'Love.'

'You understand love.'

'He prolly went to a church,' she said. 'I don't know the names. I want to shower –'

'A church.'

Silence.

'Valerie, I know these questions are a pain, but they're important. Did Cherish get mad at Drew a lot?'

'Sometimes.'

'About what?'

'Not making money.' She let go of the hair, held up a fist, and glanced at the main house.

'She felt he didn't make enough money.'

'Yeah.'

'For what?'

'She wanted a trip to Vegas.'

'She told you that?'

Silence.

'Drew told you.'

Back to hair-twisting.

'Drew told you Cherish wanted to go to Vegas.'

Shrug.

I said, 'Sounds like he talked to you about everything.'

'Uh-huh.'

'Did he want money?'

She faced me. 'No *way*. He was for the soul.'

'The soul?'

'God's work,' she said, touching a breast. 'He got chosen.'

'And Cherish?'

'She did it for the money, but tough shit, he won't give it to her.'

'Drew has money he won't give her?'

A smile spread across her lips.

I said, 'Secret money.'

She shut her eyes.

'Valerie?'

'I *got* to take a shower.'

She clamped her arms across her chest, kept her eyes shut, and when I spoke she hummed. We'd been sitting in silence for several minutes when Milo came out of the cube with Crandall Wascomb. He glanced at me while walking. Escorted the old man out.

He returned with uplifted eyebrows. 'Everything okay?'

'Valerie's been helpful but she and I are finished for now.'

Movement under the girl's eyelids.

Milo said, 'Helpful?'

'Valerie says Drew has money Cherish doesn't know about.'

Valerie's eyes opened. 'It's *his*. You can't have it.'

'Never heard of finders keepers?' said Milo.

She didn't reply. Clamped her eyes shut.

Noise from the front of the property opened them.

A uniformed officer came through the gate.

Milo said, 'Now it gets noisy.'

The Van Nuys patrol officer was followed by his partner, then six members of the newly formed downtown crimes-against-juveniles squad arrived wearing dark blue LAPD windbreakers. Five female detectives, one man, each of them bright-eyed and hyped, ready to arrest someone. Shortly after, a Van Nuys sex crimes detective named Sam Crawford showed up looking put-upon. He conferred with the head juvey cop and left.

The head was a stocky wire-haired brunette in her forties. Milo briefed her, she gave the word, and all but one of her squad entered the cube. A younger detective who introduced herself as Martha Vasquez took custody of Valerie, saying, 'Sure, hon, you can do that,' when the girl asked to shower. Walking her to the converted garage while scanning the rest of the property.

Milo motioned me over, introduced the brunette as Judy Weisvogel and told her who I was.

'Psychologist,' she said. 'That can come in handy.'

Milo briefed her some more, emphasizing Drew Daney's abuse of the girls, mentioning suspected homicides but staying spare with the details.

Weisvogel said, 'Good morning world, it's going to get complicated. Do we have a crime scene, over there?' Indicating the main house.

'Haven't had time to look around yet,' said Milo. 'At the very least it's a fugitive thing.'

'Missing perv and wife. Definitely separate cars?'

'The girls say they left separately and both cars are gone.'

'How much time elapsed between their respective rabbits?'

'From what the kids say a day or so.'

'Okay, I'll phone in for a warrant and we'll get

techies over to toss the place. I'll need a bunch of social workers, too, but they don't get in the office till nine.'

'Civilian life,' said Milo.

Weisvogel said, 'Ain't it a party? No idea where Mr and Mrs Perv are off to?'

'Nope. She may not be a perv.'

'Whatever.' Weisvogel took out her pad. 'Give me their names for a BOLO.'

Milo recited. 'Drew Daney. He could also be traveling as Moore Daney Andruson.'

'Anderson e-n or o-n?'

He spelled it. 'His wheels are a white Jeep. She drives a Toyota. C-H-E-R-I-S-H.'

'Some name. You don't think they met up somewhere and split?'

'One of the kids said she was mad at him,' said Milo.

''Cause she figured out what he was about?'

'Don't know. The kids are aware of what's been going on. They taunted two girls who were sexually active with him.'

'If missus did figure it out she sure took her sweet time about it, didn't she?' said Weisvogel. 'What do you think, Doctor, one of those see-no-evil pathological denial head cases?'

I said, 'Could be.'

'I walked into that room, saw those girls, first thing came to mind was "harem." God only knows what we're going to find when they get examined.'

'It sounds as if he was selective. Chose one or two girls who got special privileges. The girl I spoke to thinks she loves him.'

Weisvogel slapped her hands on her hips. Her wrists were as thick as a man's. 'So how long have you been looking at this fine citizen, Milo?'

'Been looking at him for murder for a week or so. The other stuff just came up.'

'The other *stuff*,' said Weisvogel. 'Well, it's obviously gonna take a long time to unravel. Speaking of which, Doctor, any chance you could be available, therapy-wise? I don't care how many girls he actually fooled with, they're all going to be affected, right? The department psychologists are pretty much tied up doing personnel evaluations and we could use some help.'

'Sure,' I said.

She seemed surprised by my easy assent. 'Okay, good, thanks. I'll be in touch. Meanwhile, let's keep each other posted, Milo.'

'Will do, Judy. Speaking of which, there's a safe-deposit box on a desk in the bedroom. Cherish left it out in the open next to her instructions. Those instructions were set out on a piece of blotter paper – like a presentation. To me that says looky here, clear invitation to scrutinize.'

'Those instructions,' said Weisvogel, 'reminded me of some stupid memo you'd get in the service. She abandons these kids and writes out a manual. Hubby rapes the kids but they need their medicine and their nutritious breakfasts. What a whack job.'

'Be interesting to see what's in the box, Judy.'

She shook her head. 'Before the warrant and the techies get here? Tsk tsk.'

'Daney's a suspect in six murders, maybe seven. I can make a case for exigent circumstances.'

Weisvogel looked doubtful.

Milo said, 'Judy, he took the girls off the property to molest them, so the house won't be your primary crime scene, his Jeep will. We need to find him asap and there could be something in the box that gets us closer.'

'What, you think the whack job left a map?'

'There are all kinds of maps, Judy.'

'That's pretty darn enigmatic, Milo. I'm not comfortable messing with the goodies prematurely. All I need is some defense attorney squawking about chain of evidence.'

'It's in plain view, despite obvious opportunities to conceal,' said Milo. 'Ain't that an invitation to search?'

Weisvogel smiled. 'You should've gone to law school. Beats honest labor.'

'I could've opened the box before you got here, Judy.'

'You certainly could've.' Weisvogel stared up at him. Her eyes were green, lighter than Milo's, almost khaki, with specks of blue scattered near the rims. Unwavering. 'What if the box is locked?'

'I've got tools.'

'That wasn't my question.'

Milo smiled.

Weisvogel said, 'Hell, what if it's ticking – I know, you'll bring in a robot. Seriously, it could cause evidentiary problems, Milo.'

'Problems can be solved. Let's find the bastard before he does more damage, then sort out the details.'

Weisvogel looked over at the house. Clicked her teeth together. Ran her hand through her terrier hair. 'So you're ordering me, as my superior, to open this alleged box.'

'I'm asking you to be a little flexible –'

'What I'm *hearing* is you pulling rank on me. Seeing as I'm merely a D-two and you're brass.'

Weisvogel's turn to smile. Tobacco teeth.

'I'm brass?' said Milo, as if he'd been diagnosed with a noxious disease.

'Sorry to drop it on you so suddenly,' said Weisvogel. 'So am I getting this whole chain-of-command thing right?'

Still smiling.

Milo said, 'Yeah, yeah. Someone bitches, it was all my idea.'

'Then I suppose I have no choice,' said Weisvogel, 'Lieu*ten*ant.'

She joined her detectives in the cube and Milo told me, 'Out to the car.'

'For what?'

'Tools.'

'Don't have any.'

'You've got a crowbar. And I've got this.' Reaching into a jacket pocket, he brought out a small penlight and a ring of stainless-steel burglar picks.

'You carry those all the time?'

'Some of the time,' he said. 'When I think important objects are gonna be left in plain sight.'

The house was tidy, just as it had been the first time, kitchen scrubbed, hallways vacuumed.

As we entered the master bedroom, I sighted down the hall at the windowless, converted laundry room where Rand had slept.

Milo went into the bedroom and I joined him. The desk sat to the left of the double bed. Plain and rickety, painted brown, a thrift-shop piece that barely managed to fit in Drew and Cherish Daney's cramped sleeping chamber.

Milo gloved up and checked the closet.

'His duds are here, but hers aren't. Looks like she packed up for the long haul.'

'And he didn't.'

'Ain't that thought-provoking.' He sidled over to the desk. The legs were wobbly and the top slanted downward. A jam glass held pens and pencils. The green blotter paper Cherish had used to frame her instructions was still there. One of its corners was held in place by the box.

Gunmetal safe-deposit box. Extra-large size, the kind banks offered preferred customers.

Milo examined the lock, lifted the box, and inspected the bottom.

'Columbia Savings stamp. They've been out of business for years.'

'Surplus, like the school lockers,' I said. 'They're parsimonious.'

He frowned. 'All that county money and they're living like this.'

'If Valerie's right, there was a lot of conflict about money. Maybe because Drew was siphoning funds and stashing it away.'

'His secret cache. That coulda been bullshit he gave the kid to impress her.'

'I'd bet on reality. He had all the power right from the start with Valerie, didn't need to prove himself.' I pointed to the box.

He set it down. Looked at the lock again. Examined his picks and selected one. Lifting the box, he hefted. 'Kinda light. Maybe Cherish found the dough, took it, and split. The question is, Where'd *he* go with all his clothes still here?'

'He could've gotten to the money first. Picked up on Cherish's suspicion, sensed the walls closing in and left.'

'With no clothes?'

'He travels light. I'm thinking Vegas because he told Valerie that Cherish wanted to go there.'

'The old projection game? Yeah, Vegas would fit his style, easy for a scumbag to blend in. Okay, enough conjecture. Gimme that.' Pocketing the burglar picks and reaching for the crowbar.

He wedged the point under the box's lid and bore down. The lid popped up with no resistance and threw him off balance. He fought for equilibrium and I had to swerve to avoid being hit by the bar.

'She left it unlocked,' he said.

'There's your invitation to search.'

First came a gray felt cloth, the kind used to keep tarnish off silverware. No money under that, but the box was half-full.

Milo removed each object and placed it on the desk.

Nothing that weighed much.

A yellowed Stockton newspaper clipping, seven and a half years old. Local coverage of Troy Turner's murder in prison. Troy's name underlined in red pencil, along with a sentence connecting him to the Malley case. Kristal Malley's name double underlined.

A pair of woman's jade drop earrings.

'Any guesses?' he said.

'Maybe Lara's.'

A black hard-shell eyeglass case. Inside was half a blackened spoon, a cheap lighter, a crude syringe fashioned from an eyedropper, and a hypodermic needle. Brown gunk soiled the glass. In the red velvet lining of the case, the gold-lettered address of an optometrist on Alvarado.

Under the address, a scrap of paper taped to the inside lid.

Property of Maria Teresa Almedeira.

'Nestor's mother,' I said. 'Nestor swiped it to house his works. After Daney killed him, it became his souvenir.'

Milo reached in the box again and drew out a flimsy knit blouse, royal blue with a horizontal red stripe. Holding it aloft by the sleeves, he checked the label. 'Made in Malaysia, size S. This could also be Lara's.'

I said, 'It's Jane Hannabee's. She was wearing it the day I met her at the jail. Brand new. Weider was trying to pretty her up.'

'And Daney deprettied her ...' He examined the garment closely. 'Doesn't look like any blood.'

'He stabbed her in her sleep. She wouldn't have worn something new. He wrapped her back up in plastic, rummaged through her stuff, took a souvenir.'

'Okay, if the earrings are Lara's, maybe her mother can verify ... check this out.'

Photocopy of a county document. Application to foster a child.

The ward in question was a sixteen-year-old female named Miranda Melinda Shulte. Drew and Cherish Daney had both signed the papers but they had never been sent in.

'Number seven,' I said.

Milo rubbed his eyes. 'There's no evidence he killed any other girls. Why her, Alex?'

'She'd only been here a week, but Beth Scoggins described her as aggressive, moving in on Beth's queen-bee status. Daney needs them to be passive.

466

Maybe she asserted herself too much. Or she thought she wanted his attentions, but when the time came, she resisted.'

'Not playing the game,' he said. 'There could be a family out there somewhere, wondering.'

Or even worse, there isn't.

I said, 'When we find him, maybe we can learn where he buried her.'

'Love your optimism.' He placed the foster form on the desk. Stared at it. Returned to the box.

Pharmaceutical bubble pack. Nine bubbles, seven of them empty. Two round, white pills, scored diagonally. Stamped 'Hoffman' atop the midline, '1' below it.

The label on the pack said: Rohypnol, 1 mg (flunitrazepam).

'Party pills,' I said.

Milo said, 'Next.'

Out came Rand Duchay's C.Y.A. I.D. tag. The photo showing Rand looking baffled.

Last, at the bottom, a manila envelope not much larger than a playing card, fastened by a string and eyelet. Milo's gloved hands fumbled with the string. He cursed, finally got the string uncoiled. Brought the envelope close to the desk and shook it out carefully.

Out tumbled a tiny bracelet. Square, white plastic cubes strung on a pink thread.

Seven cubes. A letter on each.

KRISTAL

43

Like the cement cube, the converted garage had a single window. No larger than the cube, but with only two beds, it felt a lot more spacious.

I said, 'Valerie, where did Drew keep his money? It's important.'

She sat on her bed, I was three feet away in a pink plastic chair.

Real bed, not a bunk. Wood-grain headboard embossed with vines and flowers. Matching chest of drawers with the same embellishment. A threadbare gray rug covered most of the cement floor.

Particle board partitions created a corner bathroom, complete with shower, shampoo, hotel soaps, and lotions still sealed.

A host of stuffed animals on Valerie's bed. Monica's bed, across the room, had only a single blue teddy bear.

Clear hierarchy. Lodgings for the preferred ward and her next-in-line. What reason had Drew given Cherish? What had she been *thinking*?

Valerie's black hair was shiny-wet. She played with a towel that said *Sheraton Universal.* Her eyes were pond pebbles.

I said, 'In a box? Did he keep his money in a gray metal box?'

The pebbles rounded around the edges as she looked away. Constricted pupils. Her hands danced on her knees.

'We found the box, Valerie, but there was no money in it, so I guess Drew made all that up.'

'No! I saw it.'

'You saw the money?'

She avoided my eyes.

I shrugged. 'If you say so.'

'It was there.'

'It's gone, now.'

'*Bitch!*'

'You think Cherish took it.'

'She *stoled* it.'

'It wasn't hers?'

'*We* got it! At the nonprofits!'

Fire in her eyes. Devotion. Beth Scoggins had recounted how Daney had turned off after her abortion. It had been days since Valerie's abortion and she believed Daney still cared.

I said, 'Guess Cherish found where he hid it.'

Silence.

'How do you think she found out?'

Shrug.

'No idea at all, Valerie?'

'Cleaning. Prolly.'

'Cleaning where?'

She got up, paced the length of the room, then the periphery. Passed Monica's bed and tucked in a corner of blanket.

Playing housekeeper.

She circled the room again.

'Cleaning where?' I said. 'If we're going to find your money, we have to know where.'

She stopped. Paced some more. Said something I couldn't hear.

'What's that?'

Another inaudible whisper.

I walked over to her. 'Where, Valerie?'

'Underneath.'

'Underneath the house?'

Silence.

'Is there really an underneath, Valerie?'

'Here!' Running to her own bed and slapping the covers. Slapping them. Pounding them. 'I cleaned real good but she sneaked in! *Bitch!*'

I returned her to Judy Weisvogel's custody. Milo gave me a set of gloves and the two of us moved the bed away from the corner. The cement floor bordering the garage's northern wall had been patched years ago, some sort of grayish sealant slopped generously over cracks and crumbles. Grease spots shining through the white evoked the room's original function. In the corner, the sealant stain was scored by four straight-edge cuts. Shaped roughly like a square. Two foot square, scoring the floor.

Flush with the floor, no handle or protrusions, no way you'd notice if you weren't looking.

Cherish Daney had noticed. There were all kinds of ways to house-clean.

Milo got down and stared at the seams. 'Pry marks.'

He worked the crowbar into the spot. The slab pulled away easily. Underneath was a dark space, three or so feet deep.

'Empty,' said Milo. 'No, I take that back . . .'

He got down on the ground, stuck his arm in, brought out a dusty wooden case.

Smith & Wesson label inside the lid. The bottom was foam with a form-fitted indentation. Revolver-shaped indentation.

His gloved finger prodded the foam. 'Wonder who got lucky first.'

We left the property, now cordoned by tape. Judy Weisvogel stood by the side of the cube talking softly to Valerie. The girl twirled her hair and rocked from foot to foot. Weisvogel took a tissue and dabbed Valerie's eyes. As I passed, Valerie's eyes met mine and narrowed with contempt. She flipped me off. Judy Weisvogel frowned and drew her away.

What would Allison think about my technique?

What did I think?

I drove away, staying focused on a plastic baby bracelet.

Milo said, 'Looks like you made a fan, back there.'

'She's resentful Cherish entered the room. Furious at me for prying the information out of her. Another violation of her turf.'

'Turf. Like a little wife. Sick.'

'It's going to take a long time for her to realize what he did to her.'

'Oh, yeah,' he said. 'Your job's tougher than mine.'

I got on the freeway and pushed the Seville hard. 'I think you're clear on the search. Cherish definitely wanted someone to find the souvenirs. She left the box out for Wascomb, hoping he'd open it. Knew that even if he didn't pry, he'd eventually call the authorities and the truth would come out.'

'Don't think the truth means that much to her, Alex. She abandons those kids and splits with all her clothes. Maybe with the money and the gun, too, unless Drew got there first. Which, upon reflection, he probably did. Bad guy like that, his nose for trouble would be good. For all we know, he's already partying at Caesar's Palace, has himself a new identity.'

'Valerie said he was called away to moonlight. At a church. You could try to find out all the places he worked, see if his whereabouts can be traced. If the call was righteous.'

'If?' he said.

'There's the other possibility,' I said. 'Cherish got the money and the gun. And Cherish has a boyfriend.'

*

The drive to Soledad Canyon took forty minutes. I parked a ways up the road and we walked toward the campground. Milo unsnapped his gun but kept it holstered.

No ravens, no hawks, no sign of any life in a grimy gray sky flat as flannel. Despite my heavy foot, the drive had been tedious, marked by heavy stretches of silence, the gravel pits, scrap yards, and cookie-cutter houses set into dusty tracts that seemed more depressing today. Developers would chew up the desert for as long as they were allowed. Families would move in and have babies who'd grow into adolescents. Bored teens would chafe at the heat and the quiet and days that ran into each other like a tape loop. Too much of nothing would breed trouble. People like Milo would never be out of business.

Neither would people like me.

As we neared the entrance to Mountain View Sojourn, Milo stopped, got on the phone, checked to see if the BOLO had snared Drew Daney's Jeep.

'Nothing.' He seemed almost comforted by failure.

Business was slow at the campsite. Two RVs in the lot, the generator silent. That and a fresh coating of dust and the apathetic sky gave the place a desolate feel.

No sign of Bunny MacIntyre. We headed straight through the trees.

Barnett Malley's black truck was parked exactly where it had been, in front of the cedar cabin.

Windows rolled up.

Milo's gun was out. He motioned me to stay back, proceeded slowly. Looked into the truck from all sides. Continued toward the cabin's front door.

Knock knock.

No 'Who's there?'

The welcome mat was in place, covered by dry leaves and bird crap. Milo disappeared behind the south side of the cabin, same as he'd done the first time. Returned and tried the front door. It swung open. He went in. Called out, 'C'mon.'

Rustic, wood-paneled space, rubbed clean and smelling of Lysol. As vacant as Drew Daney's hiding hole.

Except for the piano. Chipped, brown Gulbransen upright, sheet music held in place on the rack with a clothespin.

Floyd Cramer's 'Last Date' on top. Beneath that: *Country Songs for Easy Playing*. 'Desperado' by the Eagles. 'Lawyers, Guns, and Money' by Warren Zevon.

Empty gun rack on the wall. Through the disinfectant came the smell of male sweat and old clothes and machine oil.

A voice behind us said, 'What the *hell* do you think you're doing!'

Bunny MacIntyre stood in the doorway. Her

auburn perm was wrapped in an orange scarf and she wore a blue-checked western shirt tucked into straight-leg jeans. A necklace encircled her wattled neck. Silver and turquoise, peace symbol dangling from the central stone.

Barnett Malley had worn it the day we'd tried to talk to him.

MacIntyre took in Milo's gun and said, 'Pfft. Put that stupid thing away.'

Milo obliged.

She said, 'I asked you a question.'

'Looks like you've got a vacancy, ma'am.'

'And it's gonna stay that way.'

'Shucks, ma'am. And here I was thinking about country living.'

'Then do it somewheres else. This is my place. Gonna be a painting studio,' said MacIntyre. 'Shoulda done it a long time ago. Now you leave right now, you don't have my permission to trespass. Go on.'

Dismissing wave.

Still smiling, Milo strode up to her quickly. When he was a foot away, the smile was gone and his face had darkened.

MacIntyre stood her ground but it took effort.

Milo said, 'When did Malley leave and where did he go? And no bullshit.'

MacIntyre's pink lashes fluttered. 'You don't scare me,' she said, but strain thinned her smoker's voice.

'Don't want to scare anyone, ma'am, but I will cuff

you and haul you in for obstructing justice if you give me any more lip.'

'You can't do that.'

He spun her around, brought her arm behind her. Gingerly. Regret weakened his eyes.

A look that said *An old woman. This is what it's come to.*

Bunny MacIntyre howled. 'You damned *bully*! What do you *want* from me?'

Her voice was all strain, an octave higher. Milo released her arm, spun her back so she faced him.

'The truth.'

She rubbed her wrist. 'Big brave guy. I'm filing a complaint.'

'I'm sure it was a thrill having him here,' said Milo. 'Younger guy, I'm not judging. But now he's gone – with a woman his own age – and things out in the real world have grown ugly, so it's time to toss the May–December fantasies and help me get to the truth.'

Bunny MacIntyre gaped. Smiled. Slapped her flank and roared with laughter.

When her breathing finally slowed, she said, 'You thought he was my *boy* toy? Man, are you *stupid*!' More laughter.

'You're covering for him,' said Milo. 'All for a platonic relationship?'

MacIntyre laughed herself hoarse. 'Stupid, stupid, stupid! He's *family*, you dolt. My sister's son. She died of cancer and so did Barnett's father. And despite what the government claims you'll never convince me it wasn't because of all that radiation.'

'Los Alamos.'

She blinked. 'Let me tell you, they got all kinds of crazy things going on there. Few years back there was a huge fire, burned thousands of acres black but spared the lab. That sound logical? Supposedly it was set on purpose by some Smokey Bear types to control forest fires and the winds blew it out of control.' She snorted. 'Tell it to the marines.'

'Barnett's your nephew.'

'Last I heard, that's what you call a sister's son. I'm all he's got left, mister. He's an *orphan,* get it? I was willing to take him in from the beginning but he didn't want a handout so I sent him over to Gilbert Grass. When Gilbert retired, I told him I could really use the help. Which was true. Is helping family illegal now?'

'He's got a sister in Ohio.'

MacIntyre pursed her lips. 'That one. Married a banker, rich snob. She always looked down on Barnett 'cause he wasn't much for schooling. Not stupid, don't go thinking he was stupid. He had trouble reading but give him a pump to fix, or something to build, and he'd do it in a flash.'

'Good for him. Now where is he?'

'He's a good boy,' said MacIntyre. 'Why don't you just leave him alone?'

'Where is he, ma'am?'

'Don't know.'

'Ms MacIntyre –'

'You *deaf*?' She rubbed her wrist some more. 'You can pull a Rodney King from today till tomorrow but I don't *know*. He didn't *tell* me.'

'He left without a word?'

'He left thanking me for everything I'd done, said it was time to go. I didn't ask questions because I don't like to ask questions and Barnett doesn't like to answer them. He's been through enough. The man's a vegetarian, that tell you something?'

'He likes animals.'

'He's peaceful.'

'When did he leave?'

'Three days ago.'

'His truck's here.'

'Gee,' said MacIntyre, 'Sherlock Holmes must've put on a few pounds.'

'What's he using for wheels?'

Silence.

'Ma'am?'

'He's got another one.'

'Another truck?' said Milo. 'It's not registered.'

'It's registered to me.'

'Then it's your responsibility, not his.'

'Suppose so.'

'What kind?'

MacIntyre didn't answer.

'Something happens,' said Milo, 'the liability is yours. And if it's registered, all I have to do is make a call.'

She twisted her mouth.

'If it's not,' he said, 'you're in trouble.'

'Haven't gotten around to it yet. It was Gilbert's, I bought it from his widow.'

'What make?'

'Also a Ford.'

'Color?'

'Also black.'

'Where does Barnett keep it?'

'Somewhere in Santa Clarita and don't ask me where 'cause I don't know.'

'Auto-storage facility?'

'One of those customizer places. He's having work done on it. Souping up the engine, big tires, you know – boy stuff. Don't you think he's entitled to have some boy fun?'

'Is he traveling alone?'

'You just said he had a girl.'

'Did you know it before I told you?' said Milo.

'He mentioned he had a friend, but that's it, don't know her name.'

'Never met her?'

'No, but she's good for Barnett and that's all I care about.'

'How do you know she's good for him?'

'He's started getting a little happy.'

44

We headed back to the road and Milo did another BOLO check as I started up the Seville. Shook his head. 'Now I'm manhandling crones.'

'She'll survive.'

'Thanks for the support,' he said. 'Where's your sensitive side?'

'Dormant. Want me to head over to Santa Clarita, find the garage that worked on Barnett's other truck?'

'Too much work for too little payoff. Malley and Cherish are already out on the open road. The question is which road.'

'There's also the matter of Cherish's Toyota.'

'You think they're traveling separately? You heard MacIntyre. Barnett's happy.'

'It would take more than romance to bring joy into his life.'

'What do you mean?'

'Maybe he refused to cooperate with you because he had his own plan. The word "closure" should be dropped from the English language, but a guy in his position might figure getting some sort of satisfaction could ease his pain. And Cherish could help him.'

'Payback,' he said.

'That's another word for it.'

By the time I made it back to the Valley, the sun was starting to drop. I drove straight to the park where Kristal Malley had been murdered, hoping for simple bloody symmetry. Instead of Drew's body we found only a scrubby, sad space pocked with trash.

Milo had his little penlight out and he washed the skinny beam over the same public lavatories described in Sue Kramer's police report, the same Dumpster, now reeking of waste.

The same swings, where a pair of young killers had sat smoking and drinking beer.

No kids here, tonight. No people at all. Off in the distance, the crumbling, flat-roofed units of 415 City were top-lit harshly, security bulbs spanking the darkness. A police siren howled, then dopplered to silence. Shouts and laughter and drumbeats filtered through the night. The air was heavy and oppressive and dangerous, like hands around a throat.

Milo pocketed the penlight. 'Nice try. They could be anywhere. Maybe Cherish really did want to go to Vegas.'

I said, 'Where exactly was Lara found?'

He sat down on one of the swings. The chain howled in protest. Phoning Sue Kramer, he asked her the same question, listened intently. Made some notes and hung up and handed them to me. 'For what it's worth.'

*

The Sepulveda Basin Wildlife Reserve is 225 acres of what passes for natural habitat in L.A. Created by a dam filled with undrinkable water and army-engineered flood-drainage channels, and planted with native vegetation, the refuge is sandwiched between two freeways yet motion-picture gorgeous. Birds love it and a couple hundred species migrate in and out. People are welcome with qualifications. No hunting, no fishing, no bikes, no feeding the ducks. No straying off the well-marked paths.

Following Sue Kramer's directions, I entered on Balboa Boulevard, just below Birmingham High School, cruised a treeless stretch of road. A short while later, the L.A. River appeared, an empty, graffiti-marred trough in this drought-plagued winter.

Milo said, 'She parked right there.' Pointing to a spot bordering the river, half-hidden by an initial planting of eucalyptus.

No sign of any vehicles.

I kept driving.

He said, 'Where now?'

'Maybe nowhere.'

'Then why bother?'

'Got anything better to do?'

Continuing south to Burbank, I hooked a left and traversed the southern border of the reserve. Lots of trees here. Signs pointed toward the dam. No more birds than we'd seen in Soledad Canyon. Maybe they knew something.

We both saw it at the same time.

White Jeep, on the far end of a small parking lot on Burbank.

The only vehicle in the lot. Signs said legal parking had ended an hour ago.

Milo said, 'Right out in the open. Take that and stick it in your BOLO. Where are the parking nazis when you need them?'

I pulled behind the Jeep.

He said, 'Sitting right here and no one notices.'

I said, 'There's your invitation to search.'

Out came another set of plastic gloves. How many did he carry? He walked around the Jeep, checked the underbody, then the windows. The doors were locked and the interior was empty. Clear view of the rear storage area through the hatchback window. Nothing.

Milo said, 'In the mood for a hike?'

A dirt trail capped the top of the dam. Thicker trees – more eucalyptus, gnarled sycamore, wild oak that enjoyed the drought, evergreens that didn't. Plenty of opportunity to exit at paved paths feeding to Burbank and Victory but we stayed on the dirt. Twenty yards in, the planting thickened even further and the trail blackened and Milo's penlight cast a sickly beam that died three feet in front of us.

Rocks and dirt and scampering bugs.

'You came well-prepared,' I said.

'Boy Scout days,' he said. 'Made it all the way to Eagle. If they'd only known.'

We'd traipsed halfway through the reserve, finding nothing. The excitement that had pinged my chest when we'd found the Jeep began to fade.

We were just about to turn back when the sound gave it away.

Low, insistent buzzing, nearly drowned out by freeway roar.

Flies.

Milo made use of his long legs and was there within seconds.

When I caught up, the penlight was focused on a forty-foot sycamore tree.

Stout-trunked thing, with spavined, mottled branches. Unlike the surrounding evergreens and wild oaks, bare of all but a few desiccated brown leaves.

Drew Daney, dressed in dark sweats and sneakers, hung from a low branch, feet dangling two inches off the ground. His head was twisted to the side, his eyes bulged nearly out of their sockets, and his tongue was a Japanese eggplant protruding from a lopsided mouth.

Milo aimed the light at his head. Single gunshot to the left temple. Stellate entry wound. Larger exit. Tiny, hyperkinetic ants crawled in and out of both openings. The flies seemed to favor the exit.

It took awhile, but he found the hole in the tree where the slug had lodged.

Daney's eyes and tongue said he'd been hung first. I said, 'Overkill.' Thinking about Daney dangling, just short of safety. Clutching at the rope, trying to hoist himself up.

Using his big upper body. Maybe he'd managed for seconds, even minutes.

Failing, inevitably. Feeling the life force slip away.

Milo lowered the beam. 'Look at this.'

Daney's crotch was a busy place. Mangled cavity, ragged around the edges where the cotton of the sweatpants had been blasted away.

Here the flies ruled supreme.

Milo got closer and inspected. A few of the insects scattered but most of them stayed on-task. 'Looks liked gunshots . . . a bunch of them.' He stooped and checked the tree trunk, lower down. 'Yeah, here we go, looks like . . . four, no five slugs . . . yeah, five.'

'Emptying the six-shooter,' I said. 'A cowboy gun.'

'Something else in there.' He lit and peered and pointed. 'Couple of rings.'

I stepped in and saw two white gold bands specked with tiny blue gems. Same rings I'd seen at the jail eight years ago.

Thumbtacked to what was left of Daney's organ.

'Drew's and Cherish's wedding bands,' I said. 'She made her statement.'

He stepped away from the corpse. Looked it up and down. Expressionless.

Whipping out his phone he called the Van

Nuys station. 'This is Lieutenant Sturgis. Cancel the BOLO on missing fugitive Daney. *Daney*. I'll spell it for you.'

45

Milo and I moved away from the body and waited.

'Hang 'em high,' he said. 'More like hang 'em low.'

He was restless, went over and examined Daney's sneakers. The fatal two inches. 'Couldn't have been comfortable. Think they used Drew's gun or Barnett dipped into his arsenal?'

'I'd guess Drew's. The temptation of poetic justice.'

'Cherish got that along with the money. If you're already going for the irony, why hold back?'

Considering the need to proceed on foot up the dirt path, it didn't take long for the six uniforms to arrive. Then four detectives, and a white coroner's van bearing two investigators.

Milo briefed one of the D's very quickly, then came over to where I sat, just outside the tape.

'Ready for dinner?'

'That's it?'

'It's someone else's problem now.'

We had pasta and wine at Octavio's, on Ventura Boulevard, in Sherman Oaks.

No conversation until Milo had finished half his

linguini with clams. Then: 'These rolls are great.'

'Yes, they are.'

A glass of Chianti later, I said, 'Cherish may not have intended to, but she helped set Rand up to be killed. Maybe all she wanted was for him to rat out Drew, but it was a sloppy plan. She should've known he wasn't smart enough to conceal his anxiety. Her hatred for Drew overrode that.'

'Sloppiness ain't an indictable offense.' He broke off a piece of bread, sopped up sauce. 'Delicious.'

'You're really through with it.'

'Don't see any reason not to be.'

'What about Cherish and Barnett stringing up Daney and blasting his balls off?'

'Wild West kinda thing,' he said, spooling linguine around his fork. Some of it dropped and he retrieved it, ate, got sauce on his chin. 'And I ain't the sheriff of Dodge.'

'Okay,' I said.

'We don't know for a fact that Malley and Cherish were behind it, do we? Guy like Drew could make all sorts of enemies.'

I stared at him.

He wiped his chin with a napkin. 'In any case, the Valley boys will pursue it to its logical end.'

'If you say so.'

'What, *you're* not finished with it?'

'Guess I am. Except for therapy for the girls. If Detective Weisvogel calls.'

'That surprised me,' he said. 'Given your attitude

about long-term commitment. What, she catch you off guard?'

'That must've been it.'

He dove into his food again, came up for breath. 'Sorry if I'm disillusioning you, Alex, but I'm tired.'

'Don't blame you.'

'I'm talking *serious* tired. As in waking up and not wanting to get out of bed and dragging myself through the day.'

'Sorry,' I said.

He picked up a strand of linguini. Sucked it into his mouth the way little kids do. 'I'll be fine.'

Two days later, he called.

'Daney mighta wiped his Jeep down, but it's a forensic trove. Pubic hairs, semen, tiny specks of blood in the ribbing underneath the door. Also, I just got a call from downtown. My request for DNA has been approved and will be sent to Cellmark expeditiously. If I don't hear back within ninety days, give a call.'

'Any word on Cherish and Barnett?'

'Not that I've heard, but I might not hear.'

'Not in the loop.'

'The only loop of substance was the one around that bastard's neck. Anyway, Rick and I are leaving for Hawaii, thought I'd call to let you know.'

'Good for you.'

'Condo rental on the big island, ten days.'

'Thought you don't tan.'

'So I'll sauté.'

'When are you leaving?'

'Twenty minutes if the E.T.D. on the board is accurate.'

'You're at the airport?'

'Love this place. Two hours of security line worked by morons. I had to take off my shoes, they tossed my carry-on, frisked me. Meanwhile, everyone else, including a guy who could be Osama's twin, sails through.'

'Must be your dangerous demeanor.'

'If they only knew.'

Detective Judy Weisvogel didn't phone that day, but the following morning I came back from running and found a message from my service. I'd hoped it was Allison. Told myself Allison had her hands full and maybe I needed some of that, myself.

I reached Weisvogel at her downtown office.

'Thanks for calling back, Doctor. Still willing?'

'I am.'

'From what we can tell, you were right. He only molested Valerie and Monica Strunk. Valerie won't talk to you but Monica seems okay with it. You'd be more qualified to say but she seems awfully dull to me, pretty close to retarded. Or maybe it's trauma.'

'That would fit,' I said. 'Valerie was his number one choice. Monica was brought in for backup.'

'Bastard,' she said. 'Can't say I'm losing sleep over what happened to him.'

'How'd Valerie take the news?'

'She doesn't know yet. Didn't know if I should tell her, seeing as she still talks about him as if he was Jesus. Damned Stockholm syndrome. What do you think?'

'Find her someone she can relate to and ask them.'

'Good idea. She's got no family other than some distant cousins who want nothing to do with her.'

'Poor kid,' I said.

'Poor everybody. So when can you start?'

'I'll come by tomorrow.'

'Terrific. We've got the social workers involved and all the girls are staying at a youth shelter downtown. Run by a Pentecostal church, but the people in charge aren't doing the holy-roller bit and I know from past experience that they're righteous.'

She gave me an address on Sixth Street.

I said, 'I'll be there at ten.'

'Thanks again, Doctor. In terms of the long-term placement, if you have some advice, we're all open. The shelter's good but it's temporary. I can't see sending them off to new foster homes without some real careful checking.' She laughed. 'Now I'm being a social worker.'

'All part of the job.'

'Unless you keep it out of the job,' she said. 'And I'm not ready to do that yet.'

46

That night, Allison phoned. 'I'm in the car, ten minutes away. May I come by?'

'Of course.'

I left the front door open. Seven minutes later, she strode in.

Cosmetics, jewelry, hair loose and shiny. Sleek white silk blouse tucked into wine-colored slacks. Burgundy suede sandals with tiny rhinestone bows. Tiny gold chains across her instep.

She took my face in both hands and kissed my lips, but it didn't last long.

We sat down in the living room, thigh to thigh. I held her hand. She touched my knee.

'It seems like ages,' she said. 'Since we had any fun.'

'It *has* been ages.'

'I heard about Drew Daney. It was on the news — something about the Sepulveda Dam. Not a lot of details.'

'Do you want details?'

'Not really. You doing okay?'

'Fine, how about you?'

'Me too.' Her eyes dipped at the outer edges.

'What's wrong?'

'I wish I could provide fun, Alex, but I have to leave for Connecticut in a couple of days. Gram fell and broke her hip and Wes says it seems to have done something to her mind, she's just not herself. I'd be on the plane tonight but I've still got Beth to worry about. She's better, a lot better, and there's a very good resident who wants to work with her. Beth seems to like her but the rapport hasn't developed and there's the whole abandonment thing to deal with. I'm hoping to get her to accept the resident in a couple of days. To understand that my absence will be temporary.'

She sighed. 'I wouldn't tell anyone else this, but nothing would thrill me more than coming back to find she prefers the resident.'

'Know how you feel.'

'I'm so *drained*, Alex. Every minute I'm not at the office, I'm over at the hospital. Now it's Gram. Sometimes I feel I'm a host and everyone else is a parasite. Isn't that horrible? No one forced me to take this job.'

I put my arm around her. She remained stiff for a moment, then dropped her head on my shoulder. Her hair tickled my nose. I tolerated it.

A few moments later, she said, 'I know there's a lot I need to say to you, but I just don't have the energy. So could we just go to bed and not have sex? I'll understand if you say no, but if you could find it within yourself, I'd really appreciate it.'

I got up and took her hand.

'Thank you,' she said. 'At least I've got a friend.'

She's fond of her body and usually strips down in front of me. This time she undressed in the bathroom and emerged with her bra and panties on. I was nude, beneath the covers. When she crawled in and I felt the mattress bounce, I got hard and turned to keep that out of view.

She sensed it anyway, rolled over, squeezed, let go.

'It's so ready,' she said. 'Sorry.' Lying on her back, she dropped a smooth white arm over her eyes.

'No apologies necessary,' I said. I needn't have bothered. She was fast asleep, breathing through her mouth, bra cups heaving.

I knew sleep wouldn't come my way. Way off my biorhythm and too many things on my mind.

Tomorrow morning. What approach should I take with Monica Strunk?

Would Valerie be able to connect with another therapist?

Where was Miranda?

Would my role as a police surrogate make *any* approach to the girls futile and would I end up reporting failure to Judy Weisvogel?

Man in a tree.

Baby bracelet.

Trying to breathe myself calm, I worked at shutting out the case.

Thought about a call I'd need to make sooner or later.

Sooner rather than later, given the circumstances.
As Allison slept, I rehearsed mentally.

Ring ring ring.
It's me.
Oh, hi.
How're you doing?
Okay. You?
Hanging in.
That's good.
I thought I might drop over. Visit Spike.
Sure, that's fine. I'll be here, too.

Read on for a taster of

GONE

by Jonathan Kellerman

Available in hardback in Autumn 2006

'One sure way to get famous is to die the wrong way'

Los Angeles is full of performers. For psychologist Alex Delaware, finding out what's real and what's not is about to become a matter of life and horrific death ...

Called in to evaluate an aspiring actress accused – along with her boyfriend – of staging her own abduction, Alex is indifferent when the case seems to go nowhere. But then the girl is savagely murdered, and suddenly a straightforward script takes a decidedly unexpected turn. Dylan Meserve, the victim's boyfriend, has also disappeared and the caretaker at the couple's acting school has a disturbing history.

Is Dylan a deranged killer, or another victim? Alex and homicide detective Milo Sturgis begin auditioning suspects and trawling the depths of L.A.'s seedy underbelly. Then more dead wannabes start turning up ...

I

She nearly killed an innocent man.

Creighton 'Charley' Bondurant drove carefully because his life depended on it. Latigo Canyon was mile after mile of neck-wrenching, hairpin twists. Charley had no use for government meddlers but the 15 mph signs posted along the road were smart.

He lived ten miles up from Kanan Dume Road, on a four-acre remnant of the ranch his grandfather had owned during Coolidge's time. All those Arabians and Tennessee walkers and the mules Grandpa kept around because he liked the creatures' spirit. Charley had grown up with families like his. No-nonsense ranchers, a few rich folk who were still okay when they came up to ride on weekends. Now, all you had were rich pretenders.

Diabetic and rheumatoid and depressed, Charley lived in a two-room cabin with a view of oak-covered crests and the ocean beyond. Sixty-eight, never married. Poor excuse for a man, he'd scold himself on nights when the medicines mixed with the beer and his mood sank low.

On happier days, he pretended to be an old cowboy.

This morning, he was somewhere between those

extremes. His bunions hurt like hell. Two horses had died last winter and he was down to three skinny white mares and a half-blind sheepdog. Feed and hay bills ate up most of his Social Security. But the nights had been warm for October, he hadn't dreamed bad and his bones felt okay.

It was hay that got him up at seven that morning, rolling out of bed, gulping coffee, chewing on a stale sweet roll, to hell with his blood sugar. A little time-out to get the internal plumbing going and by eight he was dressed and starting up the pickup.

Coasting in neutral down the dirt road that fed to Latigo, he looked both ways a couple of times, cleared the crust from his eyes, shifted into first and rolled down. The Topanga Feed Bin was a twenty-minute ride south and he figured to stop along the way at the Malibu Stop 'n Shop for a few six-packs, a tin of Skoal and some Pringles.

Nice morning, a big old blue sky with just a few clouds from the east, sweet air blowing up from the Pacific. Switching on his eight–track, he listened to Ray Price and drove slow enough to stop for deer. Not too many of the pests before dark but you never knew what to expect up in the mountains.

The naked girl jumped out at him a lot faster than any deer.

Eyes full of terror, mouth stretched so wide Charley swore he could see her tonsils.

She ran across the road, straight in the path of his truck, hair blowing wild, waving her arms.

Stomping the brake pedal hard, Charley felt the pickup lurch, wobble and sway. Then the sharp skid to the left, straight at the battered guardrail that separated him from a thousand foot of nothing.

Hurtling toward blue sky.

He kept hitting the brake. Kept flying. Said his prayers and opened the door and prepared to bail.

His damn shirt stuck on the door handle. Eternity looked real close. What a stupid way to go!

Hands ripping at his shirt fabric, mouth working in a combination of curses and benedictions, Charley's gnarled body tightened, his legs turned to iron bars and his sore foot pressed that brake pedal down to the damn floorboard.

The truck kept going, fishtailed, slid, spattered gravel.

Shuddered. Rolled. Bumped the guard.

Charley could hear the rail groan.

The truck stopped.

Charley freed his shirt and got out. His chest was tight and he couldn't suck any breath into his lungs. Wouldn't that be the shits: spared a freefall to oblivion only to drop dead of a damned heart attack.

He gasped and swallowed air, felt his field of vision grow black and braced himself against the truck. The chassis creaked and Charley jumped back, felt himself going down again.

A scream pierced the morning. Charley opened his eyes and straightened and saw the girl. Red marks around her wrists and ankles. Bruises around her neck.

Beautiful young body, those healthy knockers bobbing as she came running toward him – sinful to think like that, she was scared, but knockers like that what else was there to notice?

She kept coming, arms wide, like she wanted Charley to hold her.

But screaming, those wild eyes, he wasn't sure what to do.

First time in a long time he'd been this close to bare female flesh.

He forgot about the knockers, nothing sexy about this. She was a kid, young enough to be his daughter. Granddaughter.

Those marks on her wrists and ankles, around her neck.

She screamed again.

'*Ohgodohgodohgod.*'

She was right up to him, now, yellow hair whipping his face. He could smell the fear on her. See the goosebumps on her pretty tan shoulders.

'*Help me!*'

Poor kid was shivering.

Charley held her.